THE FAMOUS CASES OF
DR. THORNDYKE

*Thirty-seven of his criminal
investigations as set down by*

R. AUSTIN FREEMAN

HODDER & STOUGHTON, LONDON

Volume 1

PREFACE

In the table of contents, the stories included in the present collection are divided into two groups, which I have named respectively " Inverted " and " Direct " stories ; on which classification a few explanatory comments may appropriately be offered.

The Detective Story differs from all other forms of fiction in that its interest is primarily intellectual. Emotion, dramatic action, humour, pathos, " love interest," may all be present. But they are mere accessory factors which may at will be omitted without vital injury to the story. The one essential, sine qua non, *is a problem, the solution of which shall afford the ingenious reader an agreeable exercise in intellectual gymnastics.*

But in order to attain this result, the Detective Story must conform to three indispensable conditions : 1. The problem must be susceptible of, at least approximate, solution by the reader ; 2. The solution offered by the author through the official investigator must be absolutely conclusive and convincing ; 3. No material fact must be withheld from the reader. All the cards must be honestly laid on the table before the solution is announced.

Consideration of these conditions, and especially of the last, suggested to me, many years ago, an interesting question. " Would it be possible " (I quote from the original preface to " The Singing Bone ") " to write a Detective Story in which, from the outset, the reader was taken entirely into the author's confidence, was made an actual witness of the crime and furnished with every fact that could possibly be used in its detection? Would there be any story left to tell when the reader had all the facts? I believed that there would ; and, as an experiment to test the justice of my belief, I wrote ' The Case of Oscar Brodski.' Here the usual conditions are reversed ; the

v

reader knows everything, the detective knows nothing, and the interest focuses on the unexpected significance of trivial circumstances.

" By excellent judges on both sides of the Atlantic—including the editor of Pearson's Magazine—*this story was so far approved of that I was invited to produce others of the same type."* *Six of these " inverted " stories are here included ; and connoisseurs of this class of fiction will probably agree that the separate presentation of the problem and the process of its solution add to, rather than detract from, the intellectual interest of the story as a whole ; especially if the reader should pause after reading the first part, and endeavour to assess the evidential value of the facts in his possession.*

R. A. F.

GRAVESEND,
3rd April, 1929.

CONTENTS

GROUP I—INVERTED STORIES

GROUP II—DIRECT STORIES

THE FAMOUS CASES OF
DR. THORNDYKE

GROUP
ONE

INVERTED
STORIES

I

1

I. The Mechanism of Crime

A SURPRISING amount of nonsense has been talked about conscience. On the one hand remorse (or the " again-bite," as certain scholars of ultra-Teutonic leanings would prefer to call it) ; on the other hand " an easy conscience " : these have been accepted as the determining factors of happiness or the reverse.

Of course there is an element of truth in the " easy conscience " view, but it begs the whole question. A particularly hardy conscience may be quite easy under the most unfavourable conditions—conditions in which the more feeble conscience might be severely afflicted with the " again-bite." And, then, it seems to be the fact that some fortunate persons have no conscience at all ; a negative gift that raises them above the mental vicissitudes of the common herd of humanity.

Now, Silas Hickler was a case in point. No one, looking into his cheerful, round face, beaming with benevolence and wreathed in perpetual smiles, would have imagined him to be a criminal. Least of all, his worthy, high-church housekeeper, who was a witness to his unvarying amiability, who constantly heard him carolling light-heartedly about the house and noted his appreciative zest at meal-times.

Yet it is a fact that Silas earned his modest, though comfortable, income by the gentle art of burglary. A precarious trade and risky withal, yet not so very hazardous if pursued with judgment and moderation. And Silas was eminently a man of judgment. He worked invariably alone. He kept his own counsel. No confederate had he to turn King's Evidence at a pinch ; no " doxy " who might bounce off in a fit of temper to Scotland Yard.

Nor was he greedy and thriftless, as most criminals are. His "scoops" were few and far between, carefully planned, secretly executed, and the proceeds judiciously invested in "weekly property."

In early life Silas had been connected with the diamond industry, and he still did a little rather irregular dealing. In the trade he was suspected of transactions with I.D.B.s, and one or two indiscreet dealers had gone so far as to whisper the ominous word "fence." But Silas smiled a benevolent smile and went his way. He knew what he knew, and his clients in Amsterdam were not inquisitive.

Such was Silas Hickler. As he strolled round his garden in the dusk of an October evening, he seemed the very type of modest, middle-class prosperity. He was dressed in the travelling suit that he wore on his little continental trips ; his bag was packed and stood in readiness on the sitting-room sofa. A parcel of diamonds (purchased honestly, though without impertinent questions, at Southampton) was in the inside pocket of his waistcoat, and another more valuable parcel was stowed in a cavity in the heel of his right boot. In an hour and a half it would be time for him to set out to catch the boat train at the junction ; meanwhile there was nothing to do but to stroll round the fading garden and consider how he should invest the proceeds of the impending deal. His housekeeper had gone over to Welham for the week's shopping, and would probably not be back until eleven o'clock. He was alone in the premises and just a trifle dull.

He was about to turn into the house when his ear caught the sound of footsteps on the unmade road that passed the end of the garden. He paused and listened. There was no other dwelling near, and the road led nowhere, fading away into the waste land beyond the house. Could this be a visitor ? It seemed unlikely, for visitors were few at Silas Hickler's house. Meanwhile the footsteps continued to approach, ringing out with increasing loudness on the hard, stony path.

Silas strolled down to the gate, and, leaning on it, looked out with some curiosity. Presently a glow of light showed him the face of a man, apparently lighting his pipe ; then a dim figure detached itself from the enveloping gloom, advanced towards him and halted opposite the garden. The stranger removed a cigarette from his mouth and, blowing out a cloud of smoke, asked—

" Can you tell me if this road will take me to Badsham Junction ? "

" No," replied Hickler, " but there is a footpath farther on that leads to the station."

" Footpath ! " growled the stranger. " I've had enough of footpaths. I came down from town to Catley intending to walk across to the junction. I started along the road, and then some fool directed me to a short cut, with the result that I have been blundering about in the dark for the last half-hour. My sight isn't very good, you know," he added.

" What train do you want to catch ? " asked Hickler.

" Seven fifty-eight," was the reply.

" I am going to catch that train myself," said Silas, " but I shan't be starting for another hour. The station is only three-quarters of a mile from here. If you like to come in and take a rest, we can walk down together and then you'll be sure of not missing your way."

" It's very good of you," said the stranger, peering, with spectacled eyes, at the dark house, " but—I think—— "

" Might as well wait here as at the station," said Silas in his genial way, holding the gate open, and the stranger, after a momentary hesitation, entered and, flinging away his cigarette, followed him to the door of the cottage.

The sitting-room was in darkness, save for the dull glow of the expiring fire, but, entering before his guest, Silas applied a match to the lamp that hung from the ceiling. As the flame leaped up, flooding the little interior with light, the two men regarded one another with mutual curiosity.

" Brodski, by Jingo ! " was Hickler's silent commentary, as he looked at his guest. " Doesn't know me, evidently—wouldn't, of course, after all these years and with his bad eyesight. Take a seat, sir," he added aloud. " Will you join me in a little refreshment to while away the time ? "

Brodski murmured an indistinct acceptance, and, as his host turned to open a cupboard, he deposited his hat (a hard, grey felt) on a chair in a corner, placed his bag on the edge of the table, resting his umbrella against it, and sat down in a small arm-chair.

" Have a biscuit ? " said Hickler, as he placed a whisky-bottle on the table together with a couple of his best star-pattern tumblers and a siphon.

" Thanks, I think I will," said Brodski. " The railway journey and all this confounded tramping about, you know—— "

" Yes," agreed Silas. " Doesn't do to start with an empty stomach. Hope you don't mind oat-cakes ; I see they're the only biscuits I have."

Brodski hastened to assure him that oat-cakes were his special and peculiar fancy ; and in confirmation, having mixed himself a stiff jorum, he fell to upon the biscuits with evident gusto.

Brodski was a deliberate feeder, and at present appeared to be somewhat sharp set. His measured munching being unfavourable to conversation, most of the talking fell to Silas ; and, for once, that genial transgressor found the task embarrassing. The natural thing would have been to discuss his guest's destination and perhaps the object of his journey ; but this was precisely what Hickler avoided doing. For he knew both, and instinct told him to keep his knowledge to himself.

Brodski was a diamond merchant of considerable reputation, and in a large way of business. He bought stones principally in the rough, and of these he was a most excellent judge. His fancy was for stones of somewhat unusual size and value, and it was well known to be his custom, when he had accumulated a sufficient stock, to carry them himself to Amsterdam and supervise the cutting of the rough stones. Of this Hickler was aware, and he had no doubt that Brodski was now starting on one of his periodical excursions ; that somewhere in the recesses of his rather shabby clothing was concealed a paper packet possibly worth several thousand pounds.

Brodski sat by the table munching monotonously and talking little. Hickler sat opposite him, talking nervously and rather wildly at times, and watching his guest with a growing fascination. Precious stones, and especially diamonds, were Hickler's speciality. " Hard stuff "—silver plate—he avoided entirely ; gold, excepting in the form of specie, he seldom touched ; but stones, of which he could carry off a whole consignment in the heel of his boot and dispose of with absolute safety, formed the staple of his industry. And here was a man sitting opposite him with a parcel in his pocket containing the equivalent of a dozen of his most successful " scoops " ; stones worth perhaps—— Here he pulled himself up short and began to talk rapidly, though without much coherence. For, even as he talked, other words, formed subconsciously, seemed to insinuate themselves into the interstices of the sentences, and to carry on a parallel train of thought.

" Gets chilly in the evenings now, doesn't it ? " said Hickler.

" It does indeed," Brodski agreed, and then resumed his slow munching, breathing audibly through his nose.

" Five thousand at least," the subconscious train of thought resumed ; " probably six or seven, perhaps ten." Silas fidgeted in his chair and endeavoured to concentrate his ideas on some topic of interest. He was growing disagreeably conscious of a new and unfamiliar state of mind.

" Do you take any interest in gardening ? " he asked.

Next to diamonds and " weekly property," his besetting
weakness was fuchsias.

Brodski chuckled sourly. " Hatton Garden is the
nearest approach—— " He broke off suddenly, and
then added, " I am a Londoner, you know."

The abrupt break in the sentence was not unnoticed
by Silas, nor had he any difficulty in interpreting it.
A man who carries untold wealth upon his person must
needs be wary in his speech.

" Yes," he answered absently, " it's hardly a Londoner's hobby." And then, half consciously, he began
a rapid calculation. Put it at five thousand pounds.
What would that represent in weekly property ? His last
set of houses had cost two hundred and fifty pounds
apiece, and he had let them at ten shillings and sixpence
a week. At that rate, five thousand pounds represented
twenty houses at ten and sixpence a week—say ten
pounds a week—one pound eight shillings a day—five
hundred and twenty pounds a year—for life. It was a
competency. Added to what he already had, it was
wealth. With that income he could fling the tools of his
trade into the river and live out the remainder of his life
in comfort and security.

He glanced furtively at his guest across the table,
and then looked away quickly as he felt stirring within
him an impulse the nature of which he could not mistake.
This must be put an end to. Crimes against the person
he had always looked upon as sheer insanity. There was,
it is true, that little affair of the Weybridge policeman,
but that was unforeseen and unavoidable, and it was the
constable's doing after all. And, there was the old
housekeeper at Epsom, too, but, of course, if the old
idiot would shriek in that insane fashion—well, it was
an accident, very regrettable, to be sure, and no one could
be more sorry for the mishap than himself. But deliberate homicide !—robbery from the person ! It was the
act of a stark lunatic.

Of course, if he had happened to be that sort of person,

here was the opportunity of a lifetime. The immense booty, the empty house, the solitary neighbourhood, away from the main road and from other habitations ; the time, the darkness—but, of course, there was the body to be thought of ; that was always the difficulty. What to do with the body—— Here he caught the shriek of the up express, rounding the curve in the line that ran past the waste land at the back of the house. The sound started a new train of thought, and, as he followed it out, his eyes fixed themselves on the unconscious and taciturn Brodski, as he sat thoughtfully sipping his whisky. At length, averting his gaze with an effort, he rose suddenly from his chair and turned to look at the clock on the mantelpiece, spreading out his hands before the dying fire. A tumult of strange sensations warned him to leave the house. He shivered slightly, though he was rather hot than chilly, and, turning his head, looked at the door.

" Seems to be a confounded draught," he said, with another slight shiver ; " did I shut the door properly, I wonder ? " He strode across the room and, opening the door wide, looked out into the dark garden. A desire, sudden and urgent, had come over him to get out into the open air, to be on the road and have done with this madness that was knocking at the door of his brain.

" I wonder if it is worth while to start yet," he said, with a yearning glance at the murky, starless sky.

Brodski roused himself and looked round. " Is your clock right ? " he asked.

Silas reluctantly admitted that it was.

" How long will it take us to walk to the station ? " inquired Brodski.

" Oh, about twenty-five minutes to half-an-hour," replied Silas, unconsciously exaggerating the distance.

" Well," said Brodski, " we've got more than an hour yet, and it's more comfortable here than hanging about the station. I don't see the use of starting before we need."

" No ; of course not," Silas agreed. A wave of

strange emotion, half-regretful, half-triumphant, surged through his brain. For some moments he remained standing on the threshold, looking out dreamily into the night. Then he softly closed the door ; and, seemingly without the exercise of his volition, the key turned noiselessly in the lock.

He returned to his chair and tried to open a conversation with the taciturn Brodski, but the words came faltering and disjointed. He felt his face growing hot, his brain full and tense, and there was a faint, high-pitched singing in his ears. He was conscious of watching his guest with a new and fearful interest, and, by sheer force of will, turned away his eyes ; only to find them a moment later involuntarily returning to fix the unconscious man with yet more horrible intensity. And ever through his mind walked, like a dreadful procession, the thoughts of what that other man—the man of blood and violence—would do in these circumstances. Detail by detail the hideous synthesis fitted together the parts of the imagined crime, and arranged them in due sequence until they formed a succession of events, rational, connected and coherent.

He rose uneasily from his chair, with his eyes still riveted upon his guest. He could not sit any longer opposite that man with his hidden store of precious gems. The impulse that he recognised with fear and wonder was growing more ungovernable from moment to moment. If he stayed it would presently overpower him, and then—— He shrank with horror from the dreadful thought, but his fingers itched to handle the diamonds. For Silas was, after all, a criminal by nature and habit. He was a beast of prey. His livelihood had never been earned ; it had been taken by stealth or, if necessary, by force. His instincts were predaceous, and the proximity of unguarded valuables suggested to him, as a logical consequence, their abstraction or seizure. His unwillingness to let these diamonds go away beyond his reach was fast becoming overwhelming.

But he would make one more effort to escape. He would keep out of Brodski's actual presence until the moment for starting came.

" If you'll excuse me," he said, " I will go and put on a thicker pair of boots. After all this dry weather we may get a change, and damp feet are very uncomfortable when you are travelling."

" Yes ; dangerous too," agreed Brodski.

Silas walked through into the adjoining kitchen, where, by the light of the little lamp that was burning there, he had seen his stout, country boots placed, cleaned and in readiness, and sat down upon a chair to make the change. He did not, of course, intend to wear the country boots, for the diamonds were concealed in those he had on. But he would make the change and then alter his mind ; it would all help to pass the time. He took a deep breath. It was a relief, at any rate, to be out of that room. Perhaps, if he stayed away, the temptation would pass. Brodski would go on his way—he wished that he was going alone—and the danger would be over —at least—and the opportunity would have gone—the diamonds——

He looked up as he slowly unlaced his boot. From where he sat he could see Brodski sitting by the table with his back towards the kitchen door. He had finished eating, now, and was composedly rolling a cigarette. Silas breathed heavily, and, slipping off his boot, sat for a while motionless, gazing steadily at the other man's back. Then he unlaced the other boot, still staring abstractedly at his unconscious guest, drew it off, and laid it very quietly on the floor.

Brodski calmly finished rolling his cigarette, licked the paper, put away his pouch, and, having dusted the crumbs of tobacco from his knees, began to search his pockets for a match. Suddenly, yielding to an uncontrollable impulse, Silas stood up and began stealthily to creep along the passage to the sitting-room. Not a sound came from his stockinged feet. Silently as a cat he stole forward, breathing softly with parted lips, until he stood at the threshold of the room. His face flushed duskily, his eyes, wide and staring, glittered in the lamplight, and the racing blood hummed in his ears.

Brodski struck a match—Silas noted that it was a wooden vesta—lighted his cigarette, blew out the match and flung it into the fender. Then he replaced the box in his pocket and commenced to smoke.

Slowly and without a sound Silas crept forward into the room, step by step, with catlike stealthiness, until he stood close behind Brodski's chair—so close that he had to turn his head that his breath might not stir the hair upon the other man's head. So, for half-a-minute, he stood motionless, like a symbolical statue of Murder, glaring down with horrible, glittering eyes upon the unconscious diamond merchant, while his quick breath passed without a sound through his open mouth and his fingers writhed slowly like the tentacles of a giant hydra. And then, as noiselessly as ever, he backed away to the door, turned quickly and walked back into the kitchen.

He drew a deep breath. It had been a near thing. Brodski's life had hung upon a thread. For it had been so easy. Indeed, if he had happened, as he stood behind the man's chair, to have a weapon—a hammer, for instance, or even a stone——

He glanced round the kitchen and his eye lighted on a bar that had been left by the workmen who had put up the new greenhouse. It was an odd piece cut off from a square, wrought-iron stanchion, and was about a foot long and perhaps three-quarters of an inch thick. Now, if he had had that in his hand a minute ago——

He picked the bar up, balanced it in his hand and swung it round his head. A formidable weapon this : silent, too. And it fitted the plan that had passed through his brain. Bah ! He had better put the thing down.

But he did not. He stepped over to the door and looked again at Brodski, sitting, as before, meditatively smoking, with his back towards the kitchen.

Suddenly a change came over Silas. His face flushed, the veins of his neck stood out and a sullen scowl settled on his face. He drew out his watch, glanced at it earnestly and replaced it. Then he strode swiftly but silently along the passage into the sitting-room.

A pace away from his victim's chair he halted and took deliberate aim. The bar swung aloft, but not without some faint rustle of movement, for Brodski looked round quickly even as the iron whistled through the air. The movement disturbed the murderer's aim, and the bar glanced off his victim's head, making only a trifling wound. Brodski sprang up with a tremulous, bleating cry, and clutched his assailant's arms with the tenacity of mortal terror.

Then began a terrible struggle, as the two men, locked in a deadly embrace, swayed to and fro and trampled backwards and forwards. The chair was overturned, an empty glass swept from the table and, with Brodski's spectacles, crushed beneath stamping feet. And thrice that dreadful, pitiful, bleating cry rang out into the night, filling Silas, despite his murderous frenzy, with terror lest some chance wayfarer should hear it. Gathering his great strength for a final effort, he forced his victim backwards on to the table and, snatching up a corner of the table-cloth, thrust it into his face and crammed it into his mouth as it opened to utter another shriek. And thus they remained for a full two minutes, almost motionless, like some dreadful group of tragic allegory. Then, when the last faint twitchings had died away, Silas relaxed his grasp and let the limp body slip softly on to the floor.

It was over. For good or for evil, the thing was done. Silas stood up, breathing heavily, and, as he wiped the sweat from his face, he looked at the clock. The hands stood at one minute to seven. The whole thing had taken a little over three minutes. He had nearly an hour in which to finish his task. The goods train that entered into his scheme came by at twenty minutes past, and it was only three hundred yards to the line. Still, he must not waste time. He was now quite composed, and only disturbed by the thought that Brodski's cries might have been heard. If no one had heard them it was all plain sailing.

He stooped, and, gently disengaging the table-cloth from the dead man's teeth, began a careful search of his pockets. He was not long finding what he sought, and, as he pinched the paper packet and felt the little hard bodies grating on one another inside, his faint regrets for what had happened were swallowed up in self-congratulations.

He now set about his task with business-like briskness and an attentive eye on the clock. A few large drops of blood had fallen on the table-cloth, and there was a small bloody smear on the carpet by the dead man's head. Silas fetched from the kitchen some water, a nail-brush and a dry cloth, and, having washed out the stains from the table-cover—not forgetting the deal table-top underneath—and cleaned away the smear from the carpet and rubbed the damp places dry, he slipped a sheet of paper under the head of the corpse to prevent further contamination. Then he set the table-cloth straight, stood the chair upright, laid the broken spectacles on the table and picked up the cigarette, which had been trodden flat in the struggle, and flung it under the grate. Then there was the broken glass, which he swept up into a dust-pan. Part of it was the remains of the shattered tumbler, and the rest the fragments of the broken spectacles. He turned it out on to a sheet of paper and looked it over carefully, picking out the larger recognisable pieces of the spectacle-glasses and putting them aside on a separate slip of paper, together with a sprinkling of the minute fragments. The remainder he shot back into the dust-pan and, having hurriedly put on his boots, carried it out to the rubbish-heap at the back of the house.

It was now time to start. Hastily cutting off a length of string from his string-box—for Silas was an orderly man and despised the oddments of string with which many people make shift—he tied it to the dead man's bag and umbrella and slung them from his shoulder. Then he folded up the paper of broken glass, and, slipping it and the spectacles into his pocket, picked up the body and threw it over his shoulder. Brodski was a small, spare man, weighing not more than nine stone ; not a very formidable burden for a big, athletic man like Silas.

The night was intensely dark, and, when Silas looked out of the back gate over the waste land that stretched from his house to the railway, he could hardly see twenty yards ahead. After listening cautiously and hearing no sound, he went out, shut the gate swiftly behind him and set forth at a good pace, though carefully, over the broken ground. His progress was not as silent as he could have wished, for, though the scanty turf that covered the gravelly land was thick enough to deaden his footfalls, the swinging bag and umbrella made an irritating noise ; indeed, his movements were more hampered by them than by the weightier burden.

The distance to the line was about three hundred yards. Ordinarily he would have walked it in from three to four minutes, but now, going cautiously with his burden and stopping now and again to listen, it took him just six minutes to reach the three-bar fence that separated the waste land from the railway. Arrived here he halted for a moment and once more listened attentively, peering into the darkness on all sides. Not a living creature was to be seen or heard in this desolate spot, but far away, the shriek of an engine's whistle warned him to hasten.

Lifting the corpse easily over the fence, he carried it a few yards farther to a point where the line curved sharply. Here he laid it face downwards, with the neck over the near rail. Drawing out his pocket-knife, he cut through the knot that fastened the umbrella to the string and also secured the bag ; and when he had flung the bag and umbrella on the track beside the body, he carefully pocketed the string, excepting the little loop that had fallen to the ground when the knot was cut.

The quick snort and clanking rumble of an approaching goods train began now to be clearly audible. Rapidly, Silas drew from his pockets the battered spectacles and the packet of broken glass. The former he threw down by the dead man's head, and then, emptying the packet into his hand, sprinkled the fragments of glass around the spectacles.

He was none too soon. Already the quick, laboured puffing of the engine sounded close at hand. His impulse was to stay and watch ; to witness the final catastrophe that should convert the murder into an accident or suicide. But it was hardly safe : it would be better that he should not be near lest he should not be able to get away without being seen. Hastily he climbed back over the fence and strode away across the rough fields, while the train came snorting and clattering towards the curve.

He had nearly reached his back gate when a sound from the line brought him to a sudden halt ; it was a prolonged whistle accompanied by the groan of brakes and the loud clank of colliding trucks. The snorting of the engine had ceased and was replaced by the penetrating hiss of escaping steam.

The train had stopped !

For one brief moment Silas stood with bated breath and mouth agape like one petrified ; then he strode forward quickly to the gate, and, letting himself in, silently slid the bolt. He was undeniably alarmed. What could have happened on the line ? It was practically certain that the body had been seen ; but what was happening now ? and would they come to the house ? He entered the kitchen, and having paused again to listen—for somebody might come and knock at the door at any moment—he walked through the sitting-room and looked round. All seemed in order there. There was the bar, though, lying where he had dropped it in the scuffle. He picked it up and held it under the lamp. There was no blood on it ; only one or two hairs. Somewhat absently he wiped it with the table-cover, and then, running out through the kitchen into the back garden, dropped it over the wall into a bed of nettles. Not that there was anything incriminating in the bar, but, since he had used it as a weapon, it had somehow acquired a sinister aspect to his eye.

He now felt that it would be well to start for the station at once. It was not time yet, for it was barely twenty-five minutes past seven ; but he did not wish to be found in the house if anyone should come. His soft hat was on the sofa with his bag, to which his umbrella was strapped. He put on the hat, caught up the bag and stepped over to the door ; then he came back to turn down the lamp. And it was at this moment, when he stood with his hand raised to the burner, that his eye, travelling by chance into the dim corner of the room, lighted on Brodski's grey felt hat, reposing on the chair where the dead man had placed it when he entered the house.

Silas stood for a few moments as if petrified, with the chilly sweat of mortal fear standing in beads upon his forehead. Another instant and he would have turned the lamp down and gone on his way ; and then—— He strode over to the chair, snatched up the hat and looked inside it. Yes, there was the name, " Oscar Brodski," written plainly on the lining. If he had gone away, leaving it to be discovered, he would have been lost ; indeed, even now, if a search-party should come to the house, it was enough to send him to the gallows.

His limbs shook with horror at the thought, but in spite of his panic he did not lose his self-possession. Darting through into the kitchen, he grabbed up a handful of the dry brush-wood that was kept for lighting fires and carried it to the sitting-room grate where he thrust it on the extinct, but still hot, embers, and crumpling up the paper that he had placed under Brodski's head—on which paper he now noticed, for the first time, a minute bloody smear—he poked it in under the wood, and, striking a wax match, set light to it. As the wood flared up, he hacked at the hat with his pocket knife and threw the ragged strips into the blaze.

And all the while his heart was thumping and his hands a-tremble with the dread of discovery. The fragments of felt were far from inflammable, tending rather to fuse into cindery masses that smoked and smouldered, than to burn away into actual ash. Moreover, to his dismay, they emitted a powerful resinous stench mixed with the odour of burning hair, so that he had to open the kitchen window (since he dared not unlock the front door) to disperse the reek. And still, as he fed the fire with small cut fragments, he strained his ears to catch, above the crackling of the wood, the sound of the dreaded footsteps, the knock on the door that should be as the summons of Fate.

The time, too, was speeding on. Twenty-one minutes to eight ! In a few minutes more he must set out or he would miss the train. He dropped the dismembered hat-brim on the blazing wood and ran up-stairs to open a window, since he must close that in the kitchen before he left. When he came back, the brim had already curled up into a black, clinkery mass that bubbled and hissed as the fat, pungent smoke rose from it sluggishly to the chimney.

Nineteen minutes to eight ! It was time to start. He took up the poker and carefully beat the cinders into small particles, stirring them into the glowing embers of the wood and coal. There was nothing unusual in the appearance of the grate. It was his constant custom to burn letters and other discarded articles in the sitting-room fire : his housekeeper would notice nothing out of the common. Indeed, the cinders would probably be reduced to ashes before she returned. He had been careful to notice that there were no metallic fittings of any kind in the hat, which might have escaped burning.

Once more he picked up his bag, took a last look round, turned down the lamp and, unlocking the door, held it open for a few moments. Then he went out, locked the door, pocketed the key (of which his house-keeper had a duplicate) and set off at a brisk pace for the station.

He arrived in good time after all, and, having taken his ticket, strolled through on to the platform. The train was not yet signalled, but there seemed to be an unusual stir in the place. The passengers were collected in a group at one end of the platform, and were all looking in one direction down the line ; and, even as he walked towards them, with a certain tremulous, nauseating curiosity, two men emerged from the darkness and ascended the slope to the platform, carrying a stretcher covered with a tarpaulin. The passengers parted to let the bearers pass, turning fascinated eyes upon the shape that showed faintly through the rough pall ; and, when the stretcher had been borne into the lamp-room, they fixed their attention upon a porter who followed carrying a hand-bag and an umbrella.

Suddenly one of the passengers started forward with an exclamation.

" Is that his umbrella ? " he demanded.

" Yes, sir," answered the porter, stopping and holding it out for the speaker's inspection.

" My God ! " ejaculated the passenger ; then, turning sharply to a tall man who stood close by, he said excitedly : " That's Brodski's umbrella. I could swear to it. You remember Brodski ? " The tall man nodded, and the passenger, turning once more to the porter, said : " I identify that umbrella. It belongs to a gentleman named Brodski. If you look in his hat you will see his name written in it. He always writes his name in his hat."

" We haven't found his hat yet," said the porter ;

" but here is the station-master coming up the line." He awaited the arrival of his superior and then announced : " This gentleman, sir, has identified the umbrella."

" Oh," said the station-master, " you recognise the umbrella, sir, do you ? Then perhaps you would step into the lamp-room and see if you can identify the body."

The passenger recoiled with a look of alarm.

" Is it—is he—very much injured ? " he asked tremulously.

" Well, yes," was the reply. " You see, the engine and six of the trucks went over him before they could stop the train. Took his head clean off, in fact."

" Shocking ! shocking ! " gasped the passenger. " I think, if you don't mind—I'd—I'd rather not. You don't think it's necessary, doctor, do you ? "

" Yes, I do," replied the tall man. " Early identification may be of the first importance."

" Then I suppose I must," said the passenger.

Very reluctantly he allowed himself to be conducted by the station-master to the lamp-room, as the clang of the bell announced the approaching train. Silas Hickler followed and took his stand with the expectant crowd outside the closed door. In a few moments the passenger burst out, pale and awe-stricken, and rushed up to his tall friend. " It is ! " he exclaimed breathlessly, " it's Brodski ! Poor old Brodski ! Horrible ! horrible ! He was to have met me here and come on with me to Amsterdam."

" Had he any—merchandise about him ? " the tall man asked ; and Silas strained his ears to catch the reply.

" He had some stones, no doubt, but I don't know what. His clerk will know, of course. By the way, doctor, could you watch the case for me ? Just to be sure it was really an accident or—you know what. We were old friends, you know, fellow townsmen, too ; we were both born in Warsaw. I'd like you to give an eye to the case."

" Very well," said the other. " I will satisfy myself

that—there is nothing more than appears, and let you have a report.   Will that do ? "

" Thank you.   It's excessively good of you, doctor. Ah ! here comes the train.   I hope it won't inconvenience you to stay and see to this matter."

" Not in the least," replied the doctor.   " We are not due at Warmington until to-morrow afternoon, and I expect we can find out all that is necessary to know and still keep our appointment."

Silas looked long and curiously at the tall, imposing man who was, as it were, taking his seat at the chessboard, to play against him for his life.   A formidable antagonist he looked, with his keen, thoughtful face, so resolute and calm.   As Silas stepped into his carriage he looked back at his opponent, and thinking with deep discomfort of Brodski's hat, he hoped that he had made no other oversight.

II. The Mechanism of Detection

(Related by CHRISTOPHER JERVIS, M.D.)

The singular circumstances that attended the death of Mr. Oscar Brodski, the well-known diamond merchant of Hatton Garden, illustrated very forcibly the importance of one or two points in medico-legal practice which Thorndyke was accustomed to insist were not sufficiently appreciated.   What those points were, I shall leave my friend and teacher to state at the proper place ; and meanwhile, as the case is in the highest degree instructive, I shall record the incidents in the order of their occurrence.

The dusk of an October evening was closing in as Thorndyke and I, the sole occupants of a smoking compartment, found ourselves approaching the little station of Ludham ; and, as the train slowed down, we peered out at the knot of country people who were waiting on the platform.   Suddenly Thorndyke exclaimed in a tone of surprise : " Why, that is surely Boscovitch ! "

and almost at the same moment a brisk, excitable little man darted at the door of our compartment and literally tumbled in.

"I hope I don't intrude on this learned conclave," he said, shaking hands genially and banging his Gladstone with impulsive violence into the rack; "but I saw your faces at the window, and naturally jumped at the chance of such pleasant companionship."

"You are very flattering," said Thorndyke; "so flattering that you leave us nothing to say. But what in the name of fortune are you doing at—what's the name of the place?—Ludham?"

"My brother has a little place a mile or so from here, and I have been spending a couple of days with him," Mr. Boscovitch explained. "I shall change at Badsham Junction and catch the boat train for Amsterdam. But whither are you two bound? I see you have your mysterious little green box up on the hat-rack, so I infer that you are on some romantic quest, eh? Going to unravel some dark and intricate crime?"

"No," replied Thorndyke. "We are bound for Warmington on a quite prosaic errand. I am instructed to watch the proceedings at an inquest there to-morrow on behalf of the Griffin Life Insurance Office, and we are travelling down to-night as it is rather a cross-country journey."

"But why the box of magic?" asked Boscovitch, glancing up at the hat-rack.

"I never go away from home without it," answered Thorndyke. "One never knows what may turn up; the trouble of carrying it is small when set off against the comfort of having one's appliances at hand in case of an emergency."

Boscovitch continued to stare up at the little square case covered with Willesden canvas. Presently he remarked: "I often used to wonder what you had in it when you were down at Chelmsford in connection with that bank murder—what an amazing case that was, by the way, and didn't your methods of research astonish the police ! " As he still looked up wistfully at the case, Thorndyke good-naturedly lifted it down and unlocked it. As a matter of fact he was rather proud of his " portable laboratory," and certainly it was a triumph of condensation, for, small as it was—only a foot square by four inches deep—it contained a fairly complete outfit for a preliminary investigation.

" Wonderful ! " exclaimed Boscovitch, when the case lay open before him, displaying its rows of little reagent bottles, tiny test-tubes, diminutive spirit-lamp, dwarf microscope and assorted instruments on the same Lilliputian scale ; " it's like a doll's house—everything looks as if it was seen through the wrong end of a telescope. But are these tiny things really efficient ? That microscope now——"

" Perfectly efficient at low and moderate magnifications," said Thorndyke. " It looks like a toy, but it isn't one ; the lenses are the best that can be had. Of course, a full-sized instrument would be infinitely more convenient—but I shouldn't have it with me, and should have to make shift with a pocket-lens. And so with the rest of the under-sized appliances ; they are the alternative to no appliances."

Boscovitch pored over the case and its contents, fingering the instruments delicately and asking questions innumerable about their uses ; indeed, his curiosity was but half appeased when, half-an-hour later, the train began to slow down.

" By Jove ! " he exclaimed, starting up and seizing his bag, " here we are at the junction already. You change here too, don't you ? "

" Yes," replied Thorndyke. " We take the branch train on to Warmington."

As we stepped out on to the platform, we became aware that something unusual was happening or had happened. All the passengers and most of the porters and supernumeraries were gathered at one end of the

station, and all were looking intently into the darkness
down the line.

"Anything wrong ? " asked Mr. Boscovitch, addressing the station-inspector.

"Yes, sir," the official replied ; "a man has been run
over by the goods train about a mile down the line.
The station-master has gone down with a stretcher to
bring him in, and I expect that is his lantern that you see
coming this way."

As we stood watching the dancing light grow momentarily brighter, flashing fitful reflections from the bur-
nished rails, a man came out of the booking-office and
joined the group of onlookers. He attracted my attention, as I afterwards remembered, for two reasons : in
the first place his round, jolly face was excessively pale
and bore a strained and wild expression, and, in the
second, though he stared into the darkness with eager
curiosity, he asked no questions.

The swinging lantern continued to approach, and
then suddenly two men came into sight bearing a stretcher
covered with a tarpaulin, through which the shape of a
human figure was dimly discernible. They ascended
the slope to the platform, and proceeded with their
burden to the lamp-room, when the inquisitive gaze of
the passengers was transferred to a porter who followed
carrying a hand-bag and umbrella and to the station-
master who brought up the rear with his lantern.

As the porter passed, Mr. Boscovitch started forward
with sudden excitement.

"Is that his umbrella ? " he asked.

"Yes, sir," answered the porter, stopping and holding
it out for the speaker's inspection.

"My God ! " ejaculated Boscovitch ; then, turning
sharply to Thorndyke, he exclaimed : "That's Brodski's
umbrella. I could swear to it. You remember
Brodski ? "

Thorndyke nodded, and Boscovitch, turning once
more to the porter, said : "I identify that umbrella.

It belongs to a gentleman named Brodski. If you look in his hat, you will see his name written in it. He always writes his name in his hat."

"We haven't found his hat yet," said the porter; "but here is the station-master." He turned to his superior and announced: "This gentleman, sir, has identified the umbrella."

"Oh," said the station-master, "you recognise the umbrella, sir, do you? Then perhaps you would step into the lamp-room and see if you can identify the body."

Mr. Boscovitch recoiled with a look of alarm. "Is it —is he—very much injured?" he asked nervously.

"Well, yes," was the reply. "You see, the engine and six of the trucks went over him before they could stop the train. Took his head clean off, in fact."

"Shocking! shocking!" gasped Boscovitch. "I think—if you don't mind—I'd—I'd rather not. You don't think it necessary, doctor, do you?"

"Yes, I do," replied Thorndyke. "Early identification may be of the first importance."

"Then I suppose I must," said Boscovitch; and, with extreme reluctance, he followed the station-master to the lamp-room, as the loud ringing of the bell announced the approach of the boat train. His inspection must have been of the briefest, for, in a few moments, he burst out, pale and awe-stricken, and rushed up to Thorndyke.

"It is!" he exclaimed breathlessly, "it's Brodski! Poor old Brodski! Horrible! horrible! He was to have met me here and come on with me to Amsterdam."

"Had he any—merchandise about him?" Thorndyke asked; and, as he spoke, the stranger whom I had previously noticed edged up closer as if to catch the reply.

"He had some stones, no doubt," answered Boscovitch, "but I don't know what they were. His clerk will know, of course. By the way, doctor, could you watch the case for me? Just to be sure it was really an accident or—you know what. We were old friends, you

2

know, fellow townsmen, too ; we were both born in Warsaw. I'd like you to give an eye to the case."

" Very well," said Thorndyke. " I will satisfy myself that there is nothing more than appears, and let you have a report. Will that do ? "

" Thank you," said Boscovitch. " It's excessively good of you, doctor. Ah, here comes the train. I hope it won't inconvenience you to stay and see to the matter."

" Not in the least," replied Thorndyke. " We are not due at Warmington until to-morrow afternoon, and I expect we can find out all that is necessary to know and still keep our appointment."

As Thorndyke spoke, the stranger, who had kept close to us with the evident purpose of hearing what was said, bestowed on him a very curious and attentive look ; and it was only when the train had actually come to rest by the platform that he hurried away to find a compartment.

No sooner had the train left the station than Thorndyke sought out the station-master and informed him of the instructions that he had received from Boscovitch. " Of course," he added, in conclusion, " we must not move in the matter until the police arrive. I suppose they have been informed ? "

" Yes," replied the station-master ; " I sent a message at once to the Chief Constable, and I expect him or an inspector at any moment. In fact, I think I will slip out to the approach and see if he is coming." He evidently wished to have a word in private with the police officer before committing himself to any statement.

As the official departed, Thorndyke and I began to pace the now empty platform, and my friend, as was his wont, when entering on a new inquiry, meditatively reviewed the features of the problem.

" In a case of this kind," he remarked, " we have to decide on one of three possible explanations : accident, suicide or homicide ; and our decision will be determined by inferences from three sets of facts : first, the general facts of the case ; second, the special data obtained by examination of the body, and, third, the special data obtained by examining the spot on which the body was found. Now the only general facts at present in our possession are that the deceased was a diamond merchant making a journey for a specific purpose and probably having on his person property of small bulk and great value. These facts are somewhat against the hypothesis of suicide and somewhat favourable to that of homicide. Facts relevant to the question of accident would be the existence or otherwise of a level crossing, a road or path leading to the line, an enclosing fence with or without a gate, and any other facts rendering probable or otherwise the accidental presence of the deceased at the spot where the body was found. As we do not possess these facts, it is desirable that we extend our knowledge."

"Why not put a few discreet questions to the porter who brought in the bag and umbrella ?" I suggested. "He is at this moment in earnest conversation with the ticket collector and would, no doubt, be glad of a new listener."

"An excellent suggestion, Jervis," answered Thorndyke. "Let us see what he has to tell us." We approached the porter and found him, as I had anticipated, bursting to unburden himself of the tragic story.

"The way the thing happened, sir, was this," he said, in answer to Thorndyke's question : "There's a sharpish bend in the road just at that place, and the goods train was just rounding the curve when the driver suddenly caught sight of something lying across the rails. As the engine turned, the head-lights shone on it and then he saw it was a man. He shut off steam at once, blew his whistle, and put the brakes down hard, but, as you know, sir, a goods train takes some stopping ; before they could bring her up, the engine and half-a-dozen trucks had gone over the poor beggar."

" Could the driver see how the man was lying ? "
Thorndyke asked.

" Yes, he could see him quite plain, because the head-
lights were full on him. He was lying on his face with
his neck over the near rail on the down side. His head
was in the four-foot and his body by the side of the
track. It looked as if he had laid himself out a-purpose."

" Is there a level crossing thereabouts ? " asked
Thorndyke.

" No, sir. No crossing, no road, no path, no nothing,"
said the porter, ruthlessly sacrificing grammar to empha-
sis. " He must have come across the fields and climbed
over the fence to get on to the permanent way. Deliberate suicide is what it looks like."

" How did you learn all this ? " Thorndyke inquired.

" Why, the driver, you see, sir, when him and his mate
had lifted the body off the track, went on to the next
signal-box and sent in his report by telegram. The
station-master told me all about it as we walked down
the line."

Thorndyke thanked the man for his information, and,
as we strolled back towards the lamp-room, discussed
the bearing of these new facts.

" Our friend is unquestionably right in one respect,"
he said ; " this was not an accident. The man might,
if he were near-sighted, deaf or stupid, have climbed
over the fence and got knocked down by the train. But
his position, lying across the rails, can only be explained
by one of two hypotheses : either it was, as the porter
says, deliberate suicide, or else the man was already
dead or insensible. We must leave it at that until we
have seen the body, that is, if the police will allow us to
see it. But here comes the station-master and an officer
with him. Let us hear what they have to say."

The two officials had evidently made up their minds
to decline any outside assistance. The divisional surgeon
would make the necessary examination, and information
could be obtained through the usual channels. The

production of Thorndyke's card, however, somewhat altered the situation. The police inspector hummed and hawed irresolutely, with the card in his hand, but finally agreed to allow us to view the body, and we entered the lamp-room together, the station-master leading the way to turn up the gas.

The stretcher stood on the floor by one wall, its grim burden still hidden by the tarpaulin, and the hand-bag and umbrella lay on a large box, together with the battered frame of a pair of spectacles from which the glasses had fallen out.

" Were these spectacles found by the body ? " Thorndyke inquired.

" Yes," replied the station-master. " They were close to the head and the glass was scattered about on the ballast."

Thorndyke made a note in his pocket-book, and then, as the inspector removed the tarpaulin, he glanced down on the corpse, lying limply on the stretcher and looking grotesquely horrible with its displaced head and distorted limbs. For fully a minute he remained silently stooping over the uncanny object, on which the inspector was now throwing the light of a large lantern ; then he stood up and said quietly to me : " I think we can eliminate two out of the three hypotheses."

The inspector looked at him quickly, and was about to ask a question, when his attention was diverted by the travelling-case which Thorndyke had laid on a shelf and now opened to abstract a couple of pairs of dissecting forceps.

" We've no authority to make a *post mortem*, you know," said the inspector.

" No, of course not," said Thorndyke. " I am merely going to look into the mouth." With one pair of forceps he turned back the lip and, having scrutinised its inner surface, closely examined the teeth.

" May I trouble you for your lens, Jervis ? " he said ; and, as I handed him my doublet ready opened, the inspector brought the lantern close to the dead face and leaned forward eagerly.   In his usual systematic fashion, Thorndyke slowly passed the lens along the whole range of sharp, uneven teeth, and then, bringing it back to the centre, examined with more minuteness the upper incisors.   At length, very delicately, he picked out with his forceps some minute object from between two of the upper front teeth and held it in the focus of the lens. Anticipating his next move, I took a labelled microscope-slide from the case and handed it to him together with a dissecting needle, and, as he transferred the object to the slide and spread it out with the needle, I set up the little microscope on the shelf.

" A drop of Farrant and a cover-glass, please, Jervis," said Thorndyke.

I handed him the bottle, and, when he had let a drop of the mounting fluid fall gently on the object and put on the cover-slip, he placed the slide on the stage of the microscope and examined it attentively.

Happening to glance at the inspector, I observed on his countenance a faint grin, which he politely strove to suppress when he caught my eye.

" I was thinking, sir," he said apologetically, " that it's a bit off the track to be finding out what he had for dinner.   He didn't die of unwholesome feeding."

Thorndyke looked up with a smile.   " It doesn't do, inspector, to assume that anything is off the track in an inquiry of this kind.   Every fact must have some significance, you know."

" I don't see any significance in the diet of a man who has had his head cut off," the inspector rejoined defiantly.

" Don't you ? " said Thorndyke.   " Is there no interest attaching to the last meal of a man who has met a violent death ?   These crumbs, for instance, that are scattered over the dead man's waistcoat.   Can we learn nothing from them ? "

" I don't see what you can learn," was the dogged rejoinder.

Thorndyke picked off the crumbs, one by one, with his forceps, and, having deposited them on a slide, inspected them, first with the lens and then through the microscope.

" I learn," said he, " that shortly before his death, the deceased partook of some kind of wholemeal biscuits, apparently composed partly of oatmeal."

" I call that nothing," said the inspector. " The question that we have got to settle is not what refreshments had the deceased been taking, but what was the cause of his death : did he commit suicide ? was he killed by accident ? or was there any foul play ? "

" I beg your pardon," said Thorndyke, " the questions that remain to be settled are, who killed the deceased and with what motive ? The others are already answered as far as I am concerned."

The inspector stared in sheer amazement not unmixed with incredulity.

" You haven't been long coming to a conclusion, sir," he said.

" No, it was a pretty obvious case of murder," said Thorndyke. " As to the motive, the deceased was a diamond merchant and is believed to have had a quantity of stones about his person. I should suggest that you search the body."

The inspector gave vent to an exclamation of disgust. " I see," he said. " It was just a guess on your part. The dead man was a diamond merchant and had valuable property about him ; therefore he was murdered." He drew himself up, and, regarding Thorndyke with stern reproach, added : " But you must understand, sir, that this is a judicial inquiry, not a prize competition in a penny paper. And, as to searching the body, why, that is what I principally came for." He ostentatiously turned his back on us and proceeded systematically to turn out the dead man's pockets, laying the articles, as he removed them, on the box by the side of the handbag and umbrella.

While he was thus occupied, Thorndyke looked over
the body generally, paying special attention to the soles
of the boots, which, to the inspector's undissembled
amusement, he very thoroughly examined with the lens.

" I should have thought, sir, that his feet were large
enough to be seen with the naked eye," was his comment ; " but perhaps," he added, with a sly glance at
the station-master, " you're a little near-sighted."

Thorndyke chuckled good-humouredly, and, while
the officer continued his search, he looked over the
articles that had already been laid on the box.   The
purse and pocket-book he naturally left for the inspector
to open, but the reading-glasses, pocket-knife and card-
case and other small pocket articles were subjected to a
searching scrutiny.   The inspector watched him out of
the corner of his eye with furtive amusement ; saw him
hold up the glasses to the light to estimate their refractive
power, peer into the tobacco pouch, open the cigarette
book and examine the watermark of the paper, and even
inspect the contents of the silver match-box.

" What might you have expected to find in his tobacco
pouch ? " the officer asked, laying down a bunch of
keys from the dead man's pocket.

" Tobacco," Thorndyke replied stolidly ; " but I did
not expect to find fine-cut Latakia.   I don't remember
ever having seen pure Latakia smoked in cigarettes."

" You do take an interest in things, sir," said the inspector, with a side glance at the stolid station-master.

" I do," Thorndyke agreed ; " and I note that there
are no diamonds among this collection."

" No, and we don't know that he had any about him ;
but there's a gold watch and chain, a diamond scarf-pin,
and a purse containing "—he opened it and tipped out
its contents into his hand—" twelve pounds in gold.
That doesn't look much like robbery, does it ?   What
do you say to the murder theory now ? "

" My opinion is unchanged," said Thorndyke, " and
I should like to examine the spot where the body was

found. Has the engine been inspected ? " he added,
addressing the station-master.

" I telegraphed to Bradfield to have it examined," the
official answered. " The report has probably come in
by now. I'd better see before we start down the line."

We emerged from the lamp-room and, at the door,
found the station-inspector waiting with a telegram. He
handed it to the station-master, who read it aloud.

" The engine has been carefully examined by me. I
find small smear of blood on near leading wheel and
smaller one on next wheel following. No other marks."
He glanced questioningly at Thorndyke, who nodded
and remarked : " It will be interesting to see if the line
tells the same tale."

The station-master looked puzzled and was apparently
about to ask for an explanation ; but the inspector, who
had carefully pocketed the dead man's property, was
impatient to start and, accordingly, when Thorndyke
had repacked his case and had, at his own request, been
furnished with a lantern, we set off down the permanent
way, Thorndyke carrying the light and I the indispensable green case.

" I am a little in the dark about this affair," I said,
when we had allowed the two officials to draw ahead out
of earshot ; " you came to a conclusion remarkably
quickly. What was it that so immediately determined
the opinion of murder as against suicide ? "

" It was a small matter but very conclusive," replied
Thorndyke. " You noticed a small scalp-wound above
the left temple ? It was a glancing wound, and might
easily have been made by the engine. But—the wound
had bled ; and it had bled for an appreciable time. There
were two streams of blood from it, and in both the blood
was firmly clotted and partially dried. But the man
had been decapitated ; and this wound if inflicted by
the engine, must have been made after the decapitation,
since it was on the side most distant from the engine
as it approached. Now a decapitated head does not

2*

bleed. Therefore this wound was inflicted before the decapitation.

" But not only had the wound bled : the blood had trickled down in two streams at right angles to one another. First, in the order of time as shown by the appearance of the stream, it had trickled down the side of the face and dropped on the collar. The second stream ran from the wound to the back of the head. Now, you know, Jervis, there are no exceptions to the law of gravity. If the blood ran down the face towards the chin, the face must have been upright at the time ; and if the blood trickled from the front to the back of the head, the head must have been horizontal and face upwards. But the man, when he was seen by the engine-driver, was lying *face downwards*. The only possible inference is that when the wound was inflicted, the man was in the upright position—standing or sitting ; and that subsequently, and while he was still alive, he lay on his back for a sufficiently long time for the blood to have trickled to the back of his head."

" I see. I was a duffer not to have reasoned this out for myself," I remarked contritely.

" Quick observation and rapid inference come by practice," replied Thorndyke. " But, tell me, what did you notice about the face ? "

" I thought there was a strong suggestion of asphyxia."

" Undoubtedly," said Thorndyke. " It was the face of a suffocated man. You must have noticed, too, that the tongue was very distinctly swollen and that on the inside of the upper lip were deep indentations made by the teeth, as well as one or two slight wounds, obviously caused by heavy pressure on the mouth. And now observe how completely these facts and inferences agree with those from the scalp wound. If we knew that the deceased had received a blow on the head, had struggled with his assailant and been finally borne down and suffocated, we should look for precisely those signs which we have found."

" By the way, what was it that you found wedged between the teeth ? I did not get a chance to look through the microscope."

" Ah ! " said Thorndyke, " there we not only get confirmation, but we carry our inferences a stage further. The object was a little tuft of some textile fabric. Under the microscope I found it to consist of several different fibres, differently dyed. The bulk of it consisted of wool fibres dyed crimson, but there were also cotton fibres dyed blue and a few which looked like jute, dyed yellow. It was obviously a parti-coloured fabric and might have been part of a woman's dress, though the presence of the jute is much more suggestive of a curtain or rug of inferior quality."

" And its importance ? "

" Is that, if it is not part of an article of clothing, then it must have come from an article of furniture, and furniture suggests a habitation."

" That doesn't seem very conclusive," I objected.

" It is not ; but it is valuable corroboration."

" Of what ? "

" Of the suggestion offered by the soles of the dead man's boots. I examined them most minutely and could find no trace of sand, gravel or earth, in spite of the fact that he must have crossed fields and rough land to reach the place where he was found. What I did find was fine tobacco ash, a charred mark as if a cigar or cigarette had been trodden on, several crumbs of biscuit, and, on a projecting brad, some coloured fibres, apparently from a carpet. The manifest suggestion is that the man was killed in a house with a carpeted floor, and carried from thence to the railway."

I was silent for some moments. Well as I knew Thorndyke, I was completely taken by surprise ; a sensation, indeed, that 1 experienced anew every time that I accompanied him on one of his investigations. His marvellous power of co-ordinating apparently insignificant facts, of arranging them into an ordered sequence and making them tell a coherent story, was a phenomenon that I never got used to ; every exhibition of it astonished me afresh.

" If your inferences are correct," I said, " the problem is practically solved. There must be abundant traces inside the house. The only question is, which house is it ? "

" Quite so," replied Thorndyke ; " that is the question, and a very difficult question it is. A glance at that interior would doubtless clear up the whole mystery. But how are we to get that glance ? We cannot enter houses speculatively to see if they present traces of a murder. At present, our clue breaks off abruptly. The other end of it is in some unknown house, and, if we cannot join up the two ends, our problem remains unsolved. For the question is, you remember, Who killed Oscar Brodski ? "

" Then what do you propose to do ? " I asked.

" The next stage of the inquiry is to connect some particular house with this crime. To that end, I can only gather up all available facts and consider each in all its possible bearings. If I cannot establish any such connection, then the inquiry will have failed and we shall have to make a fresh start—say, at Amsterdam, if it turns out that Brodski really had diamonds on his person, as I have no doubt he had."

Here our conversation was interrupted by our arrival at the spot where the body had been found. The station-master had halted, and he and the inspector were now examining the near rail by the light of their lanterns.

" There's remarkably little blood about," said the former. " I've seen a good many accidents of this kind and there has always been a lot of blood, both on the engine and on the road. It's very curious."

Thorndyke glanced at the rail with but slight attention : that question had ceased to interest him. But the light of his lantern flashed on to the ground at the side of the track—a loose, gravelly soil mixed with fragments of chalk—and from thence to the soles of the inspector's boots, which were displayed as he knelt by the rail.

" You observe, Jervis ? " he said in a low voice, and I nodded. The inspector's boot-soles were covered with adherent particles of gravel and conspicuously marked by the chalk on which he had trodden.

" You haven't found the hat, I suppose ? " Thorndyke asked, stooping to pick up a short piece of string that lay on the ground at the side of the track.

" No," replied the inspector, " but it can't be far off. You seem to have found another clue, sir," he added, with a grin, glancing at the piece of string.

" Who knows ? " said Thorndyke. " A short end of white twine with a green strand in it. It may tell us something later. At any rate we'll keep it," and, taking from his pocket a small tin box containing, among other things, a number of seed envelopes, he slipped the string into one of the latter and scribbled a note in pencil on the outside. The inspector watched his proceedings with an indulgent smile, and then returned to his examination of the track, in which Thorndyke now joined.

" I suppose the poor chap was near-sighted," the officer remarked, indicating the remains of the shattered spectacles ; " that might account for his having strayed on to the line."

" Possibly," said Thorndyke. He had already noticed the fragments scattered over a sleeper and the adjacent ballast, and now once more produced his " collecting-box," from which he took another seed envelope. " Would you hand me a pair of forceps, Jervis," he said ; " and perhaps you wouldn't mind taking a pair yourself and helping me to gather up these fragments."

As I complied, the inspector looked up curiously.

" There isn't any doubt that these spectacles belonged to the deceased, is there ? " he asked. " He certainly wore spectacles, for I saw the mark on his nose."

" Still, there is no harm in verifying the fact," said Thorndyke, and he added to me in a lower tone, " Pick up every particle you can find, Jervis. It may be most important."

" I don't quite see how," I said, groping amongst the shingle by the light of the lantern in search of the tiny splinters of glass.

" Don't you ? " returned Thorndyke. " Well, look at these fragments ; some of them are a fair size, but many of these on the sleeper are mere grains. And consider their number. Obviously, the condition of the glass does not agree with the circumstances in which we find it. These are thick concave spectacle-lenses broken into a great number of minute fragments. Now how were they broken ? Not merely by falling, evidently : such a lens, when it is dropped, breaks into a small number of large pieces. Nor were they broken by the wheel passing over them, for they would then have been reduced to fine powder, and that powder would have been visible on the rail, which it is not. The spectacle-frames, you may remember, presented the same incongruity : they were battered and damaged more than they would have been by falling, but not nearly so much as they would have been if the wheel had passed over them."

" What do you suggest, then ? " I asked.

" The appearances suggest that the spectacles had been trodden on. But, if the body was carried here, the probability is that the spectacles were carried here too, and that they were then already broken ; for it is more likely that they were trodden on during the struggle than that the murderer trod on them after bringing them here. Hence the importance of picking up every fragment."

" But why ? " I inquired, rather foolishly, I must admit.

" Because, if, when we have picked up every fragment that we can find, there still remains missing a larger portion of the lenses than we could reasonably expect, that would tend to support our hypothesis and we might find the missing remainder elsewhere. If, on the other hand, we find as much of the lenses as we could expect to find, we must conclude that they were broken on this spot."

While we were conducting our search, the two officials were circling around with their lanterns in quest of the missing hat ; and, when we had at length picked up the last fragment, and a careful search, even aided by a lens, failed to reveal any other, we could see their lanterns moving, like will-o'-the-wisps, some distance down the line.

"We may as well see what we have got before our friends come back," said Thorndyke, glancing at the twinkling lights. "Lay the case down on the grass by the fence ; it will serve for a table."

I did so, and Thorndyke, taking a letter from his pocket, opened it, spread it out flat on the case, securing it with a couple of heavy stones, although the night was quite calm. Then he tipped the contents of the seed envelope out on the paper, and, carefully spreading out the pieces of glass, looked at them for some moments in silence. And, as he looked, there stole over his face a very curious expression ; with sudden eagerness he began picking out the larger fragments and laying them on two visiting-cards which he had taken from his card-case. Rapidly and with wonderful deftness he fitted the pieces together, and, as the reconstituted lenses began gradually to take shape on their cards I looked on with growing excitement, for something in my colleague's manner told me that we were on the verge of a discovery.

At length the two ovals of glass lay on their respective cards, complete save for one or two small gaps ; and the little heap that remained consisted of fragments so minute as to render further reconstruction impossible. Then Thorndyke leaned back and laughed softly.

"This is certainly an unlooked-for result," said he.

"What is ? " I asked.

"Don't you see, my dear fellow ? *There's too much glass.* We have almost completely built up the broken

lenses, and the fragments that are left over are considerably more than are required to fill up the gaps."

I looked at the little heap of small fragments and saw
at once that it was as he had said.   There was a surplus
of small pieces.

"This is very extraordinary," I said.   "What do you
think can be the explanation ? "

"The fragments will probably tell us," he replied,
"if we ask them intelligently."

He lifted the paper and the two cards carefully on to
the ground, and, opening the case, took out the little
microscope, to which he fitted the lowest-power objective and eye-piece—having a combined magnification of
only ten diameters.   Then he transferred the minute
fragments of glass to a slide, and, having arranged the
lantern as a microscope-lamp, commenced his examination.

"Ha ! " he exclaimed presently.   "The plot thickens.
There is too much glass and yet too little ; that is to
say, there are only one or two fragments here that belong
to the spectacles ; not nearly enough to complete the
building up of the lenses.   The remainder consists of a
soft, uneven, moulded glass, easily distinguished from
the clear, hard optical glass.   These foreign fragments
are all curved, as if they had formed part of a cylinder,
and are, I should say, portions of a wine-glass or tumbler."
He moved the slide once or twice, and then continued :
"We are in luck, Jervis.   Here is a fragment with two
little diverging lines etched on it, evidently the points
of an eight-rayed star—and here is another with three
points—the ends of three rays.   This enables us to re-
construct the vessel perfectly.   It was a clear, thin glass
—probably a tumbler—decorated with scattered stars ;
I dare say you know the pattern.   Sometimes there is
an ornamented band in addition, but generally the stars
form the only decoration.   Have a look at the specimen."

I had just applied my eye to the microscope when the
station-master and the inspector came up.   Our appear-

ance, seated on the ground with the microscope between us, was too much for the police officer's gravity, and he laughed long and joyously.

"You must excuse me, gentlemen," he said apologetically, "but really, you know, to an old hand, like myself, it does look a little—well—you understand—I dare say a microscope is a very interesting and amusing thing, but it doesn't get you much forrader in a case like this, does it ? "

"Perhaps not," replied Thorndyke. "By the way, where did you find the hat, after all ? "

"We haven't found it," the inspector replied, a little sheepishly.

"Then we must help you to continue the search," said Thorndyke. "If you will wait a few moments, we will come with you." He poured a few drops of xylol balsam on the cards to fix the reconstituted lenses to their supports and then, packing them and the microscope in the case, announced that he was ready to start.

"Is there any village or hamlet near ? " he asked the station-master.

"None nearer than Corfield. That is about half-a-mile from here."

"And where is the nearest road ? "

"There is a half-made road that runs past a house about three hundred yards from here. It belonged to a building estate that was never built. There is a foot-path from it to the station."

"Are there any other houses near ? "

"No. That is the only house for half-a-mile round, and there is no other road near here."

"Then the probability is that Brodski approached the railway from that direction, as he was found on that side of the permanent way."

The inspector agreeing with this view, we all set off slowly towards the house, piloted by the station-master and searching the ground as we went. The waste land over which we passed was covered with patches of docks and nettles, through each of which the inspector kicked his way, searching with feet and lantern for the missing hat. A walk of three hundred yards brought us to a low wall enclosing a garden, beyond which we could see a small house ; and here we halted while the inspector waded into a large bed of nettles beside the wall and kicked vigorously. Suddenly there came a clinking sound mingled with objurgations, and the inspector hopped out holding one foot and soliloquising profanely.

" I wonder what sort of a fool put a thing like that into a bed of nettles ! " he exclaimed, stroking the injured foot. Thorndyke picked the object up and held it in the light of the lantern, displaying a piece of three-quarter inch rolled iron bar about a foot long. " It doesn't seem to have been there very long," he observed, examining it closely ; " there is hardly any rust on it."

" It has been there long enough for me," growled the inspector, " and I'd like to bang it on the head of the blighter that put it there."

Callously indifferent to the inspector's sufferings, Thorndyke continued calmly to examine the bar. At length, resting his lantern on the wall, he produced his pocket-lens, with which he resumed his investigation, a proceeding that so exasperated the inspector that that afflicted official limped off in dudgeon, followed by the station-master, and we heard him, presently, rapping at the front door of the house.

" Give me a slide, Jervis, with a drop of Farrant on it," said Thorndyke. " There are some fibres sticking to this bar."

I prepared the slide, and, having handed it to him together with a cover-glass, a pair of forceps and a needle, set up the microscope on the wall.

" I'm sorry for the inspector," Thorndyke remarked, with his eye applied to the little instrument, " but that was a lucky kick for us. Just take a look at the specimen."

I did so, and, having moved the slide about until I

had seen the whole of the object, I gave my opinion. " Red wool fibres, blue cotton fibres and some yellow, vegetable fibres that look like jute."

" Yes," said Thorndyke ; " the same combination of fibres as that which we found on the dead man's teeth and probably from the same source. This bar has probably been wiped on that very curtain or rug with which poor Brodski was stifled. We will place it on the wall for future reference, and meanwhile, by hook or by crook, we must get into that house. This is much too plain a hint to be disregarded."

Hastily repacking the case, we hurried to the front of the house, where we found the two officials looking rather vaguely up the unmade road.

" There's a light in the house," said the inspector, " but there's no one at home. I have knocked a dozen times and got no answer. And I don't see what we are hanging about here for at all. The hat is probably close to where the body was found, and we shall find it in the morning."

Thorndyke made no reply, but, entering the garden, stepped up the path, and having knocked gently at the door, stooped and listened attentively at the key-hole.

" I tell you there's no one in the house, sir," said the inspector irritably ; and, as Thorndyke continued to listen, he walked away, muttering angrily. As soon as he was gone, Thorndyke flashed his lantern over the door, the threshold, the path and the small flower-beds ; and, from one of the latter, I presently saw him stoop and pick something up.

" Here is a highly instructive object, Jervis," he said, coming out to the gate, and displaying a cigarette of which only half-an-inch had been smoked.

" How instructive ? " I asked. " What do you learn from it ? "

" Many things," he replied. " It has been lit and thrown away unsmoked ; that indicates a sudden change of purpose. It was thrown away at the entrance to the house, almost certainly by someone entering it. That person was probably a stranger, or he would have taken it in with him. But he had not expected to enter the house, or he would not have lit it. These are the general suggestions ; now as to the particular ones. The paper of the cigarette is of the kind known as the ' Zig-Zag ' brand ; the very conspicuous water-mark is quite easy to see. Now Brodski's cigarette book was a ' Zig-Zag ' book—so called from the way in which the papers pull out. But let us see what the tobacco is like." With a pin from his coat, he hooked out from the unburned end a wisp of dark, dirty brown tobacco, which he held out for my inspection.

"Fine-cut Latakia," I pronounced, without hesitation.

"Very well," said Thorndyke. "Here is a cigarette made of an unusual tobacco similar to that in Brodski's pouch and wrapped in an unusual paper similar to those in Brodski's cigarette book. With due regard to the fourth rule of the syllogism, I suggest that this cigarette was made by Oscar Brodski. But, nevertheless, we will look for corroborative detail."

"What is that ? " I asked.

"You may have noticed that Brodski's matchbox contained round wooden vestas—which are also rather unusual. As he must have lighted the cigarette within a few steps of the gate, we ought to be able to find the match with which he lighted it. Let us try up the road in the direction from which he would probably have approached."

We walked very slowly up the road, searching the ground with the lantern, and we had hardly gone a dozen paces when I espied a match lying on the rough path and eagerly picked it up. It was a round wooden vesta.

Thorndyke examined it with interest and having deposited it, with the cigarette, in his " collecting-box," turned to retrace his steps. "There is now, Jervis, no reasonable doubt that Brodski was murdered in that house. We have succeeded in connecting that house with the crime, and now we have got to force an entrance and join up the other clues." We walked quickly back to the rear of the premises, where we found the inspector conversing disconsolately with the station-master.

"I think, sir," said the former, "we had better go back now; in fact, I don't see what we came here for, but—— Here! I say, sir, you mustn't do that!" For Thorndyke, without a word of warning, had sprung up lightly and thrown one of his long legs over the wall.

"I can't allow you to enter private premises, sir," continued the inspector; but Thorndyke quietly dropped down on the inside and turned to face the officer over the wall.

"Now, listen to me, inspector," said he. "I have good reasons for believing that the dead man, Brodski, has been in this house—in fact, I am prepared to swear an information to that effect. But time is precious; we must follow the scent while it is hot. And I am not proposing to break into the house off-hand. I merely wish to examine the dust-bin."

"The dust-bin!" gasped the inspector. "Well, you really are a most extraordinary gentleman! What do you expect to find in the dust-bin?"

"I am looking for a broken tumbler or wine-glass. It is a thin glass vessel decorated with a pattern of small, eight-pointed stars. It may be in the dust-bin or it may be inside the house."

The inspector hesitated, but Thorndyke's confident manner had evidently impressed him.

"We can soon see what is in the dust-bin," he said, "though what in creation a broken tumbler has to do with the case is more than I can understand. However, here goes." He sprang up on to the wall, and, as he dropped down into the garden, the station-master and I followed.

Thorndyke lingered a few moments by the gate examining the ground, while the two officials hurried up the path. Finding nothing of interest, however, he walked towards the house, looking keenly about him as he went ; but we were hardly half-way up the path when we heard the voice of the inspector calling excitedly.

" Here you are, sir, this way," he sang out, and, as we hurried forward, we suddenly came on the two officials standing over a small rubbish-heap and looking the picture of astonishment. The glare of their lanterns illuminated the heap, and showed us the scattered fragments of a thin glass, star-pattern tumbler.

" I can't imagine how you guessed it was here, sir," said the inspector, with a new-born respect in his tone, " nor what you're going to do with it now you have found it."

" It is merely another link in the chain of evidence," said Thorndyke, taking a pair of forceps from the case and stooping over the heap. " Perhaps we shall find something else." He picked up several small fragments of glass, looked at them closely and dropped them again. Suddenly his eye caught a small splinter at the base of the heap. Seizing it with the forceps, he held it close to his eye in the strong lamplight, and, taking out his lens, examined it with minute attention. " Yes," he said at length, " this is what I was looking for. Let me have those two cards, Jervis."

I produced the two visiting-cards with the reconstructed lenses stuck to them, and, laying them on the lid of the case, threw the light of the lantern on them. Thorndyke looked at them intently for some time, and from them to the fragment that he held. Then, turning to the inspector, he said : " You saw me pick up this splinter of glass ? "

" Yes, sir," replied the officer.

" And you saw where we found these spectacle-glasses and know whose they were ? "

" Yes, sir. They are the dead man's spectacles, and you found them where the body had been."

" Very well," said Thorndyke ; " now observe " ; and, as the two officials craned forward with parted lips, he laid the little splinter in a gap in one of the lenses and then gave it a gentle push forward, when it occupied the gap perfectly, joining edge to edge with the adjacent fragments and rendering that portion of the lens complete.

" My God ! " exclaimed the inspector. " How on earth did you know ? "

" I must explain that later," said Thorndyke. " Meanwhile we had better have a look inside the house. I expect to find there a cigarette—or possibly a cigar—which has been trodden on, some whole-meal biscuits, possibly a wooden vesta, and perhaps even the missing hat."

At the mention of the hat, the inspector stepped eagerly to the back door, but, finding it bolted, he tried the window. This also was securely fastened and, on Thorndyke's advice, we went round to the front door.

" This door is locked too," said the inspector. " I'm afraid we shall have to break in. It's a nuisance, though."

" Have a look at the window," suggested Thorndyke.

The officer did so, struggling vainly to undo the patent catch with his pocket-knife.

" It's no go," he said, coming back to the door. " We shall have to——" He broke off with an astonished stare, for the door stood open and Thorndyke was putting something in his pocket.

" Your friend doesn't waste much time—even in picking a lock," he remarked to me, as we followed Thorndyke into the house ; but his reflections were soon merged in a new surprise. Thorndyke had preceded us into a small sitting-room dimly lighted by a hanging lamp turned down low.

As we entered he turned up the light and glanced about the room. A whisky-bottle was on the table, with a siphon, a tumbler and a biscuit-box. Pointing to the latter, Thorndyke said to the inspector : " See what is in that box."

The inspector raised the lid and peeped in, the station-

master peered over his shoulder, and then both stared
at Thorndyke.

"How in the name of goodness did you know that
there were whole-meal biscuits in the house, sir ? "
exclaimed the station-master.

" You'd be disappointed if I told you," replied Thorndyke. " But look at this." He pointed to the hearth,
where lay a flattened, half-smoked cigarette and a round
wooden vesta. The inspector gazed at these objects in
silent wonder, while, as to the station-master, he continued to stare at Thorndyke with what I can only
describe as superstitious awe.

"You have the dead man's property with you, I
believe ? " said my colleague.

"Yes," replied the inspector ; " I put the things in
my pocket for safety."

" Then," said Thorndyke, picking up the flattened
cigarette, " let us have a look at his tobacco-pouch."

As the officer produced and opened the pouch, Thorndyke neatly cut open the cigarette with his sharp pocket-
knife. " Now," said he, " what kind of tobacco is in
the pouch ? "

The inspector took out a pinch, looked at it and smelt
it distastefully. " It's one of those stinking tobaccos,"
he said, " that they put in mixtures—Latakia, I think."

" And what is this ? " asked Thorndyke, pointing to
the open cigarette.

" Same stuff, undoubtedly," replied the inspector.

" And now let us see his cigarette papers," said
Thorndyke.

The little book, or rather packet—for it consisted of
separated papers—was produced from the officer's pocket
and a sample paper abstracted. Thorndyke laid the
half-burnt paper beside it, and the inspector having
examined the two, held them up to the light.

" There isn't much chance of mistaking that ' Zig-
Zag ' watermark," he said. " This cigarette was made
by the deceased ; there can't be the shadow of a doubt."

" One more point," said Thorndyke, laying the burnt wooden vesta on the table. " You have his match-box ? "

The inspector brought forth the little silver casket, opened it and compared the wooden vestas that it contained with the burnt end. Then he shut the box with a snap.

" You've proved it up to the hilt," said he. " If we could only find the hat, we should have a complete case."

" I'm not sure that we haven't found the hat," said Thorndyke. " You notice that something besides coal has been burned in the grate."

The inspector ran eagerly to the fire-place and began, with feverish hands, to pick out the remains of the extinct fire. " The cinders are still warm," he said, " and they are certainly not all coal cinders. There has been wood burned here on top of the coal, and these little black lumps are neither coal nor wood. They may quite possibly be the remains of a burnt hat, but, lord ! who can tell ? You can put together the pieces of broken spectacle-glasses, but you can't build up a hat out of a few cinders." He held out a handful of little, black, spongy cinders and looked ruefully at Thorndyke, who took them from him and laid them out on a sheet of paper.

" We can't reconstitute the hat, certainly," my friend agreed, " but we may be able to ascertain the origin of these remains. They may not be cinders of a hat, after all." He lit a wax match and, taking up one of the charred fragments, applied the flame to it. The cindery mass fused at once with a crackling, seething sound, emitting a dense smoke, and instantly the air became charged with a pungent, resinous odour mingled with the smell of burning animal matter.

" Smells like varnish," the station-master remarked.

" Yes. Shellac," said Thorndyke ; " so the first test gives a positive result. The next test will take more time."

He opened the green case and took from it a little flask, fitted for Marsh's arsenic test, with a safety funnel and escape tube, a small folding tripod, a spirit lamp and a disc of asbestos to serve as a sand-bath. Dropping into the flask several of the cindery masses, selected after careful inspection, he filled it up with alcohol and placed it on the disc, which he rested on the tripod. Then he lighted the spirit lamp underneath and sat down to wait for the alcohol to boil.

" There is one little point that we may as well settle," he said presently, as the bubbles began to rise in the flask. " Give me a slide with a drop of Farrant on it, Jervis."

I prepared the slide while Thorndyke, with a pair of forceps, picked out a tiny wisp from the table-cloth. " I fancy we have seen this fabric before," he remarked, as he laid the little pinch of fluff in the mounting fluid and slipped the slide on to the stage of the microscope. " Yes," he continued, looking into the eye-piece, " here are our old acquaintances, the red wool fibres, the blue cotton and the yellow jute. We must label this at once or we may confuse it with the other specimens."

" Have you any idea how the deceased met his death ? " the inspector asked.

" Yes," replied Thorndyke. " I take it that the murderer enticed him into this room and gave him some refreshments. The murderer sat in the chair in which you are sitting, Brodski sat in that small arm-chair. Then I imagine the murderer attacked him with that iron bar that you found among the nettles, failed to kill him at the first stroke, struggled with him and finally suffocated him with the table-cloth. By the way, there is just one more point. You recognise this piece of string ? " He took from his " collecting-box " the little end of twine that had been picked up by the line. The inspector nodded. " If you look behind you, you will see where it came from."

The officer turned sharply and his eye lighted on a string-box on the mantelpiece. He lifted it down, and

Thorndyke drew out from it a length of white twine with one green strand, which he compared with the piece in his hand. " The green strand in it makes the identification fairly certain," he said. " Of course the string was used to secure the umbrella and hand-bag. He could not have carried them in his hand, encumbered as he was with the corpse. But I expect our other specimen is ready now." He lifted the flask off the tripod, and, giving it a vigorous shake, examined the contents through his lens. The alcohol had now become dark-brown in colour, and was noticeably thicker and more syrupy in consistence.

" I think we have enough here for a rough test," said he, selecting a pipette and a slide from the case. He dipped the former into the flask and, having sucked up a few drops of the alcohol from the bottom, held the pipette over the slide on which he allowed the contained fluid to drop.

Laying a cover-glass on the little pool of alcohol, he put the slide on the microscope stage and examined it attentively, while we watched him in expectant silence.

At length he looked up, and, addressing the inspector, asked : " Do you know what felt hats are made of ? "

" I can't say that I do, sir," replied the officer.

" Well, the better quality hats are made of rabbits' and hares' wool—the soft under-fur, you know— cemented together with shellac. Now there is very little doubt that these cinders contain shellac, and with the microscope I find a number of small hairs of a rabbit. I have, therefore, little hesitation in saying that these cinders are the remains of a hard felt hat ; and, as the hairs do not appear to be dyed, I should say it was a grey hat."

At this moment our conclave was interrupted by hurried footsteps on the garden path and, as we turned with one accord, an elderly woman burst into the room.

She stood for a moment in mute astonishment, and

then, looking from one to the other, demanded : " Who are you ? and what are you doing here ? "

The inspector rose. " I am a police officer, madam," said he. " I can't give you any further information just now, but, if you will excuse me asking, who are you ? "

" I am Mr. Hickler's housekeeper," she replied.

" And Mr. Hickler ; are you expecting him home shortly ? "

" No, I am not," was the curt reply. " Mr. Hickler is away from home just now. He left this evening by the boat train."

" For Amsterdam ? " asked Thorndyke.

" I believe so, though I don't see what business it is of yours," the housekeeper answered.

" I thought he might, perhaps, be a diamond broker or merchant," said Thorndyke. " A good many of them travel by that train."

" So he is," said the woman, " at least, he has something to do with diamonds."

" Ah. Well, we must be going, Jervis," said Thorndyke, " we have finished here, and we have to find an hotel or inn. Can I have a word with you, inspector ? "

The officer, now entirely humble and reverent, followed us out into the garden to receive Thorndyke's parting advice.

" You had better take possession of the house at once, and get rid of the housekeeper. Nothing must be removed. Preserve those cinders and see that the rubbish-heap is not disturbed, and, above all, don't have the room swept. The station-master or I will let them know at the police station, so that they can send an officer to relieve you."

With a friendly " good-night " we went on our way, guided by the station-master ; and here our connection with the case came to an end. Hickler (whose Christian name turned out to be Silas) was, it is true, arrested as he stepped ashore from the steamer, and a packet of diamonds, subsequently identified as the property of

Oscar Brodski, found upon his person. But he was never brought to trial, for on the return voyage he contrived to elude his guards for an instant as the ship was approaching the English coast, and it was not until three days later, when a handcuffed body was cast up on the lonely shore by Orfordness, that the authorities knew the fate of Silas Hickler.

"An appropriate and dramatic end to a singular and yet typical case," said Thorndyke, as he put down the newspaper. "I hope it has enlarged your knowledge, Jervis, and enabled you to form one or two useful corollaries."

"I prefer to hear you sing the medico-legal doxology," I answered, turning upon him like the proverbial worm and grinning derisively (which the worm does not).

"I know you do," he retorted, with mock gravity, "and I lament your lack of mental initiative. However, the points that this case illustrates are these : First, the danger of delay ; the vital importance of instant action before that frail and fleeting thing that we call a clue has time to evaporate. A delay of a few hours would have left us with hardly a single datum. Second, the necessity of pursuing the most trivial clue to an absolute finish, as illustrated by the spectacles. Third, the urgent need of a trained scientist to aid the police ; and, last," he concluded, with a smile, "we learn never to go abroad without the invaluable green case."

2   A CASE OF
                                PREMEDITATION

I. The Elimination of Mr. Pratt

THE wine merchant who should supply a consignment of *petit vin* to a customer who had ordered, and paid for, a vintage wine, would render himself subject to unambiguous comment. Nay ! more ; he would be liable to certain legal penalties. And yet his conduct would be morally indistinguishable from that of the railway company which, having accepted a first-class fare, inflicts upon the passenger that kind of company which he has paid to avoid. But the corporate conscience, as Herbert Spencer was wont to explain, is an altogether inferior product to that of the individual.

Such were the reflections of Mr. Rufus Pembury when, as the train was about to move out of Maidstone (West) station, a coarse and burly man (clearly a denizen of the third-class) was ushered into his compartment by the guard. He had paid the higher fare, not for cushioned seats, but for seclusion or, at least, select companionship. The man's entry had deprived him of both, and he resented it.

But if the presence of this stranger involved a breach of contract, his conduct was a positive affront—an indignity ; for, no sooner had the train started than he fixed upon Mr. Pembury a gaze of impertinent intensity, and continued thereafter to regard him with a stare as steady and unwinking as that of a Polynesian idol.

It was offensive to a degree, and highly disconcerting withal. Mr. Pembury fidgeted in his seat with increasing discomfort and rising temper. He looked into his pocket-book, read one or two letters and sorted a collection of visiting-cards. He even thought of opening his umbrella. Finally, his patience exhausted and his wrath mounting to boiling-point, he turned to the stranger with frosty remonstrance.

" I imagine, sir, that you will have no difficulty in recognising me, should we ever meet again—which God forbid."

" I should recognise you among ten thousand," was the reply, so unexpected as to leave Mr. Pembury speechless. " You see," the stranger continued impressively, " I've got the gift of faces. I never forget."

" That must be a great consolation," said Pembury.

" It's very useful to me," said the stranger, " at least, it used to be, when I was a warder at Portland—you remember me, I dare say : my name is Pratt. I was assistant-warder in your time. God-forsaken hole, Portland, and mighty glad I was when they used to send me up to town on reckernising duty. Holloway was the house of detention then, you remember ; that was before they moved to Brixton."

Pratt paused in his reminiscences, and Pembury, pale and gasping with astonishment, pulled himself together.

" I think," said he, " you must be mistaking me for someone else."

" I don't," replied Pratt. " You're Francis Dobbs, that's who you are. Slipped away from Portland one evening about twelve years ago. Clothes washed up on the Bill next day. No trace of fugitive. As neat a mizzle as ever I heard of. But there are a couple of photographs and a set of finger-prints at the Habitual Criminals Register. P'raps you'd like to come and see 'em ? "

" Why should I go to the Habitual Criminals Register ? " Pembury demanded faintly.

" Ah ! Exactly. Why should you ? When you are a man of means, and a little judiciously invested capital would render it unnecessary ? "

Pembury looked out of the window, and for a minute or more preserved a stony silence. At length he turned suddenly to Pratt. " How much ? " he asked.

" I shouldn't think a couple of hundred a year would hurt you," was the calm reply.

Pembury reflected awhile. " What makes you think I am a man of means ? " he asked presently.

Pratt smiled grimly. " Bless you, Mr. Pembury," said he, " I know all about you. Why, for the last six months I have been living within half-a-mile of your house."

" The devil you have ! "

" Yes. When I retired from the service, General

O'Gorman engaged me as a sort of steward or caretaker of his little place at Baysford—he's very seldom there himself—and the very day after I came down, I met you and spotted you, but, naturally, I kept out of sight myself. Thought I'd find out whether you were good for anything before I spoke, so I've been keeping my ears open and I find you are good for a couple of hundred."

There was an interval of silence, and then the ex-warder resumed—

" That's what comes of having a memory for faces. Now there's Jack Ellis, on the other hand ; he must have had you under his nose for a couple of years, and yet he's never twigged—he never will either," added Pratt, already regretting the confidence into which his vanity had led him.

" Who is Jack Ellis ? " Pembury demanded sharply.

" Why, he's a sort of supernumary at the Baysford Police Station ; does odd jobs ; rural detective, helps in the office and that sort of thing. He was in the Civil Guard at Portland, in your time, but he got his left forefinger chopped off, so they pensioned him, and, as he was a Baysford man, he got this billet. But he'll never reckernise you, don't you fear."

" Unless you direct his attention to me," suggested Pembury.

" There's no fear of that," laughed Pratt. " You can trust me to sit quiet on my own nest-egg. Besides, we're not very friendly. He came nosing round our place after the parlourmaid—him a married man, mark you ! But I soon boosted him out, I can tell you ; and Jack Ellis don't like me now."

" I see," said Pembury reflectively ; then, after a pause, he asked : " Who is this General O'Gorman ? I seem to know the name."

" I expect you do," said Pratt. " He was governor of Dartmoor when I was there—that was my last billet— and, let me tell you, if he'd been at Portland in your time, you'd never have got away."

" How is that ? "

" Why, you see, the general is a great man on blood-hounds. He kept a pack at Dartmoor and, you bet, those lags knew it. There were no attempted escapes in those days. They wouldn't have had a chance."

" He has the pack still, hasn't he ? " asked Pembury.

" Rather. Spends any amount of time on training 'em, too. He's always hoping there'll be a burglary or a murder in the neighbourhood so as he can try 'em, but he's never got a chance yet. P'raps the crooks have heard about 'em. But, to come back to our little arrange-ment : what do you say to a couple of hundred, paid quarterly, if you like ? "

" I can't settle the matter off-hand," said Pembury. " You must give me time to think it over."

" Very well," said Pratt. " I shall be back at Baysford to-morrow evening. That will give you a clear day to think it over. Shall I look in at your place to-morrow night ? "

" No," replied Pembury ; " you'd better not be seen at my house, nor I at yours. If I meet you at some quiet spot, where we shan't be seen, we can settle our business without anyone knowing that we have met. It won't take long, and we can't be too careful."

" That's true," agreed Pratt. " Well, I'll tell you what. There's an avenue leading up to our house ; you know it, I expect. There's no lodge, and the gates are always ajar, excepting at night. Now I shall be down by the six-thirty at Baysford. Our place is a quarter of an hour from the station. Say you meet me in the avenue at a quarter to seven. How will that do ? "

" That will suit me," said Pembury ; " that is, if you are sure the bloodhounds won't be straying about the grounds."

" Lord bless you, no ! " laughed Pratt. " D'you suppose the general lets his precious hounds stray about for any casual crook to feed with poisoned sausage ? No, they're locked up safe in the kennels at the back of

3

the house. Hallo! This'll be Swanley, I expect. I'll
change into a smoker here and leave you time to turn
the matter over in your mind. So long. To-morrow
evening in the avenue at a quarter to seven. And, I say,
Mr. Pembury, you might as well bring the first instalment with you—fifty, in small notes or gold."

"Very well," said Mr. Pembury. He spoke coldly
enough, but there was a flush on his cheeks and an angry
light in his eyes, which, perhaps, the ex-warder noticed;
for when he had stepped out and shut the door, he thrust
his head in at the window and said threateningly—

"One more word, Mr. Pembury-Dobbs: no hanky-
panky, you know. I'm an old hand and pretty fly, I
am. So don't you try any chickery-pokery on me.
That's all." He withdrew his head and disappeared,
leaving Pembury to his reflections.

The nature of those reflections, if some telepathist—
transferring his attention for the moment from hidden
court-cards or missing thimbles to more practical matters
—could have conveyed them into the mind of Mr. Pratt,
would have caused that quondam official some surprise
and, perhaps, a little disquiet. For long experience of
the criminal, as he appears when in durance, had produced
some rather misleading ideas as to his behaviour when at
large. In fact, the ex-warder had considerably under-
estimated the ex-convict.

Rufus Pembury, to give him his real name—for Dobbs
was literally a *nom de guerre*—was a man of strong
character and intelligence. So much so that, having
tried the criminal career and found it not worth pursuing,
he had definitely abandoned it. When the cattle-boat
that picked him up off Portland Bill had landed him at
an American port, he brought his entire ability and
energy to bear on legitimate commercial pursuits, and
with such success that, at the end of ten years, he was
able to return to England with a moderate competence.
Then he had taken a modest house near the little town
of Baysford, where he had lived quietly on his savings

for the last two years, holding aloof without much difficulty from the rather exclusive local society; and here he might have lived out the rest of his life in peace but for the unlucky chance that brought the man Pratt into the neighbourhood. With the arrival of Pratt his security was utterly destroyed.

There is something eminently unsatisfactory about a blackmailer. No arrangement with him has any permanent validity. No undertaking that he gives is binding. The thing which he has sold remains in his possession to sell over again. He pockets the price of emancipation, but retains the key of the fetters. In short, the blackmailer is a totally impossible person.

Such were the considerations that had passed through the mind of Rufus Pembury, even while Pratt was making his proposals; and those proposals he had never for an instant entertained. The ex-warder's advice to him to " turn the matter over in his mind " was unnecessary. For his mind was already made up. His decision was arrived at in the very moment when Pratt had disclosed his identity. The conclusion was self-evident. Before Pratt appeared he was living in peace and security. While Pratt remained, his liberty was precarious from moment to moment. If Pratt should disappear, his peace and security would return. Therefore Pratt must be eliminated.

It was a logical consequence.

The profound meditations, therefore, in which Pembury remained immersed for the remainder of the journey had nothing whatever to do with the quarterly allowance; they were concerned exclusively with the elimination of ex-warder Pratt.

Now Rufus Pembury was not a ferocious man. He was not even cruel. But he was gifted with a certain magnanimous cynicism which ignored the trivialities of sentiment and regarded only the main issues. If a wasp hummed over his tea-cup, he would crush that wasp; but not with his bare hand. The wasp carried

the means of aggression.   That was the wasp's look-out.
His concern was to avoid being stung.

So it was with Pratt.   The man had elected, for his
own profit, to threaten Pembury's liberty.   Very well.
He had done it at his own risk.   That risk was no
concern of Pembury's.   *His* concern was his own
safety.

When Pembury alighted at Charing Cross, he directed
his steps (after having watched Pratt's departure from
the station) to Buckingham Street, Strand, where he
entered a quiet private hotel.   He was apparently
expected, for the manageress greeted him by his name as
she handed him his key.

" Are you staying in town, Mr. Pembury ? " she asked.

" No," was the reply.   " I go back to-morrow
morning, but I may be coming up again shortly.   By
the way, you used to have an encyclopædia in one of the
rooms.   Could I see it for a moment ? "

" It is in the drawing-room," said the manageress.
" Shall I show you ?—but you know the way, don't
you ? "

Certainly Mr. Pembury knew the way.   It was on
the first floor ; a pleasant old-world room looking on
the quiet old street, and on a shelf, amidst a collect ion
of novels, stood the sedate volumes of *Chambers's
Encyclopædia*.

That a gentleman from the country should desire to
look up the subject of " hounds " would not, to a casual
observer, have seemed unnatural.   But when from
hounds the student proceeded to the article on blood,
and thence to one devoted to perfumes, the observer
might reasonably have felt some surprise ; and this
surprise might have been augmented if he had followed
Mr. Pembury's subsequent proceedings, and especially
if he had considered them as the actions of a man whose
immediate aim was the removal of a superfluous unit of
the population.

Having deposited his bag and umbrella in his room,

Pembury set forth from the hotel as one with a definite purpose ; and his footsteps led, in the first place, to an umbrella shop in the Strand, where he selected a thick rattan cane. There was nothing remarkable in this, perhaps ; but the cane was of an uncomely thickness and the salesman protested. " I like a thick cane," said Pembury.

" Yes, sir ; but for a gentleman of your height " (Pembury was a small, slightly-built man) " I would venture to suggest——— "

" I like a thick cane," repeated Pembury. " Cut it down to the proper length and don't rivet the ferrule on. I'll cement it on when I get home."

His next investment would have seemed more to the purpose, though suggestive of unexpected crudity of method. It was a large Norwegian knife. But not content with this he went on forthwith to a second cutler's and purchased a second knife, the exact duplicate of the first. Now, for what purpose could he want two identically similar knives ? And why not have bought them both at the same shop ? It was highly mysterious.

Shopping appeared to be a positive mania with Rufus Pembury. In the course of the next half-hour he acquired a cheap hand-bag, an artist's black-japanned brush-case, a three-cornered file, a stick of elastic glue and a pair of iron crucible-tongs. Still insatiable, he repaired to an old-fashioned chemist's shop in a by-street, where he further enriched himself with a packet of absorbent cotton-wool and an ounce of permanganate of potash ; and, as the chemist wrapped up these articles, with the occult and necromantic air peculiar to chemists, Pembury watched him impassively.

" I suppose you don't keep musk ? " he asked carelessly.

The chemist paused in the act of heating a stick of sealing-wax, and appeared as if about to mutter an incantation. But he merely replied : " No, sir. Not the solid musk ; it's so very costly. But I have the essence."

" That isn't as strong as the pure stuff, I suppose ? "

" No," replied the chemist, with a cryptic smile, " not *so* strong, but strong enough. These animal perfumes are so very penetrating, you know ; and so lasting. Why, I venture to say that if you were to sprinkle a table-spoonful of the essence in the middle of St. Paul's, the place would smell of it six months hence."

" You don't say so ! " said Pembury. " Well, that ought to be enough for anybody. I'll take a small quantity, please, and, for goodness' sake, see that there isn't any on the outside of the bottle. The stuff isn't for myself, and I don't want to go about smelling like a civet cat."

" Naturally you don't, sir," agreed the chemist. He then produced an ounce bottle, a small glass funnel and a stoppered bottle labelled " Ess. Moschi," with which he proceeded to perform a few trifling feats of legerdemain.

" There, sir," said he, when he had finished the performance, " there is not a drop on the outside of the bottle, and, if I fit it with a rubber cork, you will be quite secure."

Pembury's dislike of musk appeared to be excessive, for, when the chemist had retired into a secret cubicle as if to hold converse with some familiar spirit (but actually to change half-a-crown), he took the brush-case from his bag, pulled off its lid, and then, with the crucible-tongs, daintily lifted the bottle off the counter, slid it softly into the brush case, and, replacing the lid, returned the case and tongs to the bag. The other two packets he took from the counter and dropped into his pocket, and when the presiding wizard, having miraculously transformed a single half-crown into four pennies, handed him the product, he left the shop and walked thoughtfully back towards the Strand. Suddenly a new idea seemed to strike him. He halted, considered

for a few moments and then strode away northward
to make the oddest of all his purchases.

The transaction took place in a shop in the Seven
Dials, whose strange stock-in-trade ranged the whole
zoological gamut, from water-snails to Angora cats.
Pembury looked at a cage of guinea-pigs in the window
and entered the shop.

"Do you happen to have a dead guinea-pig?" he
asked.

"No; mine are all alive," replied the man, adding,
with a sinister grin : "but they're not immortal, you
know."

Pembury looked at the man distastefully. There is
an appreciable difference between a guinea-pig and a
blackmailer. "Any small mammal would do," he said.

"There's a dead rat in that cage, if he's any good,"
said the man. "Died this morning, so he's quite fresh."

"I'll take the rat," said Pembury ; "he'll do quite
well."

The little corpse was accordingly made into a parcel
and deposited in the bag, and Pembury, having tendered
a complimentary fee, made his way back to the hotel.

After a modest lunch he went forth and spent the
remainder of the day transacting the business which had
originally brought him to town. He dined at a restaurant
and did not return to his hotel until ten o'clock, when
he took his key, and tucking under his arm a parcel that
he had brought in with him, retired for the night. But
before undressing—and after locking his door—he did
a very strange and unaccountable thing. Having pulled
off the loose ferrule from his newly-purchased cane, he
bored a hole in the bottom of it with the spike end of
the file. Then, using the latter as a broach, he enlarged
the hole until only a narrow rim of the bottom was left.
He next rolled up a small ball of cotton-wool and pushed
it into the ferrule ; and, having smeared the end of the
cane with elastic glue, he replaced the ferrule, warming
it over the gas to make the glue stick.

When he had finished with the cane, he turned his attention to one of the Norwegian knives. First, he carefully removed with the file most of the bright, yellow varnish from the wooden case or handle.

Then he opened the knife, and, cutting the string of the parcel that he had brought in, took from it the dead rat which he had bought at the zoologist's. Laying the animal on a sheet of paper, he cut off its head, and, holding it up by the tail, allowed the blood that oozed from the neck to drop on the knife, spreading it over both sides of the blade and handle with his finger.

Then he laid the knife on the paper and softly opened the window. From the darkness below came the voice of a cat, apparently perfecting itself in the execution of chromatic scales ; and in that direction Pembury flung the body and head of the rat, and closed the window. Finally, having washed his hands and stuffed the paper from the parcel into the fire-place, he went to bed.

But his proceedings in the morning were equally mysterious. Having breakfasted betimes, he returned to his bedroom and locked himself in. Then he tied his new cane, handle downwards, to the leg of the dressing-table. Next, with the crucible-tongs, he drew the little bottle of musk from the brush-case, and, having assured himself, by sniffing at it, that the exterior was really free from odour, he withdrew the rubber cork. Then, slowly and with infinite care, he poured a few drops—perhaps half-a-teaspoonful—of the essence on the cotton-wool that bulged through the hole in the ferrule, watching the absorbent material narrowly as it soaked up the liquid. When it was saturated he proceeded to treat the knife in the same fashion, letting fall a drop of the essence on the wooden handle—which soaked it up readily. This done, he slid up the window and looked out. Immediately below was a tiny yard in which grew, or rather survived, a couple of faded laurel bushes. The body of the rat was nowhere to be seen ; it had apparently been spirited away in the night. Holding out the bottle, which he still held, he dropped it into the bushes, flinging the rubber cork after it.

His next proceeding was to take a tube of vaseline from his dressing-bag and squeeze a small quantity on to his fingers. With this he thoroughly smeared the shoulder of the brush-case and the inside of the lid, so as to ensure an air-tight joint. Having wiped his fingers, he picked the knife up with the crucible-tongs, and, dropping it into the brush-case, immediately pushed on the lid. Then he heated the tips of the tongs in the gas flame, to destroy the scent, packed the tongs and brush-case in the bag, untied the cane—carefully avoiding contact with the ferrule—and, taking up the two bags, went out, holding the cane by its middle.

There was no difficulty in finding an empty compartment, for first-class passengers were few at that time in the morning. Pembury waited on the platform until the guard's whistle sounded, when he stepped into the compartment, shut the door and laid the cane on the seat with its ferrule projecting out of the off-side window, in which position it remained until the train drew up in Baysford station.

Pembury left his dressing-bag at the cloakroom, and, still grasping the cane by its middle, he sallied forth. The town of Baysford lay some half-a-mile to the east of the station ; his own house was a mile along the road to the west ; and half-way between his house and the station was the residence of General O'Gorman. He knew the place well. Originally a farmhouse, it stood on the edge of a great expanse of flat meadows and communicated with the road by an avenue, nearly three hundred yards long, of ancient trees. The avenue was shut off from the road by a pair of iron gates, but these were merely ornamental, for the place was unenclosed and accessible from the surrounding meadows—indeed, an indistinct footpath crossed the meadows and intersected the avenue about half-way up.

On this occasion Pembury, whose objective was the

3*

avenue, elected to approach it by the latter route ; and at each stile or fence that he surmounted, he paused to survey the country. Presently the avenue arose before him, lying athwart the narrow track, and, as he entered it between two of the trees, he halted and looked about him.

He stood listening for a while. Beyond the faint rustle of leaves no sound was to be heard. Evidently there was no one about, and, as Pratt was at large, it was probable that the general was absent.

And now Pembury began to examine the adjacent trees with more than a casual interest. The two between which he had entered were respectively an elm and a great pollard oak, the latter being an immense tree whose huge, warty bole divided about seven feet from the ground into three limbs, each as large as a fair-sized tree, of which the largest swept outward in a great curve half-way across the avenue. On this patriarch Pembury bestowed especial attention, walking completely round it and finally laying down his bag and cane (the latter resting on the bag with the ferrule off the ground) that he might climb up, by the aid of the warty outgrowths, to examine the crown ; and he had just stepped up into the space between the three limbs, when the creaking of the iron gates was followed by a quick step in the avenue. Hastily he let himself down from the tree, and, gathering up his possessions, stood close behind the great bole.

" Just as well not to be seen," was his reflection, as he hugged the tree closely and waited, peering cautiously round the trunk. Soon a streak of moving shadow heralded the stranger's approach, and he moved round to keep the trunk between himself and the intruder. On the footsteps came, until the stranger was abreast of the tree ; and when he had passed Pembury peeped round at the retreating figure. It was only the postman, but then the man knew him, and he was glad he had kept out of sight.

Apparently the oak did not meet his requirements, for he stepped out and looked up and down the avenue.

Then, beyond the elm, he caught sight of an ancient pollard hornbeam—a strange, fantastic tree whose trunk widened out trumpet-like above into a broad crown, from the edge of which multitudinous branches uprose like the limbs of some weird hamadryad.

That tree he approved at a glance, but he lingered behind the oak until the postman, returning with brisk step and cheerful whistle, passed down the avenue and left him once more in solitude. Then he moved on with a resolute air to the hornbeam.

The crown of the trunk was barely six feet from the ground. He could reach it easily, as he found on trying. Standing the cane against the tree—ferrule downwards, this time—he took the brush-case from the bag, pulled off the lid, and, with the crucible-tongs, lifted out the knife and laid it on the crown of the tree, just out of sight, leaving the tongs—also invisible—still grasping the knife. He was about to replace the brush-case in the bag, when he appeared to alter his mind. Sniffing at it, and finding it reeking with the sickly perfume, he pushed the lid on again and threw the case up into the tree, where he heard it roll down into the central hollow of the crown. Then he closed the bag, and, taking the cane by its handle, moved slowly away in the direction whence he had come, passing out of the avenue between the elm and the oak.

His mode of progress was certainly peculiar. He walked with excessive slowness, trailing the cane along the ground, and every few paces he would stop and press the ferrule firmly against the earth, so that, to any one who should have observed him, he would have appeared to be wrapped in an absorbing reverie.

Thus he moved on across the fields, not, however, returning to the high road, but crossing another stretch of fields until he emerged into a narrow lane that led out into the High Street. Immediately opposite to the lane was the police station, distinguished from the adjacent cottages only by its lamp, its open door and the notices pasted up outside. Straight across the road Pembury walked, still trailing the cane, and halted at the station door to read the notices, resting his cane on the doorstep as he did so. Through the open doorway he could see a man writing at a desk. The man's back was towards him, but, presently, a movement brought his left hand into view, and Pembury noted that the forefinger was missing. This, then, was Jack Ellis, late of the Civil Guard at Portland.

Even while he was looking the man turned his head, and Pembury recognised him at once. He had frequently met him on the road between Baysford and the adjoining village of Thorpe, and always at the same time. Apparently Ellis paid a daily visit to Thorpe—perhaps to receive a report from the rural constable—and he started between three and four and returned between seven and a quarter past.

Pembury looked at his watch. It was a quarter past three. He moved away thoughtfully (holding his cane, now, by the middle), and began to walk slowly in the direction of Thorpe—westward.

For a while he was deeply meditative, and his face wore a puzzled frown. Then, suddenly, his face cleared and he strode forward at a brisker pace. Presently he passed through a gap in the hedge, and, walking in a field parallel with the road, took out his purse—a small pig-skin pouch. Having frugally emptied it of its contents, excepting a few shillings, he thrust the ferrule of his cane into the small compartment ordinarily reserved for gold or notes.

And thus he continued to walk on slowly, carrying the cane by the middle and the purse jammed on the end.

At length he reached a sharp double curve in the road whence he could see back for a considerable distance ; and here, opposite a small opening, he sat down to wait. The hedge screened him effectually from the gaze of passers-by—though these were few enough—without interfering with his view.

A quarter of an hour passed. He began to be uneasy. Had he been mistaken ? Were Ellis's visits only occasional instead of daily, as he had thought ? That would be tiresome though not actually disastrous. But at this point in his reflections a figure came into view, advancing along the road with a steady swing. He recognised the figure. It was Ellis.

But there was another figure advancing from the opposite direction : a labourer, apparently. He prepared to shift his ground, but another glance showed him that the labourer would pass first. He waited. The labourer came on and, at length, passed the opening, and, as he did so, Ellis disappeared for a moment in a bend of the road. Instantly Pembury passed his cane through the opening in the hedge, shook off the purse and pushed it into the middle of the footway. Then he crept forward, behind the hedge, towards the approaching official, and again sat down to wait. On came the steady tramp of the unconscious Ellis, and, as it passed, Pembury drew aside an obstructing branch and peered out at the retreating figure. The question now was, would Ellis see the purse ? It was not a very conspicuous object.

The footsteps stopped abruptly. Looking out, Pembury saw the police official stoop, pick up the purse, examine its contents and finally stow it in his trousers pocket. Pembury heaved a sigh of relief ; and, as the dwindling figure passed out of sight round a curve in the road, he rose, stretched himself and strode away briskly.

Near the gap was a group of ricks, and, as he passed them, a fresh idea suggested itself. Looking round quickly, he passed to the farther side of one and, thrusting his cane deeply into it, pushed it home with a piece of stick that he picked up near the rick, until the handle was lost among the straw. The bag was now all that was left, and it was empty—for his other purchases were in the dressing-bag, which, by the way, he must fetch from the station. He opened it and smelt the interior, but, though he could detect no odour, he resolved to be rid of it if possible.

As he emerged from the gap a wagon jogged slowly past. It was piled high with sacks, and the tail-board was down. Stepping into the road, he quickly overtook the wagon, and, having glanced round, laid the bag lightly on the tail-board. Then he set off for the station.

On arriving home he went straight up to his bedroom, and, ringing for his housekeeper, ordered a substantial meal. Then he took off all his clothes and deposited them, even to his shirt, socks and necktie, in a trunk, wherein his summer clothing was stored with a plentiful sprinkling of naphthol to preserve it from the moth. Taking the packet of permanganate of potash from his dressing-bag, he passed into the adjoining bathroom, and, tipping the crystals into the bath, turned on the water. Soon the bath was filled with a pink solution of the salt, and into this he plunged, immersing his entire body and thoroughly soaking his hair. Then he emptied the bath and rinsed himself in clear water, and, having dried himself, returned to the bedroom and dressed himself in fresh clothing. Finally he took a hearty meal, and then lay down on the sofa to rest until it should be time to start for the rendezvous.

Half-past six found him lurking in the shadow by the station-approach, within sight of the solitary lamp. He heard the train come in, saw the stream of passengers emerge, and noted one figure detach itself from the throng and turn on to the Thorpe road. It was Pratt, as the lamplight showed him ; Pratt, striding forward to the meeting-place with an air of jaunty satisfaction and an uncommonly creaky pair of boots.

Pembury followed him at a safe distance, and rather by sound than sight, until he was well past the stile at the entrance to the footpath. Evidently he was going on to the gates. Then Pembury vaulted over the stile and strode away swiftly across the dark meadows.

When he plunged into the deep gloom of the avenue,

his first act was to grope his way to the hornbeam and slip his hand up on to the crown and satisfy himself that the tongs were as he had left them. Reassured by the touch of his fingers on the iron loops, he turned and walked slowly down the avenue. The duplicate knife—ready opened—was in his left inside breast-pocket, and he fingered its handle as he walked.

Presently the iron gate squeaked mournfully, and then the rhythmical creak of a pair of boots was audible, coming up the avenue. Pembury walked forward slowly until a darker smear emerged from the surrounding gloom, when he called out—

" Is that you, Pratt ? "

" That's me," was the cheerful, if ungrammatical response, and, as he drew nearer, the ex-warder asked : " Have you brought the rhino, old man ? "

The insolent familiarity of the man's tone was agreeable to Pembury : it strengthened his nerve and hardened his heart. " Of course," he replied ; " but we must have a definite understanding, you know."

" Look here," said Pratt, " I've got no time for jaw. The general will be here presently ; he's riding over from Bingfield with a friend. You hand over the dibs and we'll talk some other time."

" That is all very well," said Pembury, " but you must understand—— " He paused abruptly and stood still. They were now close to the hornbeam, and, as he stood, he stared up into the dark mass of foliage.

" What's the matter ? " demanded Pratt. " What are you staring at ? " He, too, had halted and stood gazing intently into the darkness.

Then, in an instant, Pembury whipped out the knife and drove it, with all his strength, into the broad back of the ex-warder, below the left shoulder-blade.

With a hideous yell Pratt turned and grappled with his assailant. A powerful man and a competent wrestler, too, he was far more than a match for Pembury unarmed, and, in a moment, he had him by the throat. But

Pembury clung to him tightly, and, as they trampled to and fro round and round, he stabbed again and again with the viciousness of a scorpion, while Pratt's cries grew more gurgling and husky. Then they fell heavily to the ground, Pembury underneath. But the struggle was over. With a last bubbling groan, Pratt relaxed his hold and in a moment grew limp and inert. Pembury pushed him off and rose, trembling and breathing heavily.

But he wasted no time. There had been more noise than he had bargained for. Quickly stepping up to the hornbeam, he reached up for the tongs. His fingers slid into the looped handles ; the tongs grasped the knife, and he lifted it out from its hiding-place and carried it to where the corpse lay, depositing it in the ground a few feet from the body. Then he went back to the tree and carefully pushed the tongs over into the hollow of the crown.

At this moment a woman's voice sounded shrilly from the top of the avenue.

" Is that you, Mr. Pratt ? " it called.

Pembury started and then stepped back quickly, on tiptoe, to the body. For there was the duplicate knife. He must take that away at all costs.

The corpse was lying on its back. The knife was underneath it, driven in to the very haft. He had to use both hands to lift the body, and even then he had some difficulty in disengaging the weapon. And, meanwhile, the voice, repeating its question, drew nearer.

At length he succeeded in drawing out the knife and thrust it into his breast-pocket. The corpse fell back, and he stood up gasping.

" Mr. Pratt ! Are you there ? " The nearness of the voice startled Pembury, and, turning sharply, he saw a light twinkling between the trees. And then the gates creaked loudly and he heard the crunch of a horse's hoofs on the gravel.

He stood for an instant bewildered—utterly taken by surprise. He had not reckoned on a horse. His intended flight across the meadows towards Thorpe was now impracticable. If he were overtaken he was lost, for he knew there was blood on his clothes and his hands were wet and slippery—to say nothing of the knife in his pocket.

But his confusion lasted only for an instant. He remembered the oak tree ; and, turning out of the avenue, he ran to it, and, touching it as little as he could with his bloody hands, climbed quickly up into the crown. The great horizontal limb was nearly three feet in diameter, and, as he lay out on it, gathering his coat closely round him, he was quite invisible from below.

He had hardly settled himself when the light which he had seen came into full view, revealing a woman advancing with a stable lantern in her hand. And, almost at the same moment, a streak of brighter light burst from the opposite direction. The horseman was accompanied by a man on a bicycle.

The two men came on apace, and the horseman, sighting the woman, called out : " Anything the matter, Mrs. Parton ? " But, at that moment, the light of the bicycle lamp fell full on the prostrate corpse. The two men uttered a simultaneous cry of horror ; the woman shrieked aloud : and then the horseman sprang from the saddle and ran forward to the body.

" Why," he exclaimed, stooping over it, " it's Pratt " ; and, as the cyclist came up and the glare of his lamp shone on a great pool of blood, he added : " There's been foul play here, Hanford."

Hanford flashed his lamp around the body, lighting up the ground for several yards.

" What is that behind you, O'Gorman ? " he said suddenly ; " isn't it a knife ? " He was moving quickly towards it when O'Gorman held up his hand.

" Don't touch it ! " he exclaimed. " We'll put the hounds on it. They'll soon track the scoundrel, whoever he is. By God ! Hanford, this fellow has fairly delivered himself into our hands." He stood for a few moments looking down at the knife with something uncommonly like exultation, and then turning quickly to his friend, said : " Look here, Hanford ; you ride off to the police station as hard as you can pelt. It is only three-quarters of a mile ; you'll do it in five minutes. Send or bring an officer and I'll scour the meadows meanwhile. If I haven't got the scoundrel when you come back, we'll put the hounds on to this knife and run the beggar down."

" Right," replied Hanford, and without another word he wheeled his machine about, mounted and rode away into the darkness.

" Mrs. Parton," said O'Gorman, " watch that knife. See that nobody touches it while I go and examine the meadows."

" Is Mr. Pratt dead, sir ? " whimpered Mrs. Parton.

" Gad ! I hadn't thought of that," said the general. " You'd better have a look at him ; but mind ! nobody is to touch that knife or they will confuse the scent."

He scrambled into the saddle and galloped away across the meadows in the direction of Thorpe ; and, as Pembury listened to the diminuendo of the horse's hoofs, he was glad that he had not attempted to escape ; for that was the direction in which he had meant to go, and he would surely have been overtaken.

As soon as the general was gone, Mrs. Parton, with many a terror-stricken glance over her shoulder, approached the corpse and held the lantern close to the dead face. Suddenly she stood up, trembling violently, for footsteps were audible coming down the avenue. A familiar voice reassured her.

" Is anything wrong, Mrs. Parton ? " The question proceeded from one of the maids who had come in search of the elder woman, escorted by a young man, and the pair now came out into the circle of light.

" Good God ! " ejaculated the man. " Who's that ? "

" It's Mr. Pratt," replied Mrs. Parton. " He's been murdered."

The girl screamed, and then the two domestics approached on tiptoe, staring at the corpse with the fascination of horror.

"Don't touch that knife," said Mrs. Parton, for the man was about to pick it up. "The general's going to put the bloodhounds on to it."

"Is the general here, then?" asked the man; and, as he spoke, the drumming of hoofs, growing momentarily louder, answered him from the meadow.

O'Gorman reined in his horse as he perceived the group of servants gathered about the corpse. "Is he dead, Mrs. Parton?" he asked.

"I am afraid so, sir," was the reply.

"Ha! Somebody ought to go for the doctor; but not you, Bailey. I want you to get the hounds ready and wait with them at the top of the avenue until I call you."

He was off again into the Baysford meadows, and Bailey hurried away, leaving the two women staring at the body and talking in whispers.

Pembury's position was cramped and uncomfortable. He dared not move, hardly dared to breathe, for the women below him were not a dozen yards away; and it was with mingled feelings of relief and apprehension that he presently saw from his elevated station a group of lights approaching rapidly along the road from Baysford. Presently they were hidden by the trees, and then, after a brief interval, the whirr of wheels sounded on the drive and streaks of light on the tree-trunks announced the new arrivals. There were three bicycles, ridden respectively by Mr. Hanford, a police inspector and a sergeant; and, as they drew up, the general came thundering back into the avenue.

"Is Ellis with you?" he asked, as he pulled up.

"No, sir," was the reply. "He hadn't come in from Thorpe when we left. He's rather late to-night."

"Have you sent for a doctor?"

"Yes, sir, I've sent for Dr. Hills," said the inspector,

resting his bicycle against the oak. Pembury could smell
the reek of the lamp as he crouched. " Is Pratt dead ? "

" Seems to be," replied O'Gorman, " but we'd better
leave that to the doctor. There's the murderer's knife.
Nobody has touched it. I'm going to fetch the bloodhounds now."

" Ah ! that's the thing," said the inspector. " The
man can't be far away." He rubbed his hands with a
satisfied air as O'Gorman cantered away up the avenue.

In less than a minute there came out from the darkness
the deep baying of a hound followed by quick footsteps
on the gravel. Then into the circle of light emerged
three sinister shapes, loose-limbed and gaunt, and two
men advancing at a shambling trot.

" Here, inspector," shouted the general, " you take
one ; I can't hold 'em both."

The inspector ran forward and seized one of the
leashes, and the general led his hound up to the knife,
as it lay on the ground. Pembury, peering cautiously
round the bough, watched the great brute with almost
impersonal curiosity ; noted its high poll, its wrinkled
forehead and melancholy face as it stooped to snuff
suspiciously at the prostrate knife.

For some moments the hound stood motionless,
sniffing at the knife ; then it turned away and walked to
and fro with its muzzle to the ground. Suddenly it
lifted its head, bayed loudly, lowered its muzzle and
started forward between the oak and the elm, dragging
the general after it at a run.

The inspector next brought his hound to the knife,
and was soon bounding away to the tug of the leash in
the general's wake.

" They don't make no mistakes, they don't," said
Bailey, addressing the gratified sergeant, as he brought
forward the third hound ; " you'll see—— " But his
remark was cut short by a violent jerk of the leash, and
the next moment he was flying after the others, followed
by Mr. Hanford.

The sergeant daintily picked the knife up by its ring, wrapped it in his handkerchief and bestowed it in his pocket. Then he ran off after the hounds.

Pembury smiled grimly. His scheme was working out admirably in spite of the unforeseen difficulties. If those confounded women would only go away, he could come down and take himself off while the course was clear. He listened to the baying of the hounds, gradually growing fainter in the increasing distance, and cursed the dilatoriness of the doctor. Confound the fellow! Didn't he realise that this was a case of life or death ? These infernal doctors had no sense of responsibility.

Suddenly his ear caught the tinkle of a bicycle bell ; a fresh light appeared coming up the avenue and then a bicycle swept up swiftly to the scene of the tragedy, and a small elderly man jumped down by the side of the body. Giving his machine to Mrs. Parton, he stooped over the dead man, felt the wrist, pushed back an eyelid, held a match to the eye and then rose. " This is a shocking affair, Mrs. Parton," said he. " The poor fellow is quite dead. You had better help me to carry him to the house. If you two take the feet I will take the shoulders."

Pembury watched them raise the body and stagger away with it up the avenue. He heard their shuffling steps die away and the door of the house shut. And still he listened. From far away in the meadows came, at intervals, the baying of the hounds. Other sound there was none. Presently the doctor would come back for his bicycle, but, for the moment, the coast was clear. Pembury rose stiffly. His hands had stuck to the tree where they had pressed against it, and they were still sticky and damp. Quickly he let himself down to the ground, listened again for a moment, and then, making a small circuit to avoid the lamplight, softly crossed the avenue and stole away across the Thorpe meadows.

The night was intensely dark, and not a soul was stirring in the meadows. He strode forward quickly, peering into the darkness and stopping now and again to listen; but no sound came to his ears, save the now faint baying of the distant hounds. Not far from his house, he remembered, was a deep ditch spanned by a wooden bridge, and towards this he now made his way; for he knew that his appearance was such as to convict him at a glance. Arrived at the ditch, he stooped to wash his hands and wrists; and, as he bent forward, the knife fell from his breast-pocket into the shallow water at the margin. He groped for it, and, having found it, drove it deep into the mud as far out as he could reach. Then he wiped his hands on some water-weed, crossed the bridge and started homewards.

He approached his house from the rear, satisfied himself that his housekeeper was in the kitchen, and, letting himself in very quietly with his key, went quickly up to his bedroom. Here he washed thoroughly—in the bath, so that he could get rid of the discoloured water— changed his clothes and packed those that he took off in a portmanteau.

By the time he had done this the gong sounded for supper. As he took his seat at the table, spruce and fresh in appearance, quietly cheerful in manner, he addressed his housekeeper. " I wasn't able to finish my business in London," he said. " I shall have to go up again to-morrow."

" Shall you come home the same day? " asked the housekeeper.

" Perhaps," was the reply, " and perhaps not. It will depend on circumstances."

He did not say what the circumstances might be, nor did the housekeeper ask. Mr. Pembury was not addicted to confidences. He was an eminently discreet man : and discreet men say little.

II. *Rival Sleuth-hounds*
(Related by CHRISTOPHER JERVIS, M.D.)

The half-hour that follows breakfast, when the fire has, so to speak, got into its stride, and the morning pipe throws up its clouds of incense, is, perhaps, the most agreeable in the whole day. Especially so when a sombre sky, brooding over the town, hints at streets pervaded by the chilly morning air, and hoots from protesting tugs upon the river tell of lingering mists, the legacy of the lately-vanished night.

The autumn morning was raw : the fire burned jovially. I thrust my slippered feet towards the blaze and meditated, on nothing in particular, with cat-like enjoyment. Presently a disapproving grunt from Thorndyke attracted my attention, and I looked round lazily. He was extracting, with a pair of office shears, the readable portions of the morning paper, and had paused with a small cutting between his finger and thumb.

" Bloodhounds again," said he. " We shall be hearing presently of the revival of the ordeal by fire."

" And a deuced comfortable ordeal, too, on a morning like this," I said, stroking my legs ecstatically. " What is the case ? "

He was about to reply when a sharp rat-tat from the little brass knocker announced a disturber of our peace. Thorndyke stepped over to the door and admitted a police inspector in uniform, and I stood up, and, presenting my dorsal aspect to the fire, prepared to combine bodily comfort with attention to business.

" I believe I am speaking to Dr. Thorndyke," said the officer, and, as Thorndyke nodded, he went on : " My name, sir, is Fox, Inspector Fox of the Baysford Police. Perhaps you've seen the morning paper ? "

Thorndyke held up the cutting, and, placing a chair by the fire, asked the inspector if he had breakfasted.

" Thank you, sir, I have," replied Inspector Fox. " I came up to town by the late train last night so as to be here early, and stayed at an hotel. You see, from the paper, that we have had to arrest one of our own men. That's rather awkward, you know, sir."

" Very," agreed Thorndyke.

" Yes ; it's bad for the force and bad for the public

too. But we had to do it. There was no way out that we could see. Still, we should like the accused to have every chance, both for our sake and his own, so the chief constable thought he'd like to have your opinion on the case, and he thought that, perhaps, you might be willing to act for the defence."

" Let us have the particulars," said Thorndyke, taking a writing-pad from a drawer and dropping into his arm-chair. " Begin at the beginning," he added, " and tell us all you know."

" Well," said the inspector, after a preliminary cough, " to begin with the murdered man : his name is Pratt. He was a retired prison warder, and was employed as steward by General O'Gorman, who is a retired prison governor—you may have heard of him in connection with his pack of bloodhounds. Well, Pratt came down from London yesterday evening by a train arriving at Baysford at six-thirty. He was seen by the guard, the ticket collector and the outside porter. The porter saw him leave the station at six thirty-seven. General O'Gorman's house is about half-a-mile from the station. At five minutes to seven the general and a gentleman named Hanford and the general's housekeeper, a Mrs. Parton, found Pratt lying dead in the avenue that leads up to the house. He had apparently been stabbed, for there was a lot of blood about, and a knife—a Norwegian knife—was lying on the ground near the body. Mrs. Parton had thought she heard someone in the avenue calling out for help, and, as Pratt was just due, she came out with a lantern. She met the general and Mr. Hanford, and all three seem to have caught sight of the body at the same moment. Mr. Hanford cycled down to us, at once, with the news ; we sent for a doctor, and I went back with Mr. Hanford and took a sergeant with me. We arrived at twelve minutes past seven, and then the general, who had galloped his horse over the meadows each side of the avenue without having seen anybody, fetched out his bloodhounds and led them up to the knife. All three hounds took up the scent at once—I held the leash of one of them—and they took us across the meadows without a pause or a falter, over stiles and fences, along a lane, out into the town, and then, one after the other, they crossed the road in a bee-line to the police station, bolted in at the door, which stood open, and made straight for the desk, where a supernumerary officer, named Ellis, was writing. They made a rare to-do, struggling to get at him, and it was as much as we could manage to hold them back. As for Ellis, he turned as pale as a ghost."

" Was anyone else in the room ? " asked Thorndyke.

" Oh, yes. There were two constables and a messenger. We led the hounds up to them, but the brutes wouldn't take any notice of them. They wanted Ellis."

" And what did you do ? "

" Why, we arrested Ellis, of course. Couldn't do anything else—especially with the general there."

" What had the general to do with it ? " asked Thorndyke.

" He's a J.P. and a late governor of Dartmoor, and it was his hounds that had run the man down. But we must have arrested Ellis in any case."

" Is there anything against the accused man ? "

" Yes, there is. He and Pratt were on distinctly unfriendly terms. They were old comrades, for Ellis was in the Civil Guard at Portland when Pratt was warder there—he was pensioned off from the service because he got his left forefinger chopped off—but lately they had had some unpleasantness about a woman, a parlourmaid of the general's. It seems that Ellis, who is a married man, paid the girl too much attention—or Pratt thought he did—and Pratt warned Ellis off the premises. Since then they had not been on speaking terms."

" And what sort of a man is Ellis ? "

" A remarkably decent fellow he always seemed ; quiet, steady, good-natured ; I should have said he wouldn't have hurt a fly. We all liked him—better than we liked Pratt, in fact ; for poor Pratt was what you'd call an old soldier—sly, you know, sir—and a bit of a sneak."

" You searched and examined Ellis, of course ? "

" Yes. There was nothing suspicious about him except that he had two purses. But he says he picked up one of them—a small, pigskin pouch—on the foot-path of the Thorpe road yesterday afternoon ; and there's no reason to disbelieve him. At any rate, the purse was not Pratt's."

Thorndyke made a note on his pad, and then asked : " There were no blood-stains or marks on his clothing ? "

" No. His clothing was not marked or disarranged in any way."

" Any cuts, scratches or bruises on his person ? "

" None whatever," replied the inspector.

" At what time did you arrest Ellis ? "

" Half-past seven exactly."

" Have you ascertained what his movements were ? Had he been near the scene of the murder ? "

" Yes ; he had been to Thorpe and would pass the gates of the avenue on his way back. And he was later than usual in returning, though not later than he has often been before."

" And now, as to the murdered man : has the body been examined ? "

" Yes ; I had Dr. Hills's report before I left. There were no less than seven deep knife-wounds, all on the left side of the back. There was a great deal of blood on the ground, and Dr. Hills thinks Pratt must have bled to death in a minute or two."

" Do the wounds correspond with the knife that was found ? "

" I asked the doctor that, and he said ' Yes,' though he wasn't going to swear to any particular knife. However, that point isn't of much importance. The knife was covered with blood, and it was found close to the body."

" What has been done with it, by the way ? " asked Thorndyke.

" The sergeant who was with me picked it up and rolled it in his handkerchief to carry in his pocket. I took it from him, just as it was, and locked it in a dispatch-box, handkerchief and all."

" Has the knife been recognised as Ellis's property ? "

" No, sir, it has not."

" Were there any recognisable footprints or marks of a struggle ? " Thorndyke asked.

The inspector grinned sheepishly. " I haven't examined the spot, of course, sir," said he, " but, after the general's horse and the bloodhounds and the general on foot and me and the gardener and the sergeant and Mr. Hanford had been over it twice, going and returning, why, you see, sir——"

" Exactly, exactly," said Thorndyke. " Well, inspector, I shall be pleased to act for the defence ; it seems to me that the case against Ellis is in some respects rather inconclusive."

The inspector was frankly amazed. " It certainly hadn't struck me in that light, sir," he said.

" No ? Well, that is my view ; and I think the best plan will be for me to come down with you and investigate matters on the spot."

The inspector assented cheerfully, and, when we had provided him with a newspaper, we withdrew to the laboratory to consult time-tables and prepare for the expedition.

" You are coming, I suppose, Jervis ? " said Thorndyke.

" If I shall be of any use," I replied.

" Of course you will," said he. " Two heads are better than one, and, by the look of things, I should say that ours will be the only ones with any sense in them. We will take the research case, of course, and we may as well have a camera with us. I see there is a train from Charing Cross in twenty minutes."

For the first half-hour of the journey Thorndyke sat in his corner, alternately conning over his notes and gazing with thoughtful eyes out of the window. I could see that the case pleased him, and was careful not to break in upon his train of thought. Presently, however, he put away his notes and began to fill his pipe with a more companionable air, and then the inspector, who had been wriggling with impatience, opened fire.

" So you think, sir, that you see a way out for Ellis ? "

" I think there is a case for the defence," replied Thorndyke. " In fact, I call the evidence against him rather flimsy."

The inspector gasped. " But the knife, sir ? What about the knife ? "

" Well," said Thorndyke, " what about the knife ? Whose knife was it ? You don't know. It was covered with blood. Whose blood ? You don't know. Let us assume, for the sake of argument, that it was the murderer's knife. Then the blood on it was Pratt's blood. But if it was Pratt's blood, when the hounds had smelt it they should have led you to Pratt's body, for blood gives a very strong scent. But they did not. They ignored the body. The inference seems to be that the blood on the knife was not Pratt's blood."

The inspector took off his cap and gently scratched the back of his head. " You're perfectly right, sir," he said. " I'd never thought of that. None of us had."

" Then," pursued Thorndyke, " let us assume that the knife was Pratt's. If so, it would seem to have been used in self-defence. But this was a Norwegian knife, a clumsy tool—not a weapon at all—which takes an appreciable time to open and requires the use of two free hands. Now, had Pratt both hands free ? Certainly not after the attack had commenced. There were seven wounds, all on the left side of the back ; which indicates that he held the murderer locked in his arms and that the murderer's arms were around him. Also, incidentally, that the murderer is right-handed. But, still, let us assume that the knife was Pratt's. Then the blood on it was that of the murderer. Then the murderer must have been wounded. But Ellis was not wounded. Then Ellis is not the murderer. The knife doesn't help us at all."

The inspector puffed out his cheeks and blew softly. "This is getting out of my depth," he said. "Still, sir, you can't get over the bloodhounds. They tell us distinctly that the knife is Ellis's knife and I don't see any answer to that."

"There is no answer because there has been no statement. The bloodhounds have told you nothing. You have drawn certain inferences from their actions, but those inferences may be totally wrong and they are certainly not evidence."

"You don't seem to have much opinion of bloodhounds," the inspector remarked.

"As agents for the detection of crime," replied Thorndyke, "I regard them as useless. You cannot put a bloodhound in the witness-box. You can get no intelligible statement from it. If it possesses any knowledge, it has no means of communicating it. The fact is," he continued, "that the entire system of using bloodhounds for criminal detection is based on a fallacy. In the American plantations these animals were used with great success for tracking runaway slaves. But the slave was a known individual. All that was required was to ascertain his whereabouts. That is not the problem that is presented in the detection of a crime. The detective is not concerned in establishing the whereabouts of a known individual, but in discovering the identity of an unknown individual. And for this purpose bloodhounds are useless. They may discover such identity, but they cannot communicate their knowledge. If the criminal is unknown they cannot identify him : if he is known, the police have no need of the bloodhound.

"To return to our present case," Thorndyke resumed after a pause ; "we have employed certain agents—the hounds—with whom we are not *en rapport*, as the spiritualists would say ; and we have no 'medium.' The hound possesses a special sense—the olfactory—which in man is quite rudimentary. He thinks, so to speak, in terms of smell, and his thoughts are untranslatable to beings in whom the sense of smell is undeveloped. We have presented to the hound a knife, and he discovers in it certain odorous properties ; he discovers similar or related odorous properties in a tract of land and a human individual—Ellis. We cannot verify his discoveries or ascertain their nature. What remains ? All that we can say is that there appears to exist some odorous relation between the knife and the man Ellis. But until we can ascertain the nature of that relation, we cannot estimate its evidential value or bearing. All the other ' evidence ' is the product of your imagination and that of the general. There is, at present, no case against Ellis."

" He must have been pretty close to the place when the murder happened," said the inspector.

" So, probably, were many other people," answered Thorndyke ; " but had he time to wash and change ? Because he would have needed it."

" I suppose he would," the inspector agreed dubiously.

" Undoubtedly. There were seven wounds which would have taken some time to inflict. Now we can't suppose that Pratt stood passively while the other man stabbed him—indeed, as I have said, the position of the wounds shows that he did not. There was a struggle. The two men were locked together. One of the murderer's hands was against Pratt's back ; probably both hands were, one clasping and the other stabbing. There must have been blood on one hand and probably on both. But you say there was no blood on Ellis, and there doesn't seem to have been time or opportunity for him to wash."

" Well, it's a mysterious affair," said the inspector ; " but I don't see how you are going to get over the bloodhounds."

Thorndyke shrugged his shoulders impatiently. " The bloodhounds are an obsession," he said. " The whole problem really centres around the knife. The questions are, Whose knife was it ? and what was the connection between it and Ellis ? There is a problem, Jervis," he continued, turning to me, " that I submit for your consideration. Some of the possible solutions are exceedingly curious."

As we set out from Baysford station, Thorndyke looked at his watch and noted the time. " You will take us the way that Pratt went," he said.

" As to that," said the inspector, " he may have gone by the road or by the footpath ; but there's very little difference in the distance."

Turning away from Baysford, we walked along the road westward, towards the village of Thorpe, and presently passed on our right a stile at the entrance to a footpath.

" That path," said the inspector, " crosses the avenue about half-way up. But we'd better keep to the road." A quarter of a mile farther on we came to a pair of rusty iron gates, one of which stood open, and, entering, we found ourselves in a broad drive bordered by two rows of trees, between the trunks of which a long stretch of pasture meadows could be seen on either hand. It was a fine avenue, and, late in the year as it was, the yellowing foliage clustered thickly overhead.

When we had walked about a hundred and fifty yards from the gates, the inspector halted.

" This is the place," he said ; and Thorndyke again noted the time.

" Nine minutes exactly," said he. " Then Pratt arrived here about fourteen minutes to seven, and his body was found at five minutes to seven—nine minutes after his arrival. The murderer couldn't have been far away then."

" No, it was a pretty fresh scent," replied the inspector. " You'd like to see the body first, I think you said, sir ? "

"Yes ; and the knife, if you please."

"I shall have to send down to the station for that. It's locked up in the office."

He entered the house, and, having dispatched a messenger to the police station, came out and conducted us to the outbuilding where the corpse had been deposited. Thorndyke made a rapid examination of the wounds and the holes in the clothing, neither of which presented anything particularly suggestive. The weapon used had evidently been a thick-backed, single-edged knife similar to the one described, and the discoloration around the wounds indicated that the weapon had a definite shoulder like that of a Norwegian knife, and that it had been driven in with savage violence.

"Do you find anything that throws any light on the case ? " the inspector asked, when the examination was concluded.

"That is impossible to say until we have seen the knife," replied Thorndyke ; " but while we are waiting for it, we may as well go and look at the scene of the tragedy. These are Pratt's boots, I think ? " He lifted a pair of stout laced boots from the table and turned them up to inspect the soles.

"Yes, those are his boots," replied Fox, " and pretty easy they'd have been to track, if the case had been the other way about. Those Blakey's protectors are as good as a trademark."

"We'll take them, at any rate," said Thorndyke ; and, the inspector having taken the boots from him, we went out and retraced our steps down the avenue.

The place where the murder had occurred was easily identified by a large dark stain on the gravel at one side of the drive, half-way between two trees, an ancient pollard hornbeam and an elm. Next to the elm was a pollard oak with a squat, warty bole about seven feet high, and three enormous limbs, of which one slanted half-way across the avenue ; and between these two trees the ground was covered with the tracks of men

and hounds superimposed upon the hoof-prints of a
horse.

"Where was the knife found ?" Thorndyke asked.

The inspector indicated a spot near the middle of
the drive, almost opposite the hornbeam and Thorndyke,.
picking up a large stone, laid it on the spot. Then he
surveyed the scene thoughtfully, looking up and down
the drive and at the trees that bordered it, and, finally,
walked slowly to the space between the elm and the oak,
scanning the ground as he went. "There is no dearth
of footprints," he remarked grimly, as he looked down
at the trampled earth.

"No, but the question is, whose are they ?" said the
inspector.

"Yes, that is the question," agreed Thorndyke ; "and
we will begin the solution by identifying those of Pratt."

"I don't see how that will help us," said the inspector.
"We know he was here."

Thorndyke looked at him in surprise, and I must
confess that the foolish remark astonished me too, accustomed as I was to the quick-witted officers from Scotland
Yard.

"The hue-and-cry procession," remarked Thorndyke,.
"seems to have passed out between the elm and the oak ;.
elsewhere the ground seems pretty clear." He walked
round the elm, still looking earnestly at the ground, and
presently continued : "Now here, in the soft earth
bordering the turf, are the prints of a pair of smallish
feet wearing pointed boots ; a rather short man, evidently, by the size of foot and length of stride, and he
doesn't seem to have belonged to the procession. But
I don't see any of Pratt's ; he doesn't seem to have come
off the hard gravel." He continued to walk slowly towards the hornbeam with his eyes fixed on the ground..
Suddenly he halted and stooped with an eager look at
the earth ; and, as Fox and I approached, he stood up
and pointed. "Pratt's footprints—faint and fragmen-
tary, but unmistakable. And now, inspector, you see

4

their importance. They furnish the time factor in respect of the other footprints. Look at this one and then look at that." He pointed from one to another of the faint impressions of the dead man's foot.

"You mean that there are signs of a struggle?" said Fox.

"I mean more than that," replied Thorndyke. "Here is one of Pratt's footprints treading into the print of a small, pointed foot; and there at the edge of the gravel is another of Pratt's nearly obliterated by the tread of a pointed foot. Obviously the first pointed footprint was made before Pratt's, and the second one after his; and the necessary inference is that the owner of the pointed foot was here at the same time as Pratt."

"Then he must have been the murderer!" exclaimed Fox.

"Presumably," answered Thorndyke; "but let us see whither he went. You notice, in the first place, that the man stood close to this tree"—he indicated the hornbeam—"and that he went towards the elm. Let us follow him. He passes the elm, you see, and you will observe that these tracks form a regular series leading from the hornbeam and not mixed up with the marks of the struggle. They were, therefore, probably made after the murder had been perpetrated. You will also notice that they pass along the backs of the trees—outside the avenue, that is; what does that suggest to you?"

"It suggests to me," I said, when the inspector had shaken his head hopelessly, "that there was possibly someone in the avenue when the man was stealing off."

"Precisely," said Thorndyke. "The body was found not more than nine minutes after Pratt arrived here. But the murder must have taken some time. Then the housekeeper thought she heard someone calling and came out with a lantern, and, at the same time, the general and Mr. Hanford came up the drive. The suggestion is that the man sneaked along outside the trees to avoid being seen. However, let us follow the tracks. They pass the elm and they pass on behind the next tree ; but wait ! There is something odd here." He passed behind the great pollard oak and looked down at the soft earth by its roots. " Here is a pair of impressions much deeper than the rest, and they are not a part of the track since their toes point towards the tree. What do you make of that ? " Without waiting for an answer he began closely to scan the bole of the tree and especially a large, warty protuberance about three feet from the ground. On the bark above this was a vertical mark, as if something had scraped down the tree, and from the wart itself a dead twig had been newly broken off and lay upon the ground. Pointing to these marks Thorndyke set his foot on the protuberance, and, springing up, brought his eye above the level of the crown, whence the great boughs branched off.

" Ah ! " he exclaimed. " Here is something much more definite." With the aid of another projection, he scrambled up into the crown of the tree, and, having glanced quickly round, beckoned to us. I stepped up on the projecting lump and, as my eyes rose above the crown, I perceived the brown, shiny impression of a hand on the edge. Climbing into the crown, I was quickly followed by the inspector, and we both stood up by Thorndyke between the three boughs. From where we stood we looked on the upper side of the great limb that swept out across the avenue ; and there on its lichen-covered surface, we saw the imprints in reddish-brown of a pair of open hands.

" You notice," said Thorndyke, leaning out upon the bough, " that he is a short man ; I cannot conveniently place my hands so low. You also note that he has both forefingers intact, and so is certainly not Ellis."

" If you mean to say, sir, that these marks were made by the murderer," said Fox, " I say it's impossible. Why, that would mean that he was here looking down at us when we were searching for him with the hounds.

The presence of the hounds proves that this man could
not have been the murderer."

" On the contrary," said Thorndyke, " the presence
of this man with bloody hands confirms the other evidence, which all indicates that the hounds were never on
the murderer's trail at all.   Come now, inspector, I put
it to you : Here is a murdered man ; the murderer has
almost certainly blood upon his hands ; and here is a
man with bloody hands, lurking in a tree within a few
feet of the corpse and within a few minutes of its discovery (as is shown by the footprints) ; what are the
reasonable probabilities ? "

" But you are forgetting the bloodhounds, sir, and the
murderer's knife," urged the inspector.

" Tut, tut, man ! " exclaimed Thorndyke ; " those
bloodhounds are a positive obsession.   But I see a sergeant coming up the drive, with the knife, I hope.
Perhaps that will solve the riddle for us."

The sergeant, who carried a small dispatch-box,
halted opposite the tree in some surprise while we descended, when he came forward with a military salute
and handed the box to the inspector, who forthwith
unlocked it, and, opening the lid, displayed an object
wrapped in a pocket-handkerchief.

" There is the knife, sir," said he, " just as I received
it.   The handkerchief is the sergeant's."

Thorndyke unrolled the handkerchief and took from
it a large-sized Norwegian knife, which he looked at
critically and then handed to me.   While I was inspecting the blade, he shook out the handkerchief and, having
looked it over on both sides, turned to the sergeant.

" At what time did you pick up this knife ? " he
asked.

" About seven-fifteen, sir ; directly after the hounds
had started.   I was careful to pick it up by the ring,
and I wrapped it in the handkerchief at once."

" Seven-fifteen," said Thorndyke.   " Less than half-
an-hour after the murder.   That is very singular.   Do

you observe the state of this handkerchief ? There is not a mark on it. Not a trace of any bloodstain ; which proves that when the knife was picked up, the blood on it was already dry. But things dry slowly, if they dry at all, in the saturated air of an autumn evening. The appearances seem to suggest that the blood on the knife was dry when it was thrown down. By the way, sergeant, what do you scent your handkerchief with ? "

" Scent, sir ! " exclaimed the astonished officer in indignant accents ; " me scent my handkerchief ! No, sir, certainly not. Never used scent in my life, sir."

Thorndyke held out the handkerchief, and the sergeant sniffed at it incredulously. " It certainly does seem to smell of scent," he admitted, " but it must be the knife." The same idea having occurred to me, I applied the handle of the knife to my nose and instantly detected the sickly-sweet odour of musk.

" The question is," said the inspector, when the two articles had been tested by us all, " was it the knife that scented the handkerchief or the handkerchief that scented the knife ? "

" You heard what the sergeant said," replied Thorndyke. " There was no scent on the handkerchief when the knife was wrapped in it. Do you know, inspector, this scent seems to me to offer a very curious suggestion. Consider the facts of the case : the distinct trail leading straight to Ellis, who is, nevertheless, found to be without a scratch or a spot of blood ; the inconsistencies in the case that I pointed out in the train, and now this knife, apparently dropped with dried blood on it and scented with musk. To me it suggests a carefully-planned, coolly-premeditated crime. The murderer knew about the general's bloodhounds and made use of them as a blind. He planted this knife, smeared with blood and tainted with musk, to furnish a scent. No doubt some object, also scented with musk, would be drawn over the ground to give the trail. It is only a suggestion, of course, but it is worth considering."

" But, sir," the inspector objected eagerly, " if the murderer had handled the knife, it would have scented him too."

" Exactly ; so, as we are assuming that the man is not a fool, we may assume that he did not handle it. He will have left it here in readiness, hidden in some place whence he could knock it down, say, with a stick, without touching it."

" Perhaps in this very tree, sir," suggested the sergeant, pointing to the oak.

" No," said Thorndyke, " he would hardly have hidden in the tree where the knife had been. The hounds might have scented the place instead of following the trail at once. The most likely hiding-place for the knife is the one nearest the spot where it was found." He walked over to the stone that marked the spot, and, looking round, continued : " You see, that hornbeam is much the nearest, and its flat crown would be very convenient for the purpose—easily reached even by a short man, as he appears to be. Let us see if there are any traces of it. Perhaps you will give me a ' back up,' sergeant, as we haven't a ladder."

The sergeant assented with a faint grin, and, stooping beside the tree in an attitude suggesting the game of leap-frog, placed his hands firmly on his knees. Grasping a stout branch, Thorndyke swung himself up on the sergeant's broad back, whence he looked down into the crown of the tree. Then, parting the branches, he stepped on to the ledge and disappeared into the central hollow.

When he reappeared he held in his hands two very singular objects : a pair of iron crucible-tongs and an artist's brush-case of black-japanned tin. The former article he handed down to me, but the brush-case he held carefully by its wire handle as he dropped to the ground.

" The significance of these things is, I think, obvious," he said. " The tongs were used to handle the knife with and the case to carry it in, so that it should not scent his clothes or bag. It was very carefully planned."

" If that is so," said the inspector, " the inside of the case ought to smell of musk."

" No doubt," said Thorndyke ; " but before we open it, there is a rather important matter to be attended to. Will you give me the Vitogen powder, Jervis ? "

I opened the canvas-covered " research case " and took from it an object like a diminutive pepper-caster— an iodoform dredger in fact—and handed it to him. Grasping the brush-case by its wire handle, he sprinkled the pale yellow powder from the dredger freely all round the pull-off lid, tapping the top with his knuckles to make the fine particles spread. Then he blew off the superfluous powder, and the two police officers gave a simultaneous gasp of joy ; for now, on the black background, there stood out plainly a number of finger-prints, so clear and distinct that the ridge-pattern could be made out with perfect ease.

" These will probably be his right hand," said Thorndyke. " Now for the left." He treated the body of the case in the same way, and, when he had blown off the powder, the entire surface was spotted with yellow, oval impressions. " Now, Jervis," said he, " if you will put on a glove and pull off the lid, we can test the inside."

There was no difficulty in getting the lid off, for the shoulder of the case had been smeared with vaseline— apparently to produce an airtight joint—and, as it separated with a hollow sound, a faint, musky odour exhaled from its interior.

" The remainder of the inquiry," said Thorndyke, when I had pushed the lid on again, " will be best conducted at the police station, where, also, we can photograph these finger-prints."

" The shortest way will be across the meadows," said Fox ; " the way the hounds went."

By this route we accordingly travelled, Thorndyke carrying the brush-case tenderly by its handle.

" I don't quite see where Ellis comes in in this job,"
said the inspector, as we walked along, " if the fellow
had a grudge against Pratt. They weren't chums."

" I think I do," said Thorndyke. " You say that
both men were prison officers at Portland at the same
time. Now doesn't it seem likely that this is the work
of some old convict who had been identified—and perhaps blackmailed—by Pratt, and possibly by Ellis too ?
That is where the value of the finger-prints comes in.
If he is an old ' lag ' his prints will be at Scotland Yard.
Otherwise they are not of much value as a clue."

" That's true, sir," said the inspector. " I suppose
you want to see Ellis."

" I want to see that purse that you spoke of, first,"
replied Thorndyke. " That is probably the other end
of the clue."

As soon as we arrived at the station, the inspector
unlocked a safe and brought out a parcel. " These are
Ellis's things," said he, as he unfastened it, " and that
is the purse."

He handed Thorndyke a small pigskin pouch, which
my colleague opened, and, having smelt the inside, passed
to me. The odour of musk was plainly perceptible,
especially in the small compartment at the back.

" It has probably tainted the other contents of the
parcel," said Thorndyke, sniffing at each article in turn,
" but my sense of smell is not keen enough to detect
any scent. They all seem odourless to me, whereas the
purse smells quite distinctly. Shall we have Ellis in
now ? "

The sergeant took a key from a locked drawer and
departed for the cells, whence he presently reappeared
accompanied by the prisoner—a stout, burly man, in
the last stage of dejection.

" Come, cheer up, Ellis," said the inspector. " Here's
Dr. Thorndyke come down to help us and he wants to
ask you one or two questions."

Ellis looked piteously at Thorndyke, and exclaimed :

" I know nothing whatever about this affair, sir, I swear to God I don't."

" I never supposed you did," said Thorndyke. " But there are one or two things that I want you to tell me. To begin with, that purse : where did you find it ? "

" On the Thorpe road, sir. It was lying in the middle of the footway."

" Had anyone else passed the spot lately ? Did you meet or pass anyone ? "

" Yes, sir, I met a labourer about a minute before I saw the purse. I can't imagine why he didn't see it."

" Probably because it wasn't there," said Thorndyke. " Is there a hedge there ? "

" Yes, sir ; a hedge on a low bank."

" Ha ! Well, now, tell me : is there anyone about here whom you knew when you and Pratt were together at Portland ? Any old lag—to put it bluntly—whom you and Pratt have been putting the screw on."

" No, sir, I swear there isn't. But I wouldn't answer for Pratt. He had a rare memory for faces."

Thorndyke reflected. " Were there any escapes from Portland in your time ? " he asked.

" Only one—a man named Dobbs. He made off to the sea in a sudden fog and he was supposed to be drowned. His clothes washed up on the Bill, but not his body. At any rate, he was never heard of again."

" Thank you, Ellis. Do you mind my taking your finger-prints ? "

" Certainly not, sir," was the almost eager reply ; and the office inking-pad being requisitioned, a rough set of finger-prints was produced ; and when Thorndyke had compared them with those on the brush-case and found no resemblance, Ellis returned to his cell in quite buoyant spirits.

Having made several photographs of the strange finger-prints, we returned to town that evening, taking the negatives with us ; and while we waited for our train, Thorndyke gave a few parting injunctions to the inspector.

4*

" Remember," he said, " that the man must have washed his hands before he could appear in public. Search the banks of every pond, ditch and stream in the neighbourhood for footprints like those in the avenue ; and, if you find any, search the bottom of the water thoroughly, for he is quite likely to have dropped the knife into the mud."

The photographs, which we handed in at Scotland Yard that same night, enabled the experts to identify the finger-prints as those of Francis Dobbs, an escaped convict. The two photographs—profile and full-face —which were attached to his record, were sent down to Baysford with a description of the man, and were, in due course, identified with a somewhat mysterious individual, who passed by the name of Rufus Pembury and who had lived in the neighbourhood as a private gentleman for some two years. But Rufus Pembury was not to be found either at his genteel house or elsewhere. All that was known was, that on the day after the murder, he had converted his entire " personalty " into " bearer securities," and then vanished from mortal ken. Nor has he ever been heard of to this day.

" And, between ourselves," said Thorndyke, when we were discussing the case some time after, " he deserved to escape. It was clearly a case of blackmail, and to kill a blackmailer—when you have no other defence against him—is hardly murder. As to Ellis, he could never have been convicted, and Dobbs or Pembury must have known it. But he would have been committed to the Assizes, and that would have given time for all traces to disappear. No, Dobbs was a man of courage, ingenuity and resource ; and, above all, he knocked the bottom out of the great bloodhound superstition."

I. *Death on the Girdler*

POPULAR belief ascribes to infants and the lower animals
certain occult powers of divining character denied to the
reasoning faculties of the human adult ; and is apt to
accept their judgment as finally over-riding the pro-
nouncements of mere experience.

Whether this belief rests upon any foundation other
than the universal love of paradox it is unnecessary to
inquire. It is very generally entertained, especially by
ladies of a certain social status ; and by Mrs. Thomas
Solly it was loyally maintained as an article of faith.

"Yes," she moralised, "it's surprisin' how they
know, the little children and the dumb animals. But
they do. There's no deceivin' *them*. They can tell the
gold from the dross in a moment, they can, and they
reads the human heart like a book. Wonderful, I call it.
I suppose it's instinct."

Having delivered herself of this priceless gem of philosophic thought, she thrust her arms elbow-deep into the
foaming wash-tub and glanced admiringly at her lodger
as he sat in the doorway, supporting on one knee an
obese infant of eighteen months and on the other a fine
tabby cat.

James Brown was an elderly seafaring man, small and
slight in build and in manner suave, insinuating and
perhaps a trifle sly. But he had all the sailor's love of
children and animals, and the sailor's knack of making
himself acceptable to them, for, as he sat with an empty
pipe wobbling in the grasp of his toothless gums, the
baby beamed with humid smiles, and the cat, rolled into a
fluffy ball and purring like a stocking-loom, worked its
fingers ecstatically as if it were trying on a new pair of
gloves.

" It must be mortal lonely out at the lighthouse," Mrs.
Solly resumed. " Only three men and never a neigh-

bour to speak to ; and, Lord ! what a muddle they must be in with no woman to look after them and keep 'em tidy. But you won't be overworked, Mr. Brown, in these long days ; daylight till past nine o'clock. I don't know what you'll do to pass the time."

" Oh, I shall find plenty to do, I expect," said Brown, " what with cleanin' the lamps and glasses and paintin' up the ironwork. And that reminds me," he added, looking round at the clock, " that time's getting on. High water at half-past ten, and here it's gone eight o'clock."

Mrs. Solly, acting on the hint, began rapidly to fish out the washed garments and wring them out into the form of short ropes. Then, having dried her hands on her apron, she relieved Brown of the protesting baby.

" Your room will be ready for you, Mr. Brown," said she, " when your turn comes for a spell ashore ; and main glad me and Tom will be to see you back."

" Thank you, Mrs. Solly, ma'am," answered Brown, tenderly placing the cat on the floor ; " you won't be more glad than what I will." He shook hands warmly with his landlady, kissed the baby, chucked the cat under the chin, and, picking up his little chest by its becket, swung it on to his shoulder and strode out of the cottage.

His way lay across the marshes, and, like the ships in the offing, he shaped his course by the twin towers of Reculver that stood up grotesquely on the rim of the land ; and as he trod the springy turf, Tom Solly's fleecy charges looked up at him with vacant stares and valedictory bleatings. Once, at a dyke-gate, he paused to look back at the fair Kentish landscape : at the grey tower of St. Nicholas-at-Wade peeping above the trees and the far-away mill at Sarre, whirling slowly in the summer breeze ; and, above all, at the solitary cottage where, for a brief spell in his stormy life, he had known the homely joys of domesticity and peace. Well, that was over for the present, and the lighthouse loomed ahead. With a half-sigh he passed through the gate and walked on towards Reculver.

Outside the whitewashed cottages with their official black chimneys a petty-officer of the coast-guard was adjusting the halyards of the flagstaff. He looked round as Brown approached, and hailed him cheerily.

"Here you are, then," said he, "all figged out in your new togs, too. But we're in a bit of a difficulty, d'ye see. We've got to pull up to Whitstable this morning, so I can't send a man out with you and I can't spare a boat."

"Have I got to swim out, then?" asked Brown.

The coast-guard grinned. "Not in them new clothes, mate," he answered. "No, but there's old Willett's boat; he isn't using her to-day; he's going over to Minster to see his daughter, and he'll let us have the loan of the boat. But there's no one to go with you, and I'm responsible to Willett."

"Well, what about it?" asked Brown, with the deep-sea sailor's (usually misplaced) confidence in his power to handle a sailing-boat. "D'ye think I can't manage a tub of a boat? Me what's used the sea since I was a kid of ten?"

"Yes," said the coast-guard; "but who's to bring her back?"

"Why, the man that I'm going to relieve," answered Brown. "He don't want to swim no more than what I do."

The coast-guard reflected with his telescope pointed at a passing barge. "Well, I suppose it'll be all right," he concluded; "but it's a pity they couldn't send the tender round. However, if you undertake to send the boat back, we'll get her afloat. It's time you were off."

He strolled away to the back of the cottages, whence he presently returned with two of his mates, and the four men proceeded along the shore to where Willett's boat lay just above high-water mark.

The *Emily* was a beamy craft of the type locally known

as a "half-share skiff," solidly built of oak, with varnished planking and fitted with main and mizzen lugs. She was a good handful for four men, and, as she slid over the soft chalk rocks with a hollow rumble, the coast-guards debated the advisability of lifting out the bags of shingle with which she was ballasted.   However, she was at length dragged down, ballast and all, to the water's edge, and then, while Brown stepped the mainmast, the petty-officer gave him his directions.   " What you've got to do," said he, " is to make use of the floodtide.   Keep her nose nor'-east, and with this trickle of nor'-westerly breeze you ought to make the lighthouse in one board.   Anyhow, don't let her get east of the lighthouse, or, when the ebb sets in, you'll be in a fix."

To these admonitions Brown listened with jaunty indifference as he hoisted the sails and watched the incoming tide creep over the level shore.   Then the boat lifted on the gentle swell.   Putting out an oar, he gave a vigorous shove off that sent the boat, with a final scrape, clear of the beach, and then, having dropped the rudder on to its pintles, he seated himself and calmly belayed the main-sheet.

" There he goes," growled the coast-guard ; " makin' fast his sheet.   They *will* do it " (he invariably did it himself), " and that's how accidents happen.   I hope old Willett 'll see his boat back all right."

He stood for some time watching the dwindling boat as it sidled across the smooth water ; then he turned and followed his mates towards the station.

Out on the south-western edge of the Girdler Sand, just inside the two-fathom line, the spindle-shanked lighthouse stood a-straddle on its long screw-piles like some uncouth red-bodied wading-bird.   It was now nearly half-flood tide.   The highest shoals were long since covered, and the lighthouse rose above the smooth sea as solitary as a slaver becalmed in the " middle passage."

On the gallery outside the lantern were two men,

the entire staff of the building, of whom one sat huddled in a chair with his left leg propped up with pillows on another, while his companion rested a telescope on the rail and peered at the faint grey line of the distant land and the two tiny points that marked the twin spires of Reculver.

"I don't see any signs of the boat, Harry," said he.

The other man groaned. "I shall lose the tide," he complained, "and then there's another day gone."

"They can pull you down to Birchington and put you in the train," said the first man.

"I don't want no trains," growled the invalid. "The boat 'll be bad enough. I suppose there's nothing coming our way, Tom?"

Tom turned his face eastward and shaded his eyes. "There's a brig coming across the tide from the north," he said. "Looks like a collier." He pointed his telescope at the approaching vessel, and added: "She's got two new cloths in her upper fore top-sail, one on each leech."

The other man sat up eagerly. "What's her trysail like, Tom?" he asked.

"Can't see it," replied Tom. "Yes, I can, now: it's tanned. Why, that'll be the old *Utopia*, Harry; she's the only brig I know that's got a tanned trysail."

"Look here, Tom," exclaimed the other, "if that's the *Utopia*, she's going to my home and I'm going aboard of her. Captain Mockett 'll give me a passage, I know."

"You oughtn't to go until you're relieved, you know, Barnett," said Tom doubtfully; "it's against regulations to leave your station."

"Regulations be blowed!" exclaimed Barnett. "My leg's more to me than the regulations. I don't want to be a cripple all my life. Besides, I'm no good here, and this new chap, Brown, will be coming out presently. You run up the signal, Tom, like a good comrade, and hail the brig."

"Well, it's your look-out," said Tom, "and I don't

mind saying that if I was in your place I should cut off home and see a doctor, if I got the chance." He sauntered off to the flag-locker, and, selecting the two code-flags, deliberately toggled them on to the halyards. Then, as the brig swept up within range, he hoisted the little balls of bunting to the flagstaff-head and jerked the halyards, when the two flags blew out making the signal " Need assistance."

Promptly a coal-soiled answering pennant soared to the brig's main-truck ; less promptly the collier went about, and, turning her nose down stream, slowly drifted stern-forwards towards the lighthouse. Then a boat slid out through her gangway, and a couple of men plied the oars vigorously.

" Lighthouse ahoy ! " roared one of them, as the boat came within hail. " What's amiss ? "

" Harry Barnett has broke his leg," shouted the light-house keeper, " and he wants to know if Captain Mockett will give him a passage to Whitstable."

The boat turned back to the brig, and after a brief and bellowed consultation, once more pulled towards the lighthouse.

" Skipper says yus," roared the sailor, when he was within ear-shot, " and he says look alive, 'cause he don't want to miss his tide."

The injured man heaved a sigh of relief. " That's good news," said he, " though, how the blazes I'm going to get down the ladder is more than I can tell. What do you say, Jeffreys ? "

" I say you'd better let me lower you with the tackle," replied Jeffreys. " You can sit in the bight of a rope and I'll give you a line to steady yourself with."

" Ah, that'll do, Tom," said Barnett ; " but, for the Lord's sake, pay out the fall-rope gently."

The arrangements were made so quickly that by the time the boat was fast alongside everything was in readiness, and a minute later the injured man, dangling like a gigantic spider from the end of the tackle, slowly descended, cursing volubly to the accompaniment of the creaking of the blocks. His chest and kit-bag followed, and, as soon as these were unhooked from the tackle, the boat pulled off to the brig, which was now slowly creeping stern-foremost past the lighthouse. The sick man was hoisted up the side, his chest handed up after him, and then the brig was put on her course due south across the Kentish Flats.

Jeffreys stood on the gallery watching the receding vessel and listening to the voices of her crew as they grew small and weak in the increasing distance. Now that his gruff companion was gone, a strange loneliness had fallen on the lighthouse. The last of the homeward-bound ships had long since passed up the Princes Channel and left the calm sea desolate and blank. The distant buoys, showing as tiny black dots on the glassy surface, and the spindly shapes of the beacons which stood up from invisible shoals, but emphasised the solitude of the empty sea, and the tolling of the bell buoy on the Shivering Sand, stealing faintly down the wind, sounded weird and mournful. The day's work was already done. The lenses were polished, the lamps had been trimmed, and the little motor that worked the fog-horn had been cleaned and oiled. There were several odd jobs, it is true, waiting to be done, as there always are in a lighthouse ; but, just now, Jeffreys was not in a working humour. A new comrade was coming into his life to-day, a stranger with whom he was to be shut up alone, night and day, for a month on end, and whose temper and tastes and habits might mean for him pleasant companionship or jangling and discord without end. Who was this man Brown ? What had he been ? and what was he like ? These were the questions that passed, naturally enough, through the lighthouse-keeper's mind and distracted him from his usual thoughts and occupations.

Presently a speck on the landward horizon caught his eye. He snatched up the telescope eagerly to inspect it. Yes, it was a boat ; but not the coast-guard's cutter, for which he was looking. Evidently a fisherman's boat and with only one man in it. He laid down the telescope with a sigh of disappointment, and, filling his pipe, leaned on the rail with a dreamy eye bent on the faint grey line of the land.

Three long years had he spent in this dreary solitude, so repugnant to his active, restless nature : three blank, interminable years, with nothing to look back on but the endless succession of summer calms, stormy nights and the chilly fogs of winter, when the unseen steamers hooted from the void and the fog-horn bellowed its hoarse warning.

Why had he come to this God-forgotten spot ? and why did he stay, when the wide world called to him ? And then memory painted him a picture on which his mind's eye had often looked before and which once again arose before him, shutting out the vision of the calm sea and the distant land. It was a brightly-coloured picture. It showed a cloudless sky brooding over the deep blue · tropic sea ; and in the middle of the picture, see-sawing gently on the quiet swell, a white-painted barque.

Her sails were clewed up untidily, her swinging yards jerked at the slack braces and her untended wheel revolved to and fro to the oscillations of the rudder.

She was not a derelict, for more than a dozen men were on her deck ; but the men were all drunk and mostly asleep, and there was never an officer among them.

Then he saw the interior of one of her cabins. The chart-rack, the tell-tale compass and the chronometers marked it as the captain's cabin. In it were four men, and two of them lay dead on the deck. Of the other two, one was a small, cunning-faced man, who was, at the moment, kneeling beside one of the corpses to wipe a knife upon its coat. The fourth man was himself.

Again, he saw the two murderers stealing off in a quarter-boat, as the barque with her drunken crew drifted towards the spouting surf of a river-bar. He saw the ship melt away in the surf like an icicle in the sunshine ; and, later, two shipwrecked mariners, picked up in an open boat and set ashore at an American port.

That was why he was here. Because he was a murderer. The other scoundrel, Amos Todd, had turned Queen's Evidence and denounced him, and he had barely managed to escape. Since then he had hidden himself from the great world, and here he must continue to hide, not from the law—for his person was unknown now that his shipmates were dead—but from the partner of his crime. It was the fear of Todd that had changed him from Jeffrey Rorke to Tom Jeffreys and had sent him to the Girdler, a prisoner for life. Todd might die—might even now be dead—but he would never hear of it : would never hear the news of his release.

. He roused himself and once more pointed his telescope at the distant boat. She was considerably nearer now and seemed to be heading out towards the lighthouse. Perhaps the man in her was bringing a message ; at any rate, there was no sign of the coast-guard's cutter.

He went in, and, betaking himself to the kitchen, busied himself with a few simple preparations for dinner. But there was nothing to cook, for there remained the cold meat from yesterday's cooking, which he would make sufficient, with some biscuit in place of potatoes. He felt restless and unstrung ; the solitude irked him, and the everlasting wash of the water among the piles jarred on his nerves.

When he went out again into the gallery the ebb-tide had set in strongly and the boat was little more than a mile distant ; and now, through the glass, he could see that the man in her wore the uniform cap of the Trinity House. Then the man must be his future comrade, Brown ; but this was very extraordinary. What were they to do with the boat ? There was no one to take her back.

The breeze was dying away. As he watched the boat, he saw the man lower the sail and take to his oars ; and something of hurry in the way the man pulled over the gathering tide, caused Jeffreys to look round the horizon. And then, for the first time, he noticed a bank of fog creeping up from the east and already so near that the beacon on the East Girdler had faded out of sight. He hastened in to start the little motor that compressed the air for the fog-horn and waited awhile to see that the mechanism was running properly. Then, as the deck vibrated to the roar of the horn, he went out once more into the gallery.

The fog was now all round the lighthouse and the boat was hidden from view. He listened intently. The enclosing wall of vapour seemed to have shut out sound as well as vision. At intervals the horn bellowed its note of warning, and then all was still save the murmur of the water among the piles below, and, infinitely faint and far away, the mournful tolling of the bell on the Shivering Sand.

At length there came to his ear the muffled sound of oars working in the tholes ; then, at the very edge of the circle of grey water that was visible, the boat appeared through the fog, pale and spectral, with a shadowy figure pulling furiously. The horn emitted a hoarse growl ; the man looked round, perceived the lighthouse and altered his course towards it.

Jeffreys descended the iron stairway, and, walking along the lower gallery, stood at the head of the ladder earnestly watching the approaching stranger. Already he was tired of being alone. The yearning for human companionship had been growing ever since Barnett left. But what sort of comrade was this stranger who was coming into his life ? And coming to occupy so dominant a place in it. It was a momentous question.

The boat swept down swiftly athwart the hurrying tide. Nearer it came and yet nearer : and still Jeffreys could catch no glimpse of his new comrade's face. At length it came fairly alongside and bumped against the fender-posts ; the stranger whisked in an oar and grabbed a rung of the ladder, and Jeffreys dropped a coil of rope into the boat. And still the man's face was hidden.

Jeffreys leaned out over the ladder and watched him anxiously, as he made fast the rope, unhooked the sail from the traveller and unstepped the mast. When he had set all in order, the stranger picked up a small chest, and, swinging it over his shoulder, stepped on to the ladder. Slowly, by reason of his encumbrance, he mounted, rung by rung, with never an upward glance, and Jeffreys gazed down at the top of his head with growing curiosity. At last he reached the top of the ladder and Jeffreys stooped to lend him a hand. Then, for the first time, he looked up, and Jeffreys started back with a blanched face.

" God Almighty ! " he gasped ; " it's Amos Todd ! "

As the newcomer stepped on the gallery, the fog-horn emitted a roar like that of some hungry monster. Jeffreys turned abruptly without a word, and walked to the stairs, followed by Todd, and the two men ascended with never a sound but the hollow clank of their footsteps on the iron plates. Silently Jeffreys stalked into the living-room and, as his companion followed, he turned and motioned to the latter to set down his chest.

" You ain't much of a talker, mate," said Todd, looking round the room in some surprise ; " ain't you going to say ' good-morning ' ? We're going to be good comrades, I hope. I'm Jim Brown, the new hand, I am ; what might your name be ? "

Jeffreys turned on him suddenly and led him to the window. " Look at me carefully, Amos Todd," he said sternly, " and then ask yourself what my name is."

At the sound of his voice Todd looked up with a start and turned pale as death. " It can't be," he whispered, " it can't be Jeff Rorke ! "

The other man laughed harshly, and, leaning forward, said in a low voice : " Hast thou found me, O mine enemy ! "

" Don't say that ! " exclaimed Todd. " Don't call

me your enemy, Jeff. Lord knows but I'm glad to see you, though I'd never have known you without your beard, and with that grey hair. I've been to blame, Jeff, and I know it; but it ain't no use raking up old grudges. Let bygones be bygones, Jeff, and let us be pals as we used to be." He wiped his face with his handkerchief and watched his companion apprehensively.

"Sit down," said Rorke, pointing to a shabby rep-covered arm-chair; "sit down and tell us what you've done with all that money. You've blued it all, I suppose, or you wouldn't be here."

"Robbed, Jeff," answered Todd; "robbed of every penny. Ah! that was an unfortunate affair, that job on board the old *Sea-flower*. But it's over and done with and we'd best forget it. They're all dead but us, Jeff, so we're safe enough so long as we keep our mouths shut; all at the bottom of the sea—and the best place for 'em, too."

"Yes," Rorke replied fiercely, "that's the best place for your shipmates when they know too much; at the bottom of the sea or swinging at the end of a rope." He paced up and down the little room with rapid strides, and each time that he approached Todd's chair the latter shrank back with an expression of alarm.

"Don't sit there staring at me," said Rorke. "Why don't you smoke or do something?"

Todd hastily produced a pipe from his pocket, and having filled it from a moleskin pouch, stuck it in his mouth while he searched for a match. Apparently he carried his matches loose in his pocket, for he presently brought one forth—a red-headed match, which, when he struck it on the wall, lighted with a pale-blue flame. He applied it to his pipe, sucking in his cheeks while he kept his eyes fixed on his companion. Rorke, meanwhile, halted in his walk to cut some shavings from a cake of hard tobacco with a large clasp-knife; and, as he stood, he gazed with frowning abstraction at Todd.

"This pipe's stopped," said the latter, sucking ineffectually at the mouthpiece. "Have you got such a thing as a piece of wire, Jeff ? "

" No, I haven't," replied Rorke ; " not up here. I'll get a bit from the store presently. Here, take this pipe till you can clean your own : I've got another in the rack there." The sailor's natural hospitality overcoming for the moment his animosity, he thrust the pipe that he had just filled towards Todd, who took it with a mumbled " Thank you " and an anxious eye on the open knife. On the wall beside the chair was a roughly-carved pipe-rack containing several pipes, one of which Rorke lifted out ; and, as he leaned over the chair to reach it, Todd's face went several shades paler.

" Well, Jeff," he said, after a pause, while Rorke cut a fresh " fill " of tobacco, " are we going to be pals same as what we used to be ? "

Rorke's animosity lighted up afresh. " Am I going to be pals with the man that tried to swear away my life ? " he said sternly ; and after a pause he added : " That wants thinking about, that does ; and meantime I must go and look at the engine."

When Rorke had gone the new hand sat, with the two pipes in his hands, reflecting deeply. Abstractedly he stuck the fresh pipe into his mouth, and, dropping the stopped one into the rack, felt for a match. Still with an air of abstraction he lit the pipe, and, having smoked for a minute or two, rose from the chair and began softly to creep across the room, looking about him and listening intently. At the door he paused to look out into the fog, and then, having again listened attentively, he stepped on tip-toe out on to the gallery and along towards the stairway. Of a sudden the voice of Rorke brought him up with a start.

" Hallo, Todd ! where are you off to ? "

" I'm just going down to make the boat secure," was the reply.

" Never you mind about the boat," said Rorke. " I'll see to her."

" Right O, Jeff," said Todd, still edging towards the stairway. " But I say, mate, where's the other man— the man that I'm to relieve ? "

" There ain't any other man," replied Rorke ; " he went off aboard a collier."

Todd's face suddenly became grey and haggard. " Then, there's no one here but us two ! " he gasped ; and then, with an effort to conceal his fear, he asked : " But who's going to take the boat back ? "

" We'll see about that presently," replied Rorke ; " you get along in and unpack your chest."

He came out on the gallery as he spoke, with a lowering frown on his face. Todd cast a terrified glance at him, and then turned and ran for his life towards the stairway.

" Come back ! " roared Rorke, springing forward along the gallery ; but Todd's feet were already clattering down the iron steps. By the time Rorke reached the head of the stairs, the fugitive was near the bottom ; but here, in his haste, he stumbled, barely saving himself by the handrail, and when he recovered his balance Rorke was upon him. Todd darted to the head of the ladder, but, as he grasped the stanchion, his pursuer seized him by the collar. In a moment he had turned with his hand under his coat. There was a quick blow, a loud curse from Rorke, an answering yell from Todd, and a knife fell spinning through the air and dropped into the fore-peak of the boat below.

" You murderous little devil ! " said Rorke in an ominously quiet voice, with his bleeding hand gripping his captive by the throat. " Handy with your knife as ever, eh ? So you were off to give information, were you ? "

" No, I wasn't, Jeff," replied Todd in a choking voice ; " I wasn't, s'elp me God. Let go, Jeff. I didn't mean no harm. I was only—— " With a sudden wrench he freed one hand and struck out frantically at his captor's face. But Rorke warded off the blow, and, grasping the other wrist, gave a violent push and let go.

Todd staggered backward a few paces along the staging, bringing up at the extreme edge ; and here, for a sensible time, he stood with wide-open mouth and starting eye-balls, swaying and clutching wildly at the air. Then, with a shrill scream, he toppled backwards and fell, striking a pile in his descent and rebounding into the water.

In spite of the audible thump of his head on the pile, he was not stunned, for, when he rose to the surface, he struck out vigorously, uttering short, stifled cries for help. Rorke watched him with set teeth and quickened breath, but made no move. Smaller and still smaller grew the head with its little circle of ripples, swept away on the swift ebb-tide, and fainter the bubbling cries that came across the smooth water. At length as the small black spot began to fade in the fog, the drowning man, with a final effort, raised his head clear of the surface and sent a last, despairing shriek towards the lighthouse. The fog-horn sent back an answering bellow ; the head sank below the surface and was seen no more ; and in the dreadful stillness that settled down upon the sea there sounded faint and far away the muffled tolling of a bell.

Rorke stood for some minutes immovable, wrapped in thought. Presently the distant hoot of a steamer's whistle aroused him. The ebb-tide shipping was beginning to come down and the fog might lift at any moment ; and there was the boat still alongside. She must be disposed of at once. No one had seen her arrive and no one must see her made fast to the lighthouse. Once get rid of the boat and all traces of Todd's visit would be destroyed.

He ran down the ladder and stepped into the boat. It was perfectly simple. She was heavily ballasted and would go down like a stone if she filled.

He shifted some of the bags of shingle, and, lifting the bottom boards, pulled out the plug. Instantly a large jet of water spouted up into the bottom. Rorke looked at it critically, and, deciding that it would fill her in a few minutes, replaced the bottom boards ; and having secured the mast and sail with a few turns of the sheet round a thwart, to prevent them from floating away, he cast off the mooring-rope and stepped on the ladder.

As the released boat began to move away on the tide, he ran up and mounted to the upper gallery to watch her disappearance. Suddenly he remembered Todd's chest. It was still in the room below. With a hurried glance around into the fog, he ran down to the room, and snatching up the chest, carried it out on the lower gallery. After another nervous glance around to assure himself that no craft was in sight, he heaved the chest over the handrail, and, when it fell with a loud splash into the sea, he waited to watch it float away after its owner and the sunken boat. But it never rose ; and presently he returned to the upper gallery.

The fog was thinning perceptibly now, and the boat remained plainly visible as she drifted away. But she sank more slowly than he had expected, and presently as she drifted farther away, he fetched the telescope and peered at her with growing anxiety. It would be unfortunate if any one saw her ; if she should be picked up here, with her plug out, it would be disastrous.

He was beginning to be really alarmed. Through the glass he could see that the boat was now rolling in a sluggish, water-logged fashion, but she still showed some inches of free-board, and the fog was thinning every moment.

Presently the blast of a steamer's whistle sounded close at hand. He looked round hurriedly and, seeing nothing, again pointed the telescope eagerly at the dwindling boat. Suddenly he gave a gasp of relief. The boat had rolled gunwale under ; had staggered back for a moment and then rolled again, slowly, finally, with the water pouring in over the submerged gunwale.

In a few more seconds she had vanished. Rorke lowered the telescope and took a deep breath. Now he was safe. The boat had sunk unseen. But he was better than safe : he was free.

His evil spirit, the standing menace of his life, was gone, and the wide world, the world of life, of action, of pleasure, called to him.

In a few minutes the fog lifted. The sun shone brightly on the red-funnelled cattle-boat whose whistle had startled him just now, the summer blue came back to sky and sea, and the land peeped once more over the edge of the horizon.

He went in, whistling cheerfully, and stopped the motor ; returned to coil away the rope that he had thrown to Todd ; and, when he had hoisted a signal for assistance, he went in once more to eat his solitary meal in peace and gladness.

II. " The Singing Bone "
(Related by CHRISTOPHER JERVIS, M.D.)

To every kind of scientific work a certain amount of manual labour naturally appertains, labour that cannot be performed by the scientist himself, since art is long but life is short. A chemical analysis involves a laborious " clean up " of apparatus and laboratory, for which the chemist has no time ; the preparation of a skeleton—the maceration, bleaching, " assembling," and riveting together of bones—must be carried out by someone whose time is not too precious. And so with other scientific activities. Behind the man of science with his outfit of knowledge is the indispensable mechanic with his out- fit of manual skill.

Thorndyke's laboratory assistant, Polton, was a fine example of the latter type, deft, resourceful, ingenious and untiring. He was somewhat of an inventive genius, too ; and it was one of his inventions that connected us with the singular case that I am about to record.

Though by trade a watchmaker, Polton was, by choice, an optician. Optical apparatus was the passion of his

life ; and when, one day, he produced for our inspection
an improved prism for increasing the efficiency of gas-
buoys, Thorndyke at once brought the invention to the
notice of a friend at the Trinity House.

As a consequence, we three—Thorndyke, Polton and
I—found ourselves early on a fine July morning making
our way down Middle Temple Lane bound for the
Temple Pier. A small oil-launch lay alongside the
pontoon, and, as we made our appearance, a red-faced,
white-whiskered gentleman stood up in the cockpit.

" Here's a delightful morning, doctor," he sang out
in a fine, brassy, resonant, sea-faring voice ; " sort of
day for a trip to the lower river, hey ? Hallo, Polton !
Coming down to take the bread out of our mouths, are
you ? Ha, ha ! " The cheery laugh rang out over the
river and mingled with the throb of the engine as the
little launch moved off from the pier.

Captain Grumpass was one of the Elder Brethren of
the Trinity House. Formerly a client of Thorndyke's,
he had subsided, as Thorndyke's clients were apt to do,
into the position of a personal friend, and his hearty
regard included our invaluable assistant.

" Nice state of things," continued the captain, with
a chuckle, " when a body of nautical experts have got
to be taught their business by a parcel of lawyers or
doctors, what ? I suppose trade's slack and ' Satan
findeth mischief still,' hey, Polton ? "

" There isn't much doing on the civil side, sir," replied
Polton, with a quaint, crinkly smile, " but the criminals
are still going strong."

" Ha ! mystery department still flourishing, what ?
And, by Jove ! talking of mysteries, doctor, our people
have got a queer problem to work out ; something quite
in your line—quite. Yes, and, by the Lord Moses,
since I've got you here, why shouldn't I suck your
brains ? "

" Exactly," said Thorndyke. " Why shouldn't you ? "

" Well, then, I will," said the captain, " so here goes.

All hands to the pump ! " He lit a cigar, and, after a few preliminary puffs, began : " The mystery, shortly stated, is this : one of our lighthousemen has disappeared—vanished off the face of the earth and left no trace. He may have bolted, he may have been drowned accidentally or he may have been murdered. But I'd better give you the particulars in order. At the end of last week a barge brought into Ramsgate a letter from the screw-pile lighthouse on the Girdler. There are only two men there, and it seems that one of them, a man named Barnett, had broken his leg, and he asked that the tender should be sent to bring him ashore. Well, it happened that the local tender, the *Warden*, was up on the slip in Ramsgate Harbour, having a scrape down, and wouldn't be available for a day or two, so, as the case was urgent, the officer at Ramsgate sent a letter to the lighthouse by one of the pleasure steamers saying that the man should be relieved by boat on the following morning, which was Saturday. He also wrote to a new hand who had just been taken on, a man named James Brown, who was lodging near Reculver, waiting his turn, telling him to go out on Saturday morning in the coast-guard's boat ; and he sent a third letter to the coast-guard at Reculver asking him to take Brown out to the lighthouse and bring Barnett ashore. Well, between them, they made a fine muddle of it. The coast-guard couldn't spare either a boat or a man, so they borrowed a fisherman's boat, and in this the man Brown started off alone, like an idiot, on the chance that Barnett would be able to sail the boat back in spite of his broken leg.

" Meanwhile Barnett, who is a Whitstable man, had signalled a collier bound for his native town, and got taken off ; so that the other keeper, Thomas Jeffreys, was left alone until Brown should turn up.

" But Brown never did turn up. The coast-guard helped him to put off and saw him well out to sea, and the keeper, Jeffreys, saw a sailing-boat with one man in

her, making for the lighthouse. Then a bank of fog
came up and hid the boat, and when the fog cleared she
was nowhere to be seen. Man and boat had vanished
and left no sign."

" He may have been run down in the fog," Thorndyke
suggested.

" He may," agreed the captain, " but no accident
has been reported. The coast-guards think he may have
capsized in a squall—they saw him make the sheet fast.
But there weren't any squalls : the weather was quite
calm."

" Was he all right and well when he put off ? " inquired
Thorndyke.

" Yes," replied the captain, " the coast-guards' report
is highly circumstantial ; in fact, it's full of silly details
that have no bearing on anything. This is what they
say." He pulled out an official letter and read : " ' When
last seen, the missing man was seated in the boat's stern
to windward of the helm. He had belayed the sheet.
He was holding a pipe and tobacco-pouch in his hands
and steering with his elbow. He was filling the pipe
from the tobacco-pouch.' There ! ' He was holding
the pipe in his hand,' mark you ! not with his toes ;
and he was filling it from a tobacco-pouch, whereas
you'd have expected him to fill it from a coal-scuttle or
a feeding-bottle. Bah ! " The captain rammed the letter
back in his pocket and puffed scornfully at his cigar.

" You are hardly fair to the coast-guard," said Thorndyke, laughing at the captain's vehemence. " The duty
of a witness is to give *all* the facts, not a judicious
selection."

" But, my dear sir," said Captain Grumpass, " what
the deuce can it matter what the poor devil filled his
pipe from ? "

" Who can say ? " answered Thorndyke. " It may
turn out to be a highly material fact. One never knows
beforehand. The value of a particular fact depends on
its relation to the rest of the evidence."

" I suppose it does," grunted the captain; and he continued to smoke in reflective silence until we opened Blackwall Point, when he suddenly stood up.

" There's a steam trawler alongside our wharf," he announced. " Now what the deuce can she be doing there ? " He scanned the little steamer attentively, and continued : " They seem to be landing something, too. Just pass me those glasses, Polton. Why, hang me ! it's a dead body ! But why on earth are they landing it on our wharf ? They must have known you were coming, doctor."

As the launch swept alongside the wharf, the captain sprang up lightly and approached the group gathered round the body. " What's this ? " he asked. " Why have they brought this thing here ? "

The master of the trawler, who had superintended the landing, proceeded to explain.

" It's one of your men, sir," said he. " We saw the body lying on the edge of the South Shingles Sand, close to the beacon, as we passed at low water, so we put off the boat and fetched it aboard. As there was nothing to identify the man by, I had a look in his pockets and found this letter." He handed the captain an official envelope addressed to " Mr. J. Brown, c/o Mr. Solly, Shepherd, Reculver, Kent."

" Why, this is the man we were speaking about, doctor," exclaimed Captain Grumpass. " What a very singular coincidence. But what are we to do with the body ? "

" You will have to write to the coroner," replied Thorndyke. " By the way, did you turn out all the pockets ? " he asked, turning to the skipper of the trawler.

" No, sir," was the reply. " I found the letter in the first pocket that I felt in, so I didn't examine any of the others. Is there anything more that you want to know, sir ? "

" Nothing but your name and address, for the coroner," replied Thorndyke, and the skipper, having given this

information and expressed the hope that the coroner
would not keep him " hanging about," returned to his
vessel and pursued his way to Billingsgate.

" I wonder if you would mind having a look at the
body of this poor devil, while Polton is showing us his
contraptions," said Captain Grumpass.

" I can't do much without a coroner's order," replied
Thorndyke ; " but if it will give you any satisfaction,
Jervis and I will make a preliminary inspection with
pleasure."

" I should be glad if you would," said the captain.
" We should like to know that the poor beggar met his
end fairly."

The body was accordingly moved to a shed, and, as
Polton was led away, carrying the black bag that contained his precious model, we entered the shed and
commenced our investigation.

The deceased was a small, elderly man, decently
dressed in a somewhat nautical fashion. He appeared
to have been dead only two or three days, and the body,
unlike the majority of seaborne corpses, was uninjured
by fish or crabs. There were no fractured bones or
other gross injuries, and no wounds, excepting a ragged
tear in the scalp at the back of the head.

" The general appearance of the body," said Thorndyke, when he had noted these particulars, " suggests
death by drowning, though, of course, we can't give a
definite opinion until a *post mortem* has been made."

" You don't attach any significance to that scalp-
wound, then ? " I asked.

" As a cause of death ? No. It was obviously
inflicted during life, but it seems to have been an oblique
blow that spent its force on the scalp, leaving the skull
uninjured. But it is very significant in another way."

" In what way ? " I asked.

Thorndyke took out his pocket-case and extracted a
pair of forceps. " Consider the circumstances," said he.
" This man put off from the shore to go to the lighthouse,

but never arrived there. The question is, where did he arrive ? " As he spoke he stooped over the corpse and turned back the hair round the wound with the beak of the forceps. " Look at those white objects among the hair, Jervis, and inside the wound. They tell us something, I think."

I examined, through my lens, the chalky fragments to which he pointed. " These seem to be bits of shells and the tubes of some marine worm," I said.

" Yes," he answered ; " the broken shells are evidently those of the acorn barnacle, and the other fragments are mostly pieces of the tubes of the common serpula. The inference that these objects suggest is an important one. It is that this wound was produced by some body encrusted by acorn barnacles and serpulæ ; that is to say, by a body that is periodically submerged. Now, what can that body be, and how can the deceased have knocked his head against it ? "

" It might be the stem of a ship that ran him down," I suggested.

" I don't think you would find many serpulæ on the stem of a ship," said Thorndyke. " The combination rather suggests some stationary object between tide-marks, such as a beacon. But one doesn't see how a man could knock his head against a beacon, while, on the other hand, there are no other stationary objects out in the estuary to knock against except buoys, and a buoy presents a flat surface that could hardly have produced this wound. By the way, we may as well see what there is in his pockets, though it is not likely that robbery had anything to do with his death."

" No," I agreed, " and I see his watch is in his pocket ; quite a good silver one," I added, taking it out. " It has stopped at 12.13."

" That may be important," said Thorndyke, making a note of the fact ; " but we had better examine the pockets one at a time, and put the things back when we have looked at them."

5

The first pocket that we turned out was the left hip-pocket of the monkey jacket. This was apparently the one that the skipper had rifled, for we found in it two letters, both bearing the crest of the Trinity House. These, of course, we returned without reading, and then passed on to the right pocket. The contents of this were commonplace enough, consisting of a briar pipe, a moleskin pouch and a number of loose matches.

"Rather a casual proceeding, this," I remarked, "to carry matches loose in the pocket, and a pipe with them, too."

"Yes," agreed Thorndyke; "especially with these very inflammable matches. You notice that the sticks had been coated at the upper end with sulphur before the red phosphorus heads were put on. They would light with a touch, and would be very difficult to extinguish; which, no doubt, is the reason that this type of match is so popular among seamen, who have to light their pipes in all sorts of weather." As he spoke he picked up the pipe and looked at it reflectively, turning it over in his hand and peering into the bowl. Suddenly he glanced from the pipe to the dead man's face and then, with the forceps, turned back the lips to look into the mouth.

"Let us see what tobacco he smokes," said he.

I opened the sodden pouch and displayed a mass of dark, fine-cut tobacco. "It looks like shag," I said.

"Yes, it is shag," he replied; "and now we will see what is in the pipe. It has been only half smoked out." He dug out the "dottle" with his pocket-knife on to a sheet of paper, and we both inspected it. Clearly it was not shag, for it consisted of coarsely-cut shreds and was nearly black.

"Shavings from a cake of 'hard,'" was my verdict, and Thorndyke agreed as he shot the fragments back into the pipe.

The other pockets yielded nothing of interest, except a pocket-knife, which Thorndyke opened and examined closely. There was not much money, though as much as one would expect, and enough to exclude the idea of robbery.

" Is there a sheath-knife on that strap ? " Thorndyke asked, pointing to a narrow leather belt. I turned back the jacket and looked.

" There is a sheath," I said, " but no knife. It must have dropped out."

" That is rather odd," said Thorndyke. " A sailor's sheath-knife takes a deal of shaking out as a rule. It is intended to be used in working on the rigging when the man is aloft, so that he can get it out with one hand while he is holding on with the other. It has to be and usually is very secure, for the sheath holds half the handle as well as the blade. What makes one notice the matter in this case is that the man, as you see, carried a pocket-knife ; and, as this would serve all the ordinary purposes of a knife, it seems to suggest that the sheath-knife was carried for defensive purposes : as a weapon, in fact. However, we can't get much further in the case without a *post mortem*, and here comes the captain."

Captain Grumpass entered the shed and looked down commiseratingly at the dead seaman.

" Is there anything, doctor, that throws any light on the man's disappearance ? " he asked.

" There are one or two curious features in the case," Thorndyke replied ; " but, oddly enough, the only really important point arises out of that statement of the coast-guard's, concerning which you were so scornful."

" You don't say so ! " exclaimed the captain.

" Yes," said Thorndyke ; " the coast-guard states that when last seen deceased was filling his pipe from his tobacco-pouch. Now his pouch contains shag ; but the pipe in his pocket contains hard cut."

" Is there no cake tobacco in any of the pockets ? "

" Not a fragment. Of course, it is possible that he might have had a piece and used it up to fill the pipe ;

but there is no trace of any on the blade of his pocket-knife, and you know how this juicy black cake stains a knife-blade. His sheath-knife is missing, but he would hardly have used that to shred tobacco when he had a pocket-knife."

"No," assented the captain ; "but are you sure he hadn't a second pipe ? "

" There was only one pipe," replied Thorndyke, " and that was not his own."

" Not his own ! " exclaimed the captain, halting by a huge, chequered buoy to stare at my colleague ; " how do you know it was not his own ? "

" By the appearance of the vulcanite mouthpiece," said Thorndyke. " It showed deep toothmarks ; in fact, it was nearly bitten through. Now a man who bites through his pipe usually presents certain definite physical peculiarities, among which is, necessarily, a fairly good set of teeth. But the dead man had not a tooth in his head."

The captain cogitated a while, and then remarked : " I don't quite see the bearing of this."

" Don't you ? " said Thorndyke. " It seems to me highly suggestive. Here is a man who, when last seen, was filling his pipe with a particular kind of tobacco. He is picked up dead, and his pipe contains a totally different kind of tobacco. Where did that tobacco come from ? The obvious suggestion is that he had met some one."

" Yes, it does look like it," agreed the captain.

" Then," continued Thorndyke, " there is the fact that his sheath-knife is missing. That may mean nothing, but we have to bear it in mind. And there is another curious circumstance : there is a wound on the back of the head caused by a heavy bump against some body that was covered with acorn barnacles and marine worms. Now there are no piers or stages out in the open estuary. The question is, what could he have struck ? "

" Oh, there is nothing in that," said the captain.

"When a body has been washing about in a tideway for close on three days——"

"But this is not a question of a body," Thorndyke interrupted. "The wound was made during life."

"The deuce it was!" exclaimed the captain. "Well, all I can suggest is that he must have fouled one of the beacons in the fog, stove in his boat and bumped his head, though, I must admit, that's rather a lame explanation." He stood for a minute gazing at his toes with a cogitative frown and then looked up at Thorndyke.

"I have an idea," he said. "From what you say, this matter wants looking into pretty carefully. Now, I am going down on the tender to-day to make inquiries on the spot. What do you say to coming with me as adviser—as a matter of business, of course—you and Dr. Jervis? I shall start about eleven; we shall be at the lighthouse by three o'clock, and you can get back to town to-night, if you want to. What do you say?"

"There's nothing to hinder us," I put in eagerly, for even at Bugsby's Hole the river looked very alluring on this summer morning.

"Very well," said Thorndyke, "we will come. Jervis is evidently hankering for a sea-trip, and so am I, for that matter."

"It's a business engagement, you know," the captain stipulated.

"Nothing of the kind," said Thorndyke; "it's unmitigated pleasure; the pleasure of the voyage and your high well-born society."

"I didn't mean that," grumbled the captain, "but, if you are coming as guests, send your man for your night-gear and let us bring you back to-morrow evening."

"We won't disturb Polton," said my colleague; "we can take the train from Blackwall and fetch our things ourselves. Eleven o'clock, you said?"

"Thereabouts," said Captain Grumpass; "but don't put yourselves out."

The means of communication in London have reached

an almost undesirable state of perfection. With the aid of the snorting train and the tinkling, two-wheeled "gondola," we crossed and re-crossed the town with such celerity that it was barely eleven when we re-appeared on Trinity Wharf with a joint Gladstone and Thorndyke's little green case.

The tender had hauled out of Bow Creek, and now lay alongside the wharf with a great striped can buoy dangling from her derrick, and Captain Grumpass stood at the gangway, his jolly, red face beaming with pleasure. The buoy was safely stowed forward, the derrick hauled up to the mast, the loose shrouds rehooked to the screw-lanyards, and the steamer, with four jubilant hoots, swung round and shoved her sharp nose against the incoming tide.

For near upon four hours the ever-widening stream of the "London River" unfolded its moving panorama. The smoke and smell of Woolwich Reach gave place to lucid air made soft by the summer haze; the grey huddle of factories fell away and green levels of cattle-spotted marsh stretched away to the high land bordering the river valley. Venerable training ships displayed their chequered hulls by the wooded shore, and whispered of the days of oak and hemp, when the tall three-decker, comely and majestic, with her soaring heights of canvas, like towers of ivory, had not yet given place to the mud-coloured saucepans that fly the white ensign nowadays and devour the substance of the British taxpayer : when a sailor was a sailor and not a mere sea-faring mechanic. Sturdily breasting the flood-tide, the tender threaded her way through the endless procession of shipping ; barges, billy-boys, schooners, brigs ; lumpish Black-seamen, blue-funnelled China tramps, rickety Baltic barques with twirling windmills, gigantic liners, staggering under a mountain of top-hamper. Erith, Purfleet, Greenhithe, Grays greeted us and passed astern. The chimneys of Northfleet, the clustering roofs of Gravesend, the populous anchorage and the lurking batteries, were left behind, and, as we swung out of the Lower Hope, the wide expanse of sea reach spread out before us like a great sheet of blue-shot satin.

About half-past twelve the ebb overtook us and helped us on our way, as we could see by the speed with which the distant land slid past, and the freshening of the air as we passed through it.

But sky and sea were hushed in a summer calm. Balls of fleecy cloud hung aloft, motionless in the soft blue ; the barges drifted on the tide with drooping sails, and a big, striped bell buoy—surmounted by a staff and cage and labelled " Shivering Sand "—sat dreaming in the sun above its motionless reflection, to rouse for a moment as it met our wash, nod its cage drowsily, utter a solemn ding-dong, and fall asleep again.

It was shortly after passing the buoy that the gaunt shape of a screw-pile lighthouse began to loom up ahead, its dull-red paint turned to vermilion by the early after-noon sun. As we drew nearer, the name *Girdler*, painted in huge, white letters, became visible, and two men could be seen in the gallery around the lantern, inspecting us through a telescope.

" Shall you be long at the lighthouse, sir ? " the master of the tender inquired of Captain Grumpass ; " because we're going down to the North-East Pan Sand to fix this new buoy and take up the old one."

" Then you'd better put us off at the lighthouse and come back for us when you've finished the job," was the reply. " I don't know how long we shall be."

The tender was brought to, a boat lowered, and a couple of hands pulled us across the intervening space of water.

" It will be a dirty climb for you in your shore-going clothes," the captain remarked—he was as spruce as a new pin himself—" but the stuff will all wipe off." We looked up at the skeleton shape. The falling tide had exposed some fifteen feet of the piles, and piles and ladder alike were swathed in sea-grass and encrusted with barnacles and worm-tubes. But we were not such town-sparrows as the captain seemed to think, for we both followed his lead without difficulty up the slippery ladder, Thorndyke clinging tenaciously to his little green case, from which he refused to be separated even for an instant.

"These gentlemen and I," said the captain, as we stepped on the stage at the head of the ladder, "have come to make inquiries about the missing man, James Brown. Which of you is Jeffreys?"

"I am, sir," replied a tall, powerful, square-jawed, beetle-browed man, whose left hand was tied up in a rough bandage.

"What have you been doing to your hand?" asked the captain.

"I cut it while I was peeling some potatoes," was the reply. "It isn't much of a cut, sir."

"Well, Jeffreys," said the captain, "Brown's body has been picked up and I want particulars for the inquest. You'll be summoned as a witness, I suppose, so come in and tell us all you know."

We entered the living-room and seated ourselves at the table. The captain opened a massive pocket-book, while Thorndyke, in his attentive, inquisitive fashion, looked about the odd, cabin-like room as if making a mental inventory of its contents.

Jeffreys' statement added nothing to what we already knew. He had seen a boat with one man in it making for the lighthouse. Then the fog had drifted up and he had lost sight of the boat. He started the fog-horn and kept a bright look-out, but the boat never arrived. And that was all he knew. He supposed that the man must have missed the lighthouse and been carried away on the ebb-tide, which was running strongly at the time.

"What time was it when you last saw the boat?" Thorndyke asked.

"About half-past eleven," replied Jeffreys.

"What was the man like?" asked the captain.

" I don't know, sir : he was rowing, and his back was towards me."

" Had he any kit-bag or chest with him ? " asked Thorndyke.

" He'd got his chest with him," said Jeffreys.

" What sort of chest was it ? " inquired Thorndyke.

" A small chest, painted green, with rope beckets."

" Was it corded ? "

" It had a single cord round, to hold the lid down."

" Where was it stowed ? "

" In the stern-sheets, sir."

" How far off was the boat when you last saw it ? "

" About half-a-mile."

" Half-a-mile ! " exclaimed the captain. " Why, how the deuce could you see what the chest was like half-a-mile away ? "

The man reddened and cast a look of angry suspicion at Thorndyke. " I was watching the boat through the glass, sir," he replied sulkily.

" I see," said Captain Grumpass. " Well, that will do, Jeffreys. We shall have to arrange for you to attend the inquest. Tell Smith I want to see him."

The examination concluded, Thorndyke and I moved our chairs to the window, which looked out over the sea to the east. But it was not the sea or the passing ships that engaged my colleague's attention. On the wall, beside the window, hung a rudely-carved pipe-rack containing five pipes. Thorndyke had noted it when we entered the room, and now, as we talked, I observed him regarding it from time to time with speculative interest.

" You men seem to be inveterate smokers," he remarked to the keeper, Smith, when the captain had concluded the arrangements for the " shift."

" Well, we do like our bit of 'baccy, sir, and that's a fact," answered Smith. " You see, sir," he continued, " it's a lonely life, and tobacco's cheap out here."

" How is that ? " asked Thorndyke.

" Why, we get it given to us. The small craft from

5*

foreign; especially the Dutchmen, generally heave us a cake or two when they pass close. We're not ashore, you see, so there's no duty to pay."

" So you don't trouble the tobacconists much ? Don't go in for cut tobacco ? "

" No, sir ; we'd have to buy it, and then the cut stuff wouldn't keep. No, it's hard tack to eat out here and hard tobacco to smoke."

" I see you've got a pipe-rack, too, quite a stylish affair."

" Yes," said Smith, " I made it in my off-time. Keeps the place tidy and looks more ship-shape than letting the pipes lay about anywhere."

" Someone seems to have neglected his pipe," said Thorndyke, pointing to one at the end of the rack which was coated with green mildew.

" Yes ; that's Parsons, my mate. He must have left it when we went off near a month ago. Pipes do go mouldy in the damp air out here."

" How soon does a pipe go mouldy if it is left untouched ? " Thorndyke asked.

" It's according to the weather," said Smith. " When it's warm and damp they'll begin to go in about a week. Now here's Barnett's pipe that he's left behind—the man that broke his leg, you know, sir—it's just beginning to spot a little. He couldn't have used it for a day or two before he went."

" And are all these other pipes yours ? "

" No, sir. This here one is mine. The end one is Jeffreys', and I suppose the middle one is his too, but I don't know it."

" You're a demon for pipes, doctor," said the captain, strolling up at this moment ; " you seem to make a special study of them."

" ' The proper study of mankind is man,' " replied Thorndyke, as the keeper retired, " and ' man ' includes those objects on which his personality is impressed. Now a pipe is a very personal thing. Look at that row in the rack. Each has its own physiognomy which, in a measure, reflects the peculiarities of the owner. There is Jeffreys' pipe at the end, for instance. The mouth-piece is nearly bitten through, the bowl scraped to a shell and scored inside and the brim battered and chipped. The whole thing speaks of rude strength and rough handling. He chews the stem as he smokes, he scrapes the bowl violently, and he bangs the ashes out with unnecessary force. And the man fits the pipe exactly : powerful, square-jawed and, I should say, violent on occasion."

"Yes, he looks a tough customer, does Jeffreys," agreed the captain.

"Then," continued Thorndyke, "there is Smith's pipe, next to it ; ' coked ' up until the cavity is nearly filled and burnt all round the edge ; a talker's pipe, constantly going out and being relit. But the one that interests me most is the middle one."

"Didn't Smith say that that was Jeffreys' too ? " I said.

"Yes," replied Thorndyke, "but he must be mis-taken. It is the very opposite of Jeffreys' pipe in every respect. To begin with, although it is an old pipe, there is not a sign of any toothmark on the mouth-piece. It is the only one in the rack that is quite unmarked. Then the brim is quite uninjured : it has been handled gently, and the silver band is jet-black, whereas the band on Jeffreys' pipe is quite bright."

" I hadn't noticed that it had a band," said the captain. " What has made it so black ? "

Thorndyke lifted the pipe out of the rack and looked at it closely. " Silver sulphide," said he, " the sulphur no doubt derived from something carried in the pocket."

" I see," said Captain Grumpass, smothering a yawn and gazing out of the window at the distant tender. " Incidentally it's full of tobacco. What moral do you draw from that ? "

Thorndyke turned the pipe over and looked closely

at the mouth-piece. "The moral is," he replied, "that you should see that your pipe is clear before you fill it." He pointed to the mouth-piece, the bore of which was completely stopped up with fine fluff.

"An excellent moral too," said the captain, rising with another yawn. "If you'll excuse me a minute I'll just go and see what the tender is up to. She seems to be crossing to the East Girdler." He reached the telescope down from its brackets and went out on to the gallery.

As the captain retreated, Thorndyke opened his pocket-knife, and, sticking the blade into the bowl of the pipe, turned the tobacco out into his hand.

"Shag, by Jove!" I exclaimed.

"Yes," he answered, poking it back into the bowl. "Didn't you expect it to be shag?"

"I don't know that I expected anything," I admitted. "The silver band was occupying my attention."

"Yes, that is an interesting point," said Thorndyke, "but let us see what the obstruction consists of." He opened the green case, and, taking out a dissecting needle, neatly extracted a little ball of fluff from the bore of the pipe. Laying this on a glass slide, he teased it out in a drop of glycerine and put on a cover-glass while I set up the microscope.

"Better put the pipe back in the rack," he said, as he laid the slide on the stage of the instrument. I did so and then turned, with no little excitement, to watch him as he examined the specimen. After a brief inspection he rose and waved his hand towards the microscope.

"Take a look at it, Jervis," he said, "and let us have your learned opinion."

I applied my eye to the instrument, and, moving the slide about, identified the constituents of the little mass of fluff. The ubiquitous cotton fibre was, of course, in evidence, and a few fibres of wool, but the most remarkable objects were two or three hairs—very minute hairs of a definite zigzag shape and having a flat expansion near the free end like the blade of a paddle.

" These are the hairs of some small animal," I said ;
" not a mouse or rat or any rodent, I should say. Some
small insectivorous animal, I fancy. Yes ! Of course !
They are the hairs of a mole." I stood up, and, as the
importance of the discovery flashed on me, I looked at
my colleague in silence.

" Yes," he said, " they are unmistakable ; and they
furnish the keystone of the argument."

" You think that this is really the dead man's pipe,
then ? " I said.

" According to the law of multiple evidence," he
replied, " it is practically a certainty. Consider the
facts in sequence. Since there is no sign of mildew on
it, this pipe can have been here only a short time, and
must belong either to Barnett, Smith, Jeffreys or Brown.
It is an old pipe, but it has no tooth-marks on it. Therefore it has been used by a man who has no teeth. But
Barnett, Smith and Jeffreys all have teeth and mark
their pipes, whereas Brown had no teeth. The tobacco
in it is shag. But these three men do not smoke shag,
whereas Brown had shag in his pouch. The silver band
is encrusted with sulphide ; and Brown carried sulphur-
tipped matches loose in his pocket with his pipe. We
find hairs of a mole in the bore of the pipe ; and Brown
carried a mole-skin pouch in the pocket in which he
appears to have carried his pipe. Finally, Brown's
pocket contained a pipe which was obviously not his and
which closely resembled that of Jeffreys ; it contained
tobacco similar to that which Jeffreys smokes and different
from that in Brown's pouch. It appears to me quite
conclusive, especially when we add to this evidence the
other items that are in our possession."

" What items are they ? " I asked.

" First there is the fact that the dead man had knocked
his head heavily against some periodically submerged
body covered with acorn barnacles and serpulæ. Now
the piles of this lighthouse answer to the description
exactly, and there are no other bodies in the neighbour-

hood that do : for even the beacons are too large to have
produced that kind of wound. Then the dead man's
sheath-knife is missing, and Jeffreys has a knife-wound
on his hand. You must admit that the circumstantial
evidence is overwhelming."

At this moment the captain bustled into the room
with the telescope in his hand. " The tender is coming
up towing a strange boat," he said. " I expect it's the
missing one, and, if it is, we may learn something.
You'd better pack up your traps and get ready to go on
board."

We packed the green case and went out into the
gallery, where the two keepers were watching the
approaching tender ; Smith frankly curious and interested, Jeffreys restless, fidgety and noticeably pale.
As the steamer came opposite the lighthouse, three men
dropped into the boat and pulled across, and one of
them—the mate of the tender—came climbing up the
ladder.

" Is that the missing boat ? " the captain sang out.

" Yes, sir," answered the officer, stepping on to the
staging and wiping his hands on the reverse aspect of
his trousers, " we saw her lying on the dry patch of the
East Girdler. There's been some hanky-panky in this
job, sir."

" Foul play, you think, hey ? "

" Not a doubt of it, sir. The plug was out and lying
loose in the bottom, and we found a sheath-knife sticking
into the kelson forward among the coils of the painter.
It was stuck in hard as if it had dropped from a height."

" That's odd," said the captain. " As to the plug,
it might have got out by accident."

" But it hadn't, sir," said the mate. " The ballast-
bags had been shifted along to get the bottom boards
up. Besides, sir, a seaman wouldn't let the boat fill ;
he'd have put the plug back and baled out."

" That's true," replied Captain Grumpass ; " and
certainly the presence of the knife looks fishy. But

where the deuce could it have dropped from, out in the open sea ? Knives don't drop from the clouds— fortunately. What do you say, doctor ? "

" I should say that it is Brown's own knife, and that it probably fell from this staging."

Jeffreys turned swiftly, crimson with wrath. " What d'ye mean ? " he demanded. " Haven't I said that the boat never came here ? "

" You have," replied Thorndyke ; " but if that is so how do you explain the fact that your pipe was found in the dead man's pocket and that the dead man's pipe is at this moment in your pipe-rack ? "

The crimson flush on Jeffreys' face faded as quickly as it had come. " I don't know what you're talking about," he faltered.

" I'll tell you," said Thorndyke. " I will relate what happened and you shall check my statements. Brown brought his boat alongside and came up into the living-room, bringing his chest with him. He filled his pipe and tried to light it, but it was stopped and wouldn't draw. Then you lent him a pipe of yours and filled it for him. Soon afterwards you came out on this staging and quarrelled. Brown defended himself with his knife, which dropped from his hand into the boat. You pushed him off the staging and he fell, knocking his head on one of the piles. Then you took the plug out of the boat and sent her adrift to sink, and you flung the chest into the sea. This happened about ten minutes past twelve. Am I right ? "

Jeffreys stood staring at Thorndyke, the picture of amazement and consternation ; but he uttered no word in reply.

" Am I right ? " Thorndyke repeated.

" Strike me blind ! " muttered Jeffreys. " Was you here, then ? You talk as if you had been. Anyhow," he continued, recovering somewhat, " you seem to know all about it. But you're wrong about one thing. There was no quarrel. This chap, Brown, didn't take to me and he didn't mean to stay out here. He was going to put off and go ashore again and I wouldn't let him. Then he hit out at me with his knife and I knocked it out of his hand and he staggered backwards and went overboard."

"And did you try to pick him up?" asked the captain.

"How could I," demanded Jeffreys, "with the tide racing down and me alone on the station? I'd never have got back."

"But what about the boat, Jeffreys? Why did you scuttle her?"

"The fact is," replied Jeffreys, "I got in a funk, and I thought the simplest plan was to send her to the cellar and know nothing about it. But I never shoved him over. It was an accident, sir; I swear it!"

"Well, that sounds a reasonable explanation," said the captain. "What do you say, doctor?"

"Perfectly reasonable," replied Thorndyke, "and, as to its truth, that is no affair of ours."

"No. But I shall have to take you off, Jeffreys, and hand you over to the police. You understand that?"

"Yes, sir, I understand," answered Jeffreys.

"That was a queer case, that affair on the Girdler," remarked Captain Grumpass, when he was spending an evening with us some six months later. "A pretty easy let off for Jeffreys, too—eighteen months, wasn't it?"

"Yes, it was a very queer case indeed," said Thorndyke. "There was something behind that 'accident,' I should say. Those men had probably met before."

"So I thought," agreed the captain. "But the queerest part of it to me was the way you nosed it all out. I've had a deep respect for briar pipes since then. It was a remarkable case," he continued. "The way in which you made that pipe tell the story of the murder seems to me like sheer enchantment."

"Yes," said I; "it spoke like the magic pipe—only

that wasn't a tobacco-pipe—in the German folk-story of
the ' Singing Bone.'   Do you remember it ?   A peasant
found the bone of a murdered man and fashioned it into
a pipe.   But when he tried to play on it, it burst into a
song of its own—

> ' My brother slew me and buried my bones
> Beneath the sand and under the stones.' "

" A pretty story," said Thorndyke, " and one with an
excellent moral.   The inanimate things around us have
each of them a song to sing to us if we are but ready
with attentive ears."

4

A WASTREL'S
ROMANCE

I. The Spinsters' Guest

THE lingering summer twilight was fast merging into
night as a solitary cyclist, whose evening-dress suit was
thinly disguised by an overcoat, rode slowly along a
pleasant country road.   From time to time he had been
overtaken and passed by a carriage, a car or a closed cab
from the adjacent town, and from the festive garb of the
occupants he had made shrewd guesses at their destination.   His own objective was a large house, standing in
somewhat extensive grounds just off the road, and the
peculiar circumstances that surrounded his visit to it
caused him to ride more and more slowly as he approached his goal.

Willowdale—such was the name of the house—was,
to-night, witnessing a temporary revival of its past glories.
For many months it had been empty and a notice-board
by the gate-keeper's lodge had silently announced its
forlorn state ; but, to-night, its rooms, their bare walls
clothed in flags and draperies, their floors waxed or
carpeted, would once more echo the sound of music and
cheerful voices and vibrate to the tread of many feet.

For on this night the spinsters of Raynesford were giving a dance ; and chief amongst the spinsters was Miss Halli-well, the owner of Willowdale.

It was a great occasion. The house was large and imposing ; the spinsters were many and their purses were long. The guests were numerous and distinguished, and included no less a person than Mrs. Jehu B. Chater. This was the crowning triumph of the function, for the beautiful American widow was the lion (or should we say lioness ?) of the season. Her wealth was, if not beyond the dreams of avarice, at least beyond the powers of common British arithmetic, and her diamonds were, at once, the glory and the terror of her hostesses.

All these attractions notwithstanding, the cyclist approached the vicinity of Willowdale with a slowness almost hinting at reluctance ; and when, at length, a curve of the road brought the gates into view, he dis-mounted and halted irresolutely. He was about to do a rather risky thing, and, though by no means a man of weak nerve, he hesitated to make the plunge.

The fact is, he had not been invited.

Why, then, was he going ? And how was he to gain admittance ? To which questions the answer involves a painful explanation.

Augustus Bailey lived by his wits. That is the common phrase, and a stupid phrase it is. For do we not all live by our wits, if we have any ? And does it need any specially brilliant wits to be a common rogue ? However, such as his wits were, Augustus Bailey lived by them, and he had not hitherto made a fortune.

The present venture arose out of a conversation over-heard at a restaurant table and an invitation-card care-lessly laid down and adroitly covered with the menu. Augustus had accepted the invitation that he had not received (on a sheet of Hotel Cecil notepaper that he had among his collection of stationery) in the name of Geof-frey Harrington-Baillie ; and the question that exercised his mind at the moment was, would he or would he not be spotted ? He had trusted to the number of guests and the probable inexperience of the hostesses. He knew that the cards need not be shown, though there was the awkward ceremony of announcement.

But perhaps it wouldn't get as far as that. Probably not, if his acceptance had been detected as emanating from an uninvited stranger.

He walked slowly towards the gates with growing discomfort. Added to his nervousness as to the present were certain twinges of reminiscence. He had once held a commission in a line regiment—not for long, indeed ; his " wits " had been too much for his brother officers —but there had been a time when he would have come to such a gathering as this an invited guest. Now, a common thief, he was sneaking in under a false name, with a fair prospect of being ignominiously thrown out by the servants.

As he stood hesitating, the sound of hoofs on the road was followed by the aggressive bellow of a motor-horn. The modest twinkle of carriage lamps appeared round the curve and then the glare of acetylene headlights. A man came out of the lodge and drew open the gates ; and Mr. Bailey, taking his courage in both hands, boldly trundled his machine up the drive.

Half-way up—it was quite a steep incline—the car whizzed by ; a large Napier filled with a bevy of young men who economised space by sitting on the backs of the seats and on one another's knees. Bailey looked at them and decided that this was his chance, and, pushing forward, he saw his bicycle safely bestowed in the empty coach-house and then hurried on to the cloak-room. The young men had arrived there before him, and, as he entered, were gaily peeling off their overcoats and flinging them down on a table. Bailey followed their example, and, in his eagerness to enter the reception-room with the crowd, let his attention wander from the business of the moment, and, as he pocketed the ticket and hurried away, he failed to notice that the bewildered attendant had put his hat with another man's coat and affixed his duplicate to them both.

"Major Podbury, Captain Barker-Jones, Captain Sparker, Mr. Watson, Mr. Goldsmith, Mr. Smart, *Mr. Harrington-Baillie !* "

As Augustus swaggered up the room, hugging the party of officers and quaking inwardly, he was conscious that his hostesses glanced from one man to another with more than common interest.

But at that moment the footman's voice rang out, sonorous and clear—

"Mrs. Chater, Colonel Crumpler ! " and, as all eyes were turned towards the new arrivals, Augustus made his bow and passed into the throng. His little game of bluff had " come off," after all.

He withdrew modestly into the more crowded portion of the room, and there took up a position where he would be shielded from the gaze of his hostesses. Presently, he reflected, they would forget him, if they had really thought about him at all, and then he would see what could be done in the way of business. He was still rather shaky, and wondered how soon it would be decent to steady his nerves with a " refresher." Meanwhile he kept a sharp look-out over the shoulders of neighbouring guests, until a movement in the crowd of guests disclosed Mrs. Chater shaking hands with the presiding spinster. Then Augustus got a most uncommon surprise.

He knew her at the first glance. He had a good memory for faces, and Mrs. Chater's face was one to remember. Well did he recall the frank and lovely American girl with whom he had danced at the regimental ball years ago. That was in the old days when he was a subaltern, and before that little affair of the pricked court-cards that brought his military career to an end. They had taken a mutual liking, he remembered, that sweet-faced Yankee maid and he ; had danced many dances and had sat out others, to talk

mystical nonsense which, in their innocence, they had
believed to be philosophy. He had never seen her since.
She had come into his life and gone out of it again, and
he had forgotten her name, if he had ever known it.
But here she was, middle-aged now, it was true, but still
beautiful and a great personage withal. And, ye gods !
what diamonds ! And here was he, too, a common
rogue, lurking in the crowd that he might, perchance,
snatch a pendant or " pinch " a loose brooch.

Perhaps she might recognise him. Why not ? He
had recognised her. But that would never do. And
thus reflecting, Mr. Bailey slipped out to stroll on the
lawn and smoke a cigarette. Another man, somewhat
older than himself, was pacing to and fro thoughtfully,
glancing from time to time through the open windows
into the brilliantly-lighted rooms. When they had passed
once or twice, the stranger halted and addressed him.

" This is the best place on a night like this," he remarked ; " it's getting hot inside already. But perhaps
you're keen on dancing."

" Not so keen as I used to be," replied Bailey ; and
then, observing the hungry look that the other man
was bestowing on his cigarette, he produced his case and
offered it.

" Thanks awfully ! " exclaimed the stranger, pounc-
ing with avidity on the open case. " Good Samaritan,
by Jove. Left my case in my overcoat. Hadn't the
cheek to ask, though I was starving for a smoke." He
inhaled luxuriously, and, blowing out a cloud of smoke,
resumed : " These chits seem to be running the show
pretty well, hm ? Wouldn't take it for an empty house
to look at it, would you ? "

" I have hardly seen it," said Bailey ; " only just
come, you know."

" We'll have a look round, if you like," said the
genial stranger, " when we've finished our smoke, that
is. Have a drink too ; may cool us a bit. Know many
people here ? "

"Not a soul," replied Bailey. "My hostess doesn't seem to have turned up."

"Well, that's easily remedied," said the stranger. "My daughter's one of the spinsters—Granby, my name; when we've had a drink, I'll make her find you a partner—that is, if you care for the light fantastic."

"I should like a dance or two," said Bailey, "though I'm getting a bit past it now, I suppose. Still, it doesn't do to chuck up the sponge prematurely."

"Certainly not," Granby agreed jovially; "a man's as young as he feels. Well, come and have a drink and then we'll hunt up my little girl." The two men flung away the stumps of their cigarettes and headed for the refreshments.

The spinsters' champagne was light, but it was well enough if taken in sufficient quantity; a point to which Augustus—and Granby too—paid judicious attention; and when he had supplemented the wine with a few sandwiches, Mr. Bailey felt in notably better spirits. For, to tell the truth, his diet, of late, had been somewhat meagre. Miss Granby, when found, proved to be a blonde and guileless "flapper" of some seventeen summers, childishly eager to play her part of hostess with due dignity; and presently Bailey found himself gyrating through the eddying crowd in company with a comely matron of thirty or thereabouts.

The sensations that this novel experience aroused rather took him by surprise. For years past he had been living a precarious life of mean and sordid shifts that oscillated between mere shabby trickery and down-right crime; now conducting a paltry swindle just inside the pale of the law, and now, when hard pressed, descending to actual theft; consorting with shady characters, swindlers and knaves and scurvy rogues like himself; gambling, borrowing, cadging and, if need be, stealing, and always slinking abroad with an apprehensive eye upon "the man in blue."

And now, amidst the half-forgotten surroundings, once

so familiar ; the gaily-decorated rooms, the rhythmic music, the twinkle of jewels, the murmur of gliding feet and the rustle of costly gowns, the moving vision of honest gentlemen and fair ladies ; the shameful years seemed to drop away and leave him to take up the thread of his life where it had snapped so disastrously. After all, these were his own people. The seedy knaves in whose steps he had walked of late were but aliens met by the way.

He surrendered his partner, in due course, with regret —which was mutual—to an inarticulate subaltern, and was meditating another pilgrimage to the refreshment-room, when he felt a light touch upon his arm. He turned swiftly. A touch on the arm meant more to him than to some men. But it was no wooden-faced plain-clothes man that he confronted ; it was only a lady. In short, it was Mrs. Chater, smiling nervously and a little abashed by her own boldness.

" I expect you've forgotten me," she began apologetically, but Augustus interrupted her with an eager disclaimer.

" Of course I haven't," he said ; " though I have forgotten your name, but I remember that Portsmouth dance as well as if it were yesterday ; at least one incident in it—the only one that was worth remembering. I've often hoped that I might meet you again, and now, at last, it has happened."

" It's nice of you to remember," she rejoined. " I've often and often thought of that evening and all the wonderful things that we talked about. You were a nice boy then ; I wonder what you are like now. Dear, dear, what a long time ago it is ! "

" Yes," Augustus agreed gravely, " it *is* a long time. I know it by myself ; but when I look at you, it seems as if it could only have been last season."

" Oh, fie ! " she exclaimed. " You are not simple as you used to be. You didn't flatter then ; but perhaps there wasn't the need." She spoke with gentle reproach, but her pretty face flushed with pleasure nevertheless, and there was a certain wistfulness in the tone of her concluding sentence.

" I wasn't flattering," Augustus replied, quite sin-cerely ; " I knew you directly you entered the room and marvelled that Time had been so gentle with you. He hasn't been as kind to me."

" No. You have got a few grey hairs, I see, but after all, what are grey hairs to a man ? Just the badges of rank, like the crown on your collar or the lace on your cuffs, to mark the steps of your promotion—for I guess you'll be a colonel by now."

" No," Augustus answered quickly, with a faint flush. " I left the army some years ago."

" My ! what a pity ! " exclaimed Mrs. Chater. " You must tell me all about it—but not now. My partner will be looking for me. We will sit out a dance and have a real gossip. But I've forgotten your name —never could recall it, in fact, though that didn't prevent me from remembering you ; but, as our dear W. S. remarks, ' What's in a name ? ' "

" Ah, indeed," said Mr. Harrington-Baillie ; and apropos of that sentiment, he added : " mine is Rowland —Captain Rowland. You may remember it now."

Mrs. Chater did not, however, and said so. " Will number six do ? " she asked, opening her programme ; and, when Augustus had assented, she entered his pro-visional name, remarking complacently : " We'll sit out and have a right-down good talk, and you shall tell me all about yourself and if you still think the same about free-will and personal responsibility. You had very lofty ideals, I remember, in those days, and I hope you have still. But one's ideals get rubbed down rather faint in the friction of life. Don't you think so ? "

" Yes, I am afraid you're right," Augustus assented gloomily. " The wear and tear of life soon fetches the gilt off the gingerbread. Middle age is apt to find us a bit patchy, not to say naked."

" Oh, don't be pessimistic," said Mrs. Chater ; " that is the attitude of the disappointed idealist, and I am sure you have no reason, really, to be disappointed in yourself. But I must run away now. Think over all the things you have to tell me, and don't forget that it is number six." With a bright smile and a friendly nod she sailed away, a vision of glittering splendour, compared with which Solomon in all his glory was a mere matter of commonplace bullion.

The interview, evidently friendly and familiar, between the unknown guest and the famous American widow had by no means passed unnoticed ; and in other circumstances, Bailey might have endeavoured to profit by the reflected glory that enveloped him. But he was not in search of notoriety ; and the same evasive instinct that had led him to sink Mr. Harrington-Baillie in Captain Rowland, now advised him to withdraw his dual personality from the vulgar gaze. He had come here on very definite business. For the hundredth time he was " stony-broke," and it was the hope of picking up some " unconsidered trifles " that had brought him. But, somehow, the atmosphere of the place had proved unfavourable. Either opportunities were lacking or he failed to seize them. In any case, the game pocket that formed an unconventional feature of his dress-coat was still empty, and it looked as if a pleasant evening and a good supper were all that he was likely to get. Nevertheless, be his conduct never so blameless, the fact remained that he was an uninvited guest, liable at any moment to be ejected as an impostor, and his recognition by the widow had not rendered this possibility any the more remote.

He strayed out on to the lawn, whence the grounds fell away on all sides. But there were other guests there, cooling themselves after the last dance, and the light from the rooms streamed through the windows, illuminating their figures, and among them, that of the too-companionable Granby. Augustus quickly drew away from the lighted area, and, chancing upon a narrow path, strolled away along it in the direction of a copse or shrubbery that he saw ahead. Presently he came to an ivy-covered arch, lighted by one or two fairy lamps, and, passing through this, he entered a winding path, bordered by trees and shrubs and but faintly lighted by an occasional coloured lamp suspended from a branch.

Already he was quite clear of the crowd ; indeed, the deserted condition of the pleasant retreat rather surprised him, until he reflected that to couples desiring seclusion there were whole ranges of untenanted rooms and galleries available in the empty house.

The path sloped gently downwards for some distance ; then came a long flight of rustic steps and, at the bottom, a seat between two trees. In front of the seat the path extended in a straight line, forming a narrow terrace ; on the right the ground sloped up steeply towards the lawn ; on the left it fell away still more steeply towards the encompassing wall of the grounds ; and on both sides it was covered with trees and shrubs.

Bailey sat down on the seat to think over the account of himself that he should present to Mrs. Chater. It was a comfortable seat, built into the trunk of an elm, which formed one end and part of the back. He leaned against the tree, and, taking out his silver case, selected a cigarette. But it remained unlighted between his fingers as he sat and meditated upon his unsatisfactory past and the melancholy tale of what might have been. Fresh from the atmosphere of refined opulence that pervaded the dancing-rooms, the throng of well-groomed men and dainty women, his mind travelled back to his sordid little flat in Bermondsey, encompassed by poverty and squalor, jostled by lofty factories, grimy with the smoke of the river and the reek from the great chimneys. It was a hideous contrast. Verily the way of the transgressor was not strewn with flowers.

At that point in his meditations he caught the sound of voices and footsteps on the path above and rose to

walk on along the path. He did not wish to be seen
wandering alone in the shrubbery. But now a woman's
laugh sounded from somewhere down the path. There
were people approaching that way too. He put the
cigarette back in the case and stepped round behind the
seat, intending to retreat in that direction, but here the
path ended, and beyond was nothing but a rugged slope
down to the wall thickly covered with bushes. And
while he was hesitating, the sound of feet descending
the steps and the rustle of a woman's dress left him to
choose between staying where he was or coming out to
confront the new-comers. He chose the former, drawing up close behind the tree to wait until they should
have passed on.

But they were not going to pass on. One of them—
a woman—sat down on the seat, and then a familiar voice
smote on his ear.

" I guess I'll rest here quietly for a while ; this tooth
of mine is aching terribly ; and, see here, I want you
to go and fetch me something. Take this ticket to the
cloak-room and tell the woman to give you my little
velvet bag. You'll find in it a bottle of chloroform and
a packet of cotton-wool."

" But I can't leave you here all alone, Mrs. Chater,"
her partner expostulated.

" I'm not hankering for society just now," said Mrs.
Chater. " I want that chloroform. Just you hustle off
and fetch it, like a good boy. Here's the ticket."

The young officer's footsteps retreated rapidly, and
the voices of the couple advancing along the path grew
louder. Bailey, cursing the chance that had placed him
in his ridiculous and uncomfortable position, heard them
approach and pass on up the steps ; and then all was
silent, save for an occasional moan from Mrs. Chater
and the measured creaking of the seat as she rocked
uneasily to and fro. But the young man was uncommonly prompt in the discharge of his mission, and in a
very few minutes Bailey heard him approaching at a

run along the path above and then bounding down the steps.

"Now I call that real good of you," said the widow gratefully. "You must have run like the wind. Cut the string of the packet and then leave me to wrestle with this tooth."

"But I can't leave you here all——"

"Yes, you can," interrupted Mrs. Chater. "There won't be anyone about—the next dance is a waltz. Besides, you must go and find your partner."

"Well, if you'd really rather be alone," the subaltern began ; but Mrs. Chater interrupted him.

"Of course I would, when I'm fixing up my teeth. Now go along, and a thousand thanks for your kindness."

With mumbled protestations the young officer slowly retired, and Bailey heard his reluctant feet ascending the steps. Then a deep silence fell on the place in which the rustle of paper and the squeak of a withdrawn cork seemed loud and palpable. Bailey had turned with his face towards the tree, against which he leaned with his lips parted scarcely daring to breathe. He cursed himself again and again for having thus entrapped himself for no tangible reason, and longed to get away. But there was no escape now without betraying himself. He must wait for the woman to go.

Suddenly, beyond the edge of the tree, a hand appeared holding an open packet of cotton-wool. It laid the wool down on the seat, and, pinching off a fragment, rolled it into a tiny ball. The fingers of the hand were encircled by rings, its wrist enclosed by a broad bracelet ; and from rings and bracelet the light of the solitary fairy-lamp, that hung from a branch of the tree, was reflected in prismatic sparks. The hand was withdrawn and Bailey stared dreamily at the square pad of cotton-wool. Then the hand came again into view. This time it held a small phial which it laid softly on the seat, setting the cork beside it. And again the light flashed in many-coloured scintillations from the encrusting gems.

Bailey's knees began to tremble, and a chilly moisture broke out upon his forehead.

The hand drew back, but, as it vanished, Bailey moved his head silently until his face emerged from behind the tree. The woman was leaning back, her head resting against the trunk only a few inches away from his face. The great stones of the tiara flashed in his very eyes. Over her shoulder, he could even see the gorgeous pendant, rising and falling on her bosom with ever-changing fires ; and both her raised hands were a mass of glitter and sparkle, only the deeper and richer for the subdued light.

His heart throbbed with palpable blows that drummed aloud in his ears. The sweat trickled clammily down his face, and he clenched his teeth to keep them from chattering. An agony of horror—of deadly fear—was creeping over him—a terror of the dreadful impulse that was stealing away his reason and his will.

The silence was profound. The woman's soft breathing, the creak of her bodice, were plainly—grossly—audible ; and he checked his own breath until he seemed on the verge of suffocation.

Of a sudden through the night air was borne faintly the dreamy music of a waltz. The dance had begun. The distant sound but deepened the sense of solitude in this deserted spot.

Bailey listened intently. He yearned to escape from the invisible force that seemed to be clutching at his wrists, and dragging him forward inexorably to his doom.

He gazed down at the woman with a horrid fascination. He struggled to draw back out of sight—and struggled in vain.

Then, at last, with a horrible, stealthy deliberation, a clammy, shaking hand crept forward towards the seat. Without a sound it grasped the wool, and noiselessly, slowly drew back. Again it stole forth. The fingers twined snakily around the phial, lifted it from the seat and carried it back into the shadow.

After a few seconds it reappeared and softly replaced the bottle—now half empty. There was a brief pause. The measured cadences of the waltz stole softly through the quiet night and seemed to keep time with the woman's breathing. Other sound there was none. The place was wrapped in the silence of the grave.

Suddenly, from his hiding-place, Bailey leaned forward over the back of the seat. The pad of cotton-wool was in his hand.

The woman was now leaning back as if dozing, and her hands rested in her lap. There was a swift movement. The pad was pressed against her face and her head dragged back against the chest of the invisible assailant. A smothered gasp burst from her hidden lips as her hands flew up to clutch at the murderous arm ; and then came a frightful struggle, made even more frightful by the gay and costly trappings of the writhing victim. And still there was hardly a sound ; only muffled gasps, the rustle of silk, the creaking of the seat, the clink of the falling bottle and, afar off, with dreadful irony, the dreamy murmur of the waltz.

The struggle was but brief. Quite suddenly the jewelled hands dropped, the head lay resistless on the crumpled shirt-front, and the body, now limp and inert, began to slip forward off the seat. Bailey, still grasping the passive head, climbed over the back of the seat and, as the woman slid gently to the ground, he drew away the pad and stooped over her. The struggle was over now ; the mad fury of the moment was passing swiftly into the chill of mortal fear.

He stared with incredulous horror into the swollen face, but now so comely, the sightless eyes that but a little while since had smiled into his with such kindly recognition.

He had done this ! He, the sneaking wastrel, discarded of all the world, to whom this sweet woman had held out the hand of friendship. She had cherished his memory, when to all others he was sunk deep under the waters of oblivion. And he had killed her—for to his ear no breath of life seemed to issue from those purple lips.

A sudden hideous compunction for this irrevocable thing that he had done surged through him, and he stood up clutching at his damp hair with a hoarse cry that was like the cry of the damned.

The jewels passed straightway out of his consciousness. Everything was forgotten now but the horror of this unspeakable thing that he had done. Remorse incurable and haunting fear were all that were left to him.

The sound of voices far away along the path aroused him, and the vague horror that possessed him materialised into abject, bodily fear. He lifted the limp body to the edge of the path and let it slip down the steep declivity among the bushes. A soft, shuddering sigh came from the parted lips as the body turned over, and he paused a moment to listen. But there was no other sound of life. Doubtless that sigh was only the result of the passive movement.

Again he stood for an instant as one in a dream, gazing at the huddled shape half hidden by the bushes, before he climbed back to the path ; and even then he looked back once more, but now she was hidden from sight. And, as the voices drew nearer, he turned, and, with stealthy swiftness, ran up the rustic steps.

As he came out on the edge of the lawn the music ceased, and, almost immediately, a stream of people issued from the house. Shaken as he was, Bailey yet had wits enough left to know that his clothes and hair were disordered and that his appearance must be wild. Accordingly he avoided the dancers, and, keeping to the margin of the lawn, made his way to the cloak-room by the least frequented route. If he had dared, he would have called in at the refreshment-room, for he was deadly faint and his limbs shook as he walked. But a haunting fear pursued him and, indeed, grew from moment to moment. He found himself already listening for the rumour of the inevitable discovery.

He staggered into the cloak-room, and, flinging his ticket down on the table, dragged out his watch. The attendant looked at him curiously and, pausing with the ticket in his hand, asked sympathetically : " Not feeling very well, sir ? "

" No," said Bailey. " So beastly hot in there."

" You ought to have a glass of champagne, sir, before you start," said the man.

" No time," replied Bailey, holding out a shaky hand for his coat. " Shall lose my train if I'm not sharp."

At this hint the attendant reached down the coat and hat, holding up the former for its owner to slip his arms into the sleeves. But Bailey snatched it from him, and, flinging it over his arm, put on his hat and hurried away to the coach-house. Here, again, the attendant stared at him in astonishment ; which was not lessened when Bailey, declining his offer to help him on with his coat, bundled the latter under his arm, clicked the lever of the " variable " on to the ninety gear, sprang on to the machine and whirled away down the steep drive, a grotesque vision of flying coat-tails.

" You haven't lit your lamp, sir," roared the attendant ; but Bailey's ears were deaf to all save the clamour of the expected pursuit.

Fortunately the drive entered the road obliquely, or Bailey must have been flung into the opposite hedge. As it was, the machine, rushing down the slope, flew out into the road with terrific velocity ; nor did its speed diminish then, for its rider, impelled by mortal terror, trod the pedals with the fury of a madman. And still, as the machine whizzed along the dark and silent road, his ears were strained to catch the clatter of hoofs or the throb of a motor from behind.

He knew the country well—in fact, as a precaution, he had cycled over the district only the day before ; and he was ready, at any suspicious sound, to slip down any of the lanes or byways, secure of finding his way. But still he sped on, and still no sound from the rear came to tell him of the dread discovery.

When he had ridden about three miles, he came to the foot of a steep hill. Here he had to dismount and push his machine up the incline, which he did at such speed that he arrived at the top quite breathless. Before mounting again he determined to put on his coat, for his appearance was calculated to attract attention, if nothing more. It was only half-past eleven, and presently he would pass through the streets of a small town. Also he would light his lamp. It would be fatal to be stopped by a patrol or rural constable.

Having lit his lamp and hastily put on his coat he once more listened intently, looking back over the country that was darkly visible from the summit of the hill. No moving lights were to be seen, no ringing hoofs or throbbing engines to be heard, and, turning to mount, he instinctively felt in his overcoat pocket for his gloves.

A pair of gloves came out in his hand, but he was instantly conscious that they were not his. A silk muffler was there also ; a white one. But his muffler was black.

With a sudden shock of terror he thrust his hand into the ticket-pocket, where he had put his latch-key. There was no key there ; only an amber cigar-holder, which he had never seen before. He stood for a few moments in utter consternation. He had taken the wrong coat. Then he had left his own coat behind. A cold sweat of fear broke out afresh on his face as he realised this. His Yale latch-key was in its pocket ; not that that mattered very much. He had a duplicate at home, and, as to getting in, well, he knew his own outside door and his tool-bag contained one or two trifles not usually found in cyclists' tool-bags. The question was whether that coat contained anything that could disclose his identity. And then suddenly he remembered, with a gasp of relief,

6

that he had carefully turned the pockets out before starting, with this very idea.

No ; once let him attain the sanctuary of his grimy little flat, wedged in as it was between the great factories by the river-side, and he would be safe : safe from everything but the horror of himself, and the haunting vision of a jewelled figure huddled up in a glittering, silken heap beneath the bushes.

With a last look round he mounted his machine, and, driving it over the brow of the hill, swept away into the darkness.

II. *Munera Pulveris*

(Related by CHRISTOPHER JERVIS, M.D.)

It is one of the drawbacks of medicine as a profession that one is never rid of one's responsibilities. The merchant, the lawyer, the civil servant, each at the appointed time locks up his desk, puts on his hat and goes forth a free man with an interval of uninterrupted leisure before him. Not so the doctor. Whether at work or at play, awake or asleep, he is the servant of humanity, at the instant disposal of friend or stranger alike whose need may make the necessary claim.

When I agreed to accompany my wife to the spinsters' dance at Raynesford, I imagined that, for that evening, at least, I was definitely off duty ; and in that belief I continued until the conclusion of the eighth dance. To be quite truthful, I was not sorry when the delusion was shattered. My last partner was a young lady of a slanginess of speech that verged on the inarticulate. Now it is not easy to exchange ideas in " pidgin " English ; and the conversation of a person to whom all things are either " ripping " or " rotten " is apt to lack subtlety. In fact, I was frankly bored ; and, reflecting on the utility of the humble sandwich as an aid to conversation, I was about to entice my partner to the refreshment-room when I felt someone pluck at my sleeve. I turned quickly and looked into the anxious and rather frightened face of my wife.

" Miss Halliwell is looking for you," she said. " A lady has been taken ill. Will you come and see what is the matter ? " She took my arm and, when I had made my apologies to my partner, she hurried me on to the lawn.

" It's a mysterious affair," my wife continued. " The sick lady is a Mrs. Chater, a very wealthy American widow. Edith Halliwell and Major Podbury found her lying in the shrubbery all alone and unable to give any account of herself. Poor Edith is dreadfully upset. She doesn't know what to think."

" What do you mean ? " I began ; but at this moment Miss Halliwell, who was waiting by an ivy-covered rustic arch, espied us and ran forward.

" Oh, do hurry, please, Dr. Jervis," she exclaimed ; " such a shocking thing has happened. Has Juliet told you ? " Without waiting for an answer, she darted through the arch and preceded us along a narrow path at the curious, flat-footed, shambling trot common to most adult women. Presently we descended a flight of rustic steps which brought us to a seat, from whence extended a straight path cut like a miniature terrace on a steep slope, with a high bank rising to the right and a declivity falling away to the left. Down in the hollow, his head and shoulders appearing above the bushes, was a man holding in his hand a fairy-lamp that he had apparently taken down from a tree. I climbed down to him, and, as I came round the bushes, I perceived a richly-dressed woman lying huddled on the ground. She was not completely insensible, for she moved slightly at my approach, muttering a few words in thick, indistinct accents. I took the lamp from the man, whom I assumed to be Major Podbury, and, as he delivered it to me with a significant glance and a faint lift of the eyebrows, I understood Miss Halliwell's agitation. Indeed, for one horrible moment I thought that she was right—that the prostrate woman was intoxicated. But when I approached nearer, the flickering light of the lamp made visible a square reddened patch on her face, like the impression of a mustard plaster, covering the nose and mouth ; and then I scented mischief of a more serious kind.

"We had better carry her up to the seat," I said, handing the lamp to Miss Halliwell. "Then we can consider moving her to the house." The major and I lifted the helpless woman and, having climbed cautiously up to the path, laid her on the seat.

"What is it, Dr. Jervis ? " Miss Halliwell whispered.

"I can't say at the moment," I replied ; "but it's not what you feared."

"Thank God for that ! " was her fervent rejoinder. "It would have been a shocking scandal."

I took the dim little lamp and once more bent over the half-conscious woman.

Her appearance puzzled me not a little. She looked like a person recovering from an anæsthetic, but the square red patch on her face, recalling, as it did, the Burke murders, rather suggested suffocation. As I was thus reflecting, the light of the lamp fell on a white object lying on the ground behind the seat, and holding the lamp forward, I saw that it was a square pad of cotton-wool. The coincidence of its shape and size with that of the red patch on the woman's face instantly struck me, and I stooped down to pick it up ; and then I saw, lying under the seat, a small bottle. This also I picked up and held in the lamplight. It was a one-ounce phial, quite empty, and was labelled " Methylated Chloroform." Here seemed to be a complete explanation of the thick utterance and drunken aspect ; but it was an explanation that required, in its turn, to be explained. Obviously no robbery had been committed. for the woman literally glittered with diamonds. Equally obviously she had not administered the chloroform to herself.

There was nothing for it but to carry her indoors and await her further recovery, so, with the major's help, we conveyed her through the shrubbery and kitchen garden to a side door, and deposited her on a sofa in a half-furnished room.

Here, under the influence of water dabbed on her face and the plentiful use of smelling-salts, she quickly revived, and was soon able to give an intelligible account of herself.

The chloroform and cotton-wool were her own. She had used them for an aching tooth ; and she was sitting alone on the seat with the bottle and the wool beside her when the incomprehensible thing had happened. Without a moment's warning a hand had come from behind her and pressed the pad of wool over her nose and mouth. The wool was saturated with chloroform, and she had lost consciousness almost immediately.

" You didn't see the person, then ? " I asked.

" No, but I know he was in evening dress, because I felt my head against his shirt-front."

" Then," said I, " he is either here still or he has been to the cloak-room. He couldn't have left the place without an overcoat."

" No, by Jove ! " exclaimed the major ; " that's true. I'll go and make inquiries." He strode away all agog, and I, having satisfied myself that Mrs. Chater could be left safely, followed him almost immediately.

I made my way straight to the cloak-room, and here I found the major and one or two of his brother officers putting on their coats in a flutter of gleeful excitement.

" He's gone," said Podbury, struggling frantically into his overcoat ; " went off nearly an hour ago on a bicycle. Seemed in a deuce of a stew, the attendant says, and no wonder. We're goin' after him in our car. Care to join the hunt ? "

" No, thanks. I must stay with the patient. But how do you know you're after the right man ? "

" Isn't any other. Only one Johnnie's left. Besides

—here, confound it ! you've given me the wrong coat ! "

He tore off the garment and handed it back to the attendant, who regarded it with an expression of dismay.

" Are you sure, sir ? " he asked.

" Perfectly," said the major. " Come, hurry up, my man."

" I'm afraid, sir," said the attendant, " that the gentleman who has gone has taken your coat. They were on the same peg, I know. I am very sorry, sir."

The major was speechless with wrath. What the devil was the good of being sorry ? and how the deuce was he to get his coat back ?

" But," I interposed, " if the stranger has got your coat, then this coat must be his."

" I know," said Podbury ; " but I don't want his beastly coat."

" No," I replied, " but it may be useful for identification."

This appeared to afford the bereaved officer little consolation, but as the car was now ready, he bustled away, and I, having directed the man to put the coat away in a safe place, went back to my patient.

Mrs. Chater was by now fairly recovered, and had developed a highly vindictive interest in her late assailant. She even went so far as to regret that he had not taken at least some of her diamonds, so that robbery might have been added to the charge of attempted murder, and expressed the earnest hope that the officers would not be foolishly gentle in their treatment of him when they caught him.

" By the way, Dr. Jervis," said Miss Halliwell, " I think I ought to mention a rather curious thing that happened in connection with this dance. We received an acceptance from a Mr. Harrington-Baillie, who wrote from the Hotel Cecil. Now I am certain that no such name was proposed by any of the spinsters."

" But didn't you ask them ? " I inquired.

" Well, the fact is," she replied, " that one of them, Miss Waters, had to go abroad suddenly, and we had not got her address ; and as it was possible that she might have invited him, I did not like to move in the matter. I am very sorry I didn't now. We may have let in a regular criminal—though why he should have wanted to murder Mrs. Chater I cannot imagine."

It was certainly a mysterious affair, and the mystery was in no wise dispelled by the return of the search party an hour later. It seemed that the bicycle had been tracked for a couple of miles towards London, but then, at the cross-roads, the tracks had become hopelessly mixed with the impressions of other machines, and the officers, after cruising about vaguely for a while, had given up the hunt and returned.

" You see, Mrs. Chater," Major Podbury explained apologetically, " the fellow must have had a good hour's start, and, with a high-geared machine, that would have brought him pretty close to London."

" Do you mean to tell me," exclaimed Mrs. Chater, regarding the major with hardly concealed contempt, " that that villain has got off scot-free ? "

" Looks rather like it," replied Podbury, " but if I were you I should get the man's description from the attendants who saw him and go up to Scotland Yard to-morrow. They may know the Johnnie there, and they may even recognise the coat if you take it with you."

" That doesn't seem very likely," said Mrs. Chater, and it certainly did not ; but since no better plan could be suggested the lady decided to adopt it ; and I supposed that I had heard the last of the matter.

In this, however, I was mistaken. On the following day, just before noon, as I was drowsily considering the points in a brief dealing with a question of survivorship while Thorndyke drafted his weekly lecture, a smart rat-tat at the door of our chambers announced a visitor. I rose wearily—I had had only four hours' sleep—and opened the door, whereupon there sailed into the room no less a person than Mrs. Chater followed by Superintendent Miller, with a grin on his face and a brown-paper parcel under his arm.

The lady was not in the best of tempers, though wonderfully lively and alert considering the severe shock that she had suffered so recently, and her disapproval of Miller was frankly obvious.

"Dr. Jervis has probably told you about the attempt to murder me last night," she said, when I had introduced her to my colleague. "Well, now, will you believe it? I have been to the police, I have given them a description of the murderous villain, and I have even shown them the very coat that he wore, and they tell me that nothing can be done. That, in short, this scoundrel must be allowed to go his way free and unmolested."

"You will observe, doctor," said Miller, "that this lady has given us a description that would apply to fifty per cent. of the middle-class men of the United Kingdom, and has shown us a coat without a single identifying mark of any kind on it, and expects us to lay our hands on the owner without a solitary clue to guide us. Now we are not sorcerers at the Yard; we're only policemen. So I have taken the liberty of referring Mrs. Chater to you." He grinned maliciously and laid the parcel on the table.

"And what do you want me to do?" Thorndyke asked.

"Why, sir," said Miller, "there is a coat. In the pockets were a pair of gloves, a muffler, a box of matches, a tram-ticket and a Yale key. Mrs. Chater would like to know whose coat it is." He untied the parcel, with his eye cocked at our rather disconcerted client, and Thorndyke watched him with a faint smile.

"This is very kind of you, Miller," said he, "but I think a clairvoyant would be more to your purpose."

The superintendent instantly dropped his facetious manner.

"Seriously, sir," he said, "I should be glad if you would take a look at the coat. We have absolutely nothing to go on, and yet we don't want to give up the case. I have gone through it most thoroughly and can't find any clue to guide us. Now I know that nothing escapes you, and perhaps you might notice something that I have overlooked ; something that would give us a hint where to start on our inquiry. Couldn't you turn the microscope on it, for instance ? " he added, with a deprecating smile.

Thorndyke reflected, with an inquisitive eye on the coat. I saw that the problem was not without its attractions to him ; and when the lady seconded Miller's request with persuasive eagerness, the inevitable consequence followed.

" Very well," he said. " Leave the coat with me for an hour or so and I will look it over. I am afraid there is not the remotest chance of our learning anything from it, but even so, the examination will have done no harm. Come back at two o'clock ; I shall be ready to report my failure by then."

He bowed our visitors out and, returning to the table, looked down with a quizzical smile on the coat and the large official envelope containing the articles from the pockets.

" And what does my learned brother suggest ? " he asked, looking up at me.

" I should look at the tram-ticket first," I replied, " and then—well, Miller's suggestion wasn't such a bad one ; to explore the surface with the microscope."

" I think we will take the latter measure first," said he. " The tram-ticket might create a misleading bias. A man may take a tram anywhere, whereas the indoor dust on a man's coat appertains mostly to a definite locality."

" Yes," I replied ; " but the information that it yields is excessively vague."

" That is true," he agreed, taking up the coat and envelope to carry them to the laboratory, " and yet, you know, Jervis, as I have often pointed out, the evidential value of dust is apt to be under-estimated. The naked-

6*

eye appearances—which are the normal appearances—are misleading. Gather the dust, say, from a table-top, and what have you ? A fine powder of a characterless grey, just like any other dust from any other table-top. But, under the microscope, this grey powder is resolved into recognisable fragments of definite substances, which fragments may often be traced with certainty to the masses from which they have been detached. But you know all this as well as I do."

" I quite appreciate the value of dust as evidence in certain circumstances," I replied, " but surely the information that could be gathered from dust on the coat of an unknown man must be too general to be of any use in tracing the owner."

" I am afraid you are right," said Thorndyke, laying the coat on the laboratory bench ; " but we shall soon see, if Polton will let us have his patent dust-extractor."

The little apparatus to which my colleague referred was the invention of our ingenious laboratory assistant, and resembled in principle the " vacuum cleaners " used for restoring carpets. It had, however, one special feature : the receiver was made to admit a microscope-slide, and on this the dust-laden air was delivered from a jet.

The " extractor " having been clamped to the bench by its proud inventor, and a wetted slide introduced into the receiver, Thorndyke applied the nozzle of the instrument to the collar of the coat while Polton worked the pump. The slide was then removed and, another having been substituted, the nozzle was applied to the right sleeve near the shoulder, and the exhauster again worked by Polton. By repeating this process, half-a-dozen slides were obtained charged with dust from different parts of the garment, and then, setting up our respective microscopes, we proceeded to examine the samples.

A very brief inspection showed me that this dust contained matter not usually met with—at any rate, in appreciable quantities. There were, of course, the usual fragments of wool, cotton and other fibres derived from clothing and furniture, particles of straw, husk, hair, various mineral particles and, in fact, the ordinary constituents of dust from clothing. But, in addition to these, and in much greater quantity, were a number of other bodies, mostly of vegetable origin and presenting well-defined characters and considerable variety, and especially abundant were various starch granules.

I glanced at Thorndyke and observed he was already busy with a pencil and a slip of paper, apparently making a list of the objects visible in the field of the microscope. I hastened to follow his example, and for a time we worked on in silence. At length my colleague leaned back in his chair and read over his list.

" This is a highly interesting collection, Jervis," he remarked. " What do you find on your slides out of the ordinary ? "

" I have quite a little museum here," I replied, referring to my list. " There is, of course, chalk from the road at Raynesford. In addition to this I find various starches, principally wheat and rice, especially rice, fragments of the cortices of several seeds, several different stone-cells, some yellow masses that look like turmeric, black pepper resin-cells, one ' port wine ' pimento cell, and one or two particles of graphite."

" Graphite ! " exclaimed Thorndyke. " I have found no graphite, but I have found traces of cocoa—spiral vessels and starch grains—and of hops—one fragment of leaf and several lupulin glands. May I see the graphite ? "

I passed him the slide and he examined it with keen interest. " Yes," he said, " this is undoubtedly graphite, and no less than six particles of it. We had better go over the coat systematically. You see the importance of this ? "

" I see that this is evidently factory dust and that it may fix a locality, but I don't see that it will carry us any farther."

" Don't forget that we have a touchstone," said he ; and, as I raised my eyebrows inquiringly, he added, " the Yale latch-key. If we can narrow the locality down sufficiently, Miller can make a tour of the front doors."

" But can we ? " I asked incredulously. " I doubt it."

" We can try," answered Thorndyke. " Evidently some of these substances are distributed over the entire coat, inside and out, while others, such as the graphite, are present only on certain parts. We must locate those parts exactly and then consider what this special distribution means." He rapidly sketched out on a sheet of paper a rough diagram of the coat, marking each part with a distinctive letter, and then, taking a number of labelled slides, he wrote a single letter on each. The samples of dust taken on the slides could thus be easily referred to the exact spots whence they had been obtained.

Once more we set to work with the microscope, making now and again an addition to our lists of discoveries, and, at the end of nearly an hour's strenuous search, every slide had been examined and the lists compared.

" The net result of the examination," said Thorndyke, " is this. The entire coat, inside and out, is evenly powdered with the following substances : Rice-starch in abundance, wheat-starch in less abundance, and smaller quantities of the starches of ginger, pimento and cinnamon ; bast fibre of cinnamon, various seed cortices, stone-cells of pimento, cinnamon, cassia and black pepper, with other fragments of similar origin, such as resin-cells and ginger pigment—not turmeric. In addition there are, on the right shoulder and sleeve, traces of cocoa and hops, and on the back below the shoulders a few fragments of graphite. Those are the data ; and now, what are the inferences ? Remember this is not mere surface dust, but the accumulation of months, beaten into the cloth by repeated brushing—dust that nothing but a vacuum apparatus could extract."

" Evidently," I said, " the particles that are all over the coat represent dust that is floating in the air of the place where the coat habitually hangs. The graphite has obviously been picked up from a seat, and the cocoa and hops from some factories that the man passes frequently, though I don't see why they are on the right side only."

" That is a question of time," said Thorndyke, " and incidentally throws some light on our friend's habits. Going from home, he passes the factories on his right ; returning home, he passes them on his left, but they have then stopped work. However, the first group of sub-stances is the more important as they indicate the locality of his dwelling—for he is clearly not a workman or factory employee. Now rice-starch, wheat-starch and a group of substances collectively designated ' spices ' suggest a rice-mill, a flour-mill and a spice factory. Polton, may I trouble you for the Post Office Directory ? "

He turned over the leaves of the " Trades " section and resumed : " I see there are four rice-mills in London, of which the largest is Carbutt's at Dockhead. Let us look at the spice-factors." He again turned over the leaves and read down the list of names. " There are six spice-grinders in London," said he. " One of them, Thomas Williams & Co., is at Dockhead. None of the others is near any rice-mill. The next question is as to the flour-mill. Let us see. Here are the names of several flour millers, but none of them is near either a rice-mill or a spice-grinder, with one exception : Seth Taylor's, St. Saviour's Flour Mills, Dockhead."

" This is really becoming interesting," said I.

" It has become interesting," Thorndyke retorted. " You observe that at Dockhead we find the peculiar combination of factories necessary to produce the com-posite dust in which this coat has hung ; and the directory shows us that this particular combination exists nowhere else in London. Then the graphite, the cocoa and the hops tend to confirm the other suggestions. They all appertain to industries of the locality. The trams which pass Dockhead, also, to my knowledge, pass at no great distance from the black-lead works of Pearce Duff & Co. in Rouel Road, and will probably collect a few particles of black-lead on the seats in certain states of the wind. I see, too, that there is a cocoa factory—Payne's—in Goat Street, Horsleydown, which lies to the right of the tram line going west, and I have noticed several hop warehouses on the right side of Southwark Street, going west. But these are mere suggestions ; the really important data are the rice and flour mills and the spice-grinders, which seem to point unmistakably to Dockhead."

" Are there any private houses at Dockhead ? " I asked.

" We must look up the ' Street ' list," he replied. " The Yale latch-key rather suggests a flat, and a flat with a single occupant, and the probable habits of our absent friend offer a similar suggestion." He ran his eye down the list and presently turned to me with his finger on the page.

" If the facts that we have elicited—the singular series of agreements with the required conditions—are only a string of coincidences, here is another. On the south side of Dockhead, actually next door to the spice-grinders and opposite to Carbutt's rice-mills, is a block of work-men's flats, Hanover Buildings. They fulfil the conditions exactly. A coat hung in a room in those flats, with the windows open (as they would probably be at this time of year), would be exposed to air containing a composite dust of precisely the character of that which we have found. Of course, the same conditions obtain in other dwellings in this part of Dockhead, but the probability is in favour of the buildings. And that is all that we can say. It is no certainty. There may be some radical fallacy in our reasoning. But, on the face of it, the chances are a thousand to one that the door that that key will open is in some part of Dockhead, and most probably in Hanover Buildings. We must leave the verification to Miller."

"Wouldn't it be as well to look at the tram-ticket?" I asked.

"Dear me!" he exclaimed. "I had forgotten the ticket. Yes, by all means." He opened the envelope and, turning its contents out on the bench, picked up the dingy slip of paper. After a glance at it he handed it to me. It was punched for the journey from Tooley Street to Dockhead.

"Another coincidence," he remarked; "and, by yet another, I think I hear Miller knocking at our door."

It was the superintendent, and, as we let him into the room, the hum of a motor-car entering from Tudor Street announced the arrival of Mrs. Chater. We waited for her at the open door, and, as she entered, she held out her hands impulsively.

"Say, now, Dr. Thorndyke," she exclaimed, "have you got something to tell us?"

"I have a suggestion to make," replied Thorndyke. "I think that if the superintendent will take this key to Hanover Buildings, Dockhead, Bermondsey, he may possibly find a door that it will fit."

"The deuce!" exclaimed Miller. "I beg your pardon, madam; but I thought I had gone through that coat pretty completely. What was it that I had overlooked, sir? Was there a letter hidden in it, after all?"

"You overlooked the dust on it, Miller; that is all," said Thorndyke.

"Dust!" exclaimed the detective, staring round-eyed at my colleague. Then he chuckled softly. "Well," said he, "as I said before, I'm not a sorcerer; I'm only a policeman." He picked up the key and asked: "Are you coming to see the end of it, sir?"

"Of course he is coming," said Mrs. Chater, "and Dr. Jervis too, to identify the man. Now that we have got the villain we must leave him no loophole for escape."

Thorndyke smiled dryly. "We will come if you wish it, Mrs. Chater," he said, "but you mustn't look upon our quest as a certainty. We may have made an entire miscalculation, and I am, in fact, rather curious to see if the result works out correctly. But even if we run the man to earth, I don't see that you have much evidence against him. The most that you can prove is that he was at the house and that he left hurriedly."

Mrs. Chater regarded my colleague for a moment in scornful silence, and then, gathering up her skirts, stalked out of the room. If there is one thing that the average woman detests more than another, it is an entirely reasonable man.

The big car whirled us rapidly over Blackfriars Bridge into the region of the Borough, whence we presently turned down Tooley Street towards Bermondsey.

As soon as Dockhead came into view, the detective, Thorndyke and I alighted and proceeded on foot, leaving our client, who was now closely veiled, to follow at a little distance in the car. Opposite the head of St. Saviour's Dock, Thorndyke halted and, looking over the wall, drew my attention to the snowy powder that had lodged on every projection on the backs of the tall buildings and on the decks of the barges that were loading with the flour and ground rice. Then, crossing the road, he pointed to the wooden lantern above the roof of the spice works, the louvres of which were covered with greyish-buff dust.

"Thus," he moralised, "does commerce subserve the ends of justice—at least, we hope it does," he added quickly, as Miller disappeared into the semi-basement of the buildings.

We met the detective returning from his quest as we entered the building.

"No go there," was his report. "We'll try the next floor."

This was the ground-floor or it might be considered the first floor. At any rate, it yielded nothing of interest, and, after a glance at the doors that opened on the landing, he strode briskly up the stone stairs. The next floor was equally unrewarding, for our eager inspection disclosed nothing but the gaping keyholes associated with the common type of night-latch.

"What name was you wanting?" inquired a dusty knight of industry who emerged from one of the flats.

"Muggs," replied Miller, with admirable promptness.

"Don't know 'im," said the workman. "I expect it's farther up."

Farther up we accordingly went, but still from each door the artless grin of the invariable keyhole saluted us with depressing monotony. I began to grow uneasy, and when the fourth floor had been explored with no better result, my anxiety became acute. A mare's nest may be an interesting curiosity, but it brings no kudos to its discoverer.

"I suppose you haven't made any mistake, sir?" said Miller, stopping to wipe his brow.

"It's quite likely that I have," replied Thorndyke, with unmoved composure. "I only proposed this search as a tentative proceeding, you know."

The superintendent grunted. He was accustomed—as was I too, for that matter—to regard Thorndyke's "tentative suggestions" as equal to another man's certainties.

"It will be an awful suck-in for Mrs. Chater if we don't find him after all," he growled as we climbed up the last flight. "She's counted her chickens to a feather." He paused at the head of the stairs and stood for a few moments looking round the landing. Suddenly he turned eagerly, and, laying his hand on Thorndyke's arm, pointed to a door in the farthest corner.

"Yale lock!" he whispered impressively.

We followed him silently as he stole on tip-toe across the landing, and watched him as he stood for an instant with the key in his hand looking gloatingly at the brass disc. We saw him softly apply the nose of the fluted key-blade to the crooked slit in the cylinder, and, as we watched, it slid in noiselessly up to the shoulder. The detective looked round with a grin of triumph, and, silently withdrawing the key, stepped back to us.

"You've run him to earth, sir," he whispered, "but I don't think Mr. Fox is at home. He can't have got back yet."

"Why not?" asked Thorndyke.

Miller waved his hand towards the door. "Nothing has been disturbed," he replied. "There's not a mark on the paint. Now he hadn't got the key, and you can't pick a Yale lock. He'd have had to break in, and he hasn't broken in."

Thorndyke stepped up to the door and softly pushed in the flap of the letter-slit, through which he looked into the flat.

"There's no letter-box," said he. "My dear Miller, I would undertake to open that door in five minutes with a foot of wire and a bit of resined string."

Miller shook his head and grinned once more. "I am glad you're not on the lay, sir; you'd be one too many for us. Shall we signal to the lady?"

I went out on to the gallery and looked down at the waiting car. Mrs. Chater was staring intently up at the building, and the little crowd that the car had collected stared alternately at the lady and at the object of her regard. I wiped my face with my handkerchief—the signal agreed upon—and she instantly sprang out of the car, and in an incredibly short time she appeared on the landing, purple and gasping, but with the fire of battle flashing from her eyes.

"We've found his flat, madam," said Miller, "and we're going to enter. You're not intending to offer any violence, I hope," he added, noting with some uneasiness the lady's ferocious expression.

"Of course I'm not," replied Mrs. Chater. "In

the States ladies don't have to avenge insults themselves. If you were American men you'd hang the ruffian from his own bedpost."

"We're not American men, madam," said the superintendent stiffly. "We are law-abiding Englishmen, and, moreover, we are all officers of the law. These gentlemen are barristers and I am a police officer."

With this preliminary caution, he once more inserted the key, and as he turned it and pushed the door open, we all followed him into the sitting-room.

"I told you so, sir," said Miller, softly shutting the door; "he hasn't come back yet."

Apparently he was right. At any rate, there was no one in the flat, and we proceeded unopposed on our tour of inspection. It was a miserable spectacle, and, as we wandered from one squalid room to another, a feeling of pity for the starving wretch into whose lair we were intruding stole over me and began almost to mitigate the hideousness of his crime. On all sides poverty—utter, grinding poverty—stared us in the face. It looked at us hollow-eyed in the wretched sitting-room, with its bare floor, its solitary chair and tiny deal table; its unfurnished walls and windows destitute of blind or curtain. A piece of Dutch cheese-rind on the table, scraped to the thinness of paper, whispered of starvation; and famine lurked in the gaping cupboard, in the empty bread-tin, in the tea-caddy with its pinch of dust at the bottom, in the jam-jar, wiped clean, as a few crumbs testified, with a crust of bread. There was not enough food in the place to furnish a meal for a healthy mouse.

The bedroom told the same tale, but with a curious variation. A miserable truckle-bed with a straw mattress and a cheap jute rug for bed-clothes, an orange-case, stood on end, for a dressing-table, and another, bearing a tin washing-bowl, formed the wretched furniture. But the suit that hung from a couple of nails was well-cut and even fashionable, though shabby; and another suit lay on the floor, neatly folded and covered with a newspaper ; and, most incongruous of all, a silver cigarette-case reposed on the dressing-table.

" Why on earth does this fellow starve," I exclaimed, " when he has a silver case to pawn ? "

" Wouldn't do," said Miller. " A man doesn't pawn the implements of his trade."

Mrs. Chater, who had been staring about her with the mute amazement of a wealthy woman confronted, for the first time, with abject poverty, turned suddenly to the superintendent. " This can't be the man ! " she exclaimed. " You have made some mistake. This poor creature could never have made his way into a house like Willowdale."

Thorndyke lifted the newspaper. Beneath it was a dress suit with the shirt, collar and tie all carefully smoothed out and folded. Thorndyke unfolded the shirt and pointed to the curiously crumpled front. Suddenly he brought it close to his eye and then, from the sham diamond stud, he drew a single hair—a woman's hair.

" That is rather significant," said he, holding it up between his finger and thumb ; and Mrs. Chater evidently thought so too, for the pity and compunction suddenly faded from her face, and once more her eyes flashed with vindictive fire.

" I wish he would come," she exclaimed viciously. " Prison won't be much hardship to him after this, but I want to see him in the dock all the same."

" No," the detective agreed, " it won't hurt him much to swap this for Portland. Listen ! "

A key was being inserted into the outer door, and as we all stood like statues, a man entered and closed the door after him. He passed the door of the bedroom without seeing us, and with the dragging steps of a weary, dis-dispirited man. Almost immediately we heard him go to the kitchen and draw water into some vessel. Then he went back to the sitting-room.

" Come along," said Miller, stepping silently towards

the door. We followed closely, and as he threw the door open, we looked in over his shoulder.

The man had seated himself at the table, on which now lay a hunk of household bread resting on the paper in which he had brought it, and a tumbler of water. He half rose as the door opened, and as if petrified remained staring at Miller with a dreadful expression of terror upon his livid face.

At this moment I felt a hand on my arm, and Mrs. Chater brusquely pushed past me into the room. But at the threshold she stopped short ; and a singular change crept over the man's ghastly face, a change so remarkable that I looked involuntarily from him to our client. She had turned, in a moment, deadly pale, and her face had frozen into an expression of incredulous horror.

The dramatic silence was broken by the matter-of-fact voice of the detective.

" I am a police officer," said he, " and I arrest you for—— "

A peal of hysterical laughter from Mrs. Chater interrupted him, and he looked at her in astonishment. " Stop, stop ! " she cried in a shaky voice. " I guess we've made a ridiculous mistake. This isn't the man. This gentleman is Captain Rowland, an old friend of mine."

" I'm sorry he's a friend of yours," said Miller, " because I shall have to ask you to appear against him."

" You can ask what you please," replied Mrs. Chater. " I tell you he's not the man."

The superintendent rubbed his nose and looked hungrily at his quarry. " Do I understand, madam," he asked stiffly, " that you refuse to prosecute ? "

" Prosecute ! " she exclaimed. " Prosecute my friends for offences that I know they have not committed ? Certainly I refuse."

The superintendent looked at Thorndyke, but my

colleague's countenance had congealed into a state of absolute immobility and was as devoid of expression as the face of a Dutch clock.

"Very well," said Miller, looking sourly at his watch. "Then we have had our trouble for nothing. I wish you good afternoon, madam."

"I am sorry I troubled you, now," said Mrs. Chater.

"I am sorry you did," was the curt reply; and the superintendent, flinging the key on the table, stalked out of the room.

As the outer door slammed the man sat down with an air of bewilderment; and then, suddenly flinging his arms on the table, he dropped his head on them and burst into a passion of sobbing.

It was very embarrassing. With one accord Thorndyke and I turned to go, but Mrs. Chater motioned us to stay. Stepping over to the man, she touched him lightly on the arm.

"Why did you do it?" she asked in a tone of gentle reproach.

The man sat up and flung out one arm in an eloquent gesture that comprehended the miserable room and the yawning cupboard.

"It was the temptation of a moment," he said. "I was penniless, and those accursed diamonds were thrust in my face; they were mine for the taking. I was mad, I suppose."

"But why didn't you take them?" she said. "Why didn't you?"

"I don't know. The madness passed; and then— when I saw you lying there—— Oh, God! Why don't you give me up to the police?" He laid his head down and sobbed afresh.

Mrs. Chater bent over him with tears standing in her pretty grey eyes. "But tell me," she said, "why didn't you take the diamonds? You could if you'd liked, I suppose?"

"What good were they to me?" he demanded passionately. " What did anything matter to me ? I thought you were dead."

" Well, I'm not, you see," she said, with a rather tearful smile ; " I'm just as well as an old woman like me can expect to be. And I want your address, so that I can write and give you some good advice."

The man sat up and produced a shabby card-case from his pocket, and, as he took out a number of cards and spread them out like the " hand " of a whist player, I caught a twinkle in Thorndyke's eye.

" My name is Augustus Bailey," said the man. He selected the appropriate card, and, having scribbled his address on it with a stump of lead pencil, relapsed into his former position.

" Thank you," said Mrs. Chater, lingering for a moment by the table. " Now we'll go. Good-bye, Mr. Bailey. I shall write to-morrow, and you must attend seriously to the advice of an old friend."

I held open the door for her to pass out and looked back before I turned to follow. Bailey still sat sobbing quietly, with his head resting on his arms ; and a little pile of gold stood on the corner of the table.

" I expect, doctor," said Mrs. Chater, as Thorndyke handed her into the car, " you've written me down a sentimental fool."

Thorndyke looked at her with an unwonted softening of his rather severe face and answered quietly, " It is written : Blessed are the Merciful."

5 THE MISSING
MORTGAGEE

Part 1

EARLY in the afternoon of a warm, humid November day, Thomas Elton sauntered dejectedly along the Margate esplanade, casting an eye now on the slate-coloured sea with its pall of slate-coloured sky, and now on the harbour, where the ebb tide was just beginning to expose the mud. It was a dreary prospect, and Elton varied it by observing the few fishermen and fewer promenaders who walked foot to foot with their distorted reflections in the wet pavement; and thus it was that his eye fell on a smartly-dressed man who had just stepped into a shelter to light a cigar.

A contemporary joker has classified the Scotsmen who abound in South Africa into two groups: those, namely, who hail from Scotland, and those who hail from Palestine. Now, something in the aspect of the broad back that was presented to his view, in that of the curly, black hair and the exuberant raiment, suggested to Elton a Scotsman of the latter type. In fact, there was a suspicion of disagreeable familiarity in the figure which caused him to watch it and slacken his pace. The man backed out of the shelter, diffusing azure clouds, and, drawing an envelope from his pocket, read something that was written on it. Then he turned quickly—and so did Elton, but not quickly enough. For he was a solitary figure on that bald and empty expanse, and the other had seen him at the first glance. Elton walked away slowly, but he had not gone a dozen paces when he felt the anticipated slap on the shoulder and heard the too well-remembered voice.

"Blow me, if I don't believe you were trying to cut me, Tom," it said.

Elton looked round with ill-assumed surprise.

"Hallo, Gordon! Who the deuce would have thought of seeing you here?"

Gordon laughed thickly. "Not you, apparently; and you don't look as pleased as you might now you have seen me. Whereas I'm delighted to see you, and especially to see that things are going so well with you."

" What do you mean ? " asked Elton.

" Taking your winter holiday by the sea, like a blooming duke."

" I'm not taking a holiday," said Elton. " I was so worn out that I had to have some sort of change ; but I've brought my work down with me, and I put in a full seven hours every day."

" That's right," said Gordon. " ' Consider the ant.' Nothing like steady industry. I've brought my work down with me too ; a little slip of paper with a stamp on it. You know the article, Tom."

" I know. But it isn't due till to-morrow, is it ? "

" Isn't it, by gum ! It's due this very day, the twentieth of the month. That's why I'm here. Knowing your little weakness in the matter of dates, and having a small item to collect in Canterbury, I thought I'd just come on, and save you the useless expense that results from forgetfulness."

Elton understood the hint, and his face grew rigid.

" I can't do it, Gordon ; I can't really. Haven't got it, and shan't have it until I'm paid for the batch of drawings that I'm working on now."

" Oh, but what a pity ! " exclaimed Gordon, taking the cigar from his thick, pouting lips to utter the exclamation. " Here you are, blueing your capital on seaside jaunts and reducing your income at a stroke by a clear four pounds a year."

" How do you make that out ? " demanded Elton.

" Tut, tut," protested Gordon, " what an unbusiness-like chap you are ! Here's a little matter of twenty pounds—a quarter's interest. If it's paid now, it's twenty. If it isn't, it goes on to the principal, and there's another four pounds a year to be paid. Why don't you try to be more economical, dear boy ? "

Elton looked askance at the vampire by his side ; at the plump, blue-shaven cheeks, the thick black eyebrows, the drooping nose, and the full, red lips that embraced the cigar, and though he was a mild-tempered man he felt that he could have battered that sensual, complacent face out of all human likeness, with something uncommonly like enjoyment. But of these thoughts nothing appeared in his reply, for a man cannot afford to say all he would wish to a creditor who could ruin him with a word.

"You mustn't be too hard on me, Gordon," said he. "Give me a little time. I'm doing all I can, you know. I earn every penny that I am able, and I have kept my insurance paid up regularly. I shall be paid for this work in a week or two and then we can settle up."

Gordon made no immediate reply, and the two men walked slowly eastward, a curiously ill-assorted pair : the one prosperous, jaunty, overdressed ; the other pale and dejected, and, with his well-brushed but napless clothes, his patched boots and shiny-brimmed hat, the very type of decent, struggling poverty.

They had just passed the pier, and were coming to the base of the jetty, when Gordon next spoke.

"Can't we get off this beastly wet pavement ? " he asked, looking down at his dainty and highly-polished boots. "What's it like down on the sands ? "

"Oh, it's very good walking," said Elton, "between here and Foreness, and probably drier than the pavement."

"Then," said Gordon, "I vote we go down " ; and accordingly they descended the sloping way beyond the jetty. The stretch of sand left by the retiring tide was as smooth and firm as a sheet of asphalt, and far more pleasant to walk upon.

"We seem to have the place all to ourselves," remarked Gordon, "with the exception of some half-dozen dukes like yourself."

As he spoke, he cast a cunning black eye furtively at the dejected man by his side, considering how much further squeezing was possible, and what would be the probable product of a further squeeze ; but he quickly

averted his gaze as Elton turned on him a look eloquent
of contempt and dislike. There was another pause,
for Elton made no reply to the last observation ; then
Gordon changed over from one arm to the other the
heavy fur-lined overcoat that he was carrying. " Needn't
have brought this beastly thing," he remarked, " if I'd
known it was going to be so warm."

" Shall I carry it for you a little way ? " asked the
naturally polite Elton.

" If you would, dear boy," replied Gordon. " It's
difficult to manage an overcoat, an umbrella and cigar
all at once."

He handed over the coat with a sigh of relief, and
having straightened himself and expanded his chest,
remarked :

" I suppose you're beginning to do quite well now,
Tom ? "

Elton shook his head gloomily. " No," he answered,
" it's the same old grind."

" But surely they're beginning to recognise your
talents by this time," said Gordon, with the persuasive
air of a cross-examining counsel.

" That's just the trouble," said Elton. " You see,
I haven't any, and they recognised the fact long ago.
I'm just a journeyman, and journeyman's work is
what I get given to me."

" You mean to say that the editors don't appreciate
talent when they see it."

" I don't know about that," said Elton, " but they're
most infernally appreciative of the lack of it."

Gordon blew out a great cloud of smoke, and raised
his eyebrows reflectively. " Do you think," he said
after a brief pause, " you give 'em a fair chance ? I've
seen some of your stuff. It's blooming prim, you
know. Why don't you try something more lively ?
More skittish, you know, old chap ; something with
legs, you know, and high-heeled shoes. See what I
mean, old chap ? High-steppers, with good full calves

and not too fat in the ankle.   That ought to fetch 'em ;
don't you think so ? "

Elton scowled. "You're thinking of the drawings
in ' Hold Me Up,' " he said scornfully, " but you're
mistaken. Any fool can draw a champagne bottle
upside down with a French shoe at the end of it."

" No doubt, dear boy," said Gordon, " but I expect
that sort of fool knows what pays."

" A good many fools seem to know that much,"
retorted Elton ; and then he was sorry he had spoken,
for Gordon was not really an amiable man, and the
expression of his face suggested that he had read a
personal application into the rejoinder.   So, once more,
the two men walked on in silence.

Presently their footsteps led them to the margin
of the weed-covered rocks, and here, from under a
high heap of bladder-wrack, a large green shorecrab
rushed out and menaced them with uplifted claws.
Gordon stopped and stared at the creature with Cock-
ney surprise, prodding it with his umbrella, and speculating aloud as to whether it was good to eat.   The crab,
as if alarmed at the suggestion, suddenly darted away
and began to scuttle over the green-clad rocks, finally
plunging into a large, deep pool.   Gordon pursued it,
hobbling awkwardly over the slippery rocks, until
he came to the edge of the pool, over which he stooped,
raking inquisitively among the weedy fringe with his
umbrella.   He was so much interested in his quarry
that he failed to allow for the slippery surface on which
he stood.   The result was disastrous.   Of a sudden, one
foot began to slide forward, and when he tried to
recover his balance, was instantly followed by the
other.   For a moment he struggled frantically to regain
his footing, executing a sort of splashing, stamping
dance on the margin.   Then, the circling sea birds
were startled by a yell of terror, an ivory-handled
umbrella flew across the rocks, and Mr. Solomon
Gordon took a complete header into the deepest part

of the pool. What the crab thought of it history does not relate. What Mr. Gordon thought of it is not suitable for publication ; but, as he rose, like an extremely up-to-date merman, he expressed his senti- ments with a wealth of adjectives that brought Elton to the verge of hysteria.

"It's a good job you brought your overcoat, after all," Elton remarked for the sake of saying something, and thereby avoiding the risk of exploding into un- deniable laughter. The Hebrew made no reply—at least, no reply that lends itself to verbatim report— but staggered towards the hospitable overcoat, holding out his dripping arms. Having inducted him into the garment and buttoned him up, Elton hurried off to recover the umbrella (and, incidentally, to indulge himself in a broad grin), and, having secured it, angled with it for the smart billycock which was floating across the pool.

It was surprising what a change the last minute or two had wrought. The positions of the two men were now quite reversed. Despite his shabby clothing, Elton seemed to walk quite jauntily as compared with his shuddering companion, who trotted by his side with short miserable steps, shrinking into the uttermost depths of his enveloping coat, like an alarmed winkle into its shell, puffing out his cheeks and anathematising the Universe in general as well as his chattering teeth would let him.

For some time they hurried along towards the slope by the jetty without exchanging any further remarks ; then suddenly, Elton asked : "What are you going to do, Gordon ? You can't travel like that."

"Can't you lend me a change ? " asked Gordon.

Elton reflected. He had another suit, his best suit, which he had been careful to preserve in good condition for use on those occasions when a decent appearance was indispensable. He looked askance at the man by his side and something told him that the treasured suit would probably receive less careful treatment than it was accustomed to. Still the man couldn't be allowed to go about in wet clothes.

"I've got a spare suit," he said. "It isn't quite up to your style, and may not be much of a fit, but I daresay you'll be able to put up with it for an hour or two."

"It'll be dry anyhow," mumbled Gordon, "so we won't trouble about the style. How far is it to your rooms?"

The plural number was superfluous. Elton's room was in a little ancient flint house at the bottom of a narrow close in the old quarter of the town. You reached it without any formal preliminaries of bell or knocker by simply letting yourself in by a street door, crossing a tiny room, opening the door of what looked like a narrow cupboard, and squeezing up a diminutive flight of stairs, which was unexpectedly exposed to view. By following this procedure, the two men reached a small bed-sitting-room; that is to say, it was a bedroom, but by sitting down on the bed, you converted it into a sitting-room.

Gordon puffed out his cheeks and looked round distastefully.

"You might just ring for some hot water, old chappie," he said.

Elton laughed aloud. "Ring!". he exclaimed. "Ring what? Your clothes are the only things that are likely to get wrung."

"Well, then, sing out for the servant," said Gordon.

Elton laughed again. "My dear fellow," said he, "we don't go in for servants. There is only my landlady and she never comes up here. She's too fat to get up the stairs, and besides, she's got a game leg. I look after my room myself. You'll be all right if you have a good rub down."

Gordon groaned, and emerged reluctantly from the depths of his overcoat, while Elton brought forth from the chest of drawers the promised suit and the necessary undergarments. One of these latter Gordon held up with a sour smile, as he regarded it with extreme disfavour.

" I shouldn't think," said he, " you need have been at the trouble of marking them so plainly. No one's likely to want to run away with them."

The undergarments certainly contrasted very un-favourably with the delicate garments which he was peeling off, excepting in one respect ; they were dry ; and that had to console him for the ignominious change.

The clothes fitted quite fairly, notwithstanding the difference between the figures of the two men ; for while Gordon was a slender man grown fat, Elton was a broad man grown thin ; which, in a way, averaged their superficial area.

Elton watched the process of investment and noted the caution with which Gordon smuggled the various articles from his own pockets into those of the borrowed garments without exposing them to view ; heard the jingle of money ; saw the sumptuous gold watch and massive chain transplanted, and noted with interest the large leather wallet that came forth from the breast pocket of the wet coat. He got a better view of this from the fact that Gordon himself examined it narrowly, and even opened it to inspect its contents.

" Lucky that wasn't an ordinary pocket-book," he remarked. " If it had been, your receipt would have got wet, and so would one or two other little articles that wouldn't have been improved by salt water. And, talking of the receipt, Tom, shall I hand it over now ? "

" You can if you like," said Elton ; " but as I told you, I haven't got the money " ; on which Gordon muttered :

" Pity, pity," and thrust the wallet into his, or rather, Elton's breast pocket.

A few minutes later, the two men came out together into the gathering darkness, and as they walked slowly up the close, Elton asked : " Are you going up to town to-night, Gordon ? "

" How can I ? " was the reply. " I can't go without my clothes. No, I shall run over to Broadstairs. A client of mine keeps a boarding-house there. He'll have to put me up for the night, and if you can get my clothes cleaned and dried I can come over for them to-morrow."

These arrangements having been settled, the two men adjourned, at Gordon's suggestion, for tea at one of the restaurants on the Front ; and after that, again at Gordon's suggestion, they set forth together along the cliff path that leads to Broadstairs by way of Kingsgate.

" You may as well walk with me into Broadstairs," said Gordon ; " I'll stand you the fare back by rail " ; and to this Elton had agreed, not because he was desirous of the other man's company, but because he still had some lingering hopes of being able to adjust the little difficulty respecting the instalment.

He did not, however, open the subject at once. Profoundly as he loathed and despised the human spider whom necessity made his associate for the moment, he exerted himself to keep up a current of amusing conversation. It was not easy ; for Gordon, like most men whose attention is focussed on the mere acquirement of money, looked with a dull eye on the ordinary interests of life. His tastes in art he had already hinted at, and his other tastes lay much in the same direction. Money first, for its own sake, and then those coarser and more primitive gratifications that it was capable of purchasing. This was the horizon that bounded Mr. Solomon Gordon's field of vision.

Nevertheless, they were well on their way before Elton alluded to the subject that was uppermost in both their minds.

" Look here, Gordon," he said at length, " can't you manage to give me a bit more time to pay up this instalment ? It doesn't seem quite fair to keep sending up the principal like this."

" Well, dear boy," replied Gordon, " it's your own fault, you know. If you would only bear the dates in mind, it wouldn't happen."

" But," pleaded Elton, " just consider what I'm paying you. I originally borrowed fifty pounds from you, and I'm now paying you eighty pounds a year in addition to the insurance premium. That's close on a hundred a year ; just about half that I manage to earn by slaving like a nigger. If you stick it up any farther you won't leave me enough to keep body and soul together ; which really means that I shan't be able to pay you at all."

There was a brief pause ; then Gordon said dryly :

" You talk about not paying, dear boy, as if you had forgotten about that promissory note."

Elton set his teeth. His temper was rising rapidly. But he restrained himself.

" I should have a pretty poor memory if I had," he replied, " considering the number of reminders you've given me."

" You've needed them, Tom," said the other. " I've never met a slacker man in keeping to his engagements."

At this Elton lost his temper completely.

" That's a damned lie ! " he exclaimed, " and you know it, you infernal, dirty, blood-sucking parasite ! "

Gordon stopped dead.

" Look here, my friend," said he ; " none of that. If I've any of your damned sauce, I'll give you a sound good hammering."

" The deuce you will ! " said Elton, whose fingers were itching, not for the first time, to take some recompense for all that he had suffered from the insatiable usurer. " Nothing's preventing you now, you know, but I fancy cent. per cent. is more in your line than fighting."

7

" Give me any more sauce and you'll see," said Gordon.

" Very well," was the quiet rejoinder. " I have great pleasure in informing you that you are a human maw-worm. How does that suit you ? "

For reply, Gordon threw down his overcoat and umbrella on the grass at the side of the path, and deliberately slapped Elton on the cheek.

The reply followed instantly in the form of a smart left-hander, which took effect on the bridge of the Hebrew's rather prominent nose. Thus the battle was fairly started, and it proceeded with all the fury of accumulated hatred on the one side and sharp physical pain on the other. What little science there was appertained to Elton, in spite of which, however, he had to give way to his heavier, better nourished and more excitable opponent. Regardless of the punishment he received, the infuriated Jew rushed at him and, by sheer weight of onslaught, drove him backward across the little green.

Suddenly, Elton, who knew the place by daylight, called out in alarm.

" Look out, Gordon ! Get back, you fool ! "

But Gordon, blind with fury, and taking this as a manœuvre to escape, only pressed him harder. Elton's pugnacity died out instantly in mortal terror. He shouted out another warning and as Gordon still pressed him, battering furiously, he did the only thing that was possible : he dropped to the ground. And then, in the twinkling of an eye came the catastrophe. Borne forward by his own momentum, Gordon stumbled over Elton's prostrate body, staggered forward a few paces, and fell. Elton heard a muffled groan that faded quickly, and mingled with the sound of falling earth and stones. He sprang to his feet and looked round and saw that he was alone.

For some moments he was dazed by the suddenness of the awful thing that had happened. He crept timorously towards the unseen edge of the cliff, and listened.

But there was no sound save the distant surge of the breakers, and the scream of an invisible sea-bird. It was useless to try to look over. Near as he was, he could not, even now, distinguish the edge of the cliff from the dark beach below. Suddenly he bethought him of a narrow cutting that led down from the cliff to the shore. Quickly crossing the green, and mechanically stooping to pick up Gordon's overcoat and umbrella, he made his way to the head of the cutting and ran down the rough chalk roadway. At the bottom he turned to the right and, striding hurriedly over the smooth sand, peered into the darkness at the foot of the cliff.

Soon there loomed up against the murky sky the shadowy form of the little headland on which he and Gordon had stood ; and, almost at the same moment, there grew out of the darkness of the beach a darker spot amidst a constellation of smaller spots of white. As he drew nearer the dark spot took shape ; a horrid shape with sprawling limbs and a head strangely awry. He stepped forward, trembling, and spoke the name that the thing had borne. He grasped the flabby hand, and laid his fingers on the wrist ; but it only told him the same tale as did that strangely misplaced head. The body lay face downwards, and he had not the courage to turn it over ; but that his enemy was dead he had not the faintest doubt. He stood up amidst the litter of fallen chalk and earth and looked down at the horrible, motionless thing, wondering numbly and vaguely what he should do. Should he go and seek assistance ? The answer to that came in another question. How came that body to be lying on the beach ? And what answer should he give to the inevitable questions ? And swiftly there grew up in his mind, born of the horror of the thing that was, a yet greater horror of the thing that might be.

A minute later, a panic-stricken man stole with stealthy swiftness up the narrow cutting and set forth towards Margate, stopping anon to listen, and stealing away off the path into the darkness, to enter the town by the inland road.

Little sleep was there that night for Elton in his room in the old flint house. The dead man's clothes, which greeted him on his arrival, hanging limply on the towel-horse where he had left them, haunted him through the night. In the darkness, the sour smell of damp cloth assailed him with an endless reminder of their presence, and after each brief doze, he would start up in alarm and hastily light his candle ; only to throw its flickering light on those dank, drowned-looking vestments. His thoughts, half-controlled, as night thoughts are, flitted erratically from the unhappy past to the unstable present, and thence to the incalculable future. Once he lighted the candle specially to look at his watch to see if the tide had yet crept up to that solitary figure on the beach ; nor could he rest again until the time of high-water was well past. And all through these wanderings of his thoughts there came, recurring like a horrible refrain, the question what would happen when the body was found ? Could he be connected with it and, if so, would he be charged with murder ? At last he fell asleep and slumbered on until the landlady thumped at the staircase door to announce that she had brought his breakfast.

As soon as he was dressed he went out. Not, however, until he had stuffed Gordon's still damp clothes and boots, the cumbrous overcoat and the smart billy-cock hat into his trunk, and put the umbrella into the darkest corner of the cupboard. Not that anyone ever came up to the room, but that, already, he was possessed with the uneasy secretiveness of the criminal. He went straight down to the beach ; with what purpose he could hardly have said, but an irresistible impulse drove him thither to see if it was there. He went down by the jetty and struck out eastward over the smooth sand, looking about him with dreadful expectation for some small crowd or hurrying messenger. From the foot of the cliffs, over the rocks to the distant line of breakers, his eye roved with eager dread, and still he hurried eastward, always drawing nearer to the place that he feared to look on. As he left the town behind, so he left behind the one or two idlers on the beach, and when he turned Foreness Point he lost sight of the last of them and went forward alone.

It was less than half an hour later that the fatal head-land opened out beyond Whiteness. Not a soul had he met along that solitary beach, and though, once or twice, he had started at the sight of some mass of drift-wood or heap of seaweed, the dreadful thing that he was seeking had not yet appeared. He passed the opening of the cutting and approached the headland, breathing fast and looking about him fearfully. Already he could see the larger lumps of chalk that had fallen, and looking up, he saw a clean, white patch at the sum-mit of the cliff. But still there was no sign of the corpse. He walked on more slowly now, considering whether it could have drifted out to sea, or whether he should find it in the next bay. And then, rounding the head-land, he came in sight of a black hole at the cliff foot, the entrance to a deep cave. He approached yet more slowly, sweeping his eye round the little bay, and looking apprehensively at the cavity before him. Suppose the thing should have washed in there. It was quite possible. Many things did wash into that cave, for he had once visited it and had been astonished at the quantity of seaweed and jetsam that had accumulated within it. But it was an uncomfortable thought. It would be doubly horrible to meet the awful thing in the dim twi-light of the cavern. And yet, the black archway seemed to draw him on, step by step, until he stood at the portal and looked in. It was an eerie place, chilly and damp, the clammy walls and roof stained green and purple and black with encrusting lichens. At one time, Elton had been told, it used to be haunted by smugglers, and then communicated with an underground passage ; and the old smuggler's look-out still remained ; a narrow tunnel, high up the cliff, looking out into Kingsgate Bay; and even some vestiges of the rude steps that led up to the look-out platform could still be traced, and were not impossible to climb. Indeed, Elton had, at his last visit, climbed to the platform and looked out through the spy-hole. He recalled the circumstance now, as he stood, peering nervously into the darkness, and straining his eyes to see what jetsam the ocean had brought since then.

At first he could see nothing but the smooth sand near the opening; then, as his eyes grew more accustomed to the gloom, he could make out the great heap of seaweed on the floor of the cave. Insensibly, he crept in, with his eyes riveted on the weedy mass and, as he left the daylight behind him, so did the twilight of the cave grow clearer. His feet left the firm sand and trod the springy mass of weed, and in the silence of the cave he could now hear plainly the rain-like patter of the leaping sand-hoppers. He stopped for a moment to listen to the unfamiliar sound, and still the gloom of the cave grew lighter to his more accustomed eyes.

And then, in an instant, he saw it. From a heap of weed, a few paces ahead, projected a boot; his own boot; he recognised the patch on the sole; and at the sight, his heart seemed to stand still. Though he had somehow expected to find it here, its presence seemed to strike him with a greater shock of horror from that very circumstance.

He was standing stock still, gazing with fearful fascination at the boot and the swelling mound of weed, when, suddenly, there struck upon his ear the voice of a woman, singing.

He started violently. His first impulse was to run out of the cave. But a moment's reflection told him what madness this would be. And then the voice drew nearer, and there broke out the high, rippling laughter of a child. Elton looked in terror at the bright opening of the cavern's mouth, expecting every moment to see it frame a group of figures. If that happened, he was lost, for he would have been seen actually with the body. Suddenly he bethought him of the spy-hole and the platform, both of which were invisible from the entrance ; and turning, he ran quickly over the sodden weed till he came to the remains of the steps. Climbing hurriedly up these, he reached the platform, which was enclosed in a large niche, just as the reverberating sound of voices told him that the strangers were within the mouth of the cave. He strained his ears to catch what they were saying and to make out if they were entering farther. It was a child's voice that he had first heard, and very weird were the hollow echoes of the thin treble that were flung back from the rugged walls. But he could not hear what the child had said. The woman's voice, however, was quite distinct, and the words seemed significant in more senses than one.

" No, dear," it said, " you had better not go in. It's cold and damp. Come out into the sunshine."

Elton breathed more freely. But the woman was more right than she knew. It was cold and damp : that thing under the black tangle of weed. Better far to be out in the sunshine. He himself was already longing to escape from the chill and gloom of the cavern. But he could not escape yet. Innocent as he actually was, his position was that of a murderer. He must wait until the coast was clear, and then steal out, to hurry away unobserved.

He crept up cautiously to the short tunnel and peered out through the opening across the bay. And then his heart sank. Below him, on the sunny beach, a small party of visitors had established themselves just within view of the mouth of the cave ; and even as he looked, a man approached from the wooden stairway down the cliff, carrying a couple of deck chairs. So, for the present his escape was hopelessly cut off.

He went back to the platform and sat down to wait for his release ; and, as he sat, his thoughts went back once more to the thing that lay under the weed. How long would it lie there undiscovered ? And what would happen when it was found ? What was there to connect him with it ? Of course, there was his name on the clothing, but there was nothing incriminating in that, if he had only had the courage to give information at once. But it was too late to think of that now. Besides, it suddenly flashed upon him, there was the receipt in the wallet. That receipt mentioned him by name and referred to a loan. Obviously, its suggestion was most sinister, coupled with his silence. It was a deadly item of evidence against him. But no sooner had he realised the appalling significance of this document than he also realised that it was still within his reach. Why should he leave it there to be brought in evidence—in false evidence, too—against him ?

Slowly he rose and, creeping down the tunnel, once more looked out. The people were sitting quietly in their chairs, the man was reading, and the child was digging in the sand. Elton looked across the bay to make sure that no other person was approaching, and then, hastily climbing down the steps, walked across the great bed of weed, driving an army of sand-hoppers before him. He shuddered at the thought of what he was going to do, and the clammy chill of the cave seemed to settle on him in a cold sweat.

He came to the little mound from which the boot projected, and began, shudderingly and with faltering hand, to lift the slimy, tangled weed. As he drew aside the first bunch, he gave a gasp of horror and quickly replaced it. The body was lying on its back, and, as he lifted the weed he had uncovered—not the face, for the thing had no face. It had struck either the cliff or a stone upon the beach and—but there is no need to go into particulars : it had no face. When he had recovered a little, Elton groped shudderingly among the weed until he found the breast-pocket from which he quickly drew out the wallet, now clammy, sodden and loathsome. He was rising with it in his hand when an apparition, seen through the opening of the cave, arrested his movement as if he had been suddenly turned into stone. A man, apparently a fisherman or sailor, was sauntering past some thirty yards from the mouth of the cave, and at his heels trotted a mongrel dog. The dog stopped, and, lifting his nose, seemed to sniff the air ; and then he began to walk slowly and suspiciously towards the cave. The man sauntered on and soon passed out of view ; but the dog still came on towards the cave, stopping now and again with upraised nose.

The catastrophe seemed inevitable. But just at that moment the man's voice rose, loud and angry, evidently calling the dog. The animal hesitated, looking wistfully from his master to the cave ; but when the summons was repeated, he turned reluctantly and trotted away.

Elton stood up and took a deep breath. The chilly sweat was running down his face, his heart was thumping and his knees trembled, so that he could hardly get back to the platform. What hideous peril had he escaped and how narrowly ! For there he had stood ; and had the man entered, he would have been caught in the very act of stealing the incriminating document from the body. For that matter, he was little better off now, with the dead man's property on his person, and he resolved instantly to take out and destroy the receipt and put back the wallet. But this was easier thought of than done. The receipt was soaked with sea water, and refused utterly to light when he applied a match to it. In the end, he tore it up into little fragments and deliberately swallowed them, one by one.

But to restore the wallet was more than he was equal to just now. He would wait until the people had gone home to lunch, and then he would thrust it under the weed as he ran past. So he sat down again and once more took up the endless thread of his thoughts.

The receipt was gone now, and with it the immediate suggestion of motive. There remained only the clothes

7*

with their too legible markings. They certainly connected him with the body, but they offered no proof
of his presence at the catastrophe. And then, suddenly,
another most startling idea occurred to him. Who could
identify the body—the body that had no face? There
was the wallet, it was true, but he could take that away
with him, and there was a ring on the finger and some
articles in the pockets which might be identified. But—
a voice seemed to whisper to him—these things were
removable, too. And if he removed them, what then?
Why, then, the body was that of Thomas Elton, a friend-
less, poverty-stricken artist, about whom no one would
trouble to ask any questions.

He pondered on this new situation profoundly. It
offered him a choice of alternatives. Either he might
choose the imminent risk of being hanged for a murder
that he had not committed, or he might surrender his
identity for ever and move away to a new environment.

He smiled faintly. His identity! What might that
be worth to barter against his life? Only yesterday
he would gladly have surrendered it as the bare price of
emancipation from the vampire who had fastened on to
him.

He thrust the wallet into his pocket and buttoned his
coat. Thomas Elton was dead; and that other man,
as yet unnamed, should go forth, as the woman had
said, into the sunshine.

Part II

(Related by CHRISTOPHER JERVIS, M.D.)

From various causes, the insurance business that
passed through Thorndyke's hands had, of late, considerably increased. The number of societies which
regularly employed him had grown larger, and, since
the remarkable case of Percival Bland, the " Griffin "
had made it a routine practice to send all inquest cases
to us for report.

It was in reference to one of these latter that Mr. Stalker, a senior member of the staff of that office, called on us one afternoon in December ; and when he had laid his bag on the table and settled himself comfortably before the fire, he opened the business without preamble.

" I've brought you another inquest case," said he ; " a rather queer one, quite interesting from your point of view.   As far as we can see, it has no particular interest for us excepting that it does rather look as if our examining medical officer had been a little casual."

" What is the special interest of the case from our point of view ? " asked Thorndyke.

" I'll just give you a sketch of it," said Stalker, " and I think you will agree that it's a case after your own heart.

" On the 24th of last month, some men who were collecting seaweed, to use as manure, discovered in a cave at Kingsgate, in the Isle of Thanet, the body of a man, lying under a mass of accumulated weed.   As the tide was rising, they put the body into their cart and conveyed it to Margate, where, of course, an inquest was held, and the following facts were elicited.   The body was that of a man named Thomas Elton.   It was identified by the name-marks on the clothing, by the visiting-cards and a couple of letters which were found in the pockets.   From the address on the letters it was seen that Elton had been staying in Margate, and on inquiry at that address, it was learnt from the old woman who let the lodgings, that he had been missing about four days.   The landlady was taken to the mortuary, and at once identified the body as that of her lodger.   It remained only to decide how the body came into the cave ; and this did not seem to present much difficulty ; for the neck had been broken by a tremendous blow, which had practically destroyed the face, and there were distinct' evidences of a breaking away of a portion of the top of the cliff, only a few yards from the position of the cave.   There was apparently no doubt that Elton had fallen sheer from the top of the over-hanging cliff on to the beach. Now, one would suppose with the evidence of this fall of about a hundred and fifty feet, the smashed face and broken neck, there was not much room for doubt as to the cause of death. I think you will agree with me, Dr. Jervis ? "

" Certainly," I replied ; " it must be admitted that a broken neck is a condition that tends to shorten life."

" Quite so," agreed Stalker ; " but our friend, the local coroner, is a gentleman who takes nothing for granted—a very Thomas Didymus, who apparently agrees with Dr. Thorndyke that if there is no post-mortem, there is no inquest. So he ordered a post-mortem, which would have appeared to me an absurdly unnecessary proceeding, and I think that even you will agree with me, Dr. Thorndyke."

But Thorndyke shook his head.

" Not at all," said he. " It might, for instance, be much more easy to push a drugged or poisoned man over a cliff than to put over the same man in his normal state. The appearance of violent accident is an excellent mask for the less obvious forms of murder."

" That's perfectly true," said Stalker ; " and I suppose that is what the coroner thought. At any rate, he had the post-mortem made, and the result was most curious ; for it was found, on opening the body, that the deceased had suffered from a smallish thoracic aneurism, which had burst. Now, as the aneurism must obviously have burst during life, it leaves the cause of death—so I understand—uncertain ; at any rate, the medical witness was unable to say whether the deceased fell over the cliff in consequence of the bursting of the aneurism or burst the aneurism in consequence of falling over the cliff. Of course, it doesn't matter to us which way the thing happened ; the only question which interests us is, whether a comparatively recently insured man ought to have had an aneurism at all."

" Have you paid the claim ? " asked Thorndyke.

" No, certainly not. We never pay a claim until we have had your report. But, as a matter of fact, there is another circumstance that is causing delay. It seems that Elton had mortgaged his policy to a money-lender, named Gordon, and it is by him that the claim has been made, or rather, by a clerk of his, named Hyams. Now, we have had a good many dealings with this man Gordon, and hitherto he has always acted in person ; and as he is a somewhat slippery gentleman, we have thought it desirable to have the claim actually signed by him. And that is the difficulty. For it seems that Mr. Gordon is abroad, and his whereabouts unknown to Hyams ; so, as we certainly couldn't take Hyams's receipt for payment, the matter is in abeyance until Hyams can communicate with his principal. And now, I must be running away. I have brought you, as you will see, all the papers, including the policy and the mortgage deed."

As soon as he was gone, Thorndyke gathered up the bundle of papers and sorted them out in what he apparently considered the order of their importance. First he glanced quickly through the proposal form, and then took up the copy of the coroner's depositions.

" The medical evidence," he remarked, " is very full and complete. Both the coroner and the doctor seem to know their business."

" Seeing that the man apparently fell over a cliff," said I, " the medical evidence would not seem to be of first importance. It would seem to be more to the point to ascertain how he came to fall over."

" That's quite true," replied Thorndyke ; " and yet, this report contains some rather curious matter. The deceased had an aneurism of the arch ; that was probably rather recent. But he also had some slight, old-standing aortic disease, with full compensatory hypertrophy. He also had a nearly complete set of false teeth. Now, doesn't it strike you, Jervis, as rather odd that a man who was passed only five years ago as a first-class life, should, in that short interval, have become actually uninsurable ? "

" It certainly does look," said I, " as if the fellow had had rather bad luck. What does the proposal form say ? "

I took the document up and ran my eyes over it. On Thorndyke's advice, medical examiners for the " Griffin " were instructed to make a somewhat fuller report than is usual in some companies. In this case, the ordinary answers to questions set forth that the heart was perfectly healthy and the teeth rather exceptionally good, and then, in the summary at the end, the examiner remarked : " the proposer seems to be a completely sound and healthy man ; he presents no physical defects whatever, with the exception of a bony ankylosis of the first joint of the third finger of the left hand, which he states to have been due to an injury."

Thorndyke looked up quickly. " Which finger, did you say ? " he asked.

" The third finger of the left hand," I replied.

Thorndyke looked thoughtfully at the paper that he was reading. " It's very singular," said he, " for I see that the Margate doctor states that the deceased wore a signet ring on the third finger of the left hand. Now, of course, you couldn't get a ring on to a finger with bony ankylosis of the joint."

" He must have mistaken the finger," said I, " or else the insurance examiner did."

" That is quite possible," Thorndyke replied ; " but, doesn't it strike you as very singular that, whereas the insurance examiner mentions the ankylosis, which was of no importance from an insurance point of view, the very careful man who made the post-mortem should not have mentioned it, though, owing to the unrecognisable condition of the face, it was of vital importance for the purpose of identification ? "

I admitted that it was very singular indeed, and we

then resumed our study of the respective papers. But presently I noticed that Thorndyke had laid the report upon his knee, and was gazing speculatively into the fire.

" I gather," said I, " that my learned friend finds some matter of interest in this case."

For reply, he handed me the bundle of papers, recommending me to look through them.

" Thank you," said I, rejecting them firmly, " but I think I can trust you to have picked out all the plums."

Thorndyke smiled indulgently. " They're not plums, Jervis," said he ; " they're only currants, but they make quite a substantial little heap."

I disposed myself in a receptive attitude (somewhat after the fashion of the juvenile pelican) and he continued :

" If we take the small and unimpressive items and add them together, you will see that a quite considerable sum of discrepancy results, thus :

" *In* 1903, *Thomas Elton, aged thirty-one, had a set of sound teeth. In* 1908, *at the age of thirty-six, he was more than half toothless.*

" *Again, at the age of thirty-one, his heart was perfectly healthy. At the age of thirty-six, he had old aortic disease, with fully established compensation, and an aneurism that was possibly due to it.*

" *When he was examined he had a noticeable incurable malformation ; no such malformation is mentioned in connection with the body.*

" *He appears to have fallen over a cliff ; and he had also burst an aneurism. Now, the bursting of the aneurism must obviously have occurred during life ; but it would occasion practically instantaneous death. Therefore, if the fall was accidental, the rupture must have occurred either as he stood at the edge of the cliff, as he was in the act of falling, or on striking the beach.*

" *At the place where he apparently fell, the footpath is some thirty yards distant from the edge of the cliff.*

" *It is not known how he came to that spot, or whether he was alone at the time.*

" *Someone is claiming five hundred pounds as the immediate result of his death.*

" There, you see, Jervis, are seven propositions, none of them extremely striking, but rather suggestive when taken together."

" You seem," said I, " to suggest a doubt as to the identity of the body."

" I do," he replied. " The identity was not clearly established."

" You don't think the clothing and the visiting-cards conclusive."

" They're not parts of the body," he replied. " Of course, substitution is highly improbable. But it is not impossible."

" And the old woman," I suggested, but he interrupted me.

" My dear Jervis," he exclaimed ; " I'm surprised at you. How many times has it happened within our knowledge that women have identified the bodies of total strangers as those of their husbands, fathers or brothers. The thing happens almost every year. As to this old woman, she saw a body with an unrecognisable face, dressed in the clothes of her missing lodger. Of course, it was the clothes that she identified."

" I suppose it was," I agreed ; and then I said : " You seem to suggest the possibility of foul play."

" Well," he replied, " if you consider those seven points, you will agree with me that they present a cumulative discrepancy which it is impossible to ignore. The whole significance of the case turns on the question of identity ; for, if this was not the body of Thomas Elton, it would appear to have been deliberately prepared

to counterfeit that body. And such deliberate preparation would manifestly imply an attempt to conceal the
identity of some other body.

" Then," he continued, after a pause, " there is this
deed. It looks quite regular and is correctly stamped,
but it seems to me that the surface of the paper is
slightly altered in one or two places, and if one holds
the document up to the light, the paper looks a little
more transparent in those places." He examined
the document for a few seconds with his pocket lens,
and then passing lens and document to me, said :
" Have a look at it, Jervis, and tell me what you
think."

I scrutinised the paper closely, taking it over to the
window to get a better light ; and to me, also, the
paper appeared to be changed in certain places.

" Are we agreed as to the position of the altered
places ? " Thorndyke asked when I announced the
fact.

" I only see three patches," I answered. " Two
correspond to the name, Thomas Elton, and the third
to one of the figures in the policy number."

" Exactly," said Thorndyke, " and the significance
is obvious. If the paper has really been altered, it
means that some other name has been erased and
Elton's substituted ; by which arrangement, of course,
the correctly dated stamp would be secured. And this
—the alteration of an old document—is the only form
of forgery that is possible with a dated, impressed
stamp."

" Wouldn't it be rather a stroke of luck," I asked,
" for a forger to happen to have in his possession a
document needing only these two alterations ? "

" I see nothing remarkable in it," Thorndyke replied.
" A money-lender would have a number of documents
of this kind in hand, and you observe that he was not
bound down to any particular date. Any date within
a year or so of the issue of the policy would answer

his purpose. This document is, in fact, dated, as you see, about six months after the issue of the policy."

"I suppose," said I, "that you will draw Stalker's attention to this matter."

"He will have to be informed, of course," Thorndyke replied ; "but I think it would be interesting in the first place to call on Mr. Hyams. You will have noticed that there are some rather mysterious features in this case, and Mr. Hyams's conduct, especially if this docu- ment should turn out to be really a forgery, suggests that he may have some special information on the subject." He glanced at his watch and, after a few moments' reflection, added : "I don't see why we shouldn't make our little ceremonial call at once. But it will be a delicate business, for we have mighty little to go upon. Are you coming with me ? "

If I had had any doubts, Thorndyke's last remark disposed of them ; for the interview promised to be quite a sporting event. Mr. Hyams was presumably not quite newly-hatched, and Thorndyke, who utterly despised bluff of any kind, and whose exact mind refused either to act or speak one hair's breadth beyond his knowledge, was admittedly in somewhat of a fog. The meeting promised to be really entertaining.

Mr. Hyams was "discovered," as the playwrights have it, in a small office at the top of a high building in Queen Victoria Street. He was a small gentleman, of sallow and greasy aspect, with heavy eyebrows and a still heavier nose.

"Are you Mr. Gordon ? " Thorndyke suavely inquired as we entered.

Mr. Hyams seemed to experience a momentary doubt on the subject, but finally decided that he was not. "But perhaps," he added brightly, "I can do your business for you as well."

"I daresay you can," Thorndyke agreed significantly ; on which we were conducted into an inner den, where

I noticed Thorndyke's eye rest for an instant on a large iron safe.

" Now," said Mr. Hyams, shutting the door ostentatiously, " what can I do for you ? "

" I want you," Thorndyke replied, " to answer one or two questions with reference to the claim made by you on the ' Griffin ' Office in respect of Thomas Elton."

Mr. Hyams's manner underwent a sudden change. He began rapidly to turn over papers, and opened and shut the drawers of his desk, with an air of restless preoccupation.

" Did the ' Griffin ' people send you here ? " he demanded brusquely.

" They did not specially instruct me to call on you," replied Thorndyke.

" Then," said Hyams, bouncing out of his chair, " I can't let you occupy my time.   I'm not here to answer conundrums from Tom, Dick or Harry."

Thorndyke rose from his chair.   " Then I am to understand," he said, with unruffled suavity, " that you would prefer me to communicate with the Directors, and leave them to take any necessary action."

This gave Mr. Hyams pause.   " What action do you refer to ? " he asked.   " And, who are you ? "

Thorndyke produced a card and laid it on the table. Mr. Hyams had apparently seen the name before, for he suddenly grew rather pale and very serious.

" What is the nature of the questions that you wished to ask ? " he inquired.

" They refer to this claim," replied Thorndyke. " The first question is, where is Mr. Gordon ? "

" I don't know," said Hyams.

" Where do you think he is ? " asked Thorndyke.

" I don't think at all," replied Hyams, turning a shade paler and looking everywhere but at Thorndyke.

" Very well," said the latter, " then the next question is, are you satisfied that this claim is really payable ? "

" I shouldn't have made it if I hadn't been," replied Hyams.

" Quite so," said Thorndyke ; " and the third question is, are you satisfied that the mortgage deed was executed as it purports to have been ? "

" I can't say anything about that," replied Hyams, who was growing every moment paler and more fidgety, " it was done before my time."

" Thank you," said Thorndyke. " You will, of course, understand why I am making these inquiries."

" I don't," said Hyams.

" Then," said Thorndyke, " perhaps I had better explain. We are dealing, you observe, Mr. Hyams, with the case of a man who has met with a violent death under somewhat mysterious circumstances. We are dealing, also, with another man who has disappeared, leaving his affairs to take care of themselves ; and with a claim, put forward by a third party, on behalf of the one man in respect of the other. When I say that the dead man has been imperfectly identified, and that the document supporting the claim presents certain peculiarities, you will see that the matter calls for further inquiry."

There was an appreciable interval of silence. Mr. Hyams had turned a tallowy white, and looked furtively about the room, as if anxious to avoid the stony gaze that my colleague had fixed on him.

" Can you give us no assistance ? " Thorndyke inquired, at length. Mr. Hyams chewed a pen-holder ravenously, as he considered the question. At length, he burst out in an agitated voice : " Look here, sir, if I tell you what I know, will you treat the information as confidential ? "

" I can't agree to that, Mr. Hyams," replied Thorndyke. " It might amount to compounding a felony. But you will be wiser to tell me what you know. The document is a side-issue, which my clients may never raise, and my own concern is with the death of this man."

Hyams looked distinctly relieved. " If that's so," said he, " I'll tell you all I know, which is precious little, and which just amounts to this : Two days after Elton was killed, someone came to this office in my absence and opened the safe. I discovered the fact the next morning. Someone had been to the safe and rummaged over all the papers. It wasn't Gordon, because he knew where to find everything ; and it wasn't an ordinary thief, because no cash or valuables had been taken. In fact, the only thing that I missed was a promissory note, drawn by Elton."

" You didn't miss a mortgage deed ? " suggested Thorndyke, and Hyams, having snatched a little further refreshment from the pen-holder, said he did not.

" And the policy," suggested Thorndyke, " was apparently not taken ? "

" No," replied Hyams ; " but it was looked for. Three bundles of policies had been untied, but this one happened to be in a drawer of my desk and I had the only key."

" And what do you infer from this visit ? " Thorndyke asked.

" Well," replied Hyams, " the safe was opened with keys, and they were Gordon's keys—or, at any rate, they weren't mine—and the person who opened it wasn't Gordon ; and the things that were taken—at least the thing, I mean—chiefly concerned Elton. Naturally I smelt a rat ; and when I read of the finding of the body, I smelt a fox."

" And have you formed any opinion about the body that was found ? "

" Yes, I have," he replied. " My opinion is that it was Gordon's body : that Gordon had been putting the screw on Elton, and Elton had just pitched him over the cliff and gone down and changed clothes with the body. Of course, that's only my opinion. I may be wrong ; but I don't think I am."

As a matter of fact, Mr. Hyams was not wrong. An exhumation, consequent on Thorndyke's challenge of the identity of the deceased, showed that the body was that of Solomon Gordon. A hundred pounds reward was offered for information as to Elton's whereabouts. But no one ever earned it. A letter, bearing the post-mark of Marseilles, and addressed by the missing man to Thorndyke, gave a plausible account of Gordon's death ; which was represented as having occurred accidentally at the moment when Gordon chanced to be wearing a suit of Elton's clothes.

Of course, this account may have been correct, or again, it may have been false ; but whether it was true or false, Elton, from that moment, vanished from our ken and has never since been heard of.

6

PERCIVAL BLAND'S
PROXY

Part I

MR. PERCIVAL BLAND was a somewhat uncommon type of criminal. In the first place he really had an appreci-able amount of common-sense. If he had only had a little more, he would not have been a criminal at all. As it was, he had just sufficient judgment to perceive that the consequences of unlawful acts accumulate as the acts are repeated ; to realise that the criminal's position must, at length, become untenable ; and to take what he considered fair precautions against the inevitable catastrophe.

But in spite of these estimable traits of character and the precautions aforesaid, Mr. Bland found himself in rather a tight place and with a prospect of increasing tightness. The causes of this uncomfortable tension do not concern us, and may be dismissed with the remark, that, if one perseveringly distributes flash Bank of England notes among the money-changers of the

Continent, there will come a day of reckoning when those notes are tendered to the exceedingly knowing old lady who lives in Threadneedle Street.

Mr. Bland considered uneasily the approaching storm-cloud as he raked over the " miscellaneous property " in the Sale-rooms of Messrs. Plimpton. He was a confirmed frequenter of auctions, as was not unnatural ; for the criminal is essentially a gambler. And criminal and auction-frequenter have one quality in common : each hopes to get something of value without paying the market price for it.

So Percival turned over the dusty oddments and his own difficulties at one and the same time. The vital questions were : When would the storm burst ? And would it pass by the harbour of refuge that he had been at such pains to construct ? Let us inspect that harbour of refuge.

A quiet flat in the pleasant neighbourhood of Battersea bore a name-plate inscribed, Mr. Robert Lindsay ; and the tenant was known to the porter and the char-woman who attended to the flat, as a fair-haired gentle-man who was engaged in the book trade as a travelling agent, and was consequently a good deal away from home. Now Mr. Robert Lindsay bore a distinct resemblance to Percival Bland ; which was not sur-prising seeing that they were first cousins (or, at any rate, they said they were ; and we may presume that they knew). But they were not very much alike. Mr. Lindsay had flaxen, or rather sandy, hair ; Mr. Bland's hair was black. Mr. Bland had a mole under his left eye ; Mr. Lindsay had no mole under his eye—but carried one in a small box in his waistcoat pocket.

At somewhat rare intervals the cousins called on one another ; but they had the very worst of luck, for neither of them ever seemed to find the other at home. And what was even more odd was that whenever Mr. Bland spent an evening at home in his lodgings over the oil

shop in Bloomsbury, Mr. Lindsay's flat was empty ;
and as sure as Mr. Lindsay was at home in his flat so
surely were Mr. Bland's lodgings vacant for the time
being. It was a queer coincidence, if anyone had
noticed it ; but nobody ever did.

However, if Percival saw little of his cousin, it was
not a case of " out of sight, out of mind." On the
contrary ; so great was his solicitude for the latter's
welfare that he not only had made a will constituting
him his executor and sole legatee, but he had actually
insured his life for no less a sum than three thousand
pounds ; and this will, together with the insurance
policy, investment securities and other necessary documents, he had placed in the custody of a highly respectable solicitor. All of which did him great credit. It
isn't every man who is willing to take so much trouble
for a mere cousin.

Mr. Bland continued his perambulations, pawing
over the miscellaneous raffle from sheer force of habit,
reflecting on the coming crisis in his own affairs, and
on the provisions that he had made for his cousin
Robert. As for the latter, they were excellent as far
as they went, but they lacked definiteness and perfect
completeness. There was the contingency of a
" stretch," for instance ; say fourteen years' penal
servitude. The insurance policy did not cover that.
And, meanwhile, what was to become of the estimable
Robert ?

He had bruised his thumb somewhat severely in a
screw-cutting lathe, and had abstractedly turned the
handle of a bird-organ until politely requested by an
attendant to desist, when he came upon a series of
boxes containing, according to the catalogue, " a
collection of surgical instruments the property of a
lately deceased practitioner." To judge by the appearance of the instruments, the practitioner must have
commenced practice in his early youth and died at a
very advanced age. They were an uncouth set of tools,

of no value whatever excepting as testimonials to the amazing tenacity of life of our ancestors ; but Percival fingered them over according to his wont, working the handle of a complicated brass syringe and ejecting a drop of greenish fluid on to the shirt-front of a dressy Hebrew (who requested him to " point the dam' thing at thomeone elth nectht time "), opening musty leather cases, clicking off spring scarifiers and feeling the edges of strange, crooked-bladed knives. Then he came upon a largish black box, which, when he raised the lid, breathed out an ancient and fish-like aroma and exhibited a collection of bones, yellow, greasy-looking and spotted in places with mildew. The catalogue described them as " a complete set of human osteology " ; but they were not an ordinary " student's set," for the bones of the hands and feet, instead of being strung together on cat-gut, were united by their original liga-ments and were of an unsavoury brown colour.

" I thay, misther," expostulated the Hebrew, " shut that bocth. Thmellth like a blooming inquetht."

But the contents of the black box seemed to have a fascination for Percival. He looked in at those greasy remnants of mortality, at the brown and mouldy hands and feet and the skull that peeped forth eerily from the folds of a flannel wrapping ; and they breathed out something more than that stale and musty odour. A suggestion—vague and general at first, but rapidly crystallising into distinct shape—seemed to steal out of the black box into his consciousness ; a suggestion that somehow seemed to connect itself with his estimable cousin Robert.

For upwards of a minute he stood motionless, as one immersed in reverie, the lid poised in his hand and a dreamy eye fixed on the half-uncovered skull. A stir in the room roused him. The sale was about to begin. The members of the knock-out and other habitués seated themselves on benches around a long, baize-covered table ; the attendants took possession

of the first lots and opened their catalogues as if about
to sing an introductory chorus ; and a gentleman with
a waxed moustache and a striking resemblance to his
late Majesty, the third Napoleon, having ascended to
the rostrum bespoke the attention of the assembly by
a premonitory tap with his hammer.

How odd are some of the effects of a guilty conscience ! With what absurd self-consciousness do we
read into the minds of others our own undeclared
intentions, when those intentions are unlawful ! Had
Percival Bland wanted a set of human bones for any
legitimate purpose—such as anatomical study—he
would have bought it openly and unembarrassed.
Now, he found himself earnestly debating whether he
should not bid for some of the surgical instruments,
just for the sake of appearances ; and there being
little time in which to make up his mind—for the
deceased practitioner's effects came first in the catalogue—he was already the richer by a set of cupping-
glasses, a tooth-key, and an instrument of unknown
use and diabolical aspect, before the fateful lot was
called.

At length the black box was laid on the table, an object
of obscene mirth to the knockers-out, and the auctioneer
read the entry :

" Lot seventeen ; a complete set of human osteology.
A very useful and valuable set of specimens, gentlemen."

He looked round at the assembly majestically, oblivious
of sundry inquiries as to the identity of the deceased
and the verdict of the coroner's jury, and finally suggested
five shillings.

" Six," said Percival.

An attendant held the box open, and, chanting the
mystic word " Loddlemen ! " (which, being interpreted,
meant " Lot, gentlemen "), thrust it under the rather
bulbous nose of the smart Hebrew ; who remarked
that " they 'ummed a bit too much to thoot him " and
pushed it away.

" Going at six shillings," said the auctioneer, re-proachfully ; and as nobody contradicted him, he smote the rostrum with his hammer and the box was delivered into the hands of Percival on the payment of that modest sum.

Having crammed the cupping-glasses, the tooth-key and the unknown instrument into the box, Percival obtained from one of the attendants a length of cord, with which he secured the lid. Then he carried his treasure out into the street, and, chartering a four-wheeler, directed the driver to proceed to Charing Cross Station. At the station he booked the box in the cloak-room (in the name of Simpson) and left it for a couple of hours ; at the expiration of which he returned, and, employing a different porter, had it conveyed to a hansom, in which it was borne to his lodgings over the oil-shop in Bloomsbury. There he, himself, carried it, unobserved, up the stairs, and, depositing it in a large cupboard, locked the door and pocketed the key.

And thus was the curtain rung down on the first act.

The second act opened only a couple of days later, the office of call-boy—to pursue the metaphor to the bitter end—being discharged by a Belgian police official who emerged from the main entrance to the Bank of England. What should have led Percival Bland into so unsafe a neighbourhood it is difficult to imagine, unless it was that strange fascination that seems so frequently to lure the criminal to places associated with his crime. But there he was within a dozen paces of the entrance when the officer came forth, and mutual recognition was instantaneous. Almost equally instantaneous was the self-possessed Percival's decision to cross the road.

It is not a nice road to cross. The old-fashioned horse-driver would condescend to shout a warning to the indiscreet wayfarer. Not so the modern chauffeur, who looks stonily before him and leaves you to get out of the way of Juggernaut. He knows his " exonera-ting " coroner's jury. At the moment, however, the procession of Juggernauts was at rest; but Percival had seen the presiding policeman turn to move away and he darted across the fronts of the vehicles even as they started. The foreign officer followed. But in that moment the whole procession had got in motion. A motor omnibus thundered past in front of him; another was bearing down on him relentlessly. He hesitated, and sprang back; and then a taxi-cab, darting out from behind, butted him heavily, sending him sprawling in the road, whence he scrambled as best he could back on to the pavement.

Percival, meanwhile, had swung himself lightly on to the footboard of the first omnibus just as it was gathering speed. A few seconds saw him safely across at the Mansion House, and in a few more, he was whirling down Queen Victoria Street. The danger was practically over, though he took the precaution to alight at St. Paul's, and, crossing to Newgate Street, board another west-bound omnibus.

That night he sat in his lodgings turning over his late experience. It had been a narrow shave. That sort of thing mustn't happen again. In fact, seeing that the law was undoubtedly about to be set in motion, it was high time that certain little plans of his should be set in motion, too. Only, there was a difficulty; a serious difficulty. And as Percival thought round and round that difficulty his brows wrinkled and he hummed a soft refrain.

> "Then is the time for disappearing,
> Take a header—down you go——"

A tap at the door cut his song short. It was his landlady, Mrs. Brattle; a civil woman, and particularly civil just now. For she had a little request to make.

" It was about Christmas Night, Mr. Bland," said Mrs. Brattle. " My husband and me thought of spending the evening with his brother at Hornsey, and we were going to let the maid go home to her mother's for the night, if it wouldn't put you out."

" Wouldn't put me out in the least, Mrs. Brattle,"
said Percival.

" You needn't sit up for us, you see," pursued Mrs.
Brattle, " if you'd just leave the side door unbolted.
We shan't be home before two or three ; but we'll
come in quiet not to disturb you."

" You won't disturb me," Percival replied with a
genial laugh. " I'm a sober man in general ; but
' Christmas comes but once a year.' When once
I'm tucked up in bed, I shall take a bit of waking on
Christmas Night."

Mrs. Brattle smiled indulgently. " And you won't
feel lonely, all alone in the house ? "

" Lonely ! " exclaimed Percival. " Lonely ! With
a roaring fire, a jolly book, a box of good cigars and a
bottle of sound port—ah, and a second bottle if need
be. Not I."

Mrs. Brattle shook her head. " Ah," said she,
" you bachelors ! Well, well. It's a good thing to
be independent," and with this profound reflection
she smiled herself out of the room and descended the
stairs.

As her footsteps died away Percival sprang from
his chair and began excitedly to pace the room. His
eyes sparkled and his face was wreathed with smiles.
Presently he halted before the fireplace, and, gazing
into the embers, laughed aloud.

" Damn funny ! " said he. " Deuced rich ! Neat !
Very neat ! Ha ! Ha ! " And here he resumed his
interrupted song :

> " When the sky above is clearing,
> When the sky above is clearing,
> Bob up serenely, bob up serenely,
> Bob up serenely from below ! "

Which may be regarded as closing the first scene
of the second act.

During the few days that intervened before Christmas,
Percival went abroad but little ; and yet he was a busy

man. He did a little surreptitious shopping, venturing out as far as Charing Cross Road ; and his purchases were decidedly miscellaneous. A porridge saucepan, a second-hand copy of " Gray's Anatomy," a rabbit skin, a large supply of glue and upwards of ten pounds of shin of beef seems a rather odd assortment ; and it was a mercy that the weather was frosty, for otherwise Percival's bedroom, in which these delicacies were deposited under lock and key, would have yielded odorous traces of its wealth.

But it was in the long evenings that his industry was most conspicuous ; and then it was that the big cupboard with the excellent lever lock, which he himself had fixed on, began to fill up with the fruits of his labours. In those evenings the porridge saucepan would simmer on the hob with a rich lading of good Scotch glue, the black box of the deceased practitioner would be hauled forth from its hiding-place, and the well-thumbed " Gray " laid open on the table.

It was an arduous business though ; a stiffer task than he had bargained for. The right and left bones were so confoundedly alike, and the bones that joined were so difficult to fit together. However, the plates in " Gray " were large and very clear, so it was only a question of taking enough trouble.

His method of work was simple and practical. Having fished a bone out of the box, he would compare it with the illustrations in the book until he had identified it beyond all doubt, when he would tie on it a paper label with its name and side—right or left. Then he would search for the adjoining bone, and, having fitted the two together, would secure them with a good daub of glue and lay them in the fender to dry. It was a crude and horrible method of articulation that would have made a museum curator shudder. But it seemed to answer Percival's purpose—whatever that may have been—for gradually the loose " items " came together into recognisable members such as arms and legs, the vertebræ—which were, fortunately, strung in their order on a thick cord—were joined up into a solid backbone, and even the ribs, which were the toughest job of all, fixed on in some semblance of a thorax. It was a wretched performance. The bones were plastered with gouts of glue and yet would have broken apart at a touch. But, as we have said, Percival seemed satisfied, and as he was the only person concerned, there was nothing more to be said.

In due course, Christmas Day arrived. Percival dined with the Brattles at two, dozed after dinner, woke up for tea, and then, as Mrs. Brattle, in purple and fine raiment, came in to remove the tea-tray, he spread out on the table the materials for the night's carouse. A quarter of an hour later, the side-door slammed, and, peering out of the window, he saw the shopkeeper and his wife hurrying away up the gas-lit street towards the nearest omnibus route.

Then Mr. Percival Bland began his evening's entertainment; and a most remarkable entertainment it was, even for a solitary bachelor, left alone in a house on Christmas Night. First, he took off his clothing and dressed himself in a fresh suit. Then, from the cupboard, he brought forth the reconstituted " set of osteology," and, laying the various members on the table, returned to the bedroom, whence he presently reappeared with a large, unsavoury parcel which he had disinterred from a trunk. The parcel, being opened, revealed his accumulated purchases in the matter of shin of beef.

With a large knife, providently sharpened beforehand, he cut the beef into large, thin slices which he proceeded to wrap around the various bones that formed the " complete set "; whereby their nakedness was certainly mitigated though their attractiveness was by no means increased. Having thus " clothed the dry bones," he gathered up the scraps of offal that were left, to be placed presently inside the trunk. It was an extraordinary proceeding, but the next was more extraordinary still.

Taking up the newly clothed members one by one, he began very carefully to insinuate them into the garments that he had recently shed. It was a ticklish business, for the glued joints were as brittle as glass. Very cautiously the legs were separately inducted, first into underclothing and then into trousers, the skeleton feet were fitted with the cast-off socks and delicately persuaded into the boots. The arms, in like manner, were gingerly pressed into their various sleeves and through the arm-holes of the waistcoat; and then came the most difficult task of all—to fit the garments on the trunk. For the skull and ribs, secured to the back-bone with mere spots of glue, were ready to drop off at a shake; and yet the garments had to be drawn over them with the arms enclosed in the sleeves. But Percival managed it at last by resting his " restoration " in the big, padded arm-chair and easing the garments on inch by inch.

It now remained only to give the finishing touch; which was done by cutting the rabbit-skin to the requisite shape and affixing it to the skull with a thin coat of stiff glue; and when the skull had thus been finished with a sort of crude, makeshift wig, its appearance was so appalling as even to disturb the nerves of the matter-of-fact Percival. However, this was no occasion for cherishing sentiment. A skull in an extemporised wig or false scalp might be, and in fact was, a highly unpleasant object; but so was a Belgian police officer.

Having finished the " restoration," Percival fetched the water-jug from his bedroom, and, descending to the shop, the door of which had been left unlocked, tried the taps of the various drums and barrels until he came to the one which contained methylated spirit; and from this he filled his jug and returned to the bedroom. Pouring the spirit out into the basin, he tucked a towel round his neck and filling his sponge with spirit proceeded very vigorously to wash his hair and eyebrows; and as, by degrees, the spirit in the basin grew dark and turbid, so did his hair and eyebrows grow lighter in colour until, after a final energetic rub with a towel, they had acquired a golden or sandy hue indistinguishable from that of the hair of his cousin Robert. Even the mole under his eye was susceptible to the changing conditions, for when he had wetted it thoroughly with spirit, he was able, with the blade of a penknife, to peel it off as neatly as if it had been stuck on with spirit-gum. Having done which, he deposited it in a tiny box which he carried in his waistcoat pocket.

The proceedings which followed were unmistakable as to their object. First he carried the basin of spirit through into the sitting-room and deliberately poured its contents on to the floor by the arm-chair. Then, having returned the basin to the bedroom, he again went down to the shop, where he selected a couple of galvanised buckets from the stock, filled them with paraffin oil from one of the great drums and carried them upstairs. The oil from one bucket he poured over the arm-chair and its repulsive occupant; the other bucket he simply emptied on the carpet, and then went down to the shop for a fresh supply.

When this proceeding had been repeated once or twice the entire floor and all the furniture were saturated, and such a reek of paraffin filled the air of the room that Percival thought it wise to turn out the gas. Returning to the shop, he poured a bucketful of oil over the stack of bundles of firewood, another over the counter and floor and a third over the loose articles on the walls and hanging from the ceiling. Looking up at the latter he now perceived a number of greasy patches where the oil had soaked through from the floor above, and some of these were beginning to drip on to the shop floor.

8

He now made his final preparations. Taking a bundle of "Wheel" firelighters, he made a small pile against the stack of firewood. In the midst of the firelighters he placed a ball of string saturated in paraffin ; and in the central hole of the ball he stuck a half-dozen diminutive Christmas candles. This mine was now ready. Providing himself with a stock of firelighters, a few balls of paraffined string and a dozen or so of the little candles, he went upstairs to the sitting-room, which was immediately above the shop. Here, by the glow of the fire, he built up one or two piles of firelighters around and partly under the arm-chair, placed the balls of string on the piles and stuck two or three bundles in each ball. Everything was now ready. Stepping into the bedroom, he took from the cupboard a spare overcoat, a new hat and a new umbrella—for he must leave his old hats, coat and umbrella in the hall. He put on the coat and hat, and, with the umbrella in his hand, returned to the sitting-room.

Opposite the arm-chair he stood awhile, irresolute, and a pang of horror shot through him. It was a terrible thing that he was going to do ; a thing the consequences of which no one could foresee. He glanced furtively at the awful shape that sat huddled in the chair, its horrible head all awry and its rigid limbs sprawling in hideous grotesque deformity. It was but a dummy, a mere scarecrow ; but yet, in the dim firelight, the grisly face under that horrid wig seemed to leer intelligently, to watch him with secret malice out of its shadowy eye-sockets, until he looked away with clammy skin and a shiver of half-superstitious terror.

But this would never do. The evening had run out, consumed by these engrossing labours ; it was nearly eleven o'clock, and high time for him to be gone. For if the Brattles should return prematurely he was lost. Pulling himself together with an effort, he struck a match and lit the little candles one after the other. In a quarter of an hour or so, they would have burned down to the balls of string, and then——

He walked quickly out of the room ; but, at the door, he paused for a moment to look back at the ghastly figure, seated rigidly in the chair with the lighted candles at its feet, like some foul fiend appeased by votive fires. The unsteady flames threw flickering shadows on its face that made it seem to mow and gibber and grin in mockery of all his care and caution. So he turned and tremblingly ran down the stairs— opening the staircase window as he went. Running into the shop, he lit the candles there and ran out again, shutting the door after him.

Secretly and guiltily he crept down the hall, and opening the door a few inches peered out. A blast of icy wind poured in with a light powdering of dry snow. He opened his umbrella, flung open the door, looked up and down the empty street, stepped out, closed the door softly and strode away over the whitening pavement.

Part II

(Related by CHRISTOPHER JERVIS, M.D.)

It was one of the axioms of medico-legal practice laid down by my colleague, John Thorndyke, that the investigator should be constantly on his guard against the effect of suggestion. Not only must all prejudices and preconceptions be avoided, but when information is received from outside, the actual, undeniable facts must be carefully sifted from the inferences which usually accompany them. Of the necessity for this precaution our insurance practice furnished an excellent instance in the case of the fire at Mr. Brattle's oil-shop.

The case was brought to our notice by Mr. Stalker of the " Griffin " Fire and Life Insurance Society a few days after Christmas. He dropped in, ostensibly to

wish us a Happy New Year, but a discreet pause in
the conversation on Thorndyke's part elicited a further
purpose.

" Did you see the account of that fire in Bloomsbury ? "
Mr. Stalker asked.

" The oil-shop ? Yes. But I didn't note any details,
excepting that a man was apparently burnt to death
and that the affair happened on the twenty-fifth of
December."

" Yes, I know," said Mr. Stalker. " It seems un-
charitable, but one can't help looking a little askance
at these quarter-day fires. And the date isn't the
only doubtful feature in this one ; the Divisional
Officer of the Fire Brigade, who has looked over the
ruins, tells me that there are some appearances suggesting that the fire broke out in two different places—
the shop and the first-floor room over it. Mind you,
he doesn't say that it actually did. The place is so
thoroughly gutted that very little is to be learned from
it ; but that is his impression ; and it occurred to me
that if you were to take a look at the ruins, your
radiographic eye might detect something that he had
overlooked."

" It isn't very likely," said Thorndyke. " Every
man to his trade. The Divisional Officer looks at a
burnt house with an expert eye, which I do not. My
evidence would not carry much weight if you were
contesting the claim."

" Perhaps not," replied Mr. Stalker, " and we are
not anxious to contest the claim unless there is
manifest fraud. Arson is a serious matter."

" It is wilful murder in this case," remarked Thorndyke.

" I know," said Stalker. " And that reminds me
that the man who was burnt happens to have been
insured in our office, too. So we stand a double
loss."

" How much ? " asked Thorndyke.

"The dead man, Percival Bland, had insured his life for three thousand pounds."

Thorndyke became thoughtful. The last statement had apparently made more impression on him than the former ones.

"If you want me to look into the case for you," said he, "you had better let me have all the papers connected with it, including the proposal forms."

Mr. Stalker smiled. "I thought you would say that—know you of old, you see—so I slipped the papers in my pocket before coming here."

He laid the documents on the table and asked : "Is there anything that you want to know about the case ? "

"Yes," replied Thorndyke. "I want to know all that you can tell me."

"Which is mighty little," said Stalker ; "but such as it is, you shall have it.

"The oil-shop man's name is Brattle and the dead man, Bland, was his lodger. Bland appears to have been a perfectly steady, sober man in general ; but it seems that he had announced his intention of spending a jovial Christmas Night and giving himself a little extra indulgence. He was last seen by Mrs. Brattle at about half-past six, sitting by a blazing fire, with a couple of unopened bottles of port on the table and a box of cigars. He had a book in his hand and two or three newspapers lay on the floor by his chair. Shortly after this, Mr. and Mrs. Brattle went out on a visit to Hornsey, leaving him alone in the house."

"Was there no servant ? " asked Thorndyke.

"The servant had the day and night off duty to go to her mother's. That, by the way, looks a trifle fishy. However, to return to the Brattles ; they spent the evening at Hornsey and did not get home until past three in the morning, by which time their house was a heap of smoking ruins. Mrs. Brattle's idea is that Bland must have drunk himself sleepy, and dropped one of the newspapers into the fender, where a chance cinder may have started the blaze. Which may or may not be the true explanation. Of course, an habitually sober man can get pretty mimsey on two bottles of port."

"What time did the fire break out?" asked Thorndyke.

"It was noticed about half-past eleven that flames were issuing from one of the chimneys, and the alarm was given at once. The first engine arrived ten minutes later, but, by that time, the place was roaring like a furnace. Then the water-plugs were found to be frozen hard, which caused some delay; in fact, before the engines were able to get to work the roof had fallen in, and the place was a mere shell. You know what an oil-shop is, when once it gets a fair start."

"And Mr. Bland's body was found in the ruins, I suppose?"

"Body!" exclaimed Mr. Stalker; "there wasn't much body! Just a few charred bones, which they dug out of the ashes next day."

"And the question of identity?"

"We shall leave that to the coroner. But there really isn't any question. To begin with, there was no one else in the house; and then the remains were found mixed up with the springs and castors of the chair that Bland was sitting in when he was last seen. Moreover, there were found, with the bones, a pocket-knife, a bunch of keys and a set of steel waistcoat buttons, all identified by Mrs. Brattle as belonging to Bland. She noticed the cut steel buttons on his waistcoat when she wished him 'good-night.'"

"By the way," said Thorndyke, "was Bland reading by the light of an oil lamp?"

"No," replied Stalker. "There was a two-branch gasalier with a porcelain shade to one burner, and he had that burner alight when Mrs. Brattle left."

Thorndyke reflectively picked up the proposal form, and, having glanced through it, remarked : " I see that Bland is described as unmarried. Do you know why he insured his life for this large amount ? "

" No ; we assumed that it was probably in connection with some loan that he had raised. I learn from the solicitor who notified us of the death, that the whole of Bland's property is left to a cousin—a Mr. Lindsay, I think. So the probability is that this cousin had lent him money. But it is not the life claim that is interesting us. We must pay that in any case. It is the fire claim that we want you to look into."

" Very well," said Thorndyke ; " I will go round presently and look over the ruins, and see if I can detect any substantial evidence of fraud."

" If you would," said Mr. Stalker, rising to take his departure, " we should be very much obliged. Not that we shall probably contest the claim in any case."

When he had gone, my colleague and I glanced through the papers, and I ventured to remark : " It seems to me that Stalker doesn't quite appreciate the possibilities of this case."

" No," Thorndyke agreed. " But, of course, it is an insurance company's business to pay, and not to boggle at anything short of glaring fraud. And we specialists, too," he added with a smile, " must beware of seeing too much. I suppose that, to a rhinologist, there is hardly such a thing as a healthy nose—unless it is his own—and the uric acid specialist is very apt to find the firmament studded with dumb-bell crystals. We mustn't forget that normal cases do exist, after all."

" That is true," said I ; " but, on the other hand, the rhinologist's business is with the unhealthy nose, and our concern is with abnormal cases."

Thorndyke laughed. " ' A Daniel come to judgment,' " said he. " But my learned friend is quite right. Our function is to pick holes. So let us pocket the documents and wend Bloomsbury way. We can talk the case over as we go."

We walked at an easy pace, for there was no hurry, and a little preliminary thought was useful. After a while, as Thorndyke made no remark, I reopened the subject.

" How does the case present itself to you ? " I asked.

" Much as it does to you, I expect," he replied. " The circumstances invite inquiry, and I do not find myself connecting them with the shopkeeper. It is true that the fire occurred on quarter-day ; but there is nothing to show that the insurance will do more than cover the loss of stock, chattels and the profits of trade. The other circumstances are much more suggestive. Here is a house burned down and a man killed. That man was insured for three thousand pounds, and, consequently, some person stands to gain by his death to that amount. The whole set of circumstances is highly favourable to the idea of homicide. The man was alone in the house when he died ; and the total destruction of both the body and its surroundings seems to render investigation impossible. The cause of death can only be inferred ; it cannot be proved ; and the most glaring evidence of a crime will have vanished utterly. I think that there is a quite strong *prima facie* suggestion of murder. Under the known conditions, the perpetration of a murder would have been easy, it would have been safe from detection, and there is an adequate motive.

" On the other hand, suicide is not impossible. The man might have set fire to the house and then killed himself by poison or otherwise. But it is intrinsically less probable that a man should kill himself for another person's benefit than that he should kill another man for his own benefit.

" Finally, there is the possibility that the fire and the man's death were the result of accident ; against which is the official opinion that the fire started in two

places. If this opinion is correct, it establishes, in
my opinion, a strong presumption of murder against
some person who may have obtained access to the
house."

This point in the discussion brought us to the ruined
house, which stood at the corner of two small streets.
One of the firemen in charge admitted us, when we had
shown our credentials, through a temporary door
and down a ladder into the basement, where we found
a number of men treading gingerly, ankle deep in
white ash, among a litter of charred wood-work, fused
glass, warped and broken china, and more or less
recognisable metal objects.

" The coroner and the jury," the fireman explained ;
" come to view the scene of the disaster." He introduced us to the former, who bowed stiffly and continued
his investigations.

" These," said the other fireman, " are the springs
of the chair that the deceased was sitting in. We
found the body—or rather the bones—lying among
them under a heap of hot ashes ; and we found the
buttons of his clothes and the things from his pockets
among the ashes, too. You'll see them in the mortuary
with the remains."

" It must have been a terrific blaze," one of the
jurymen remarked. " Just look at this, sir," and he
handed to Thorndyke what looked like part of a gas-
fitting, of which the greater part was melted into
shapeless lumps and the remainder encrusted into
fused porcelain.

" That," said the fireman, " was the gasalier of the
first-floor room, where Mr. Bland was sitting. Ah !
you won't turn that tap, sir ; nobody'll ever turn that
tap again."

Thorndyke held the twisted mass of brass towards
me in silence, and, glancing up the blackened walls,
remarked : " I think we shall have to come here again
with the Divisional Officer, but meanwhile, we had

8*

better see the remains of the body. It is just possible that we may learn something from them."

He applied to the coroner for the necessary authority to make the inspection, and, having obtained a rather ungracious and grudging permission to examine the remains when the jury had " viewed " them, began to ascend the ladder.

" Our friend would have liked to refuse permission," he remarked when we had emerged into the street, " but he knew that I could and should have insisted."

" So I gathered from his manner," said I. " But what is he doing here ? This isn't his district."

" No ; he is acting for Bettsford, who is laid up just now ; and a very poor substitute he is. A non-medical coroner is an absurdity in any case, and a coroner who is hostile to the medical profession is a public scandal. By the way, that gas-tap offers a curious problem. You noticed that it was turned off ? "

" Yes."

" And consequently that the deceased was sitting in the dark when the fire broke out. I don't see the bearing of the fact, but it is certainly rather odd. Here is the mortuary. We had better wait and let the jury go in first."

We had not long to wait. In a couple of minutes or so the " twelve good men and true " made their appearance with a small attendant crowd of raga-muffins. We let them enter first, and then we followed. The mortuary was a good-sized room, well lighted by a glass roof, and having at its centre a long table on which lay the shell containing the remains. There was also a sheet of paper on which had been laid out a set of blackened steel waistcoat buttons, a bunch of keys, a steel-handled pocket-knife, a steel-cased watch on a partly-fused rolled-gold chain, and a pocket corkscrew. The coroner drew the attention of the jury to these objects, and then took possession of them, that they might be identified by witnesses. And meanwhile the jurymen gathered round the shell and stared shudderingly at its gruesome contents.

" I am sorry, gentlemen," said the coroner, " to have to subject you to this painful ordeal. But duty is duty. We must hope, as I think we may, that this poor creature met a painless if in some respects a rather terrible death."

At this point, Thorndyke, who had drawn near to the table, cast a long and steady glance down into the shell ; and immediately his ordinarily rather impassive face seemed to congeal ; all expression faded from it, leaving it as immovable and uncommunicative as the granite face of an Egyptian statue. I knew the symptom of old and began to speculate on its present significance.

" Are you taking any medical evidence ? " he asked.

" Medical evidence ! " the coroner repeated, scornfully. " Certainly not, sir ! I do not waste the public money by employing so-called experts to tell the jury what each of them can see quite plainly for himself. I imagine," he added, turning to the foreman, " that you will not require a learned doctor to explain to you how that poor fellow mortal met his death ? " And the foreman, glancing askance at the skull, replied, with a pallid and sickly smile, that " he thought not."

" Do you, sir," the coroner continued, with a dramatic wave of the hand towards the plain coffin, " suppose that we shall find any difficulty in determining how that man came by his death ? "

" I imagine," replied Thorndyke, without moving a muscle, or, indeed, appearing to have any muscles to move, " I imagine you will find no difficulty whatever."

" So do I," said the coroner.

" Then," retorted Thorndyke, with a faint, inscrutable smile, " we are, for once, in complete agreement."

As the coroner and jury retired, leaving my colleague and me alone in the mortuary, Thorndyke remarked :

" I suppose this kind of farce will be repeated periodically so long as these highly technical medical inquiries continue to be conducted by lay persons."

I made no reply, for I had taken a long look into the shell, and was lost in astonishment.

" But my dear Thorndyke ! " I exclaimed ; " what on earth does it mean ? Are we to suppose that a woman can have palmed herself off as a man on the examining medical officer of a London Life Assurance Society ? "

Thorndyke shook his head. " I think not," said he. " Our friend, Mr. Bland, may conceivably have been a woman in disguise, but he certainly was not a negress."

" A negress ! " I gasped. " By Jove ! So it is. I hadn't looked at the skull. But that only makes the mystery more mysterious. Because, you remember, the body was certainly dressed in Bland's clothes."

" Yes, there seems to be no doubt about that. And you may have noticed, as I did," Thorndyke continued dryly, " the remarkably fire-proof character of the waistcoat buttons, watch-case, knife-handle, and other identifiable objects."

" But what a horrible affair ! " I exclaimed. " The brute must have gone out and enticed some poor devil of a negress into the house, have murdered her in cold blood and then deliberately dressed the corpse in his own clothes ! It is perfectly frightful ! "

Again Thorndyke shook his head. " It wasn't as bad as that, Jervis," said he, " though I must confess that I feel strongly tempted to let your hypothesis stand. It would be quite amusing to put Mr. Bland on trial for the murder of an unknown negress, and let him explain the facts himself. But our reputation is at stake. Look at the bones again and a little more critically. You very probably looked for the sex first ;

then you looked for racial characters. Now carry your investigations a step farther."

"There is the stature," said I. "But that is of no importance, as these are not Bland's bones. The only other point that I notice is that the fire seems to have acted very unequally on the different parts of the body."

"Yes," agreed Thorndyke, "and that is *the* point. Some parts are more burnt than others; and the parts which are burnt most are the wrong parts. Look at the back-bone, for instance. The vertebræ are as white as chalk. They are mere masses of bone ash. But, of all parts of the skeleton, there is none so completely protected from fire as the back-bone, with the great dorsal muscles behind, and the whole mass of the viscera in front. Then look at the skull. Its appearance is quite inconsistent with the suggested facts. The bones of the face are bare and calcined and the orbits contain not a trace of the eyes or other structures; and yet there is a charred mass of what may or may not be scalp adhering to the crown. But the scalp, as the most exposed and the thinnest covering, would be the first to be destroyed, while the last to be consumed would be the structures about the jaws and the base, of which, you see, not a vestige is left."

Here he lifted the skull carefully from the shell, and, peering in through the great foramen at the base, handed it to me.

"Look in," he said, "through the Foramen Magnum —you will see better if you hold the orbits towards the skylight—and notice an even more extreme inconsistency with the supposed conditions. The brain and membranes have vanished without leaving a trace. The inside of the skull is as clean as if it had been macerated. But this is impossible. The brain is not only protected from the fire; it is also protected from contact with the air. But without access of oxygen, although it might become carbonised, it could not be consumed. No, Jervis; it won't do."

I replaced the skull in the coffin and looked at him in surprise.

"What is it that you are suggesting ? " I asked.

" I suggest that this was not a body at all, but merely a dry skeleton."

" But," I objected, " what about those masses of what looks like charred muscle adhering to the bones ? "

" Yes," he replied, " I have been noticing them. They do, as you say, look like masses of charred muscle. But they are quite shapeless and structureless ; I cannot identify a single muscle or muscular group ; and there is not a vestige of any of the tendons. Moreover, the distribution is false. For instance, will you tell me what muscle you think that is ? "

He pointed to a thick, charred mass on the inner surface of the left tibia or shin-bone. " Now this portion of the bone—as many a hockey-player has had reason to realise—has no muscular covering at all. It lies immediately under the skin."

" I think you are right, Thorndyke," said I. " That lump of muscle in the wrong place gives the whole fraud away. But it was really a rather smart dodge. This fellow Bland must be an ingenious rascal."

" Yes," agreed Thorndyke ; " but an unscrupulous villain too. He might have burned down half the street and killed a score of people. He'll have to pay the piper for this little frolic."

" What shall you do now ? Are you going to notify the coroner ? "

" No ; that is not my business. I think we will verify our conclusions and then inform our clients and the police. We must measure the skull as well as we can without callipers, but it is, fortunately, quite typical. The short, broad, flat nasal bones, with the ' Simian groove,' and those large, strong teeth, worn flat by hard and gritty food, are highly characteristic." He once more lifted out the skull, and, with a spring tape, made a few measurements, while I noted the lengths of the principal long bones and the width across the hips.

"I make the cranial-nasal index 55·1," said he, as he replaced the skull, "and the cranial index about 72, which are quite representative numbers; and, as I see that your notes show the usual disproportionate length of arm and the characteristic curve of the tibia, we may be satisfied. But it is fortunate that the specimen is so typical. To the experienced eye, racial types have a physiognomy which is unmistakable on mere inspection. But you cannot transfer the experienced eye. You can only express personal conviction and back it up with measurements.

"And now we will go and look in on Stalker, and inform him that his office has saved three thousand pounds by employing us. After which it will be Westward Ho! for Scotland Yard, to prepare an unpleasant little surprise for Mr. Percival Bland."

There was joy among the journalists on the following day. Each of the morning papers devoted an entire column to an unusually detailed account of the inquest on the late Percival Bland—who, it appeared, met his death by misadventure—and a verbatim report of the coroner's eloquent remarks on the danger of solitary, fireside tippling, and the stupefying effects of port wine. An adjacent column contained an equally detailed account of the appearance of the deceased at Bow Street Police Court to answer complicated charges of arson, fraud and forgery; while a third collated the two accounts with gleeful commentaries.

Mr. Percival Bland, *alias* Robert Lindsay, now resides on the breezy uplands of Dartmoor, where, in his abundant leisure, he, no doubt, regrets his misdirected ingenuity. But he has not laboured in vain. To the Lord Chancellor he has furnished an admirable illustration of the danger of appointing lay coroners; and to me an unforgettable warning against the effects of suggestion.

THE FAMOUS CASES OF
DR. THORNDYKE

GROUP
TWO

DIRECT
STORIES

I. The Changed Immutable

AMONG the minor and purely physical pleasures of life, I am disposed to rank very highly that feeling of bodily comfort that one experiences on passing from the outer darkness of a wet winter's night to a cheerful interior made glad by mellow lamplight and blazing hearth. And so I thought when, on a dreary November night, I let myself into our chambers in the Temple and found my friend smoking his pipe in slippered ease, by a roaring fire, and facing an empty arm-chair evidently placed in readiness for me.

As I shed my damp overcoat, I glanced inquisitively at my colleague, for he held in his hand an open letter, and I seemed to perceive in his aspect something meditative and self-communing—something, in short, suggestive of a new case.

" I was just considering," he said, in answer to my inquiring look, " whether I am about to become an accessory after the fact. Read that and give me your opinion."

He handed me the letter, which I read aloud.

" DEAR SIR,—I am in great danger and distress. A warrant has been issued for my arrest on a charge of which I am entirely innocent. Can I come and see you, and will you let me leave in safety ? The bearer will wait for a reply."

" I said ' Yes,' of course ; there was nothing else to do," said Thorndyke. " But if I let him go, as I have promised to do, I shall be virtually conniving at his escape."

" Yes, you are taking a risk," I answered. " When is he coming ? "

" He was due five minutes ago—and I rather think— yes, here he is."

A stealthy tread on the landing was followed by a soft tapping on the outer door.

Thorndyke rose and, flinging open the inner door, unfastened the massive " oak."

" Dr. Thorndyke ? " inquired a breathless, quavering voice.

" Yes, come in.   You sent me a letter by hand ? "

" I did, sir," was the reply ; and the speaker entered, but at the sight of me he stopped short.

" This is my colleague, Dr. Jervis," Thorndyke explained.   " You need have no——"

" Oh, I remember him," our visitor interrupted in a tone of relief.   " I have seen you both before, you know, and you have seen me too—though I don't suppose you recognise me," he added, with a sickly smile.

" Frank Belfield ? " asked Thorndyke, smiling also.

Our visitor's jaw fell and he gazed at my colleague in sudden dismay.

" And I may remark," pursued Thorndyke, " that for a man in your perilous position, you are running most unnecessary risks.   That wig, that false beard and those spectacles—through which you obviously cannot see— are enough to bring the entire police force at your heels. It is not wise for a man who is wanted by the police to make up as though he had just escaped from a comic opera."

Mr. Belfield seated himself with a groan, and, taking off his spectacles, stared stupidly from one of us to the other.

" And now tell us about your little affair," said Thorndyke.   " You say that you are innocent ? "

" I swear it, doctor," replied Belfield ; adding, with great earnestness, " and you may take it from me, sir, that if I was not, I shouldn't be here.   It was you that convicted me last time, when I thought myself quite safe, so I know your ways too well to try to gammon you."

"If you are innocent," rejoined Thorndyke, "I will do what I can for you ; and if you are not—well, you would have been wiser to stay away."

"I know that well enough," said Belfield, "and I am only afraid that you won't believe what I am going to tell you."

"I shall keep an open mind, at any rate," replied Thorndyke.

"If you only will," groaned Belfield, "I shall have a look in, in spite of them all. You know, sir, that I have been on the crook, but I have paid in full. That job when you tripped me up was the last of it—it was, sir, so help me. It was a woman that changed me— the best and truest woman on God's earth. She said she would marry me when I came out if I promised her to go straight and live an honest life. And she kept her promise—and I have kept mine. She found me work as clerk in a warehouse and I have stuck to it ever since, earning fair wages and building up a good character as an honest, industrious man. I thought all was going well and that I was settled for life, when only this very morning the whole thing comes tumbling about my ears like a house of cards."

"What happened this morning, then ? " asked Thorndyke.

"Why, I was on my way to work when, as I passed the police station, I noticed a bill with the heading 'Wanted' and a photograph. I stopped for a moment to look at it, and you may imagine my feelings when I recognised my own portrait—taken at Holloway—and read my own name and description. I did not stop to read the bill through, but ran back home and told my wife, and she ran down to the station and read the bill carefully. Good God, sir ! What do you think I am wanted for ? " He paused for a moment, and then replied in breathless tones to his own question : " The Camberwell murder ! "

Thorndyke gave a low whistle.

" My wife knows I didn't do it," continued Belfield, " because I was at home all the evening and night ; but what use is a man's wife to prove an alibi ? "

" Not much, I fear," Thorndyke admitted ; " and you have no other witness ? "

" Not a soul. We were alone all the evening."

" However," said Thorndyke, " if you are innocent— as I am assuming—the evidence against you must be entirely circumstantial and your alibi may be quite sufficient. Have you any idea of the grounds of suspicion against you ? "

" Not the faintest. The papers said that the police had an excellent clue, but they did not say what it was. Probably someone has given false information for the——"

A sharp rapping at the outer door cut short the explanation, and our visitor rose, trembling and aghast, with beads of sweat standing upon his livid face.

" You had better go into the office, Belfield, while we see who it is," said Thorndyke. " The key is on the inside."

The fugitive wanted no second bidding, but hurried into the empty apartment, and, as the door closed, we heard the key turn in the lock.

As Thorndyke threw open the outer door, he cast a meaning glance at me over his shoulder which I under- stood when the new-comer entered the room ; for it was none other than Superintendent Miller of Scotland Yard.

" I have just dropped in," said the superintendent, in his brisk, cheerful way, " to ask you to do me a favour. Good-evening, Dr. Jervis, I hear you are reading for the bar ; learned counsel soon, sir, hey ? Medico-legal expert. Dr. Thorndyke's mantle going to fall on you, sir ? "

" I hope Dr. Thorndyke's mantle will continue to drape his own majestic form for many a long year yet," I answered ; " though he is good enough to spare me a corner—but what on earth have you got there ? " For during this dialogue the superintendent had been deftly unfastening a brown-paper parcel, from which he now drew a linen shirt, once white, but now of an unsavoury grey.

" I want to know what this is," said Miller, exhibiting a brownish-red stain on one sleeve. " Just look at that, sir, and tell me if it is blood, and, if so, is it human blood ? "

" Really, Miller," said Thorndyke, with a smile, " you flatter me ; but I am not like the wise woman of Bagdad who could tell you how many stairs the patient had tumbled down by merely looking at his tongue. I must examine this very thoroughly before I can give an opinion. When do you want to know ? "

" I should like to know to-night," replied the detective.

" Can I cut a piece out to put under the microscope ? "

" I would rather you did not," was the reply.

" Very well ; you shall have the information in about an hour."

" It's very good of you, doctor," said the detective ; and he was taking up his hat preparatory to departing, when Thorndyke said suddenly—

" By the way, there is a little matter that I was going to speak to you about. It refers to this Camberwell Murder case. I understand you have a clue to the identity of the murderer ? "

" Clue ! " exclaimed the superintendent contemptuously. " We have spotted our man all right, if we could only lay hands on him ; but he has given us the slip for the moment."

" Who is the man ? " asked Thorndyke.

The detective looked doubtfully at Thorndyke for some seconds and then said, with evident reluctance ; " I suppose there is no harm in telling you—especially

as you probably know already "—this with a sly grin ;
" it's an old crook named Belfield."

" And what is the evidence against him ? "

Again the superintendent looked doubtful and again
relented.

" Why, the case is as clear as—as cold Scotch," he
said (here Thorndyke in illustration of this figure of
speech produced a decanter, a syphon and a tumbler,
which he pushed towards the officer). " You see, sir,
the silly fool went and stuck his sweaty hand on the
window ; and there we found the marks—four fingers
and a thumb, as beautiful prints as you could wish to
see. Of course we cut out the piece of glass and took
it up to the Finger-print Department ; they turned up
their files and out came Mr. Belfield's record, with his
finger-prints and photograph all complete."

" And the finger-prints on the window-pane were
identical with those on the prison form ? "

" Identical. All five prints of the right hand."

" Hm ! " Thorndyke reflected for a while, and the
superintendent watched him foxily over the edge of his
tumbler.

" I guess you are retained to defend Belfield," the
latter observed presently.

" To look into the case generally," replied Thorndyke.

" And I expect you know where the beggar is hiding,"
continued the detective.

" Belfield's address has not yet been communicated
to me," said Thorndyke. " I am merely to investigate
the case—and there is no reason, Miller, why you and
I should be at cross purposes. We are both working at
the case ; you want to get a conviction and you want to
convict the right man."

" That's so—and Belfield's the right man—but what
do you want of us, doctor ? "

" I should like to see the piece of glass with the finger-
prints on it, and the prison form, and take a photograph
of each. And I should like to examine the room in

which the murder took place—you have it locked up, I suppose ? "

" Yes, we have the keys. Well, it's all rather irregular, letting you see the things. Still, you've always played the game fairly with us, so we might stretch a point. Yes, I will. I'll come back in an hour for your report and bring the glass and the form. I can't let them go out of my custody, you know. I'll be off now—no, thank you, not another drop."

The superintendent caught up his hat and strode away, the personification of mental alertness and bodily vigour.

No sooner had the door closed behind him than Thorndyke's stolid calm changed instantaneously into feverish energy. Darting to the electric bell that rang into the laboratories above, he pressed the button while he gave me my directions.

" Have a look at that blood-stain, Jervis, while I am finishing with Belfield. Don't wet it ; scrape it into a drop of warm normal saline solution."

I hastened to reach down the microscope and set out on the table the necessary apparatus and reagents, and, as I was thus occupied, a latch-key turned in the outer door and our invaluable helpmate, Polton, entered the room in his habitual silent, unobtrusive fashion.

" Let me have the finger-print apparatus, please, Polton," said Thorndyke ; " and have the copying camera ready by nine o'clock. I am expecting Mr. Miller with some documents."

As his laboratory assistant departed, Thorndyke rapped at the office door.

" It's all clear, Belfield," he called ; " you can come out."

The key turned and the prisoner emerged, looking ludicrously woebegone in his ridiculous wig and beard.

" I am going to take your finger-prints, to compare with some that the police found on the window."

" Finger-prints ! " exclaimed Belfield, in a tone of

dismay. "They don't say they're my finger-prints, do they, sir ?"

"They do indeed," replied Thorndyke, eyeing the man narrowly. "They have compared them with those taken when you were at Holloway, and they say that they are identical."

"Good God!" murmured Belfield, collapsing into a chair, faint and trembling. "They must have made some awful mistake. But are mistakes possible with finger-prints ?"

"Now look here, Belfield," said Thorndyke. "Were you in that house that night, or were you not ? It is of no use for you to tell me any lies."

"I was not there, sir ; I swear to God I was not."

"Then they cannot be your finger-prints, that is obvious." Here he stepped to the door to intercept Polton, from whom he received a substantial box, which he brought in and placed on the table.

"Tell me all you know about this case," he continued, as he set out the contents of the box on the table.

"I know nothing about it whatever," replied Belfield ; "nothing, at least, except——"

"Except what ?" demanded Thorndyke, looking up sharply as he squeezed a drop from a tube of finger-print ink on to a smooth copper plate.

"Except that the murdered man, Caldwell, was a retired fence."

"A fence, was he ?" said Thorndyke in a tone of interest.

"Yes ; and I suspect he was a nark too. He knew more than was wholesome for a good many."

"Did he know anything about you ?"

"Yes ; but nothing that the police don't know."

With a small roller Thorndyke spread the ink upon the plate into a thin film. Then he laid on the edge of the table a smooth white card and, taking Belfield's right hand, pressed the forefinger firmly but quickly, first on the inked plate and then on the card, leaving on the latter a clear print of the finger-tip. This process he repeated with the other fingers and thumb, and then took several additional prints of each.

"That was a nasty injury to your forefinger, Belfield," said Thorndyke, holding the finger to the light and examining the tip carefully. "How did you do it?"

"Stuck a tin-opener into it—a dirty one, too. It was bad for weeks; in fact, Dr. Sampson thought at one time that he would have to amputate the finger."

"How long ago was that?"

"Oh, nearly a year ago, sir."

Thorndyke wrote the date of the injury by the side of the finger-print and then, having rolled up the inking plate afresh, laid on the table several larger cards.

"I am now going to take the prints of the four fingers and the thumb all at once," he said.

"They only took the four fingers at once at the prison," said Belfield. "They took the thumb separately."

"I know," replied Thorndyke; "but I am going to take the impression just as it would appear on the window glass."

He took several impressions thus, and then, having looked at his watch, he began to repack the apparatus in its box. While doing this, he glanced, from time to time, in meditative fashion, at the suspected man, who sat, the living picture of misery and terror, wiping the greasy ink from his trembling fingers with his handkerchief.

"Belfield," he said at length, "you have sworn to me that you are an innocent man and are trying to live an honest life. I believe you; but in a few minutes I shall know for certain."

"Thank God for that, sir," exclaimed Belfield, brightening up wonderfully.

"And now," said Thorndyke, "you had better go back into the office, for I am expecting Superintendent Miller, and he may be here at any moment."

Belfield hastily slunk back into the office, locking the door after him, and Thorndyke, having returned the box to the laboratory and deposited the cards bearing the finger-prints in a drawer, came round to inspect my work. I had managed to detach a tiny fragment of dried clot from the bloodstained garment, and this, in a drop of normal saline solution, I now had under the microscope.

" What do you make out, Jervis ? " my colleague asked.

" Oval corpuscles with distinct nuclei," I answered.

" Ah," said Thorndyke, " that will be good hearing for some poor devil. Have you measured them ? "

" Yes. Long diameter $\frac{1}{2100}$ of an inch ; short diameter about $\frac{1}{3400}$."

Thorndyke reached down an indexed note-book from a shelf of reference volumes and consulted a table of histological measurements.

" That would seem to be the blood of a pheasant, then, or it might, more probably, be that of a common fowl." He applied his eye to the microscope and, fitting in the eye-piece micrometer, verified my measurements. He was thus employed when a sharp tap was heard on the outer door, and rising to open it he admitted the superintendent.

" I see you are at work on my little problem, doctor," said the latter, glancing at the microscope. " What do you make of that stain ? "

" It is the blood of a bird—probably a pheasant, or perhaps a common fowl."

The superintendent slapped his thigh. " Well, I'm hanged ! " he exclaimed, " you're a regular wizard, doctor, that's what you are. The fellow said he got that stain through handling a wounded pheasant, and here are you able to tell us yes or no without a hint from us to help you. Well, you've done my little job for me, sir, and I'm much obliged to you ; now I'll carry out my part of the bargain." He opened a hand-bag and drew forth a wooden frame and a blue foolscap envelope and laid them with extreme care on the table.

" There you are, sir," said he, pointing to the frame ; " you will find Mr. Belfield's trade-mark very neatly executed, and in the envelope is the finger-print sheet for comparison."

Thorndyke took up the frame and examined it. It enclosed two sheets of glass, one being the portion of the window-pane and the other a coverglass to protect the finger-prints. Laying a sheet of white paper on the table, where the light was strongest, Thorndyke held the frame over it and gazed at the glass in silence, but with that faint lighting up of his impassive face which I knew so well and which meant so much to me. I walked round, and looking over his shoulder saw upon the glass the beautifully distinct imprints of four fingers and a thumb—the finger-tips, in fact, of an open hand.

After regarding the frame attentively for some time, Thorndyke produced from his pocket a little wash-leather bag, from which he extracted a powerful doublet lens, and with the aid of this he again explored the finger-prints, dwelling especially upon the print of the forefinger.

" I don't think you will find much amiss with those finger-prints, doctor," said the superintendent, " they are as clear as if he had made them on purpose."

" They are indeed," replied Thorndyke, with an inscrutable smile, " exactly as if he had made them on purpose. And how beautifully clean the glass is—as if he had polished it before making the impression."

The superintendent glanced at Thorndyke with quick suspicion ; but the smile had faded and given place to a wooden immobility from which nothing could be gleaned.

When he had examined the glass exhaustively, Thorndyke drew the finger-print form from its envelope and scanned it quickly, glancing repeatedly from the paper to the glass and from the glass to the paper. At length he laid them both on the table, and turning to the detective looked him steadily in the face.

"I think, Miller," said he, "that I can give you a useful hint."

"Indeed, sir? And what might that be?"

"It is this : you are after the wrong man."

The superintendent snorted—not a loud snort, for that would have been rude, and no officer could be more polite than Superintendent Miller. But it conveyed a protest which he speedily followed up in words.

"You don't mean to say that the prints on that glass are not the finger-prints of Frank Belfield?"

"I say that those prints were not made by Frank Belfield," Thorndyke replied firmly.

"Do you admit, sir, that the finger-prints on the official form were made by him?"

"I have no doubt that they were."

"Well, sir, Mr. Singleton, of the Finger-print Depart-ment, has compared the prints on the glass with those on the form and he says they are identical ; and I have examined them and I say they are identical."

"Exactly," said Thorndyke ; "and I have examined them and I say they are identical—and that therefore those on the glass cannot have been made by Belfield."

The superintendent snorted again—somewhat louder this time—and gazed at Thorndyke with wrinkled brows.

"You are not pulling my leg, I suppose, sir?" he asked, a little sourly.

"I should as soon think of tickling a porcupine," Thorndyke answered, with a suave smile.

"Well," rejoined the bewildered detective, "if I didn't know you, sir, I should say you were talking confounded nonsense. Perhaps you wouldn't mind explaining what you mean."

"Supposing," said Thorndyke, "I make it clear to you that those prints on the window-pane were not made by Belfield. Would you still execute the warrant?"

"What do *you* think?" exclaimed Miller. "Do you

suppose we should go into court to have you come and knock the bottom out of our case, like you did in that Hornby affair—by the way, that was a finger-print case too, now I come to think of it," and the superintendent suddenly became thoughtful.

"You have often complained," pursued Thorndyke, "that I have withheld information from you and sprung unexpected evidence on you at the trial. Now I am going to take you into my confidence, and when I have proved to you that this clue of yours is a false one, I shall expect you to let this poor devil Belfield go his way in peace."

The superintendent grunted—a form of utterance that committed him to nothing.

"These prints," continued Thorndyke, taking up the frame once more, "present several features of interest, one of which, at least, ought not to have escaped you and Mr. Singleton, as it seems to have done. Just look at that thumb."

The superintendent did so, and then pored over the official paper. "Well," he said, "I don't see anything the matter with it. It's exactly like the print on the paper."

"Of course it is," rejoined Thorndyke, "and that is just the point. It ought not to be. The print of the thumb on the paper was taken separately from the fingers. And why? Because it was impossible to take it at the same time. The thumb is in a different plane from the fingers ; when the hand is laid flat on any surface—as this window-pane, for instance—the palmar surfaces of the fingers touch it, whereas it is the *side* of the thumb which comes in contact and not the palmar surface. But in this "—he tapped the framed glass with his finger—" the prints show the palmar surfaces of all the five digits in contact at once, which is an impossibility. Just try to put your own thumb in that position and you will see that it is so."

The detective spread out his hand on the table and

immediately perceived the truth of my colleague's statement.

" And what does that prove ? " he asked.

" It proves that the thumb-print on the window-pane was not made at the same time as the finger-prints—that it was added separately ; and that fact seems to prove that the prints were not made accidentally, but—as you ingeniously suggested just now—were put there for a purpose."

" I don't quite see the drift of all this," said the superintendent, rubbing the back of his head perplexedly ; " and you said a while back that the prints on the glass can't be Belfield's because they are identical with the prints on the form. Now that seems to me sheer nonsense, if you will excuse my saying so."

" And yet," replied Thorndyke, " it is the actual fact. Listen : these prints "—here he took up the official sheet—" were taken at Holloway six years ago. These " —pointing to the framed glass—" were made within the present week. The one is, as regards the ridge-pattern, a perfect duplicate of the other. Is that not so ? "

" That is so, doctor," agreed the superintendent.

" Very well. Now suppose I were to tell you that within the last twelve months something had happened to Belfield that made an appreciable change in the ridge-pattern on one of his fingers ? "

" But is such a thing possible ? "

" It is not only possible but it has happened. I will show you."

He brought forth from the drawer the cards on which Belfield had made his finger-prints, and laid them before the detective.

" Observe the prints of the forefinger," he said, indicating them ; " there are a dozen, in all, and you will notice in each a white line crossing the ridges and dividing them. That line is caused by a scar, which has destroyed a portion of the ridges, and is now an integral part of Belfield's finger-print. And since no such blank line is to be seen in this print on the glass—in which the ridges appear perfect, as they were before the injury—it follows that that print could not have been made by Belfield's finger."

" There is no doubt about the injury, I suppose ? "

" None whatever. There is the scar to prove it ; and I can produce the surgeon who attended Belfield at the time."

The officer rubbed his head harder than before, and regarded Thorndyke with puckered brows.

" This is a teaser," he growled, " it is indeed. What you say, sir, seems perfectly sound, and yet—there are those finger-prints on the window-glass. Now you can't get finger-prints without fingers, can you ? "

" Undoubtedly you can," said Thorndyke.

" I should want to see that done before I could believe even you, sir," said Miller.

" You shall see it done now," was the calm rejoinder. " You have evidently forgotten the Hornby case—the case of the Red Thumb-mark, as the newspapers called it."

" I only heard part of it," replied Miller, " and I didn't really follow the evidence in that."

" Well, I will show you a relic of that case," said Thorndyke. He unlocked a cabinet and took from one of the shelves a small box labelled " Hornby," which, being opened, was seen to contain a folded paper, a little red-covered oblong book and what looked like a large boxwood pawn.

" This little book," Thorndyke continued, " is a ' thumbograph '—a sort of finger-print album—I dare say you know the kind of thing."

The superintendent nodded contemptuously at the little volume.

" Now while Dr. Jervis is finding us the print we want I will run up to the laboratory for an inked slab."

He handed me the little book and, as he left the room,

9

I began to turn over the leaves—not without emotion, for it was this very " thumbograph " that first introduced me to my wife, as is related elsewhere—glancing at the various prints above the familiar names and marvelling afresh at the endless variations of pattern that they displayed. At length I came upon two thumbprints of which one—the left—was marked by a longitudinal white line—evidently the trace of a scar ; and underneath them was written the signature " Reuben Hornby."

At this moment Thorndyke re-entered the room carrying the inked slab, which he laid on the table, and, seating himself between the superintendent and me, addressed the former.

" Now, Miller, here are two thumb-prints made by a gentleman named Reuben Hornby. Just glance at the left one ; it is a highly characteristic print."

" Yes," agreed Miller, " one could swear to that from memory, I should think."

" Then look at this." Thorndyke took the paper from the box and, unfolding it, handed it to the detective. It bore a pencilled inscription, and on it were two blood-smears and a very distinct thumb-print in blood. " What do you say to that thumb-print ? "

" Why," answered Miller, " it's this one, of course ; Reuben Hornby's left thumb."

" Wrong, my friend," said Thorndyke. " It was made by an ingenious gentleman named Walter Hornby (whom you followed from the Old Bailey and lost on Ludgate Hill) ; but not with his thumb."

" How, then ? " demanded the superintendent incredulously.

" In this way." Thorndyke took the boxwood " pawn " from its receptacle and pressed its flat base on to the inked slab ; then lifted it and pressed it on to the back of a visiting-card, and again raised it ; and now the card was marked by a very distinct thumb-print.

" My God ! " exclaimed the detective, picking up

the card and viewing it with a stare of dismay, " this is the very devil, sir. This fairly knocks the bottom out of finger-print identification. May I ask, sir, how you made that stamp—for I suppose you did make it ? "

" Yes, we made it here, and the process we used was practically that used by photo-engravers in making line blocks ; that is to say, we photographed one of Mr. Hornby's thumb-prints, printed it on a plate of chrome-gelatine, developed the plate with hot water and this "—here he touched the embossed surface of the stamp—" is what remained. But we could have done it in various other ways ; for instance, with common transfer paper and lithographic stone ; indeed, I assure you, Miller, that there is nothing easier to forge than a finger-print, and it can be done with such perfection that the forger himself cannot tell his own forgery from a genuine original, even when they are placed side by side."

" Well, I'm hanged," grunted the superintendent, " you've fairly knocked me, this time, doctor." He rose gloomily and prepared to depart. " I suppose," he added, " your interest in this case has lapsed, now Belfield's out of it ? "

" Professionally, yes ; but I am disposed to finish the case for my own satisfaction. I am quite curious as to who our too-ingenious friend may be."

Miller's face brightened. " We shall give you every facility, you know—and that reminds me that Singleton gave me these two photographs for you, one of the official paper and one of the prints on the glass. Is there anything more that we can do for you ? "

" I should like to have a look at the room in which the murder took place."

" You shall, doctor ; to-morrow, if you like ; I'll meet you there in the morning at ten, if that will do."

It would do excellently, Thorndyke assured him ; and with this the superintendent took his departure in renewed spirits.

We had only just closed the door when there came a

hurried and urgent tapping upon it, whereupon I once more threw it open, and a quietly-dressed woman in a thick veil, who was standing on the threshold, stepped quickly past me into the room.

"Where is my husband?" she demanded, as I closed the door; and then, catching sight of Thorndyke, she strode up to him with a threatening air and a terrified but angry face.

"What have you done with my husband, sir?" she repeated. "Have you betrayed him, after giving your word? I met a man who looked like a police officer on the stairs."

"Your husband, Mrs. Belfield, is here and quite safe," replied Thorndyke. "He has locked himself in that room," indicating the office.

Mrs. Belfield darted across and rapped smartly at the door. "Are you there, Frank?" she called.

In immediate response the key turned, the door opened and Belfield emerged looking very pale and worn.

"You *have* kept me a long time in there, sir," he said reproachfully.

"It took me a long time to prove to Superintendent Miller that he was after the wrong man. But I succeeded, and now, Belfield, you are free. The charge against you is withdrawn."

Belfield stood for a while as one stupefied, while his wife, after a moment of silent amazement, flung her arms round his neck and burst into tears.

"But how did you know I was innocent, sir?" demanded the bewildered Belfield.

"Ah! how did I? Every man to his trade, you know. Well, I congratulate you, and now go home and have a square meal and get a good night's rest."

He shook hands with his clients—vainly endeavouring to prevent Mrs. Belfield from kissing his hand—and stood at the open door listening until the sound of their retreating footsteps died away.

"A noble little woman, Jervis," said he, as he closed

the door. " In another moment she would have scratched
my face—and I mean to find out the scoundrel who
tried to wreck her happiness."

II. The Ship of the Desert

The case which I am now about to describe has
always appeared to me a singularly instructive one, as
illustrating the value and importance of that fundamental
rule in the carrying out of investigations which Thorndyke
had laid down so emphatically—the rule that all facts,
in any way relating to a case, should be collected im-
partially and without reference to any theory, and each
fact, no matter how trivial or apparently irrelevant,
carefully studied. But I must not anticipate the remarks
of my learned and talented friend on this subject
which I have to chronicle anon ; rather let me proceed
to the case itself.

I had slept at our chambers in King's Bench Walk—
as I commonly did two or three nights a week—and on
coming down to the sitting-room, found Thorndyke's
man, Polton, putting the last touches to the breakfast-
table, while Thorndyke himself· was poring over two
photographs of finger-prints, of which he seemed to be
taking elaborate measurements with a pair of hair-
dividers. He greeted me with his quiet, genial smile
and, laying down the dividers, took his seat at the
breakfast-table.

" You are coming with me this morning, I suppose,"
said he ; " the Camberwell murder case, you know."

" Of course I am if you will have me, but I know
practically nothing of the case. Could you give me an
outline of the facts that are known ? "

Thorndyke looked at me solemnly, but with a mischievous twinkle. " This," he said, " is the old story
of the fox and the crow ; you ' bid me discourse,' and
while I ' enchant thine ear,' you claw to windward with
the broiled ham. A deep-laid plot, my learned brother."

" And such," I exclaimed, " is the result of contact
with the criminal classes ! "

" I am sorry that you regard yourself in that light,"
he retorted, with a malicious smile. " However, with
regard to this case. The facts are briefly these : The
murdered man, Caldwell, who seems to have been
formerly a receiver of stolen goods and probably a police
spy as well, lived a solitary life in a small house with only
an elderly woman to attend him.

" A week ago this woman went to visit a married
daughter and stayed the night with her, leaving Caldwell
alone in the house. When she returned on the following
morning she found her master lying dead on the floor
of his office, or study, in a small pool of blood.

" The police surgeon found that he had been dead
about twelve hours. He had been killed by a single
blow, struck from behind, with some heavy implement,
and a jemmy which lay on the floor beside him fitted the
wound exactly. The deceased wore a dressing-gown
and no collar, and a bedroom candlestick lay upside down
on the floor, although gas was laid on in the room ; and
as the window of the office appears to have been forced
with the jemmy that was found, and there were distinct
footprints on the flower-bed outside the window, the
police think that the deceased was undressing to go to
bed when he was disturbed by the noise of the opening
window ; that he went down to the office and, as he
entered, was struck down by the burglar who was lurking
behind the door. On the window-glass the police found
the greasy impression of an open right hand, and, as
you know, the finger-prints were identified by the
experts as those of an old convict named Belfield. As
you also know, I proved that those finger-prints were,
in reality, forgeries, executed with rubber or gelatine
stamps. That is a general outline of the case."

The close of this recital brought our meal to an end,
and we prepared for our visit to the scene of the crime.
Thorndyke slipped into his pocket his queer outfit—

somewhat like that of a field geologist—locked up the photographs, and we set forth by way of the Embankment.

" The police have no clue, I suppose, to the identity of the murderer, now that the finger-prints have failed ? " I asked, as we strode along together.

" I expect not," he replied, " though they might have if they examined their material. I made out a rather interesting point this morning, which is this : the man who made those sham finger-prints used two stamps, one for the thumb and the other for the four fingers ; and the original from which those stamps were made was the official finger-print form."

" How did you discover that ? " I inquired.

" It was very simple. You remember that Mr. Singleton of the Finger-print Department sent me, by Superintendent Miller, two photographs, one of the prints on the window and one of the official form with Belfield's finger-prints on it. Well, I have compared them and made the most minute measurements of each, and they are obviously duplicates. Not only are all the little imperfections on the form—due to defective inking —reproduced faithfully on the window-pane, but the relative positions of the four fingers in both cases agree to the hundredth of an inch. Of course the thumb stamp was made by taking an oval out of the rolled impression on the form."

" Then do you suggest that this murder was committed by someone connected with the Finger-print Department at Scotland Yard ? "

" Hardly. But someone has had access to the forms. There has been leakage somewhere."

When we arrived at the little detached house in which the murdered man had lived, the door was opened by an elderly woman, and our friend Superintendent Miller greeted us in the hall.

" We are all ready for you, doctor," said he. " Of course, the things have all been gone over once, but we are turning them out more thoroughly now." He led the way into the small, barely-furnished office in which the tragedy had occurred. A dark stain on the carpet and a square hole in one of the window-panes furnished memorials of the crime, which were supplemented by an odd assortment of objects laid out on the newspaper-covered table. These included silver tea-spoons, watches, various articles of jewellery, from which the stones had been removed—none of them of any considerable value —and a roughly-made jemmy.

"I don't know why Caldwell should have kept all these odds and ends," said the detective superintendent. "There is stuff here, that I can identify, from six different burglaries—and not a conviction among the six."

Thorndyke looked over the collection with languid interest; he was evidently disappointed at finding the room so completely turned out.

"Have you any idea what has been taken?" he asked.

"Not the least. We don't even know if the safe was opened. The keys were on the writing-table, so I suppose he went through everything, though I don't see why he left these things if he did. We found them all in the safe."

"Have you powdered the jemmy?"

The superintendent turned very red. "Yes," he growled, "but some half-dozen blithering idiots had handled the thing before I saw it—been trying it on the window, the blighters—so, of course, it showed nothing but the marks of their beastly paws."

"The window had not really been forced, I suppose?" said Thorndyke.

"No," replied Miller, with a glance of surprise at my colleague, "that was a plant; so were the footprints. He must have put on a pair of Caldwell's boots and gone out and made them—unless Caldwell made them himself, which isn't likely."

"Have you found any letter or telegram?"

"A letter making an appointment for nine o'clock

on the night of the murder. No signature or address, and the handwriting evidently disguised."

" Is there anything that furnishes any sort of clue ? "

" Yes, sir, there is. There's this, which we found in the safe." He produced a small parcel which he proceeded to unfasten, looking somewhat queerly at Thorndyke the while. It contained various odds and ends of jewellery, and a smaller parcel formed of a pocket-handkerchief tied with tape. This the detective also unfastened, revealing half-a-dozen silver tea-spoons, all engraved with the same crest, two salt-cellars and a gold locket bearing a monogram. There was also a half-sheet of note-paper on which was written, in a manifestly disguised hand : " These are the goods I told you about.—F. B." But what riveted Thorndyke's attention and mine was the handkerchief itself (which was not a very clean one and was sullied by one or two small bloodstains), for it was marked in one corner with the name " F. Belfield," legibly printed in marking-ink with a rubber stamp.

Thorndyke and the superintendent looked at one another and both smiled.

" I know what you are thinking, sir," said the latter.

" I am sure you do," was the reply, " and it is useless to pretend that you don't agree with me."

" Well, sir," said Miller doggedly, " if that handkerchief has been put there as a plant, it's Belfield's business to prove it. You see, doctor," he added persuasively, " it isn't this job only that's affected. Those spoons, those salt-cellars and that locket are part of the proceeds of the Winchmore Hill burglary, and we want the gentleman who did that crack—we want him very badly."

" No doubt you do," replied Thorndyke, " but this handkerchief won't help you. A sharp counsel—Mr. Anstey, for instance—would demolish it in five minutes. I assure you, Miller, that handkerchief has no evidential value whatever, whereas it might prove an invaluable

9*

instrument of research. The best thing you can do is to hand it over to me and let me see what I can learn from it."

The superintendent was obviously dissatisfied, but he eventually agreed, with manifest reluctance, to Thorndyke's suggestion.

" Very well, doctor," he said ; " you shall have it for a day or two. Do you want the spoons and things as well ? "

" No. Only the handkerchief and the paper that was in it."

The two articles were accordingly handed to him and deposited in a tin box which he usually carried in his pocket, and, after a few more words with the disconsolate detective, we took our departure.

" A very disappointing morning," was Thorndyke's comment as we walked away. " Of course the room ought to have been examined by an expert before anything was moved."

" Have you picked up anything in the way of information ? " I asked.

" Very little excepting confirmation of my original theory. You see, this man Caldwell was a receiver and evidently a police spy. He gave useful information to the police, and they, in return, refrained from inconvenient inquiries. But a spy, or ' nark,' is nearly always a blackmailer too, and the probabilities in this case are that some crook, on whom Caldwell was putting the screw rather too tightly, made an appointment for a meeting when the house was empty, and just knocked Caldwell on the head. The crime was evidently planned beforehand, and the murderer came prepared to kill several birds with one stone. Thus he brought with him the stamps to make the sham finger-prints on the window, and I have no doubt that he also brought this handkerchief and the various oddments of plate and jewellery from those burglaries that Miller is so keen about, and planted them in the safe. You noticed, I suppose, that none of the things were of any value, but all were capable of easy identification ? "

" Yes, I noticed that. His object, evidently, was to put those burglaries as well as the murder on to poor Belfield."

" Exactly. And you see what Miller's attitude is ; Belfield is the bird in the hand, whereas the other man— if there is another—is still in the bush ; so Belfield is to be followed up and a conviction obtained if possible. If he is innocent, that is his affair, and it is for him to prove it."

" And what shall you do next ? " I asked.

" I shall telegraph to Belfield to come and see us this evening. He may be able to tell us something about this handkerchief that, with the clue we already have, may put us on the right track. What time is your consultation ? "

" Twelve-thirty—and here comes my 'bus. I shall be in to lunch." I sprang on to the footboard, and as I took my seat on the roof and looked back at my friend striding along with an easy swing, I knew that he was deep in thought, though automatically attentive to all that was happening around him.

My consultation—it was a lunacy case of some importance—was over in time to allow of my return to our chambers punctually at the luncheon hour ; and as I entered, I was at once struck by something new in Thorndyke's manner—a certain elation and gaiety which I had learned to associate with a point scored successfully in some intricate and puzzling case. He made no confidences, however, and seemed, in fact, inclined to put away, for a time, all his professional cares and business.

" Shall we have an afternoon off, Jervis ? " he said gaily. " It is a fine day and work is slack just now. What say you to the Zoo ? They have a splendid chimpanzee and several specimens of that remarkable fish *Periophthalmos Kölreuteri*. Shall we go ? "

" By all means," I replied ; " and we will mount the elephant, if you like, and throw buns to the grizzly bear and generally renew our youth like the eagle."

But when, an hour later, we found ourselves in the gardens, I began to suspect my friend of some ulterior purpose in this holiday jaunt ; for it was not the chimpanzee or even the wonderful walking fish that attracted his attention. On the contrary, he hung about the vicinity of the lamas and camels in a way that I could not fail to notice ; and even there it appeared to be the sheds and houses rather than the animals themselves that interested him.

" Behold, Jervis," he said presently, as a saddled camel of seedy aspect was led towards its house, " behold the ship of the desert, with raised saloon-deck amidships, fitted internally with watertight compartments and displaying the effects of rheumatoid arthritis in his starboard hip-joint. Let us go and examine him before he hauls into dock." We took a cross-path to intercept the camel on its way to its residence, and Thorndyke moralised as we went.

" It is interesting," he remarked, " to note the way in which these specialised animals, such as the horse, the reindeer and the camel, have been appropriated by man, and their special character made to subserve human needs. Think, for instance, of the part the camel has played in history, in ancient commerce—and modern too, for that matter—and in the diffusion of culture ; and of the rôle he has enacted in war and conquest from the Egyptian campaign of Cambyses down to that of Kitchener. Yes, the camel is a very remarkable animal, though it must be admitted that this particular specimen is a scurvy-looking beast."

The camel seemed to be sensible of these disparaging remarks, for as it approached it saluted Thorndyke with a supercilious grin and then turned away its head.

" Your charge is not as young as he used to be," Thorndyke observed to the man who was leading the animal.

" No, sir, he isn't ; he's getting old, and that's the fact. He shows it too."

" I suppose," said Thorndyke, strolling towards the house by the man's side, " these beasts require a deal of attention ? "

" You're right, sir ; and nasty-tempered brutes they are."

" So I have heard ; but they are interesting creatures, the camels and lamas. Do you happen to know if complete sets of photographs of them are to be had here ? "

" You can get a good many at the lodge, sir," the man replied, " but not all, I think. If you want a complete set, there's one of our men in the camel-house that could let you have them ; he takes the photos himself, and very clever he is at it, too. But he isn't here just now."

" Perhaps you could give me his name so that I could write to him," said Thorndyke.

" Yes, sir. His name is Woodthorpe—Joseph Wood-thorpe. He'll do anything for you to order. Thank you, sir ; good-afternoon, sir ; " and pocketing an unexpected tip, the man led his charge towards its lair.

Thorndyke's absorbing interest in the camelidæ seemed now suddenly to become extinct, and he suffered me to lead him to any part of the gardens that attracted me, showing an impartial interest in all the inmates from the insects to the elephants, and enjoying his holiday— if it was one—with the gaiety and high spirits of a schoolboy. Yet he never let slip a chance of picking up a stray hair or feather, but gathered up each with care, wrapped it in its separate paper, on which was written its description, and deposited it in his tin collecting-box.

" You never know," he remarked, as we turned away from the ostrich enclosure, " when a specimen for comparison may be of vital importance. Here, for instance, is a small feather of a cassowary, and here the hair of a wapiti deer ; now the recognition of either of those might, in certain circumstances, lead to the detection of a criminal or save the life of an innocent man.

The thing has happened repeatedly, and may happen again to-morrow."

" You must have an enormous collection of hairs in your cabinet," I remarked, as we walked home.

" I have," he replied, " probably the largest in the world. And as to other microscopical objects of medico-legal interest, such as dust and mud from different localities and from special industries and manufactures, fibres, food-products and drugs, my collection is certainly unique."

" And you have found your collection useful in your work ? " I asked.

" Constantly. Over and over again I have obtained, by reference to my specimens, the most unexpected evidence, and the longer I practise, the more I become convinced that the microscope is the sheet-anchor of the medical jurist."

" By the way," I said, " you spoke of sending a telegram to Belfield. Did you send it ? "

" Yes. I asked him to come to see me to-night at half-past eight, and, if possible, bring his wife with him. I want to get to the bottom of that handkerchief mystery."

" But do you think he will tell you the truth about it ? "

" That is impossible to judge ; he will be a fool if he does not. But I think he will ; he has a godly fear of me and my methods."

As soon as our dinner was finished and cleared away, Thorndyke produced the " collecting-box " from his pocket and began to sort out the day's " catch," giving explicit directions to Polton for the disposal of each specimen. The hairs and small feathers were to be mounted as microscopic objects, while the larger feathers were to be placed, each in its separate labelled envelope, in its appropriate box. While these directions were being given, I stood by the window absently gazing out as I listened, gathering many a useful hint in the technique of preparation and preservation, and filled with admiration alike at my colleague's exhaustive knowledge of practical detail and the perfect manner in which he had trained his assistant. Suddenly I started, for a well-known figure was crossing from Crown Office Row and evidently bearing down on our chambers.

"My word, Thorndyke," I exclaimed, "here's a pretty mess!"

"What is the matter?" he asked, looking up anxiously.

"Superintendent Miller heading straight for our doorway. And it is now twenty minutes past eight."

Thorndyke laughed. "It will be a quaint position," he remarked, "and somewhat of a shock for Belfield. But it really doesn't matter; in fact, I think, on the whole, I am rather pleased that he should have come."

The superintendent's brisk knock was heard a few moments later, and when he was admitted by Polton, he entered and looked round the room a little sheepishly.

"I am ashamed to come worrying you like this, sir," he began apologetically.

"Not at all," replied Thorndyke, serenely slipping the cassowary's feather into an envelope, and writing the name, date and locality on the outside. "I am your servant in this case, you know. Polton, whisky and soda for the superintendent."

"You see, sir," continued Miller, "our people are beginning to fuss about this case, and they don't approve of my having handed that handkerchief and the paper over to you, as they will have to be put in evidence."

"I thought they might object," remarked Thorndyke.

"So did I, sir; and they do. And, in short, they say that I have got to get them back at once. I hope it won't put you out, sir."

"Not in the least," said Thorndyke. "I have asked Belfield to come here to-night—I expect him in a few minutes—and when I have heard what he has to say I shall have no further use for the handkerchief."

"You're not going to show it to him!" exclaimed the detective, aghast.

" Certainly I am."

" You mustn't do that, sir. I can't sanction it ; I can't indeed."

" Now, look you here, Miller," said Thorndyke, shaking his forefinger at the officer ; " I am working for you in this case, as I have told you. Leave the matter in my hands. Don't raise silly objections ; and when you leave here to-night you will take with you not only the handkerchief and the paper, but probably also the name and address of the man who committed this murder and those various burglaries that you are so keen about."

" Is that really so, sir ? " exclaimed the astonished detective. " Well, you haven't let the grass grow under your feet. Ah ! " as a gentle rap at the door was heard, " here's Belfield, I suppose."

It was Belfield—accompanied by his wife—and mightily disturbed they were when their eyes lighted on our visitor.

" You needn't be afraid of me, Belfield," said Miller, with ferocious geniality ; " I am not here after you." Which was not literally true, though it served to reassure the affrighted ex-convict.

" The superintendent dropped in by chance," said Thorndyke ; " but it is just as well that he should hear what passes. I want you to look at this handkerchief and tell me if it is yours. Don't be afraid, but just tell us the simple truth."

He took the handkerchief out of a drawer and spread it on the table ; and I now observed that a small square had been cut out of one of the blood-stains.

Belfield took the handkerchief in his trembling hands, and as his eye fell on the stamped name in the corner he turned deadly pale.

" It looks like mine," he said huskily. " What do you say, Liz ? " he added, passing it to his wife.

Mrs. Belfeld examined first the name and then the hem. " It's yours, right enough, Frank," said she.

" It's the one that got changed in the wash. You see, sir," she continued, addressing Thorndyke, " I bought him half-a-dozen new ones about six months ago, and I got a rubber stamp made and marked them all. Well, one day when I was looking over his things I noticed that one of his handkerchiefs had got no mark on it. I spoke to the laundress about it, but she couldn't explain it, so as the right one never came back, I marked the one that we got in exchange."

" How long ago was that ? " asked Thorndyke.

" About two months ago I noticed it."

" And you know nothing more about it."

" Nothing whatever, sir. Nor do you, Frank, do you ? "

Her husband shook his head gloomily, and Thorndyke replaced the handkerchief in the drawer.

" And now," said he, " I am going to ask you a question on another subject. When you were at Holloway there was a warder—or assistant warder—there, named Woodthorpe. Do you remember him ? "

" Yes, sir, very well indeed ; in fact, it was him that—— "

" I know," interrupted Thorndyke. " Have you seen him since you left Holloway ? "

" Yes, sir, once. It was last Easter Monday. I met him at the Zoo ; he is a keeper there now in the camel-house " (here a sudden light dawned upon me and I chuckled aloud, to Belfield's great astonishment). " He gave my little boy a ride on one of the camels and made himself very pleasant."

" Do you remember anything else happening ? " Thorndyke inquired.

" Yes, sir. The camel had a little accident ; he kicked out—he was an ill-tempered beast—and his leg hit a post ; there happened to be a nail sticking out from that post, and it tore up a little flap of skin. Then Woodthorpe got out his handkerchief to tie up the wound, but as it was none of the cleanest, I said to him :

' Don't use that, Woodthorpe ; have mine,' which was quite a clean one. So he took it and bound up the camel's leg, and he said to me : ' I'll have it washed and send it to you if you give me your address.' But I told him there was no need for that ; I should be passing the camel-house on my way out and I would look in for the handkerchief. And I did : I looked in about an hour later, and Woodthorpe gave me my handkerchief, folded up but not washed."

" Did you examine it to see if it was yours ? " asked Thorndyke.

" No, sir. I just slipped it in my pocket as it was."

" And what became of it afterwards ? "

" When I got home I dropped it into the dirty-linen basket."

" Is that all you know about it ? "

" Yes, sir ; that is all I know."

" Very well, Belfield, that will do. Now you have no reason to be uneasy. You will soon know all about the Camberwell murder—that is, if you read the papers."

The ex-convict and his wife were obviously relieved by this assurance and departed in quite good spirits. When they were gone, Thorndyke produced the handkerchief and the half-sheet of paper and handed them to the superintendent, remarking—

" This is highly satisfactory, Miller ; the whole case seems to join up very neatly indeed. Two months ago the wife first noticed the substituted handkerchief, and last Easter Monday—a little over two months ago—this very significant incident took place in the Zoological Gardens."

" That is all very well, sir," objected the superintendent, " but we've only their word for it, you know."

" Not so," replied Thorndyke. " We have excellent corroborative evidence. You noticed that I had cut a small piece out of the blood-stained portion of the handkerchief ? "

"Yes; and I was sorry you had done it. Our people won't like that."

"Well, here it is, and we will ask Dr. Jervis to give us his opinion of it."

From the drawer in which the handkerchief had been hidden he brought forth a microscope slide, and setting the microscope on the table, laid the slide on the stage.

"Now, Jervis," he said, "tell us what you see there."

I examined the edge of the little square of fabric (which had been mounted in a fluid reagent) with a high-power objective, and was, for a time, a little puzzled by the appearance of the blood that adhered to it.

"It looks like bird's blood," I said presently, with some hesitation, "but yet I can make out no nuclei." I looked again, and then, suddenly, "By Jove!" I exclaimed, "I have it; of course! It's the blood of a camel!"

"Is that so, doctor?" demanded the detective, leaning forward in his excitement.

"That is so," replied Thorndyke. "I discovered it after I came home this morning. You see," he explained, "it is quite unmistakable. The rule is that the blood-corpuscles of mammals are circular; the one exception is the camel family, in which the corpuscles are elliptical."

"Why," exclaimed Miller, "that seems to connect Woodthorpe with this Camberwell job."

"It connects him with it very conclusively," said Thorndyke. "You are forgetting the finger-prints."

The detective looked puzzled. "What about them?" he asked.

"They were made with stamps—two stamps, as a matter of fact—and those stamps were made by photographic process from the official finger-print form. I can prove that beyond all doubt."

"Well, suppose they were. What then?"

Thorndyke opened a drawer and took out a photograph, which he handed to Miller. "Here," he said, "is the photograph of the official finger-print form which you were kind enough to bring me. What does it say at the bottom there ? " and he pointed with his finger.

The superintendent read aloud : " Impressions taken by Joseph Woodthorpe. Rank, Warder ; Prison, Holloway." He stared at the photograph for a moment, and then exclaimed—

" Well, I'm hanged ! You *have* worked this out neatly, doctor ! and so quick too. We'll have Mr. Woodthorpe under lock and key the first thing to-morrow morning. But how did he do it, do you think ? "

" He might have taken duplicate finger-prints and kept one form ; the prisoners would not know there was anything wrong ; but he did not in this case. He must have contrived to take a photograph of the form before sending it in—it would take a skilful photographer only a minute or two with a suitable hand-camera placed on a table at the proper distance from the wall ; and I have ascertained that he is a skilful photographer. You will probably find the apparatus, and the stamps too, when you search his rooms."

" Well, well. You do give us some surprises, doctor. But I must be off now to see about this warrant. Good-night, sir, and many thanks for your help."

When the superintendent had gone we sat for a while looking at one another in silence. At length Thorndyke spoke. " Here is a case, Jervis," he said, " which, simple as it is, teaches a most invaluable lesson—a lesson which you should take well to heart. It is this : *The evidential value of any fact is an unknown quantity until the fact has been examined.* That seems a self-evident truth, but like many other self-evident truths, it is constantly overlooked in practice. Take this present case. When I left Caldwell's house this morning the facts in my possession were these : (1) The man who murdered Caldwell was directly or indirectly connected with the Finger-print Department. (2) He was almost certainly a skilled photographer. (3) He probably committed the Winchmore Hill and the other burglaries.

(4) He was known to Caldwell, had had professional dealings with him and was probably being blackmailed. This was all ; a very vague clue, as you see.

" There was the handkerchief, planted as I had no doubt, but could not prove ; the name stamped on it was Belfield's, but anyone can get a rubber stamp made. Then it was stained with blood, as handkerchiefs often are ; that blood might or might not be human blood ; it did not seem to matter a straw whether it was or not. Nevertheless, I said to myself : If it is human or at least mammalian blood, that is a fact ; and if it is not human blood, that is also a fact. I will have that fact, and then I shall know what its value is. I examined the stain when I reached home, and behold ! it was camel's blood ; and immediately this insignificant fact swelled up into evidence of primary importance. The rest was obvious. I had seen Woodthorpe's name on the form, and I knew several other officials. My business was to visit all places in London where there were camels, to get the names of all persons connected with them and to ascertain if any among them was a photographer. Naturally I went first to the Zoo, and at the very first cast hooked Joseph Woodthorpe. Wherefore I say again : Never call any fact irrelevant until you have examined it."

The remarkable evidence given above was not heard at the trial, nor did Thorndyke's name appear among the witnesses ; for when the police searched Woodthorpe's rooms, so many incriminating articles were found (including a pair of finger-print stamps which exactly answered to Thorndyke's description of them, and a number of photographs of finger-print forms) that his guilt was put beyond all doubt ; and society was shortly after relieved of a very undesirable member.

8

THE contrariety of human nature is a subject that has given a surprising amount of occupation to makers of proverbs and to those moral philosophers who make it their province to discover and expound the glaringly obvious ; and especially have they been concerned to enlarge upon that form of perverseness which engenders dislike of things offered under compulsion, and arouses desire of them as soon as their attainment becomes difficult or impossible. They assure us that a man who has had a given thing within his reach and put it by, will, as soon as it is beyond his reach, find it the one thing necessary and desirable ; even as the domestic cat which has turned disdainfully from the proffered saucer, may presently be seen with her head jammed hard in the milk-jug, or, secretly and with horrible relish, slaking her thirst at the scullery sink.

To this peculiarity of the human mind was due, no doubt, the fact that no sooner had I abandoned the clinical side of my profession in favour of the legal, and taken up my abode in the chambers of my friend Thorndyke, the famous medico-legal expert, to act as his assistant or junior, than my former mode of life— that of a locum tenens, or minder of other men's practices—which had, when I was following it, seemed intolerably irksome, now appeared to possess many desirable features ; and I found myself occasionally hankering to sit once more by the bedside, to puzzle out the perplexing train of symptoms, and to wield that power—the greatest, after all, possessed by man— the power to banish suffering and ward off the approach of death itself.

Hence it was that on a certain morning of the long vacation I found myself installed at The Larches, Burling, in full charge of the practice of my old friend Dr. Hanshaw, who was taking a fishing holiday in

Norway. I was not left desolate, however, for Mrs. Hanshaw remained at her post, and the roomy, old-fashioned house accommodated three visitors in addition. One of these was Dr. Hanshaw's sister, a Mrs. Haldean, the widow of a wealthy Manchester cotton factor ; the second was her niece by marriage, Miss Lucy Haldean, a very handsome and charming girl of twenty-three ; while the third was no less a person than Master Fred, the only child of Mrs. Haldean, and a strapping boy of six.

" It is quite like old times—and very pleasant old times, too—to see you sitting at our breakfast-table, Dr. Jervis." With these gracious words and a friendly smile, Mrs. Hanshaw handed me my tea-cup.

I bowed. " The highest pleasure of the altruist," I replied, " is in contemplating the good fortune of others."

Mrs. Haldean laughed. " Thank you," she said. " You are quite unchanged, I perceive. Still as suave and as—shall I say oleaginous ? "

" No, please don't ! " I exclaimed in a tone of alarm.

" Then I won't. But what does Dr. Thorndyke say to this backsliding on your part ? How does he regard this relapse from medical jurisprudence to common general practice ? "

" Thorndyke," said I, " is unmoved by any catastrophe ; and he not only regards the ' Decline and Fall-off of the Medical Jurist ' with philosophic calm, but he even favours the relapse, as you call it. He thinks it may be useful to me to study the application of medico-legal methods to general practice."

" That sounds rather unpleasant—for the patients, I mean," remarked Miss Haldean.

" Very," agreed her aunt. " Most cold-blooded. What sort of man is Dr. Thorndyke ? I feel quite curious about him. Is he at all human, for instance ? "

" He is entirely human," I replied ; " the accepted tests of humanity being, as I understand, the habitual adoption of the erect posture in locomotion, and the relative position of the end of the thumb——"

" I don't mean that," interrupted Mrs. Haldean. " I mean human in things that matter."

" I think those things matter," I rejoined. " Consider, Mrs. Haldean, what would happen if my learned colleague were to be seen in wig and gown, walking towards the Law Courts in any posture other than the erect. It would be a public scandal."

" Don't talk to him, Mabel," said Mrs. Hanshaw ; " he is incorrigible. What are you doing with yourself this morning, Lucy ? "

Miss Haldean (who had hastily set down her cup to laugh at my imaginary picture of Dr. Thorndyke in the character of a quadruped) considered a moment.

" I think I shall sketch that group of birches at the edge of Bradham Wood," she said.

" Then, in that case," said I, " I can carry your traps for you, for I have to see a patient in Bradham."

" He is making the most of his time," remarked Mrs. Haldean maliciously to my hostess. " He knows that when Mr. Winter arrives he will retire into the extreme background."

Douglas Winter, whose arrival was expected in the course of the week, was Miss Haldean's fiancé. Their engagement had been somewhat protracted, and was likely to be more so, unless one of them received some unexpected accession of means ; for Douglas was a subaltern in the Royal Engineers, living, with great difficulty, on his pay, while Lucy Haldean subsisted on an almost invisible allowance left her by an uncle.

I was about to reply to Mrs. Haldean when a patient was announced, and, as I had finished my breakfast, I made my excuses and left the table.

Half an hour later, when I started along the road to the village of Bradham, I had two companions. Master Freddy had joined the party, and he disputed with me the privilege of carrying the " traps," with the result that a compromise was effected, by which he carried the camp-stool, leaving me in possession of the easel, the bag, and a large bound sketching-block.

" Where are you going to work this morning ? " I asked, when we had trudged on some distance.

" Just off the road to the left there, at the edge of the wood. Not very far from the house of the mysterious stranger." She glanced at me mischievously as she made this reply, and chuckled with delight when I rose at the bait.

" What house do you mean ? " I inquired.

" Ha ! " she exclaimed. " the investigator of mysteries is aroused. He saith, ' Ha ! ha ! ' amidst the trumpets ; he smelleth the battle afar off."

" Explain instantly," I commanded, " or I drop your sketch-block into the very next puddle."

" You terrify me," said she. " But I will explain, only there isn't any mystery except to the bucolic mind. The house is called Lavender Cottage, and it stands alone in the fields behind the wood. A fortnight ago it was let furnished to a stranger named Whitelock, who has taken it for the purpose of studying the botany of the district ; and the only really mysterious thing about him is that no one has seen him. All arrangements with the house-agent were made by letter, and, as far as I can make out, none of the local tradespeople supply him, so he must get his things from a distance—even his bread, which really is rather odd. Now say I am an inquisitive, gossiping country bumpkin."

" I was going to," I answered, " but it is no use now."

She relieved me of her sketching appliances with pretended indignation, and crossed into the meadow, leaving me to pursue my way alone ; and when I presently looked back, she was setting up her easel and stool, gravely assisted by Freddy.

My " round," though not a long one, took up more

time than I had anticipated, and it was already past
the luncheon hour when I passed the place where I
had left Miss Haldean. She was gone, as I had expected, and I hurried homewards, anxious to be as
nearly punctual as possible. When I entered the
dining-room, I found Mrs. Haldean and our hostess
seated at the table, and both looked up at me expectantly.

" Have you seen Lucy ? " the former inquired.

" No," I answered. " Hasn't she come back ? I
expected to find her here. She had left the wood
when I passed just now."

Mrs. Haldean knitted her brows anxiously. " It
is very strange," she said, " and very thoughtless of
her. Freddy will be famished."

I hurried over my lunch, for two fresh messages had
come in from outlying hamlets, effectually dispelling
my visions of a quiet afternoon ; and as the minutes
passed without bringing any signs of the absentees,
Mrs. Haldean became more and more restless and
anxious. At length her suspense became unbearable ;
she rose suddenly, announcing her intention of cycling
up the road to look for the defaulters, but as she was
moving towards the door, it burst open, and Lucy
Haldean staggered into the room.

Her appearance filled us with alarm. She was
deadly pale, breathless, and wild-eyed ; her dress
was draggled and torn, and she trembled from head
to foot.

" Good God, Lucy ! " gasped Mrs. Haldean. " What
has happened ? And where is Freddy ? " she added in
a sterner tone.

" He is lost ! " replied Miss Haldean in a faint voice,
and with a catch in her breath. " He strayed away
while I was painting. I have searched the wood
through, and called to him, and looked in all the
meadows. Oh ! where can he have gone ? " Her
-ketching " kit," with which she was loaded, slipped

from her grasp and rattled on to the floor, and she buried her face in her hands and sobbed hysterically.

" And you have dared to come back without him ? " exclaimed Mrs. Haldean.

" I was getting exhausted. I came back for help," was the faint reply.

" Of course she was exhausted," said Mrs. Hanshaw. " Come, Lucy : come, Mabel ; don't make mountains out of molehills. The little man is safe enough. We shall find him presently, or he will come home by himself. Come and have some food, Lucy."

Miss Haldean shook her head. " I can't, Mrs. Hanshaw—really I can't," she said ; and seeing that she was in a state of utter exhaustion, I poured out a glass of wine and made her drink it.

Mrs. Haldean darted from the room, and returned immediately, putting on her hat. " You have got to come with me and show me where you lost him," she said.

" She can't do that, you know," I said rather brusquely. " She will have to lie down for the present. But I know the place, and will cycle up with you."

" Very well," replied Mrs. Haldean, " that will do. What time was it," she asked, turning to her niece, " when you lost the child ? and which way——"

She paused abruptly, and I looked at her in surprise. She had suddenly turned ashen and ghastly ; her face had set like a mask of stone, with parted lips and staring eyes that were fixed in horror on her niece.

There was a deathly silence for a few seconds. Then, in a terrible voice, she demanded : " What is that on your dress, Lucy ? " And, after a pause, her voice rose into a shriek. " What have you done to my boy ? "

I glanced in astonishment at the dazed and terrified girl, and then I saw what her aunt had seen—a good-sized blood-stain halfway down the front of her skirt, and another smaller one on her right sleeve. The girl herself looked down at the sinister patch of red and then

up at her aunt. " It looks like—like blood," she
stammered. " Yes, it is—I think—of course it is.
He struck his nose—and it bled——"

" Come," interrupted Mrs. Haldean, " let us go,"
and she rushed from the room, leaving me to follow.

I lifted Miss Haldean, who was half fainting with
fatigue and agitation, on to the sofa, and, whispering
a few words of encouragement into her ear, turned to
Mrs. Hanshaw.

" I can't stay with Mrs. Haldean," I said. " There
are two visits to be made at Rebworth. Will you
send the dogcart up the road with somebody to take
my place ? "

" Yes," she answered. " I will send Giles, or come
myself if Lucy is fit to be left."

I ran to the stables for my bicycle, and as I pedalled
out into the road I could see Mrs. Haldean already far
ahead, driving her machine at frantic speed. I followed at a rapid pace, but it was not until we approached
the commencement of the wood, when she slowed down
somewhat, that I overtook her.

" This is the place," I said, as we reached the spot
where I had parted from Miss Haldean. We dis-
mounted and wheeled our bicycles through the gate,
and, laying them down beside the hedge, crossed the
meadow and entered the wood.

It was a terrible experience, and one that I shall
never forget—the white-faced, distracted woman,
tramping in her flimsy house-shoes over the rough
ground, bursting through the bushes, regardless of
the thorny branches that dragged at skin and hair
and dainty clothing, and sending forth from time to
time a tremulous cry, so dreadfully pathetic in its
mingling of terror and coaxing softness, that a lump
rose in my throat, and I could barely keep my self-
control.

" Freddy ! Freddy-boy ! Mummy's here, darling ! "
The wailing cry sounded through the leafy solitude ;

but no answer came save the whirr of wings or the chatter of startled birds. But even more shocking than that terrible cry—more disturbing and eloquent with dreadful suggestion—was the way in which she peered, furtively, but with fearful expectation, among the roots of the bushes, or halted to gaze upon every molehill and hummock, every depression or disturbance of the ground.

So we stumbled on for a while, with never a word spoken, until we came to a beaten track or footpath leading across the wood. Here I paused to examine the footprints, of which several were visible in the soft earth, though none seemed very recent ; but, proceeding a little way down the track, I perceived, crossing it, a set of fresh imprints, which I recognised at once as Miss Haldean's. She was wearing, as I knew, a pair of brown golf-boots, with rubber pads in the leather soles, and the prints made by them were unmistakable.

" Miss Haldean crossed the path here," I said, pointing to the footprints.

" Don't speak of her before me ! " exclaimed Mrs. Haldean ; but she gazed eagerly at the footprints, nevertheless, and immediately plunged into the wood to follow the tracks.

" You are very unjust to your niece, Mrs. Haldean," I ventured to protest.

She halted, and faced me with an angry frown.

" You don't understand ! " she exclaimed. " You don't know, perhaps, that if my poor child is really dead, Lucy Haldean will be a rich woman, and may marry to-morrow if she chooses ? "

" I did not know that," I answered, " but if I had, I should have said the same."

" Of course you would," she retorted bitterly. " A pretty face can muddle any man's judgment."

She turned away abruptly to resume her pursuit, and I followed in silence. The trail which we were following zigzagged through the thickest part of the

wood, but its devious windings eventually brought us
out on to an open space on the farther side. Here
we at once perceived traces of another kind. A litter
of dirty rags, pieces of paper, scraps of stale bread,
bones and feathers, with hoof-marks, wheel ruts, and
the ashes of a large wood fire, pointed clearly to a
gipsy encampment recently broken up. I laid my
hand on the heap of ashes, and found it still warm,
and on scattering it with my foot a layer of glowing
cinders appeared at the bottom.

"These people have only been gone an hour or
two," I said. "It would be well to have them followed without delay."

A gleam of hope shone on the drawn, white face as
the bereaved mother caught eagerly at my suggestion.

"Yes," she exclaimed breathlessly; "she may have
bribed them to take him away. Let us see which way
they went."

We followed the wheel tracks down to the road, and
found that they turned towards London. At the same
time I perceived the dogcart in the distance, with
Mrs. Hanshaw standing beside it; and, as the coachman observed me, he whipped up his horse and
approached.

"I shall have to go," I said, "but Mrs. Hanshaw
will help you to continue the search."

"And you will make inquiries about the gipsies,
won't you?" she said.

I promised to do so, and as the dogcart now came
up, I climbed to the seat, and drove off briskly up the
London Road.

The extent of a country doctor's round is always an
unknown quantity. On the present occasion I picked
up three additional patients, and as one of them was
a case of incipient pleurisy, which required to have the
chest strapped, and another was a neglected dislocation
of the shoulder, a great deal of time was taken up.
Moreover, the gipsies, whom I ran to earth on Reb-

worth Common, delayed me considerably, though I
had to leave the rural constable to carry out the actual
search, and, as a result, the clock of Burling Church
was striking six as I drove through the village on my
way home.

I got down at the front gate, leaving the coachman
to take the dogcart round, and walked up the drive;
and my astonishment may be imagined when, on turning the corner, I came suddenly upon the inspector of
the local police in earnest conversation with no less a
person than John Thorndyke.

"What on earth has brought you here?" I exclaimed,
my surprise getting the better of my manners.

"The ultimate motive-force," he replied, "was an
impulsive lady named Mrs. Haldean. She telegraphed
for me—in your name."

"She oughtn't to have done that," I said.

"Perhaps not. But the ethics of an agitated woman
are not worth discussing, and she has done something
much worse—she has applied to the local J.P. (a retired
Major-General), and our gallant and unlearned friend
has issued a warrant for the arrest of Lucy Haldean on
the charge of murder."

"But there has been no murder!" I exclaimed.

"That," said Thorndyke, "is a legal subtlety that
he does not appreciate. He has learned his law in the
orderly-room, where the qualifications to practise are
an irritable temper and a loud voice. However,
the practical point is, inspector, that the warrant is
irregular. You can't arrest people for hypothetical
crimes."

The officer drew a deep breath of relief. He knew
all about the irregularity, and now joyfully took refuge
behind Thorndyke's great reputation.

When he had departed—with a brief note from my
colleague to the General—Thorndyke slipped his arm
through mine, and we strolled towards the house.

"This is a grim business, Jervis," said he. "That

boy has got to be found for everybody's sake. Can you come with me when you have had some food ? "

" Of course I can.   I have been saving myself all the afternoon with a view to continuing the search."

" Good," said Thorndyke. " Then come in and feed."

A nondescript meal, half tea and half dinner, was already prepared, and Mrs. Hanshaw, grave but self-possessed, presided at the table.

" Mabel is still out with Giles, searching for the boy," she said.   " You have heard what she has done ? "

I nodded.

" It was dreadful of her," continued Mrs. Hanshaw, " but she is half mad, poor thing.   You might run up and say a few kind words to poor Lucy while I make the tea."

I went up at once and knocked at Miss Haldean's door, and, being bidden to enter, found her lying on the sofa, red-eyed and pale, the very ghost of the merry, laughing girl who had gone out with me in the morning.   I drew up a chair, and sat down by her side, and as I took the hand she held out to me, she said :

" It is good of you to come and see a miserable wretch like me.   And Jane has been so sweet to me, Dr. Jervis ; but Aunt Mabel thinks I have killed Freddy—you know she does—and it was really my fault that he was lost.   I shall never forgive myself ! "

She burst into a passion of sobbing, and I proceeded to chide her gently.

" You are a silly little woman," I said, " to take this nonsense to heart as you are doing.   Your aunt is not responsible just now, as you must know ; but when we bring the boy home she shall make you a handsome apology.   I will see to that."

She pressed my hand gratefully, and as the bell now rang for tea, I bade her have courage and went downstairs.

"You need not trouble about the practice," said Mrs. Hanshaw, as I concluded my lightning repast, and Thorndyke went off to get our bicycles. "Dr. Symons has heard of our trouble, and has called to say that he will take anything that turns up ; so we shall expect you when we see you."

"How do you like Thorndyke ? " I asked.

"He is quite charming," she replied enthusiastically ; "so tactful and kind, and so handsome, too. You didn't tell us that. But here he is. Goodbye, and good luck."

She pressed my hand, and I went out into the drive, where Thorndyke and the coachman were standing with three bicycles.

"I see you have brought your outfit," I said as we turned into the road ; for Thorndyke's machine bore a large canvas-covered case strapped on to a strong bracket.

"Yes ; there are many things that we may want on a quest of this kind. How did you find Miss Haldean ? "

"Very miserable, poor girl. By the way, have you heard anything about her pecuniary interest in the child's death ? "

"Yes," said Thorndyke. "It appears that the late Mr. Haldean used up all his brains on his business, and had none left for the making of his will—as often happens. He left almost the whole of his property—about eighty thousand pounds—to his son, the widow to have a life-interest in it. He also left to his late brother's daughter, Lucy, fifty pounds a year, and to his surviving brother Percy, who seems to have been a good-for-nothing, a hundred a year for life. But—and here is the utter folly of the thing—if the son should die, the property was to be equally divided between the brother and the niece, with the exception of five hundred a year for life to the widow. It was an insane arrangement."

10

" Quite," I agreed, " and a very dangerous one for Lucy Haldean, as things are at present."

" Very ; especially if anything should have happened to the child."

" What are you going to do now ? " I inquired, seeing that Thorndyke rode on as if with a definite purpose.

" There is a footpath through the wood," he replied. " I want to examine that. And there is a house behind the wood which I should like to see."

" The house of the mysterious stranger," I suggested.

" Precisely. Mysterious and solitary strangers invite inquiry."

We drew up at the entrance to the footpath, leaving Willett the coachman in charge of the three machines, and proceeded up the narrow track. As we went, Thorndyke looked back at the prints of our feet, and nodded approvingly.

" This soft loam," he remarked, " yields beautifully clear impressions, and yesterday's rain has made it perfect."

We had not gone far when we perceived a set of footprints which I recognised, as did Thorndyke also, for he remarked : " Miss Haldean—running, and alone." Presently we met them again, crossing in the opposite direction, together with the prints of small shoes with very high heels. " Mrs. Haldean on the track of her niece," was Thorndyke's comment ; and a minute later we encountered them both again, accompanied by my own footprints.

" The boy does not seem to have crossed the path at all," I remarked as we walked on, keeping off the track itself to avoid confusing the footprints.

" We shall know when we have examined the whole length," replied Thorndyke, plodding on with his eyes on the ground. " Ha ! here is something new," he added, stopping short and stooping down eagerly—" a man with a thick stick—a smallish man, rather lame.

Notice the difference between the two feet, and the peculiar way in which he uses his stick. Yes, Jervis, there is a great deal to interest us in these footprints. Do you notice anything very suggestive about them ? "

" Nothing but what you have mentioned," I replied. " What do you mean ? "

" Well, first there is the very singular character of the prints themselves, which we will consider presently. You observe that this man came down the path, and at this point turned off into the wood ; then he returned from the wood and went up the path again. The imposition of the prints makes that clear. But now look at the two sets of prints, and compare them. Do you notice any difference ? "

" The returning footprints seem more distinct— better impressions."

" Yes ; they are noticeably deeper. But there is something else." He produced a spring tape from his pocket, and took half a dozen measurements. " You see," he said, " the first set of footprints have a stride of twenty-one inches from heel to heel—a short stride ; but he is a smallish man, and lame ; the returning ones have a stride of only nineteen and a half inches ; hence the returning footprints are deeper than the others, and the steps are shorter. What do you make of that ? "

" It would suggest that he was carrying a burden when he returned," I replied.

" Yes ; and a heavy one, to make that difference in the depth. I think I will get you to go and fetch Willett and the bicycles."

I strode off down the path to the entrance, and, taking possession of Thorndyke's machine, with its precious case of instruments, bade Willett follow with the other two.

When I returned, my colleague was standing with his hands behind him, gazing with intense preoccupation at the footprints. He looked up sharply as we approached, and called out to us to keep off the path if possible.

" Stay here with the machines, Willett," said he. " You and I, Jervis, must go and see where our friend went to when he left the path, and what was the burden that he picked up."

We struck off into the wood, where last year's dead leaves made the footprints almost indistinguishable, and followed the faint double track for a long distance between the dense clumps of bushes. Suddenly my eye caught, beside the double trail, a third row of tracks, smaller in size and closer together. Thorndyke had seen them, too, and already his measuring-tape was in his hand.

" Eleven and a half inches to the stride," said he. " That will be the boy, Jervis. But the light is getting weak. We must press on quickly, or we shall lose it."

Some fifty yards farther on, the man's tracks ceased abruptly, but the small ones continued alone ; and we followed them as rapidly as we could in the fading light.

" There can be no reasonable doubt that these are the child's tracks," said Thorndyke ; " but I should like to find a definite footprint to make the identification absolutely certain."

A few seconds later he halted with an exclamation, and stooped on one knee. A little heap of fresh earth from the surface-burrow of a mole had been thrown up over the dead leaves ; and fairly planted on it was the clean and sharp impression of a diminutive foot, with a rubber heel showing a central star. Thorndyke drew from his pocket a tiny shoe, and pressed it on the soft earth beside the footprint ; and when he raised it the second impression was identical with the first.

" The boy had two pairs of shoes exactly alike," he said, " so I borrowed one of the duplicate pair."

He turned, and began to retrace his steps rapidly, following our own fresh tracks, and stopping only once to point out the place where the unknown man had picked the child up. When we regained the path we proceeded without delay until we emerged from the wood within a hundred yards of the cottage.

"I see Mrs. Haldean has been here with Giles," remarked Thorndyke, as we pushed open the garden-gate. "I wonder if they saw anybody."

He advanced to the door, and having first rapped with his knuckles and then kicked at it vigorously, tried the handle.

"Locked," he observed, "but I see the key is in the lock, so we can get in if we want to. Let us try the back."

The back door was locked, too, but the key had been removed.

"He came out this way, evidently," said Thorndyke, "though he went in at the front, as I suppose you noticed. Let us see where he went."

The back garden was a small, fenced patch of ground, with an earth path leading down to the back gate. A little way beyond the gate was a small barn or outhouse.

"We are in luck," Thorndyke remarked, with a glance at the path. "Yesterday's rain has cleared away all old footprints, and prepared the surface for new ones. You see there are three sets of excellent impressions—two leading away from the house, and one set towards it. Now, you notice that both of the sets leading *from* the house are characterised by deep impressions and short steps, while the set leading *to* the house has lighter impressions and longer steps. The obvious inference is that he went down the path with a heavy burden, came back empty-handed, and went down again—and finally—with another heavy burden. You observe, too, that he walked with his stick on each occasion."

By this time we had reached the bottom of the garden. Opening the gate, we followed the tracks towards the outhouse, which stood beside a cart-

track ; but as we came round the corner we both
stopped short and looked at one another. On the
soft earth were the very distinct impressions of the
tyres of a motor-car leading from the wide door of the
outhouse. Finding that the door was unfastened,
Thorndyke opened it, and looked in, to satisfy himself
that the place was empty. Then he fell to studying
the tracks.

"The course of events is pretty plain," he observed.
" First the fellow brought down his luggage, started
the engine, and got the car out—you can see where it
stood, both by the little pool of oil, and by the widening
and blurring of the wheel-tracks from the vibration
of the free engine ; then he went back and fetched
the boy—carried him pick-a-back, I should say, judging
by the depth of the toe-marks in the last set of footprints. That was a tactical mistake. He should have
taken the boy straight into the shed."

He pointed as he spoke to one of the footprints
beside the wheel-tracks, from the toe of which projected a small segment of the print of a little rubber heel.

We now made our way back to the house, where we
found Willett pensively rapping at the front door with
a cycle-spanner. Thorndyke took a last glance, with
his hand in his pocket, at an open window above, and
then, to the coachman's intense delight, brought forth
what looked uncommonly like a small bunch of skeleton
keys. One of these he inserted into the keyhole, and
as he gave it a turn, the lock clicked, and the door
stood open.

The little sitting-room, which we now entered, was
furnished with the barest necessaries. Its centre was
occupied by an oilcloth-covered table, on which I
observed with surprise a dismembered " Bee " clock
(the works of which had been taken apart with a tin-
opener that lay beside them) and a box-wood bird-call.
At these objects Thorndyke glanced and nodded, as
though they fitted into some theory that he had

formed ; examined carefully the oilcloth around the litter of wheels and pinions, and then proceeded on a tour of inspection round the room, peering inquisitively into the kitchen and store-cupboard.

"Nothing very distinctive or personal here," he remarked. "Let us go upstairs."

There were three bedrooms on the upper floor, of which two were evidently disused, though the windows were wide open. The third bedroom showed manifest traces of occupation, though it was as bare as the others, for the water still stood in the wash-hand basin, and the bed was unmade. To the latter Thorndyke advanced, and, having turned back the bedclothes, examined the interior attentively, especially at the foot and the pillow. The latter was soiled—not to say grimy—though the rest of the bed-linen was quite clean.

"Hair-dye," remarked Thorndyke, noting my glance at it ; then he turned and looked out of the open window. "Can you see the place where Miss Haldean was sitting to sketch ? " he asked.

"Yes," I replied ; "there is the place well in view, and you can see right up the road. I had no idea this house stood so high. From the three upper windows you can see all over the country excepting through the wood."

"Yes," Thorndyke rejoined, "and he has probably been in the habit of keeping watch up here with a telescope or a pair of field-glasses. Well, there is not much of interest in this room. He kept his effects in a cabin trunk which stood there under the window. He shaved this morning. He has a white beard, to judge by the stubble on the shaving-paper, and that is all. Wait, though. There is a key hanging on that nail. He must have overlooked that, for it evidently does not belong to this house. It is an ordinary town latchkey."

He took the key down, and having laid a sheet of

notepaper, from his pocket, on the dressing-table, produced a pin, with which he began carefully to probe the interior of the key-barrel. Presently there came forth, with much coaxing, a large ball of grey fluff, which Thorndyke folded up in the paper with infinite care.

" I suppose we mustn't take away the key," he said, " but I think we will take a wax mould of it."

He hurried downstairs, and, unstrapping the case from his bicycle, brought it in and placed it on the table. As it was now getting dark, he detached the powerful acetylene lamp from his machine, and, having lighted it, proceeded to open the mysterious case. First he took from it a small insufflator, or powder-blower, with which he blew a cloud of light yellow powder over the table around the remains of the clock. The powder settled on the table in an even coating, but when he blew at it smartly with his breath, it cleared off, leaving, however, a number of smeary impressions which stood out in strong yellow against the black oilcloth. To one of these impressions he pointed significantly. It was the print of a child's hand.

He next produced a small, portable microscope and some glass slides and cover-slips, and having opened the paper and tipped the ball of fluff from the key-barrel on to a slide, set to work with a pair of mounted needles to tease it out into its component parts. Then he turned the light of the lamp on to the microscope mirror and proceeded to examine the specimen.

" A curious and instructive assortment this, Jervis," he remarked, with his eye at the microscope : " woollen fibres—no cotton or linen ; he is careful of his health to have woollen pockets—and two hairs ; very curious ones, too. Just look at them, and observe the root bulbs."

I applied my eye to the microscope, and saw, among other things, two hairs—originally white, but encrusted with a black, opaque, glistening stain. The root bulbs, I noticed, were shrivelled and atrophied.

"But how on earth," I exclaimed, "did the hairs get into his pocket ?"

"I think the hairs themselves answer that question," he replied, "when considered with the other curios. The stain is obviously lead sulphide ; but what else do you see ?"

"I see some particles of metal—a white metal apparently—and a number of fragments of woody fibre and starch granules, but I don't recognise the starch. It is not wheat-starch, nor rice, nor potato. Do you make out what it is ?"

Thorndyke chuckled. "Experientia does it," said he. "You will have, Jervis, to study the minute properties of dust and dirt. Their evidential value is immense. Let us have another look at that starch ; it is all alike, I suppose."

It was ; and Thorndyke had just ascertained the fact when the door burst open and Mrs. Haldean entered the room, followed by Mrs. Hanshaw and the police inspector. The former lady regarded my colleague with a glance of extreme disfavour.

"We heard that you had come here, sir," said she, "and we supposed you were engaged in searching for my poor child. But it seems we were mistaken, since we find you here amusing yourselves fiddling with these nonsensical instruments."

"Perhaps, Mabel," said Mrs. Hanshaw stiffly, "it would be wiser, and infinitely more polite, to ask if Dr. Thorndyke has any news for us."

"That is undoubtedly so, madam," agreed the inspector, who had apparently suffered also from Mrs. Haldean's impulsiveness.

"Then perhaps," the latter lady suggested, "you will inform us if you have discovered anything."

"I will tell you," replied Thorndyke, "all that we know. The child was abducted by the man who occupied this house, and who appears to have watched him from an upper window, probably through a glass.

10*

This man lured the child into the wood by blowing this bird-call; he met him in the wood, and induced him—by some promises, no doubt—to come with him. He picked the child up and carried him—on his back, I think—up to the house, and brought him in through the front door, which he locked after him. He gave the boy this clock and the bird-call to amuse him while he went upstairs and packed his trunk. He took the trunk out through the back door and down the garden to the shed there, in which he had a motor-car. He got the car out and came back for the boy, whom he carried down to the car, locking the back door after him. Then he drove away."

" You know he has gone," cried Mrs. Haldean, " and yet you stay here playing with these ridiculous toys. Why are you not following him ? "

" We have just finished ascertaining the facts," Thorndyke replied calmly, " and should by now be on the road if you had not come."

Here the inspector interposed anxiously. " Of course, sir, you can't give any description of the man. You have no clue to his identity, I suppose ? "

" We have only his footprints," Thorndyke answered, " and this fluff which I raked out of the barrel of his latchkey, and have just been examining. From these data I conclude that he is a rather short and thin man, and somewhat lame. He walks with the aid of a thick stick, which has a knob, not a crook, at the top, and which he carries in his left hand. I think that his left leg has been amputated above the knee, and that he wears an artificial limb. He is elderly, he shaves his beard, has white hair dyed a greyish black, is partly bald, and probably combs a wisp of hair over the bald place ; he takes snuff, and carries a leaden comb in his pocket."

As Thorndyke's description proceeded, the inspector's mouth gradually opened wider and wider, until he appeared the very type and symbol of astonishment.

But its effect on Mrs. Haldean was much more remarkable. Rising from her chair, she leaned on the table
and stared at Thorndyke with an expression of awe—
even of terror; and as he finished she sank back into
her chair, with her hands clasped, and turned to Mrs.
Hanshaw.

"Jane!" she gasped, "it is Percy—my brother-in-
law! He has described him exactly, even to his stick
and his pocket-comb. But I thought he was in Chicago."

"If that is so," said Thorndyke, hastily repacking
his case, "we had better start at once."

"We have the dogcart in the road," said Mrs.
Hanshaw.

"Thank you," replied Thorndyke. "We will ride
on our bicycles, and the inspector can borrow Willett's.
We go out at the back by the cart-track, which joins
the road farther on."

"Then we will follow in the dogcart," said Mrs.
Haldean. "Come, Jane."

The two ladies departed down the path, while we
made ready our bicycles and lit our lamps.

"With your permission, inspector," said Thorndyke,
"we will take the key with us."

"It's hardly legal, sir," objected the officer. "We
have no authority."

"It is quite illegal," answered Thorndyke; "but it
is necessary; and necessity—like your military J.P.—
knows no law."

The inspector grinned and went out, regarding me
with a quivering eyelid as Thorndyke locked the door
with his skeleton key. As we turned into the road, I
saw the lights of the dogcart behind us, and we pushed
forward at a swift pace, picking up the trail easily on
the soft, moist road.

"What beats me," said the inspector confidentially,
as we rode along, "is how he knew the man was bald.
Was it the footprints or the latchkey? And that comb,
too, that was a regular knock-out."

These points were, by now, pretty clear to me. I had seen the hairs with their atrophied bulbs—such as one finds at the margin of a bald patch ; and the comb was used, evidently, for the double purpose of keeping the bald patch covered and blackening the sulphur-charged hair. But the knobbed stick and the artificial limb puzzled me so completely that I presently overtook Thorndyke to demand an explanation.

" The stick," said he, " is perfectly simple. The ferrule of a knobbed stick wears evenly all round ; that of a crooked stick wears on one side—the side opposite the crook. The impressions showed that the ferrule of this one was evenly convex ; therefore it had no crook. The other matter is more complicated. To begin with, an artificial foot makes a very characteristic impression, owing to its purely passive elasticity, as I will show you to-morrow. But an artificial leg fitted below the knee is quite secure, whereas one fitted above the knee —that is, with an artificial knee-joint worked by a spring —is much less reliable. Now, this man had an artificial foot, and he evidently distrusted his knee-joint, as is shown by his steadying it with his stick on the same side. If he had merely had a weak leg, he would have used the stick with his right hand—with the natural swing of the arm, in fact—unless he had been very lame, which he evidently was not. Still, it was only a question of probability, though the probability was very great. Of course you understand that those particles of woody fibre and starch granules were disintegrated snuff-grains."

This explanation, like the others, was quite simple when one had heard it, though it gave me material for much thought as we pedalled on along the dark road, with Thorndyke's light flickering in front, and the dogcart pattering in our wake. But there was ample time for reflection ; for our pace rather precluded conversation, and we rode on, mile after mile, until my legs ached with fatigue. On and on we went through

village after village, now losing the trail in some frequented street, but picking it up again unfailingly as
we emerged on to the country road, until at last, in
the paved High Street of the little town of Horsefield,
we lost it for good. We rode on through the town
out on to the country road ; but although there were
several tracks of motors, Thorndyke shook his head at
them all. " I have been studying those tyres until I
know them by heart," he said. " No ; either he is in
the town, or he has left it by a side road."

There was nothing for it but to put up the horse and
the machines at the hotel, while we walked round to
reconnoitre ; and this we did, tramping up one street
and down another, with eyes bent on the ground, fruit-
lessly searching for a trace of the missing car.

Suddenly, at the door of a blacksmith's shop, Thorndyke halted. The shop had been kept open late for
the shoeing of a carriage horse, which was just being
led away, and the smith had come to the door for a
breath of air. Thorndyke accosted him genially.

" Good-evening. You are just the man I wanted to
see. I have mislaid the address of a friend of mine,
who, I think, called on you this afternoon—a lame
gentleman who walks with a stick. I expect he wanted
you to pick a lock or make him a key."

" Oh, I remember him ! " said the man. " Yes, he
had lost his latchkey, and wanted the lock picked before
he could get into his house. Had to leave his motor-
car outside while he came here. But I took some keys
round with me, and fitted one to his latch."

He then directed us to a house at the end of a street
close by, and, having thanked him, we went off in high
spirits.

" How did you know he had been there ? " I asked.

" I didn't ; but there was the mark of a stick and
part of a left foot on the soft earth inside the doorway,
and the thing was inherently probable, so I risked a
false shot."

The house stood alone at the far end of a straggling street, and was enclosed by a high wall, in which, on the side facing the street, was a door and a wide carriage-gate. Advancing to the former, Thorndyke took from his pocket the purloined key, and tried it in the lock. It fitted perfectly, and when he had turned it and pushed open the door, we entered a small courtyard. Crossing this, we came to the front door of the house, the latch of which fortunately fitted the same key; and this having been opened by Thorndyke, we trooped into the hall. Immediately we heard the sound of an opening door above, and a reedy, nasal voice sang out :

" Hello, there ! Who's that below ? "

The voice was followed by the appearance of a head projecting over the baluster rail.

" You are Mr. Percy Haldean, I think," said the inspector.

At the mention of this name, the head was withdrawn, and a quick tread was heard, accompanied by the tapping of a stick on the floor. We started to ascend the stairs, the inspector leading, as the authorised official ; but we had only gone up a few steps, when a fierce, wiry little man danced out on to the landing, with a thick stick in one hand and a very large revolver in the other.

" Move another step, either of you," he shouted, pointing the weapon at the inspector, " and I let fly ; and, mind you, when I shoot I hit."

He looked as if he meant it, and we accordingly halted with remarkable suddenness, while the inspector proceeded to parley.

" Now, what's the good of this, Mr. Haldean ? " said he. " The game's up, and you know it."

" You clear out of my house, and clear out sharp," was the inhospitable rejoinder, " or you'll give me the trouble of burying you in the garden."

I looked round to consult with Thorndyke, when, to

my amazement, I found that he had vanished—apparently through the open hall-door. I was admiring his discretion when the inspector endeavoured to reopen negotiations, but was cut short abruptly.

"I am going to count fifty," said Mr. Haldean, "and if you aren't gone then, I shall shoot."

He began to count deliberately, and the inspector looked round at me in complete bewilderment. The flight of stairs was a long one, and well lighted by gas, so that to rush it was an impossibility. Suddenly my heart gave a bound and I held my breath, for out of an open door behind our quarry, a figure emerged slowly and noiselessly on to the landing. It was Thorndyke, shoeless, and in his shirt-sleeves.

Slowly and with cat-like stealthiness, he crept across the landing until he was within a yard of the unconscious fugitive, and still the nasal voice droned on, monotonously counting out the allotted seconds.

"Forty-one, forty-two, forty-three——"

There was a lightning-like movement—a shout—a flash—a bang—a shower of falling plaster, and then the revolver came clattering down the stairs. The inspector and I rushed up, and in a moment the sharp click of the handcuffs told Mr. Percy Haldean that the game was really up.

Five minutes later Freddy-boy, half asleep, but wholly cheerful, was borne on Thorndyke's shoulders into the private sitting-room of the Black Horse Hotel. A shriek of joy saluted his entrance, and a shower of maternal kisses brought him to the verge of suffocation. Finally, the impulsive Mrs. Haldean, turning suddenly to Thorndyke, seized both his hands, and for a moment I hoped that she was going to kiss him, too. But he was spared, and I have not yet recovered from the disappointment.

THORNDYKE was not a newspaper reader. He viewed
with extreme disfavour all scrappy and miscellaneous
forms of literature, which, by presenting a disorderly
series of unrelated items of information, tended, as he
considered, to destroy the habit of consecutive mental
effort.

" It is most important," he once remarked to me,
" habitually to pursue a definite train of thought, and
to pursue it to a finish, instead of flitting indolently
from one uncompleted topic to another, as the newspaper reader is so apt to do. Still, there is no harm in
a daily paper—so long as you don't read it."

Accordingly, he patronised a morning paper, and his
method of dealing with it was characteristic. The
paper was laid on the table after breakfast, together
with a blue pencil and a pair of office shears. A preliminary glance through the sheets enabled him to
mark with the pencil those paragraphs that were to
be read, and these were presently cut out and looked
through, after which they were either thrown away or
set aside to be pasted in an indexed book.

The whole proceeding occupied, on an average, a
quarter of an hour.

On the morning of which I am now speaking he was
thus engaged. The pencil had done its work, and the
snick of the shears announced the final stage. Presently he paused with a newly-excised cutting between
his fingers, and, after glancing at it for a moment, he
handed it to me.

" Another art robbery," he remarked. " Mysterious
affairs, these—as to motive, I mean. You can't melt
down a picture or an ivory carving, and you can't put
them on the market as they stand. The very qualities
that give them their value make them totally unnegoti-
able."

" Yet I suppose," said I, " the really inveterate collector—the pottery or stamp maniac, for instance—will
buy these contraband goods even though he dare not
show them."

" Probably. No doubt the *cupiditas habendi*, the
mere desire to possess, is the motive force rather than
any intelligent purpose——"

The discussion was at this point interrupted by a
knock at the door, and a moment later my colleague
admitted two gentlemen. One of these I recognised
as a Mr. Marchmont, a solicitor, for whom we had
occasionally acted ; the other was a stranger—a typical
Hebrew of the blonde type—good-looking, faultlessly
dressed, carrying a bandbox, and obviously in a state
of the most extreme agitation.

" Good-morning to you, gentlemen," said Mr. Marchmont, shaking hands cordially. " I have brought a
client of mine to see you, and when I tell you that his
name is Solomon Löwe, it will be unnecessary for me
to say what our business is."

" Oddly enough," replied Thorndyke, " we were, at
the very moment when you knocked, discussing the
bearings of his case."

" It is a horrible affair ! " burst in Mr. Löwe. " I
am distracted ! I am ruined ! I am in despair ! "

He banged the bandbox down on the table, and
flinging himself into a chair, buried his face in his
hands.

" Come, come," remonstrated Marchmont, " we
must be brave, we must be composed. Tell Dr.
Thorndyke your story, and let us hear what he thinks
of it."

He leaned back in his chair, and looked at his client
with that air of patient fortitude that comes to us all
so easily when we contemplate the misfortunes of other
people.

" You must help us, sir," exclaimed Löwe, starting
up again—" you must, indeed or I shall go mad. But

I shall tell you what has happened, and then you must
act at once. Spare no effort and no expense. Money
is no object—at least, not in reason," he added, with
native caution. He sat down once more, and in perfect English, though with a slight German accent, proceeded volubly : " My brother Isaac is probably known
to you by name."

Thorndyke nodded.

" He is a great collector, and to some extent a dealer
—that is to say, he makes his hobby a profitable hobby."

" What does he collect ? " asked Thorndyke.

" Everything," replied our visitor, flinging his hands
apart with a comprehensive gesture—" everything that
is precious and beautiful—pictures, ivories, jewels,
watches, objects of art and *vertu*—everything. He is a
Jew, and he has that passion for things that are rich
and costly that has distinguished our race from the
time of my namesake Solomon onwards. His house
in Howard Street, Piccadilly, is at once a museum and
an art gallery. The rooms are filled with cases of
gems, of antique jewellery, of coins and historic relics
—some of priceless value—and the walls are covered
with paintings, every one of which is a masterpiece.
There is a fine collection of ancient weapons and armour,
both European and Oriental ; rare books, manuscripts,
papyri, and valuable antiquities from Egypt, Assyria,
Cyprus, and elsewhere. You see, his taste is quite
catholic, and his knowledge of rare and curious things
is probably greater than that of any other living man.
He is never mistaken. No forgery deceives him, and
hence the great prices that he obtains ; for a work of
art purchased from Isaac Löwe is a work certified as
genuine beyond all cavil."

He paused to mop his face with a silk handkerchief,
and then, with the same plaintive volubility, continued :

" My brother is unmarried. He lives for his collection, and he lives with it. The house is not a very

large one, and the collection takes up most of it ; but he keeps a suite of rooms for his own occupation, and has two servants—a man and wife—to look after him. The man, who is a retired police sergeant, acts as caretaker and watchman ; the woman as housekeeper and cook, if required, but my brother lives largely at his club. And now I come to this present catastrophe."

He ran his fingers through his hair, took a deep breath, and continued :

" Yesterday morning Isaac started for Florence by way of Paris, but his route was not certain, and he intended to break his journey at various points as circumstances determined. Before leaving, he put his collection in my charge, and it was arranged that I should occupy his rooms in his absence. Accordingly, I sent my things round and took possession.

" Now, Dr. Thorndyke, I am closely connected with the drama, and it is my custom to spend my evenings at my club, of which most of the members are actors. Consequently, I am rather late in my habits ; but last night I was earlier than usual in leaving my club, for I started for my brother's house before half-past twelve. I felt, as you may suppose, the responsibility of the great charge I had undertaken ; and you may, therefore, imagine my horror, my consternation, my despair, when, on letting myself in with my latchkey, I found a police-inspector, a sergeant, and a constable in the hall. There had been a robbery, sir, in my brief absence, and the account that the inspector gave of the affair was briefly this :

" While taking the round of his district, he had noticed an empty hansom proceeding in leisurely fashion along Howard Street. There was nothing remarkable in this, but when, about ten minutes later, he was returning, and met a hansom, which he believed to be the same, proceeding along the same street in the same direction, and at the same easy pace, the circumstance struck him as odd, and he made a note of the number of the cab in his pocket-book. It was 72,863, and the time was 11.35.

" At 11.45 a constable coming up Howard Street noticed a hansom standing opposite the door of my brother's house, and, while he was looking at it, a man came out of the house carrying something, which he put in the cab. On this the constable quickened his pace, and when the man returned to the house and reappeared carrying what looked like a portmanteau, and closing the door softly behind him, the policeman's suspicions were aroused, and he hurried forward, hailing the cabman to stop.

" The man put his burden into the cab, and sprang in himself. The cabman lashed his horse, which started off at a gallop, and the policeman broke into a run, blowing his whistle and flashing his lantern on to the cab. He followed it round the two turnings into Albemarle Street, and was just in time to see it turn into Piccadilly, where, of course, it was lost. However, he managed to note the number of the cab, which was 72,863, and he describes the man as short and thick-set, and thinks he was not wearing any hat.

" As he was returning, he met the inspector and the sergeant, who had heard the whistle, and on his report the three officers hurried to the house, where they knocked and rang for some minutes without any result. Being now more than suspicious, they went to the back of the house, through the mews, where, with great difficulty, they managed to force a window and effect an entrance into the house.

" Here their suspicions were soon changed to certainty, for, on reaching the first-floor, they heard strange muffled groans proceeding from one of the rooms, the door of which was locked, though the key had not been removed. They opened the door, and found the caretaker and his wife sitting on the floor, with their backs against the wall. Both were bound hand and foot, and the head of each was enveloped in a green-baize bag ; and when the bags were taken off, each was found to be lightly but effectively gagged.

" Each told the same story. The caretaker, fancying he heard a noise, armed himself with a truncheon, and came downstairs to the first-floor, where he found the door of one of the rooms open, and a light burning inside. He stepped on tiptoe to the open door, and was peering in, when he was seized from behind, half suffocated by a pad held over his mouth, pinioned, gagged, and blindfolded with the bag.

" His assailant—whom he never saw—was amazingly strong and skilful, and handled him with perfect ease, although he—the caretaker—is a powerful man, and a good boxer and wrestler. The same thing happened to the wife, who had come down to look for her husband. She walked into the same trap, and was gagged, pinioned, and blindfolded without ever having seen the robber. So the only description that we have of this villain is that furnished by the constable."

" And the caretaker had no chance of using his truncheon ? " said Thorndyke.

" Well, he got in one backhanded blow over his right shoulder, which he thinks caught the burglar in the face ; but the fellow caught him by the elbow, and gave his arm such a twist that he dropped the truncheon on the floor."

" Is the robbery a very extensive one ? "

" Ah ! " exclaimed Mr. Löwe, " that is just what we cannot say. But I fear it is. It seems that my brother had quite recently drawn out of his bank four thousand pounds in notes and gold. These little transactions are often carried out in cash rather than by cheque "—here I caught a twinkle in Thorndyke's eye—" and the caretaker says that a few days ago Isaac brought home several parcels, which were put away temporarily in a strong cupboard. He seemed to be very pleased with his new acquisitions, and gave the caretaker to understand that they were of extraordinary rarity and value.

"Now, this cupboard has been cleared out. Not a vestige is left in it but the wrappings of the parcels, so, although nothing else has been touched, it is pretty clear that goods to the value of four thousand pounds have been taken ; but when we consider what an excellent buyer my brother is, it becomes highly probable that the actual value of those things is two or three times that amount, or even more. It is a dreadful, dreadful business, and Isaac will hold me responsible for it all."

"Is there no further clue ? " asked Thorndyke. " What about the cab, for instance ? "

" Oh, the cab," groaned Löwe—" that clue failed. The police must have mistaken the number. They telephoned immediately to all the police stations, and a watch was set, with the result that number 72,863 was stopped as it was going home for the night. But it then turned out that the cab had not been off the rank since eleven o'clock, and the driver had been in the shelter all the time with several other men. But there *is* a clue ; I have it here."

Mr. Löwe's face brightened for once as he reached out for the bandbox.

" The houses in Howard Street," he explained, as he untied the fastening, " have small balconies to the first-floor windows at the back. Now, the thief entered by one of these windows, having climbed up a rain-water pipe to the balcony. It was a gusty night, as you will remember, and this morning, as I was leaving the house, the butler next door called to me and gave me this ; he had found it lying in the balcony of his house."

He opened the bandbox with a flourish, and brought forth a rather shabby billycock hat.

" I understand," said he, " that by examining a hat it is possible to deduce from it, not only the bodily characteristics of the wearer, but also his mental and moral qualities, his state of health, his pecuniary position, his past history, and even his domestic relations and the peculiarities of his place of abode. Am I right in this supposition ? "

The ghost of a smile flitted across Thorndyke's face as he laid the hat upon the remains of the newspaper. " We must not expect too much," he observed. " Hats, as you know, have a way of changing owners. Your own hat, for instance " (a very spruce, hard felt), " is a new one, I think."

" Got it last week," said Mr. Löwe.

" Exactly. It is an expensive hat, by Lincoln and Bennett, and I see you have judiciously written your name in indelible marking-ink on the lining. Now, a new hat suggests a discarded predecessor. What do you do with your old hats ? "

" My man has them, but they don't fit him. I suppose he sells them or gives them away."

" Very well. Now, a good hat like yours has a long life, and remains serviceable long after it has become shabby ; and the probability is that many of your hats pass from owner to owner ; from you to the shabby-genteel, and from them to the shabby ungenteel. And it is a fair assumption that there are, at this moment, an appreciable number of tramps and casuals wearing hats by Lincoln and Bennett, marked in indelible ink with the name S. Löwe ; and anyone who should examine those hats, as you suggest, might draw some very misleading deductions as to the personal habits of S. Löwe."

Mr. Marchmont chuckled audibly, and then, remembering the gravity of the occasion, suddenly became portentously solemn.

" So you think that the hat is of no use, after all ? " said Mr. Löwe, in a tone of deep disappointment.

" I won't say that," replied Thorndyke. " We may learn something from it. Leave it with me, at any

rate ; but you must let the police know that I have
it. They will want to see it, of course."

"And you will try to get those things, won't you ? "
pleaded Löwe.

"I will think over the case. But you understand,
or Mr. Marchmont does, that this is hardly in my
province. I am a medical jurist, and this is not a
medico-legal case."

"Just what I told him," said Marchmont. "But
you will do me a great kindness if you will look into
the matter. Make it a medico-legal case," he added
persuasively.

Thorndyke repeated his promise, and the two men
took their departure.

For some time after they had left, my colleague
remained silent, regarding the hat with a quizzical
smile. "It is like a game of forfeits," he remarked
at length, "and we have to find the owner of ' this
very pretty thing.' " He lifted it with a pair of
forceps into a better light, and began to look at it more
closely.

"Perhaps," said he, "we have done Mr. Löwe an
injustice, after all. This is certainly a very remarkable
hat."

"It is as round as a basin," I exclaimed. "Why,
the fellow's head must have been turned in a lathe ! "

Thorndyke laughed. "The point," said he, "is
this. This is a hard hat, and so must have fitted
fairly, or it could not have been worn ; and it was a
cheap hat, and so was not made to measure. But a
man with a head that shape has got to come to a clear
understanding with his hat. No ordinary hat would go
on at all.

"Now, you see what he has done—no doubt on the
advice of some friendly hatter. He has bought a
hat of a suitable size, and he has made it hot—probably
steamed it. Then he has jammed it, while still hot
and soft, on to his head, and allowed it to cool and set

before removing it. That is evident from the distortion of the brim. The important corollary is, that this hat fits his head exactly—is, in fact, a perfect mould of it ; and this fact, together with the cheap quality of the hat, furnishes the further corollary that it has probably only had a single owner.

" And now let us turn it over and look at the outside. You notice at once the absence of old dust. Allowing for the circumstance that it had been out all night, it is decidedly clean. Its owner has been in the habit of brushing it, and is therefore presumably a decent, orderly man. But if you look at it in a good light, you see a kind of bloom on the felt, and through this lens you can make out particles of a fine white powder which has worked into the surface."

He handed me his lens, through which I could distinctly see the particles to which he referred.

" Then," he continued, " under the curl of the brim and in the folds of the hatband, where the brush has not been able to reach it, the powder has collected quite thickly, and we can see that it is a very fine powder, and very white, like flour. What do you make of that ? "

" I should say that it is connected with some industry. He may be engaged in some factory or works, or, at any rate, may live near a factory, and have to pass it frequently."

" Yes ; and I think we can distinguish between the two possibilities. For, if he only passes the factory, the dust will be on the outside of the hat only ; the inside will be protected by his head. But if he is engaged in the works, the dust will be inside, too, as the hat will hang on a peg in the dust-laden atmosphere, and his head will also be powdered, and so convey the dust to the inside."

He turned the hat over once more, and as I brought the powerful lens to bear upon the dark lining, I could clearly distinguish a number of white particles in the interstices of the fabric.

" The powder is on the inside, too," I said.

He took the lens from me, and, having verified my statement, proceeded with the examination. " You notice," he said, " that the leather head-lining is stained with grease, and this staining is more pronounced at the sides and back. His hair, therefore, is naturally greasy, or he greases it artificially ; for if the staining were caused by perspiration, it would be most marked opposite the forehead."

He peered anxiously into the interior of the hat, and eventually turned down the head-lining ; and immediately there broke out upon his face a gleam of satisfaction.

" Ha ! " he exclaimed. " This is a stroke of luck. I was afraid our neat and orderly friend had defeated us with his brush. Pass me the small dissecting forceps, Jervis."

I handed him the instrument, and he proceeded to pick out daintily from the space behind the head-lining some half a dozen short pieces of hair, which he laid, with infinite tenderness, on a sheet of white paper.

" There are several more on the other side," I said, pointing them out to him.

" Yes, but we must leave some for the police," he answered, with a smile. " They must have the same chance as ourselves, you know."

" But, surely," I said, as I bent down over the paper, " these are pieces of horsehair ! "

" I think not," he replied ; " but the microscope will show. At any rate, this is the kind of hair I should expect to find with a head of that shape."

" Well, it is extraordinarily coarse," said I, " and two of the hairs are nearly white."

" Yes ; black hairs beginning to turn grey. And now, as our preliminary survey has given such encouraging results, we will proceed to more exact methods ; and we must waste no time, for we shall have the police here presently to rob us of our treasure."

He folded up carefully the paper containing the hairs, and taking the hat in both hands, as though it were some sacred vessel, ascended with me to the laboratory on the next floor.

"Now, Polton," he said to his laboratory assistant, "we have here a specimen for examination, and time is precious. First of all, we want your patent dust-extractor."

The little man bustled to a cupboard and brought forth a singular appliance, of his own manufacture, somewhat like a miniature vacuum cleaner. It had been made from a bicycle foot-pump, by reversing the piston-valve, and was fitted with a glass nozzle and a small detachable glass receiver for collecting the dust, at the end of a flexible metal tube.

"We will sample the dust from the outside first," said Thorndyke, laying the hat upon the work-bench. "Are you ready, Polton?"

The assistant slipped his foot into the stirrup of the pump and worked the handle vigorously, while Thorndyke drew the glass nozzle slowly along the hat-brim under the curled edge. And as the nozzle passed along, the white coating vanished as if by magic, leaving the felt absolutely clean and black, and simultaneously the glass receiver became clouded over with a white deposit.

"We will leave the other side for the police," said Thorndyke, and as Polton ceased pumping he detached the receiver, and laid it on a sheet of paper, on which he wrote in pencil, "Outside," and covered it with a small bell-glass. A fresh receiver having been fitted on, the nozzle was now drawn over the silk lining of the hat, and then through the space behind the leather head-lining on one side; and now the dust that collected in the receiver was much of the usual grey colour and fluffy texture, and included two more hairs.

"And now," said Thorndyke, when the second receiver had been detached and set aside, "we want a mould of the inside of the hat, and we must make it by the quickest method ; there is no time to make a paper mould. It is a most astonishing head," he added, reaching down from a nail a pair of large callipers, which he applied to the inside of the hat ; "six inches and nine-tenths long by six and six-tenths broad, which gives us "—he made a rapid calculation on a scrap of paper—" the extraordinarily high cephalic index of 95·6."

Polton now took possession of the hat, and, having stuck a band of wet tissue-paper round the inside, mixed a small bowl of plaster-of-Paris, and very dexterously ran a stream of the thick liquid on to the tissue-paper, where it quickly solidified. A second and third application resulted in a broad ring of solid plaster an inch thick, forming a perfect mould of the inside of the hat, and in a few minutes the slight contraction of the plaster in setting rendered the mould sufficiently loose to allow of its being slipped out on to a board to dry.

We were none too soon, for even as Polton was removing the mould, the electric bell, which I had switched on to the laboratory, announced a visitor, and when I went down I found a police-sergeant waiting with a note from Superintendent Miller, requesting the immediate transfer of the hat.

"The next thing to be done," said Thorndyke, when the sergeant had departed with the bandbox, " is to measure the thickness of the hairs, and make a transverse section of one, and examine the dust. The section we will leave to Polton—as time is an object, Polton, you had better imbed the hair in thick gum and freeze it hard on the microtome, and be very careful to cut the section at right angles to the length of the hair—meanwhile, we will get to work with the microscope."

The hairs proved on measurement to have the surprisingly large diameter of $\frac{1}{135}$ of an inch—fully double that of ordinary hairs, although they were unquestionably human. As to the white dust, it presented a problem that even Thorndyke was unable to solve. The application of reagents showed it to be carbonate of lime, but its source for a time remained a mystery.

"The larger particles," said Thorndyke, with his eye applied to the microscope, "appear to be transparent, crystalline, and distinctly laminated in structure. It is not chalk, it is not whiting, it is not any kind of cement. What can it be?"

"Could it be any kind of shell?" I suggested. "For instance——"

"Of course!" he exclaimed, starting up; "you have hit it, Jervis, as you always do. It must be mother-of-pearl. Polton, give me a pearl shirt-button out of your oddments box."

The button was duly produced by the thrifty Polton, dropped into an agate mortar, and speedily reduced to powder, a tiny pinch of which Thorndyke placed under the microscope.

"This powder," said he, "is, naturally, much coarser than our specimen, but the identity of character is unmistakable. Jervis, you are a treasure. Just look at it."

I glanced down the microscope, and then pulled out my watch. "Yes," I said, "there is no doubt about it, I think; but I must be off. Anstey urged me to be in court by 11.30 at the latest."

With infinite reluctance I collected my notes and papers and departed, leaving Thorndyke diligently copying addresses out of the Post Office Directory.

My business at the court detained me the whole of the day, and it was near upon dinner-time when I reached our chambers. Thorndyke had not yet come in, but he arrived half an hour later, tired and hungry, and not very communicative.

"What have I done?" he repeated, in answer to my inquiries. "I have walked miles of dirty pavement, and I have visited every pearl-shell cutter's in London, with one exception, and I have not found what I was looking for. The one mother-of-pearl factory that remains, however, is the most likely, and I propose to look in there to-morrow morning. Meanwhile, we have completed our data, with Polton's assistance. Here is a tracing of our friend's skull taken from the mould ; you see it is an extreme type of brachycephalic skull, and markedly unsymmetrical. Here is a transverse section of his hair, which is quite circular—unlike yours or mine, which would be oval. We have the mother-of-pearl dust from the outside of the hat, and from the inside similar dust mixed with various fibres and a few granules of rice starch. Those are our data."

"Supposing the hat should not be that of the burglar after all ?" I suggested.

"That would be annoying. But I think it is his, and I think I can guess at the nature of the art treasures that were stolen."

"And you don't intend to enlighten me ?"

"My dear fellow," he replied, "you have all the data. Enlighten yourself by the exercise of your own brilliant faculties. Don't give way to mental indolence."

I endeavoured, from the facts in my possession, to construct the personality of the mysterious burglar, and failed utterly ; nor was I more successful in my endeavour to guess at the nature of the stolen property ; and it was not until the following morning, when we had set out on our quest and were approaching Limehouse, that Thorndyke would revert to the subject.

"We are now," he said, "going to the factory of Badcomb and Martin, shell importers and cutters, in the West India Dock Road. If I don't find my man there, I shall hand the facts over to the police, and waste no more time over the case."

" What is your man like ? " I asked.

" I am looking for an elderly Japanese, wearing a new hat or, more probably, a cap, and having a bruise on his right cheek or temple. I am also looking for a cab-yard ; but here we are at the works, and as it is now close on the dinner-hour, we will wait and see the hands come out before making any inquiries."

We walked slowly past the tall, blank-faced building, and were just turning to re-pass it when a steam whistle sounded, a wicket opened in the main gate, and a stream of workmen—each powdered with white, like a miller—emerged into the street. We halted to watch the men as they came out, one by one, through the wicket, and turned to the right or left towards their homes or some adjacent coffee-shop ; but none of them answered to the description that my friend had given.

The outcoming stream grew thinner, and at length ceased ; the wicket was shut with a bang, and once more Thorndyke's quest appeared to have failed.

" Is that all of them, I wonder ? " he said, with a shade of disappointment in his tone ; but even as he spoke the wicket opened again, and a leg protruded. The leg was followed by a back and a curious globular head, covered with iron-grey hair, and surmounted by a cloth cap, the whole appertaining to a short, very thick-set man, who remained thus, evidently talking to someone inside.

Suddenly he turned his head to look across the street ; and immediately I recognised, by the pallid yellow complexion and narrow eye-slits, the physiognomy of a typical Japanese. The man remained talking for nearly another minute ; then, drawing out his other leg, he turned towards us ; and now I perceived that the right side of his face, over the prominent cheekbone, was discoloured as though by a severe bruise.

" Ha ! " said Thorndyke, turning round sharply as

the man approached, "either this is our man or it is an incredible coincidence." He walked away at a moderate pace, allowing the Japanese to overtake us slowly, and when the man had at length passed us, he increased his speed somewhat, so as to maintain the distance.

Our friend stepped along briskly, and presently turned up a side street, whither we followed at a respectful distance, Thorndyke holding open his pocket-book, and appearing to engage me in an earnest discussion, but keeping a sharp eye on his quarry.

"There he goes!" said my colleague, as the man suddenly disappeared—"the house with the green window-sashes. That will be number thirteen."

It was ; and, having verified the fact, we passed on, and took the next turning that would lead us back to the main road.

Some twenty minutes later, as we were strolling past the door of a coffee-shop, a man came out and began to fill his pipe with an air of leisurely satisfaction. His hat and clothes were powdered with white like those of the workmen whom we had seen come out of the factory. Thorndyke accosted him.

"Is that a flour-mill up the road there ?"

"No, sir ; pearl-shell. I work there myself."

"Pearl-shell, eh ?" said Thorndyke. "I suppose that will be an industry that will tend to attract the aliens. Do you find it so ?"

"No, sir ; not at all. The work's too hard. We've only got one foreigner in the place, and he ain't an alien—he's a Jap."

"A Jap!" exclaimed Thorndyke. "Really. Now, I wonder if that would chance to be our old friend Kotei—you remember Kotei ?" he added, turning to me.

"No, sir ; this man's name is Futashima. There was another Jap in the works, a chap named Itu, a pal of Futashima's, but he's left."

"Ah! I don't know either of them. By the way, usen't there to be a cab-yard just about here?"

"There's a yard up Rankin Street where they keep vans and one or two cabs. That chap Itu works there now. Taken to horseflesh. Drives a van sometimes. Queer start for a Jap."

"Very." Thorndyke thanked the man for his information, and we sauntered on towards Rankin Street. The yard was at this time nearly deserted, being occupied only by an ancient and crazy four-wheeler and a very shabby hansom.

"Curious old houses, these that back on to the yard," said Thorndyke, strolling into the enclosure. "That timber gable, now," pointing to a house, from a window of which a man was watching us suspiciously, "is quite an interesting survival."

"What's your business, mister?" demanded the man in a gruff tone.

"We are just having a look at these quaint old houses," replied Thorndyke, edging towards the back of the hansom, and opening his pocket-book, as though to make a sketch.

"Well, you can see 'em from outside," said the man.

"So we can," said Thorndyke suavely, "but not so well, you know."

At this moment the pocket-book slipped from his hand and fell, scattering a number of loose papers about the ground under the hansom, and our friend at the window laughed joyously.

"No hurry," murmured Thorndyke, as I stooped to help him to gather up the papers—which he did in the most surprisingly slow and clumsy manner. "It is fortunate that the ground is dry." He stood up with the rescued papers in his hand, and, having scribbled down a brief note, slipped the book in his pocket.

"Now you'd better mizzle," observed the man at the window.

11

"Thank you," replied Thorndyke, "I think we had"; and, with a pleasant nod at the custodian, he proceeded to adopt the hospitable suggestion.

"Mr. Marchmont has been here, sir, with Inspector Badger and another gentleman," said Polton, as we entered our chambers. "They said they would call again about five."

"Then," replied Thorndyke, "as it is now a quarter to five, there is just time for us to have a wash while you get the tea ready. The particles that float in the atmosphere of Limehouse are not all mother-of-pearl."

Our visitors arrived punctually, the third gentleman being, as we had supposed, Mr. Solomon Löwe. Inspector Badger I had not seen before, and he now impressed me as showing a tendency to invert the significance of his own name by endeavouring to "draw" Thorndyke; in which, however, he was not brilliantly successful.

"I hope you are not going to disappoint Mr. Löwe, sir," he commenced facetiously. "You have had a good look at that hat—we saw your marks on it—and he expects that you will be able to point us out the man, name and address all complete." He grinned patronisingly at our unfortunate client, who was looking even more haggard and worn than he had been on the previous morning.

"Have you—have you made any—discovery?" Mr. Löwe asked with pathetic eagerness.

"We examined the hat very carefully, and I think we have established a few facts of some interest."

"Did your examination of the hat furnish any information as to the nature of the stolen property, sir?" inquired the humorous inspector.

Thorndyke turned to the officer with a face as expressionless as a wooden mask.

"We thought it possible," said he, "that it might

consist of works of Japanese art, such as netsukes, paintings, and such like."

Mr. Löwe uttered an exclamation of delighted astonishment, and the facetiousness faded rather suddenly from the inspector's countenance.

" I don't know how you can have found out," said he. " We have only known it half an hour ourselves, and the wire came direct from Florence to Scotland Yard."

" Perhaps you can describe the thief to us," said Mr. Löwe, in the same eager tone.

" I dare say the inspector can do that," replied Thorndyke.

" Yes, I think so," replied the officer. " He is a short strong man, with a dark complexion and hair turning grey. He has a very round head, and he is probably a workman engaged at some whiting or cement works. That is all we know ; if you can tell us any more, we shall be very glad to hear it."

" I can only offer a few suggestions," said Thorndyke, " but perhaps you may find them useful. For instance, at 13, Birket Street, Limehouse, there is living a Japanese gentleman named Futashima, who works at Badcomb and Martin's mother-of-pearl factory. I think that if you were to call on him, and let him try on the hat that you have, it would probably fit him."

The inspector scribbled ravenously in his notebook, and Mr. Marchmont—an old admirer of Thorndyke's—leaned back in his chair, chuckling softly and rubbing his hands.

" Then," continued my colleague, " there is in Rankin Street, Limehouse, a cab-yard, where another Japanese gentleman named Itu is employed. You might find out where Itu was the night before last ; and if you should chance to see a hansom cab there—number 22,481 —have a good look at it. In the frame of the number-

plate you will find six small holes. Those holes may
have held brads, and the brads may have held a false
number card. At any rate, you might ascertain where
that cab was at 11.30 the night before last. That is
all I have to suggest."

Mr. Löwe leaped from his chair. " Let us go—now
—at once—there is no time to be lost. A thousand
thanks to you, doctor—a thousand million thanks.
Come ! "

He seized the inspector by the arm and forcibly
dragged him towards the door, and a few moments
later we heard the footsteps of our visitors clattering
down the stairs.

" It was not worth while to enter into explanations
with them," said Thorndyke, as the footsteps died away
—" nor perhaps with you ? "

" On the contrary," I replied, " I am waiting to be
fully enlightened."

" Well, then, my inferences in this case were perfectly
simple ones, drawn from well-known anthropological
facts. The human race, as you know, is roughly divided
into three groups—the black, the white, and the yellow
races. But apart from the variable quality of colour,
these races have certain fixed characteristics associated
especially with the shape of the skull, of the eye-sockets,
and the hair.

" Thus in the black races the skull is long and narrow,
the eye-sockets are long and narrow, and the hair is
flat and ribbon-like, and usually coiled up like a watch-
spring. In the white races the skull is oval, the eye-
sockets are oval, and the hair is slightly flattened or
oval in section, and tends to be wavy ; while in the
yellow or Mongol races, the skull is short and round,
the eye-sockets are short and round, and the hair is
straight and circular in section. So that we have,
in the black races, long skull, long orbits, flat hair ; in
the white races, oval skull, oval orbits, oval hair ; and
in the yellow races, round skull, round orbits, round hair.

" Now, in this case we had to deal with a very short round skull. But you cannot argue from races to individuals ; there are many short-skulled Englishmen. But when I found, associated with that skull, hairs which were circular in section, it became practically certain that the individual was a Mongol of some kind. The mother-of-pearl dust and the granules of rice starch from the inside of the hat favoured this view, for the pearl-shell industry is specially connected with China and Japan, while starch granules from the hat of an Englishman would probably be wheat starch.

" Then as to the hair : it was, as I mentioned to you, circular in section, and of very large diameter. Now, I have examined many thousands of hairs, and the thickest that I have ever seen came from the heads of Japanese ; but the hairs from this hat were as thick as any of them. But the hypothesis that the burglar was a Japanese received confirmation in various ways. Thus, he was short, though strong and active, and the Japanese are the shortest of the Mongol races, and very strong and active.

" Then his remarkable skill in handling the powerful caretaker—a retired police-sergeant—suggested the Japanese art of ju-jitsu, while the nature of the robbery was consistent with the value set by the Japanese on works of art. Finally, the fact that only a particular collection was taken, suggested a special, and probably national, character in the things stolen, while their portability—you will remember that goods of the value of from eight to twelve thousand pounds were taken away in two hand-packages—was much more consistent with Japanese than Chinese works, of which the latter tend rather to be bulky and ponderous. Still, it was nothing but a bare hypothesis until we had seen Futashima—and, indeed, is no more now. I may, after all, be entirely mistaken."

He was not, however ; and at this moment there reposes in my drawing-room an ancient netsuke, which came as a thank-offering from Mr. Isaac Löwe on the recovery of the booty from a back room in No. 13, Birket Street, Limehouse. The treasure, of course, was given in the first place to Thorndyke, but transferred by him to my wife on the pretence that but for my suggestion of shell-dust the robber would never have been traced. Which is, on the face of it, preposterous.

10 THE BLUE SEQUIN

THORNDYKE stood looking up and down the platform with anxiety that increased as the time drew near for the departure of the train.

" This is very unfortunate," he said, reluctantly stepping into an empty smoking compartment as the guard executed a flourish with his green flag. " I am afraid we have missed our friend." He closed the door, and, as the train began to move, thrust his head out of the window.

" Now I wonder if that will be he," he continued. " If so, he has caught the train by the skin of his teeth, and is now in one of the rear compartments."

The subject of Thorndyke's speculations was Mr. Edward Stopford, of the firm of Stopford and Myers, of Portugal Street, solicitors, and his connection with us at present arose out of a telegram that had reached our chambers on the preceding evening. It was reply-paid, and ran thus :

" Can you come here to-morrow to direct defence ? Important case. All costs undertaken by us.—STOP-FORD AND MYERS."

Thorndyke's reply had been in the affirmative, and

early on this present morning a further telegram—
evidently posted overnight—had been delivered :

" Shall leave for Woldhurst by 8.25 from Charing
Cross. Will call for you if possible.—EDWARD STOP-
FORD."

He had not called, however, and, since he was unknown
personally to us both, we could not judge whether or
not he had been among the passengers on the platform.

" It is most unfortunate," Thorndyke repeated, " for
it deprives us of that preliminary consideration of the
case which is so invaluable." He filled his pipe thoughtfully, and, having made a fruitless inspection of the
platform at London Bridge, took up the paper that he
had bought at the bookstall, and began to turn over
the leaves, running his eye quickly down the columns,
unmindful of the journalistic baits in paragraph or article.

" It is a great disadvantage," he observed, while still
glancing through the paper, " to come plump into an
inquiry without preparation—to be confronted with
the details before one has a chance of considering the
case in general terms. For instance——"

He paused, leaving the sentence unfinished, and as
I looked up inquiringly I saw that he had turned over
another page, and was now reading attentively.

" This looks like our case, Jervis," he said presently,
handing me the paper and indicating a paragraph at
the top of the page. It was quite brief, and was headed
" Terrible Murder in Kent," the account being as
follows :

" A shocking crime was discovered yesterday morning at the little town of Woldhurst, which lies on the
branch line from Halbury Junction. The discovery
was made by a porter who was inspecting the carriages
of the train which had just come in. On opening the
door of a first-class compartment, he was horrified to
find the body of a fashionably-dressed woman stretched

upon the floor. Medical aid was immediately summoned, and on the arrival of the divisional surgeon, Dr. Morton, it was ascertained that the woman had not been dead more than a few minutes.

" The state of the corpse leaves no doubt that a murder of a most brutal kind has been perpetrated, the cause of death being a penetrating wound of the head, inflicted with some pointed implement, which must have been used with terrible violence, since it has perforated the skull and entered the brain. That robbery was not the motive of the crime is made clear by the fact that an expensively fitted dressing-bag was found on the rack, and that the dead woman's jewellery, including several valuable diamond rings, was untouched. It is rumoured that an arrest has been made by the local police."

" A gruesome affair," I remarked, as I handed back the paper, " but the report does not give us much information."

" It does not," Thorndyke agreed, " and yet it gives us something to consider. Here is a perforating wound of the skull, inflicted with some pointed implement—that is, assuming that it is not a bullet wound. Now, what kind of implement would be capable of inflicting such an injury ? How would such an implement be used in the confined space of a railway-carriage, and what sort of person would be in possession of such an implement ? These are preliminary questions that are worth considering, and I commend them to you, together with the further problems of the possible motive—excluding robbery—and any circumstances other than murder which might account for the injury."

" The choice of suitable implements is not very great," I observed.

" It is very limited, and most of them, such as a plasterer's pick or a geological hammer, are associated with certain definite occupations. You have a note-book ? "

I had, and, accepting the hint, I produced it and pursued my further reflections in silence, while my companion, with his notebook also on his knee, gazed steadily out of the window. And thus he remained, wrapped in thought, jotting down an entry now and again in his book, until the train slowed down at Halbury Junction, where we had to change on to a branch line.

As we stepped out, I noticed a well-dressed man hurrying up the platform from the rear and eagerly scanning the faces of the few passengers who had alighted. Soon he espied us, and, approaching quickly, asked, as he looked from one of us to the other :

" Dr. Thorndyke ? "

" Yes," replied my colleague, adding : " And you, I presume, are Mr. Edward Stopford ? "

The solicitor bowed. " This is a dreadful affair," he said, in an agitated manner. " I see you have the paper. A most shocking affair. I am immensely relieved to find you here. Nearly missed the train, and feared I should miss you."

" There appears to have been an arrest," Thorndyke began.

" Yes—my brother. Terrible business. Let us walk up the platform ; our train won't start for a quarter of an hour yet."

We deposited our joint Gladstone and Thorndyke's travelling-case in an empty first-class compartment, and then, with the solicitor between us, strolled up to the unfrequented end of the platform.

" My brother's position," said Mr. Stopford, " fills me with dismay—but let me give you the facts in order, and you shall judge for yourself. This poor creature who has been murdered so brutally was a Miss Edith Grant. She was formerly an artist's model, and as such was a good deal employed by my brother, who is a painter—Harold Stopford, you know, A.R.A. now——"

11*

"I know his work very well, and charming work it is."

"I think so, too. Well, in those days he was quite a youngster—about twenty—and he became very intimate with Miss Grant, in quite an innocent way, though not very discreet; but she was a nice respectable girl, as most English models are, and no one thought any harm. However, a good many letters passed between them, and some little presents, amongst which was a beaded chain carrying a locket, and in this he was fool enough to put his portrait and the inscription, 'Edith, from Harold.'

"Later on Miss Grant, who had a rather good voice, went on the stage, in the comic opera line, and, in consequence, her habits and associates changed somewhat; and, as Harold had meanwhile become engaged, he was naturally anxious to get his letters back, and especially to exchange the locket for some less compromising gift. The letters she eventually sent him, but refused absolutely to part with the locket.

"Now, for the last month Harold has been staying at Halbury, making sketching excursions into the surrounding country, and yesterday morning he took the train to Shinglehurst, the third station from here, and the one before Woldhurst.

"On the platform here he met Miss Grant, who had come down from London, and was going on to Worthing. They entered the branch train together, having a first-class compartment to themselves. It seems she was wearing his locket at the time, and he made another appeal to her to make an exchange, which she refused, as before. The discussion appears to have become rather heated and angry on both sides, for the guard and a porter at Munsden both noticed that they seemed to be quarrelling; but the upshot of the affair was that the lady snapped the chain, and tossed it together with the locket to my brother, and they parted quite amiably at Shinglehurst, where Harold got out. He was then carrying his full sketching kit, including a large holland umbrella, the lower joint of which is an ash staff fitted with a powerful steel spike for driving into the ground.

" It was about half-past ten when he got out at Shinglehurst ; by eleven he had reached his pitch and got to work, and he painted steadily for three hours. Then he packed up his traps, and was just starting on his way back to the station, when he was met by the police and arrested.

" And now, observe the accumulation of circumstantial evidence against him. He was the last person seen in company with the murdered woman—for no one seems to have seen her after they left Munsden ; he appeared to be quarrelling with her when she was last seen alive, he had a reason for possibly wishing for her death, he was provided with an implement—a spiked staff—capable of inflicting the injury which caused her death, and, when he was searched, there was found in his possession the locket and broken chain, apparently removed from her person with violence.

" Against all this is, of course, his known character —he is the gentlest and most amiable of men—and his subsequent conduct—imbecile to the last degree if he had been guilty ; but, as a lawyer, I can't help seeing that appearances are almost hopelessly against him."

" We won't say ' hopelessly,' " replied Thorndyke, as we took our places in the carriage, " though I expect the police are pretty cocksure. When does the inquest open ? "

" To-day at four. I have obtained an order from the coroner for you to examine the body and be present at the post-mortem."

" Do you happen to know the exact position of the wound ? "

" Yes ; it is a little above and behind the left ear—

a horrible round hole, with a ragged cut or tear running from it to the side of the forehead."

" And how was the body lying ? "

" Right along the floor, with the feet close to the off-side door."

" Was the wound on the head the only one ? "

" No ; there was a long cut or bruise on the right cheek—a contused wound the police surgeon called it, which he believes to have been inflicted with a heavy and rather blunt weapon. I have not heard of any other wounds or bruises."

" Did anyone enter the train yesterday at Shingle-hurst ? " Thorndyke asked.

" No one entered the train after it left Halbury."

Thorndyke considered these statements in silence, and presently fell into a brown study, from which he roused only as the train moved out of Shinglehurst station.

" It would be about here that the murder was committed," said Mr. Stopford ; " at least, between here and Woldhurst."

Thorndyke nodded rather abstractedly, being engaged at the moment in observing with great attention the objects that were visible from the windows.

" I notice," he remarked presently, " a number of chips scattered about between the rails, and some of the chair-wedges look new. Have there been any platelayers at work lately ? "

" Yes," answered Stopford, " they are on the line now, I believe—at least, I saw a gang working near Woldhurst yesterday, and they are said to have set a rick on fire ; I saw it smoking when I came down."

" Indeed ; and this middle line of rails is, I suppose, a sort of siding ? "

" Yes ; they shunt the goods trains and empty trucks on to it. There are the remains of the rick—still smouldering, you see."

Thorndyke gazed absently at the blackened heap

until an empty cattle-truck on the middle track hid it from view. This was succeeded by a line of goods-waggons, and these by a passenger coach, one compartment of which—a first-class—was closed up and sealed. The train now began to slow down rather suddenly, and a couple of minutes later we brought up in Woldhurst station.

It was evident that rumours of Thorndyke's advent had preceded us, for the entire staff—two porters, an inspector, and the station-master—were waiting expectantly on the platform, and the latter came forward, regardless of his dignity, to help us with our luggage.

" Do you think I could see the carriage ? " Thorndyke asked the solicitor.

" Not the inside, sir," said the station-master, on being appealed to. " The police have sealed it up. You would have to ask the inspector."

" Well, I can have a look at the outside, I suppose ? " said Thorndyke, and to this the station-master readily agreed, and offered to accompany us.

" What other first-class passengers were there ? " Thorndyke asked.

" None, sir. There was only one first-class coach, and the deceased was the only person in it. It has given us all a dreadful turn, this affair has," he continued, as we set off up the line. " I was on the platform when the train came in. We were watching a rick that was burning up the line, and a rare blaze it made, too ; and I was just saying that we should have to move the cattle-truck that was on the mid-track, because, you see, sir, the smoke and sparks were blowing across, and I thought it would frighten the poor beasts. And Mr. Felton he don't like his beasts handled roughly. He says it spoils the meat."

" No doubt he is right," said Thorndyke. " But now, tell me, do you think it is possible for any person to board or leave the train on the off-side unobserved ?

Could a man, for instance, enter a compartment on the off-side at one station and drop off as the train was slowing down at the next, without being seen ? "

" I doubt it," replied the station-master. " Still, I wouldn't say it is impossible."

" Thank you. Oh, and there's another question. You have a gang of men at work on the line, I see. Now, do those men belong to the district ? "

" No, sir ; they are strangers, every one, and pretty rough diamonds some of 'em are. But I shouldn't say there was any real harm in 'em. If you was suspecting any of 'em of being mixed up in this——"

" I am not," interrupted Thorndyke rather shortly. " I suspect nobody ; but I wish to get all the facts of the case at the outset."

" Naturally, sir," replied the abashed official ; and we pursued our way in silence.

" Do you remember, by the way," said Thorndyke, as we approached the empty coach, " whether the off-side door of the compartment was closed and locked when the body was discovered ? "

" It was closed, sir, but not locked. Why, sir, did you think——? "

" Nothing, nothing. The sealed compartment is the one, of course ? "

Without waiting for a reply, he commenced his survey of the coach, while I gently restrained our two companions from shadowing him, as they were disposed to do. The off-side footboard occupied his attention specially, and when he had scrutinised minutely the part opposite the fatal compartment, he walked slowly from end to end with his eyes but a few inches from its surface, as though he was searching for something.

Near what had been the rear end he stopped, and drew from his pocket a piece of paper ; then, with a moistened finger-tip he picked up from the footboard some evidently minute object, which he carefully transferred to the paper, folding the latter and placing it in his pocket-book.

He next mounted the footboard, and, having peered in through the window of the sealed compartment, produced from his pocket a small insufflator or powder-blower, with which he blew a stream of impalpable smoke-like powder on to the edges of the middle window, bestowing the closest attention on the irregular dusty patches in which it settled, and even measuring one on the jamb of the window with a pocket-rule. At length he stepped down, and, having carefully looked over the near-side footboard, announced that he had finished for the present.

As we were returning down the line, we passed a working man, who seemed to be viewing the chairs and sleepers with more than casual interest.

" That, I suppose, is one of the plate-layers ? " Thorndyke suggested to the station-master.

" Yes, the foreman of the gang," was the reply.

" I'll just step back and have a word with him, if you will walk on slowly." And my colleague turned back briskly and overtook the man, with whom he remained in conversation for some minutes.

" I think I see the police inspector on the platform," remarked Thorndyke, as we approached the station.

" Yes, there he is," said our guide. " Come down to see what you are after, sir, I expect." Which was doubtless the case, although the officer professed to be there by the merest chance.

" You would like to see the weapon, sir, I suppose ? " he remarked, when he had introduced himself.

" The umbrella-spike," Thorndyke corrected. " Yes, if I may. We are going to the mortuary now."

" Then you'll pass the station on the way ; so, if you care to look in, I will walk up with you."

This proposition being agreed to, we all proceeded to the police station, including the station-master, who was on the very tiptoe of curiosity.

" There you are, sir," said the inspector, unlocking his office, and ushering us in. " Don't say we haven't given every facility to the defence. There are all the effects of the accused, including the very weapon the deed was done with."

" Come, come," protested Thorndyke ; " we mustn't be premature." He took the stout ash staff from the officer, and, having examined the formidable spike through a lens, drew from his pocket a steel calliper-gauge, with which he carefully measured the diameter of the spike, and the staff to which it was fixed. " And now," he said, when he had made a note of the measurements in his book, " we will look at the colour-box and the sketch. Ha ! a very orderly man, your brother, Mr. Stopford. Tubes all in their places, palette-knives wiped clean, palette cleaned off and rubbed bright, brushes wiped—they ought to be washed before they stiffen—all this is very significant." He unstrapped the sketch from the blank canvas to which it was pinned, and, standing it on a chair in a good light, stepped back to look at it.

" And you tell me that that is only three hours' work ! " he exclaimed, looking at the lawyer. " It is really a marvellous achievement."

" My brother is a very rapid worker," replied Stopford dejectedly.

" Yes, but this is not only amazingly rapid ; it is in his very happiest vein—full of spirit and feeling. But we mustn't stay to look at it longer." He replaced the canvas on its pins, and having glanced at the locket and some other articles that lay in a drawer, thanked the inspector for his courtesy and withdrew.

" That sketch and the colour-box appear very suggestive to me," he remarked, as we walked up the street.

" To me also," said Stopford gloomily, " for they are under lock and key, like their owner, poor old fellow."

He sighed heavily, and we walked on in silence.

The mortuary-keeper had evidently heard of our arrival, for he was waiting at the door with the key in his hand, and, on being shown the coroner's order, unlocked the door, and we entered together ; but, after a momentary glance at the ghostly, shrouded figure lying upon the slate table, Stopford turned pale and retreated, saying that he would wait for us outside with the mortuary-keeper.

As soon as the door was closed and locked on the inside, Thorndyke glanced curiously round the bare, whitewashed building. A stream of sunlight poured in through the skylight, and fell upon the silent form that lay so still under its covering-sheet, and one stray beam glanced into a corner by the door, where, on a row of pegs and a deal table, the dead woman's clothing was displayed.

" There is something unspeakably sad in these poor relics, Jervis," said Thorndyke, as we stood before them. " To me they are more tragic, more full of pathetic suggestion, than the corpse itself. See the smart, jaunty hat, and the costly skirts hanging there, so desolate and forlorn ; the dainty *lingerie* on the table, neatly folded—by the mortuary-man's wife, I hope— the little French shoes and open-work silk stockings. How pathetically eloquent they are of harmless, womanly vanity, and the gay, careless life, snapped short in the twinkling of an eye. But we must not give way to sentiment. There is another life threatened, and it is in our keeping."

He lifted the hat from its peg, and turned it over in his hand. It was, I think, what is called a " picture-hat "—a huge, flat, shapeless mass of gauze and ribbon and feather, spangled over freely with dark-blue sequins. In one part of the brim was a ragged hole, and from this the glittering sequins dropped off in little showers when the hat was moved.

" This will have been worn tilted over on the left

side," said Thorndyke, " judging by the general shape
and the position of the hole."

" Yes," I agreed.   " Like that of the Duchess of
Devonshire in Gainsborough's portrait."

" Exactly."

He shook a few of the sequins into the palm of his
hand, and, replacing the hat on its peg, dropped the
little discs into an envelope, on which he wrote, " From
the hat," and slipped it into his pocket.   Then, stepping
over to the table, he drew back the sheet reverently
and even tenderly from the dead woman's face, and
looked down at it with grave pity.   It was a comely
face, white as marble, serene and peaceful in expression, with half-closed eyes, and framed with a mass of
brassy, yellow hair ; but its beauty was marred by a
long linear wound, half cut, half bruise, running down
the right cheek from the eye to the chin.

" A   handsome   girl,"   Thorndyke   commented—" a
dark-haired blonde.   What a sin to have disfigured
herself so with that horrible peroxide."   He smoothed
the hair back from her forehead, and added : " She
seems to have applied the stuff last about ten days ago.
There is about a quarter of an inch of dark hair at the
roots.   What do you make of that wound on the cheek ? "

" It looks as if she had struck some sharp angle in
falling, though, as the seats are padded in first-class
carriages, I don't see what she could have struck."

" No.   And now let us look at the other wound.
Will you note down the description ? "   He handed
me his notebook, and I wrote down as he dictated :
" A clean-punched circular hole in skull, an inch behind
and above margin of left ear—diameter, an inch and
seven-sixteenths ;   starred fracture of parietal bone ;
membranes   perforated,   and   brain   entered   deeply ;
ragged scalp-wound, extending forward to margin of
left orbit ; fragments of gauze and sequins in edges of
wound.   That will do for the present.   Dr. Morton
will give us further details if we want them."

He pocketed his callipers and rule, drew from the bruised scalp one or two loose hairs, which he placed in the envelope with the sequins, and, having looked over the body for other wounds or bruises (of which there were none), replaced the sheet, and prepared to depart.

As we walked away from the mortuary, Thorndyke was silent and deeply thoughtful, and I gathered that he was piecing together the facts that he had acquired. At length Mr. Stopford, who had several times looked at him curiously, said :

" The post-mortem will take place at three, and it is now only half-past eleven. What would you like to do next ? "

Thorndyke, who, in spite of his mental preoccupation, had been looking about him in his usual keen, attentive way, halted suddenly.

" Your reference to the post-mortem," said he, " reminds me that I forgot to put the ox-gall into my case."

" Ox-gall ! " I exclaimed, endeavouring vainly to connect this substance with the technique of the pathologist. " What were you going to do with——"

But here I broke off, remembering my friend's dislike of any discussion of his methods before strangers.

" I suppose," he continued, " there would hardly be an artist's colourman in a place of this size ? "

" I should think not," said Stopford. " But couldn't you get the stuff from a butcher ? There's a shop just across the road."

" So there is," agreed Thorndyke, who had already observed the shop. " The gall ought, of course, to be prepared, but we can filter it ourselves—that is, if the butcher has any. We will try him, at any rate."

He crossed the road towards the shop, over which the name " Felton " appeared in gilt lettering, and, addressing himself to the proprietor, who stood at the door, introduced himself and explained his wants.

" Ox-gall ? " said the butcher. " No, sir, I haven't
any just now ; but I am having a beast killed this afternoon, and I can let you have some then. In fact," he
added, after a pause, " as the matter is of importance,
I can have one killed at once if you wish it."

" That is very kind of you," said Thorndyke, " and
it would greatly oblige me. Is the beast perfectly
healthy ? "

" They're in splendid condition, sir. I picked them
out of the herd myself. But you shall see them—ay,
and choose the one that you'd like killed."

" You are really very good," said Thorndyke warmly.
" I will just run into the chemist's next door, and get
a suitable bottle, and then I will avail myself of your
exceedingly kind offer."

He hurried into the chemist's shop, from which he
presently emerged, carrying a white paper parcel ; and
we then followed the butcher down a narrow lane by
the side of his shop. It led to an enclosure containing
a small pen, in which were confined three handsome
steers, whose glossy, black coats contrasted in a very
striking manner with their long, greyish-white, nearly
straight horns.

" These are certainly very fine beasts, Mr. Felton,"
said Thorndyke, as we drew up beside the pen, " and
in excellent condition, too."

He leaned over the pen and examined the beasts
critically, especially as to their eyes and horns ; then,
approaching the nearest one, he raised his stick and
bestowed a smart tap on the under-side of the right
horn, following it by a similar tap on the left one, a
proceeding that the beast viewed with stolid surprise.

" The state of the horns," explained Thorndyke, as
he moved on to the next steer, " enables one to judge,
to some extent, of the beast's health."

" Lord bless you, sir," laughed Mr. Felton, " they
haven't got no feeling in their horns, else what good
'ud their horns be to 'em ? "

Apparently he was right, for the second steer was as indifferent to a sounding rap on either horn as the first. Nevertheless, when Thorndyke approached the third steer, I unconsciously drew nearer to watch ; and I noticed that, as the stick struck the horn, the beast drew back in evident alarm, and that when the blow was repeated, it became manifestly uneasy.

" He don't seem to like that," said the butcher. " Seems as if—— Hullo, that's queer ! "

Thorndyke had just brought his stick up against the left horn, and immediately the beast had winced and started back, shaking his head and moaning. There was not, however, room for him to back out of reach, and Thorndyke, by leaning into the pen, was able to inspect the sensitive horn, which he did with the closest attention, while the butcher looked on with obvious perturbation.

" You don't think there's anything wrong with this beast, sir, I hope," said he.

" I can't say without a further examination," replied Thorndyke. " It may be the horn only that is affected. If you will have it sawn off close to the head, and sent up to me at the hotel, I will look at it and tell you. And, by way of preventing any mistakes I will mark it and cover it up, to protect it from injury in the slaughter-house."

He opened his parcel and produced from it a wide-mouthed bottle labelled " Ox-gall," a sheet of gutta-percha tissue, a roller bandage, and a stick of sealing-wax. Handing the bottle to Mr. Felton, he encased the distal half of the horn in a covering by means of the tissue and the bandage, which he fixed securely with the sealing-wax.

" I'll saw the horn off and bring it up to the hotel myself, with the ox-gall," said Mr. Felton. " You shall have them in half an hour."

He was as good as his word, for in half an hour Thorndyke was seated at a small table by the window of our private sitting-room in the Black Bull Hotel. The table was covered with newspaper, and on it lay the long grey horn and Thorndyke's travelling-case, now open and displaying a small microscope and its accessories. The butcher was seated solidly in an arm-chair waiting, with a half-suspicious eye on Thorndyke, for the report ; and I was endeavouring by cheerful talk to keep Mr. Stopford from sinking into utter despondency, though I, too, kept a furtive watch on my colleague's rather mysterious proceedings.

I saw him unwind the bandage and apply the horn to his ear, bending it slightly to and fro. I watched him, as he scanned the surface closely through a lens, and observed him as he scraped some substance from the pointed end on to a glass slide, and, having applied a drop of some reagent, began to tease out the scraping with a pair of mounted needles. Presently he placed the slide under the microscope, and, having observed it attentively for a minute or two, turned round sharply.

" Come and look at this, Jervis," said he.

I wanted no second bidding, being on tenterhooks of curiosity, but came over and applied my eye to the instrument.

" Well, what is it ? " he asked.

" A multipolar nerve corpuscle—very shrivelled, but unmistakable."

" And this ? "

He moved the slide to a fresh spot.

" Two pyramidal nerve corpuscles and some portions of fibres."

" And what do you say the tissue is ? "

" Cortical brain substance, I should say, without a doubt."

" I entirely agree with you. And that being so," he added, turning to Mr. Stopford, " we may say that the case for the defence is practically complete."

" What, in Heaven's name, do you mean ? " exclaimed Stopford, starting up.

" I mean that we can now prove when and where
and how Miss Grant met her death. Come and sit
down here, and I will explain. No, you needn't go
away, Mr. Felton. We shall have to subpœna you.
Perhaps," he continued, " we had better go over the
facts and see what they suggest. And first we note
the position of the body, lying with the feet close to
the off-side door, showing that, when she fell, the
deceased was sitting, or more probably standing, close
to that door. Next there is this." He drew from his
pocket a folded paper, which he opened, displaying a
tiny blue disc. " It is one of the sequins with which
her hat was trimmed, and I have in this envelope several
more which I took from the hat itself.

" This single sequin I picked up on the rear end of
the off-side footboard, and its presence there makes it
nearly certain that at some time Miss Grant had put
her head out of the window on that side.

" The next item of evidence I obtained by dusting
the margins of the off-side window with a light powder,
which made visible a greasy impression three and a
quarter inches long on the sharp corner of the right-
hand jamb (right-hand from the inside, I mean).

" And now as to the evidence furnished by the body.
The wound in the skull is behind and above the left
ear, is roughly circular, and measures one inch and
seven-sixteenths at most, and a ragged scalp-wound
runs from it towards the left eye. On the right cheek
is a linear contused wound three and a quarter inches
long. There are no other injuries.

" Our next facts are furnished by this." He took
up the horn and tapped it with his finger, while the
solicitor and Mr. Felton stared at him in speechless
wonder. " You notice it is a left horn, and you remember that it was highly sensitive. If you put your
ear to it while I strain it, you will hear the grating of a
fracture in the bony core. Now look at the pointed
end, and you will see several deep scratches running

lengthwise, and where those scratches end the diameter of the horn is, as you see by this calliper-gauge, one inch and seven-sixteenths. Covering the scratches is a dry blood-stain, and at the extreme tip is a small mass of a dried substance which Dr. Jervis and I have examined with the microscope and are satisfied is brain tissue."

" Good God ! " exclaimed Stopford eagerly. " Do you mean to say——"

" Let us finish with the facts, Mr. Stopford," Thorndyke interrupted. " Now, if you look closely at that blood-stain, you will see a short piece of hair stuck to the horn, and through this lens you can make out the root-bulb. It is a golden hair, you notice, but near the root it is black, and our calliper-gauge shows us that the black portion is fourteen sixty-fourths of an inch long. Now, in this envelope are some hairs that I removed from the dead woman's head. They also are golden hairs, black at the roots, and when I measure the black portion I find it to be fourteen sixty-fourths of an inch long. Then, finally, there is this."

He turned the horn over, and pointed to a small patch of dried blood. Embedded in it was a blue sequin.

Mr. Stopford and the butcher both gazed at the horn in silent amazement ; then the former drew a deep breath and looked up at Thorndyke.

" No doubt," said he, " you can explain this mystery, but for my part I am utterly bewildered, though you are filling me with hope."

" And yet the matter is quite simple," returned Thorndyke, " even with these few facts before us, which are only a selection from the body of evidence in our possession. But I will state my theory, and you shall judge." He rapidly sketched a rough plan on a sheet of paper, and continued : " These were the conditions when the train was approaching Woldhurst : Here was the passenger-coach, here was the burning rick, and here was a cattle-truck. This steer was in that truck. Now my hypothesis is that at that time Miss Grant was standing with her head out of the off-side window, watching the burning rick. Her wide hat, worn on the left side, hid from her view the cattle-truck which she was approaching, and then this is what happened." He sketched another plan to a larger scale. " One of the steers—this one—had thrust its long horn out through the bars. The point of that horn struck the deceased's head, driving her face violently against the corner of the window, and then, in disengaging, ploughed its way through the scalp and suffered a fracture of its core from the violence of the wrench. This hypothesis is inherently probable, it fits all the facts, and those facts admit of no other explanation."

The solicitor sat for a moment as though dazed, then he rose impulsively and seized Thorndyke's hands.

" I don't know what to say to you," he exclaimed huskily, " except that you have saved my brother's life, and for that may God reward you ! "

The butcher rose from his chair with a slow grin.

" It seems to me," said he, " as if that ox-gall was what you might call a blind, eh, sir ? "

And Thorndyke smiled an inscrutable smile.

When we returned to town on the following day we were a party of four, which included Mr. Harold Stopford. The verdict of " Death by misadventure," promptly returned by the coroner's jury, had been shortly followed by his release from custody, and he now sat with his brother and me, listening with rapt attention to Thorndyke's analysis of the case.

" So, you see," the latter concluded, " I had six possible theories of the cause of death worked out before I reached Halbury, and it only remained to select the one that fitted the facts. And when I had seen the cattle-truck, had picked up that sequin, had heard the description of the steers, and had seen the

hat and the wounds, there was nothing left to do but
the filling in of details."

" And you never doubted my innocence ? " asked
Harold Stopford.

Thorndyke smiled at his quondam client.

" Not after I had seen your colour-box and your
sketch," said he, " to say nothing of the spike."

11

THE MOABITE
CIPHER

A LARGE and motley crowd lined the pavements of
Oxford Street as Thorndyke and I made our way
leisurely eastward. Floral decorations and drooping
bunting announced one of those functions inaugurated
from time to time by a benevolent Government for
the entertainment of fashionable loungers and the
relief of distressed pickpockets. For a Russian Grand
Duke, who had torn himself away, amidst valedictory
explosions, from a loving if too demonstrative people,
was to pass anon on his way to the Guildhall ; and a
British Prince, heroically indiscreet, was expected to
occupy a seat in the ducal carriage.

Near Rathbone Place Thorndyke halted and drew
my attention to a smart-looking man who stood
lounging in a doorway, cigarette in hand.

" Our old friend Inspector Badger," said Thorndyke.
" He seems mightily interested in that gentleman in
the light overcoat. How d'ye do, Badger ? " for at
this moment the detective caught his eye and bowed.
" Who is your friend ? "

" That's what I want to know, sir," replied the
inspector. " I've been shadowing him for the last half-
hour, but I can't make him out, though I believe I've
seen him somewhere. He don't look like a foreigner,
but he has got something bulky in his pocket, so I must

keep him in sight until the Duke is safely past. I wish," he added gloomily, " these beastly Russians would stop at home. They give us no end of trouble."

" Are you expecting any—occurrences, then ? " asked Thorndyke.

" Bless you, sir," exclaimed Badger, " the whole route is lined with plain-clothes men. You see, it is known that several desperate characters followed the Duke to England, and there are a good many exiles living here who would like to have a rap at him. Hallo ! What's he up to now ? "

The man in the light overcoat had suddenly caught the inspector's too inquiring eye, and forthwith dived into the crowd at the edge of the pavement. In his haste he trod heavily on the foot of a big, rough-looking man, by whom he was in a moment hustled out into the road with such violence that he fell sprawling face downwards. It was an unlucky moment. A mounted constable was just then backing in upon the crowd, and before he could gather the meaning of the shout that arose from the bystanders, his horse had set down one hind-hoof firmly on the prostrate man's back.

The inspector signalled to a constable, who forthwith made a way for us through the crowd ; but even as we approached the injured man, he rose stiffly and looked round with a pale, vacant face.

" Are you hurt ? " Thorndyke asked gently, with an earnest look into the frightened, wondering eyes.

" No, sir," was the reply ; " only I feel queer—sinking—just here."

He laid a trembling hand on his chest, and Thorndyke, still eyeing him anxiously, said in a low voice to the inspector : " Cab or ambulance, as quickly as you can."

A cab was led round from Newman Street, and the injured man put into it. Thorndyke, Badger, and I entered, and we drove off up Rathbone Place. As we proceeded, our patient's face grew more and more

ashen, drawn, and anxious ; his breathing was shallow
and uneven, and his teeth chattered slightly. The
cab swung round into Goodge Street, and then—
suddenly, in the twinkling of an eye—there came a
change. The eyelids and jaw relaxed, the eyes became
filmy, and the whole form subsided into the corner
in a shrunken heap, with the strange gelatinous
limpness of a body that is dead as a whole, while its
tissues are still alive.

" God save us ! The man's dead ! " exclaimed the
inspector in a shocked voice—for even policemen have
their feelings. He sat staring at the corpse, as it
nodded gently with the jolting of the cab, until we
drew up inside the courtyard of the Middlesex Hospital,
when he got out briskly, with suddenly renewed cheer-
fulness, to help the porter to place the body on the
wheeled couch.

" We shall know who he is now, at any rate," said
he, as we followed the couch to the casualty-room.
Thorndyke nodded unsympathetically. The medical
instinct in him was for the moment stronger than the
legal.

The house-surgeon leaned over the couch, and made
a rapid examination as he listened to our account of
the accident. Then he straightened himself up and
looked at Thorndyke.

" Internal hæmorrhage, I expect," said he. " At
any rate, he's dead, poor beggar !—as dead as Nebu-
chadnezzar. Ah ! here comes a bobby ; it's his affair
now."

A sergeant came into the room, breathing quickly,
and looked in surprise from the corpse to the inspector.
But the latter, without loss of time, proceeded to turn
out the dead man's pockets, commencing with the
bulky object that had first attracted his attention ;
which proved to be a brown-paper parcel tied up with
red tape.

" Pork-pie, begad ! " he exclaimed with a crestfallen air as he cut the tape and opened the package. "You had better go through his other pockets, sergeant."

The small heap of odds and ends that resulted from this process tended, with a single exception, to throw little light on the man's identity ; the exception being a letter, sealed, but not stamped, addressed in an exceedingly illiterate hand to Mr. Adolf Schönberg, 213, Greek Street, Soho.

"He was going to leave it by hand, I expect," observed the inspector, with a wistful glance at the sealed envelope. "I think I'll take it round myself, and you had better come with me, sergeant."

He slipped the letter into his pocket, and, leaving the sergeant to take possession of the other effects, made his way out of the building.

"I suppose, doctor," said he, as we crossed into Berners Street, "you are not coming our way ? Don't want to see Mr. Schönberg, h'm ? "

Thorndyke reflected for a moment. "Well, it isn't very far, and we may as well see the end of the incident. Yes ; let us go together."

No. 213, Greek Street, was one of those houses that irresistibly suggest to the observer the idea of a church organ, either jamb of the doorway being adorned with a row of brass bell-handles corresponding to the stop-knobs.

These the sergeant examined with the air of an expert musician, and having, as it were, gauged the capacity of the instrument, selected the middle knob on the right-hand side and pulled it briskly ; whereupon a first-floor window was thrown up and a head protruded. But it afforded us a momentary glimpse only, for, having caught the sergeant's upturned eye, it retired with surprising precipitancy, and before we had time to speculate on the apparition, the street-door was opened and a man emerged. He was about to close the door after him when the inspector interposed.

" Does Mr. Adolf Schönberg live here ? "

The new-comer, a very typical Jew of the red-haired type, surveyed us thoughtfully through his gold-rimmed spectacles as he repeated the name.

" Schönberg—Schönberg ? Ah, yes ! I know. He lives on the third-floor. I saw him go up a short time ago. Third-floor back " ; and indicating the open door with a wave of the hand, he raised his hat and passed into the street.

" I suppose we had better go up," said the inspector, with a dubious glance at the row of bell-pulls. He accordingly started up the stairs, and we all followed in his wake.

There were two doors at the back on the third-floor, but as the one was open, displaying an un-occupied bedroom, the inspector rapped smartly on the other. It flew open almost immediately, and a fierce-looking little man confronted us with a hostile stare.

" Well ? " said he.

" Mr. Adolf Schönberg ? " inquired the inspector.

" Well ? What about him ? " snapped our new acquaintance.

" I wished to have a few words with him," said Badger.

" Then what the deuce do you come banging at *my* door for ? " demanded the other.

" Why, doesn't he live here ? "

" No. First-floor front," replied our friend, pre-paring to close the door.

" Pardon me," said Thorndyke, " but what is Mr. Schönberg like ? I mean——"

" Like ? " interrupted the resident. " He's like a blooming Sheeny, with a carroty beard and gold gig-lamps ! " and, having presented this impressionist sketch, he brought the interview to a definite close by slamming the door and turning the key.

With a wrathful exclamation, the inspector turned towards the stairs, down which the sergeant was already clattering in hot haste, and made his way back to the ground-floor, followed, as before, by Thorndyke and me. On the doorstep we found the sergeant breathlessly interrogating a smartly-dressed youth, whom I had seen alight from a hansom as we entered the house, and who now stood with a notebook tucked under his arm, sharpening a pencil with deliberate care.

"Mr. James saw him come out, sir," said the sergeant. "He turned up towards the Square."

"Did he seem to hurry?" asked the inspector.

"Rather," replied the reporter. "As soon as you were inside, he went off like a lamplighter. You won't catch him now."

"We don't want to catch him," the detective rejoined gruffly; then, backing out of earshot of the eager press-man, he said in a lower tone: "That was Mr. Schönberg, beyond a doubt, and it is clear that he has some reason for making himself scarce; so I shall consider myself justified in opening that note."

He suited the action to the word, and, having cut the envelope open with official neatness, drew out the enclosure.

"My hat!" he exclaimed, as his eye fell upon the contents. "What in creation is this? It isn't short-hand, but what the deuce is it?"

He handed the document to Thorndyke, who, having held it up to the light and felt the paper critically, proceeded to examine it with keen interest. It consisted of a single half-sheet of thin notepaper, both sides of which were covered with strange, crabbed characters, written with a brownish-black ink in continuous lines, without any spaces to indicate the divisions into words; and, but for the modern material which bore the writing, it might have been a portion of some ancient manuscript or forgotten codex.

"What do you make of it, doctor?" inquired the inspector anxiously, after a pause, during which Thorndyke had scrutinised the strange writing with knitted brows.

"Not a great deal," replied Thorndyke. "The character is the Moabite or Phœnician—primitive Semitic, in fact—and reads from right to left. The language I take to be Hebrew. At any rate, I can find no Greek words, and I see here a group of letters which *may* form one of the few Hebrew words that I know—the word *badim*, 'lies.' But you had better get it deciphered by an expert."

"If it is Hebrew," said Badger, "we can manage it all right. There are plenty of Jews at our disposal."

"You had much better take the paper to the British Museum," said Thorndyke, "and submit it to the keeper of the Phœnician antiquities for decipherment."

Inspector Badger smiled a foxy smile as he deposited the paper in his pocket-book. "We'll see what we can make of it ourselves first," he said; "but many thanks for your advice, all the same, doctor. No, Mr. James, I can't give you any information just at present; you had better apply at the hospital."

"I suspect," said Thorndyke, as we took our way homewards, "that Mr. James has collected enough material for his purpose already. He must have followed us from the hospital, and I have no doubt that he has his report, with 'full details,' mentally arranged at this moment. And I am not sure that he didn't get a peep at the mysterious paper, in spite of the inspector's precautions."

"By the way," I said, "what do you make of the document?"

"A cipher, most probably," he replied. "It is written in the primitive Semitic alphabet, which, as you know, is practically identical with primitive Greek. It is written from right to left, like the Phœnician, Hebrew, and Moabite, as well as the earliest Greek, inscriptions. The paper is common cream-laid note-paper, and the ink is ordinary indelible Chinese ink, such as is used by draughtsmen. Those are the facts, and without further study of the document itself, they don't carry us very far."

" Why do you think it is a cipher rather than a document in straightforward Hebrew ? "

" Because it is obviously a secret message of some kind. Now, every educated Jew knows more or less Hebrew, and, although he is able to read and write only the modern square Hebrew character, it is so easy to transpose one alphabet into another that the mere language would afford no security. Therefore, I expect that, when the experts translate this document, the translation or transliteration will be a mere farrago of unintelligible nonsense. But we shall see, and meanwhile the facts that we have offer several interesting suggestions which are well worth consideration."

" As, for instance—— ? "

" Now, my dear Jervis," said Thorndyke, shaking an admonitory forefinger at me, " don't, I pray you, give way to mental indolence. You have these few facts that I have mentioned. Consider them separately and collectively, and in their relation to the circumstances. Don't attempt to suck my brain when you have an excellent brain of your own to suck."

On the following morning the papers fully justified my colleague's opinion of Mr. James. All the events which had occurred, as well as a number that had not, were given in the fullest and most vivid detail, a lengthy reference being made to the paper " found on the person of the dead anarchist," and " written in a private shorthand or cryptogram."

The report concluded with the gratifying—though untrue—statement that " in this intricate and important case, the police have wisely secured the assistance of Dr. John Thorndyke, to whose acute intellect and vast experience the portentous cryptogram will doubtless soon deliver up its secret."

" Very flattering," laughed Thorndyke, to whom I

12

read the extract on his return from the hospital, " but a little awkward if it should induce our friends to deposit a few trifling mementoes in the form of nitro-compounds on our main staircase or in the cellars. By the way, I met Superintendent Miller on London Bridge. The ' cryptogram,' as Mr. James calls it, has set Scotland Yard in a mighty ferment."

" Naturally. What have they done in the matter ? "

" They adopted my suggestion, after all, finding that they could make nothing of it themselves, and took it to the British Museum. The Museum people referred them to Professor Poppelbaum, the great palæographer, to whom they accordingly submitted it."

" Did he express any opinion about it ? "

" Yes, provisionally. After a brief examination, he found it to consist of a number of Hebrew words sand-wiched between apparently meaningless groups of letters. He furnished the Superintendent off-hand with a translation of the words, and Miller forthwith struck off a number of hectograph copies of it, which he has distributed among the senior officials of his depart-ment ; so that at present "—here Thorndyke gave vent to a soft chuckle—" Scotland Yard is engaged in a sort of missing word—or, rather, missing sense—com-petition. Miller invited me to join in the sport, and to that end presented me with one of the hectograph copies on which to exercise my wits, together with a photograph of the document."

" And shall you ? " I asked.

" Not I," he replied, laughing. " In the first place, I have not been formally consulted, and consequently am a passive, though interested, spectator. In the second place, I have a theory of my own which I shall test if the occasion arises. But if you would like to take part in the competition, I am authorised to show you the photograph and the translation. I will pass them on to you, and I wish you joy of them."

He handed me the photograph and a sheet of paper

that he had just taken from his pocket-book, and watched me with grim amusement as I read out the first few lines.

THE CIPHER.

" Woe, city, lies, robbery, prey, noise, whip, rattling, vheel, horse, chariot, day, darkness, gloominess, clouds, larkness, morning, mountain, people, strong, fire, them, lame."

" It doesn't look very promising at first sight," I emarked. " What is the Professor's theory ? "

" His theory—provisionally, of course—is that the words form the message, and the groups of letters represent mere filled-up spaces between the words."

" But surely," I protested, " that would be a very transparent device."

Thorndyke laughed. " There is a childlike simplicity about it," said he, " that is highly attractive—but discouraging. It is much more probable that the words are dummies, and that the letters contain the message. Or, again, the solution may lie in an entirely different direction. But listen ! Is that cab coming here ? "

It was. It drew up opposite our chambers, and a few moments later a brisk step ascending the stairs heralded a smart rat-tat at our door. Flinging open the latter, I found myself confronted by a well-dressed stranger, who, after a quick glance at me, peered inquisitively over my shoulder into the room.

" I am relieved, Dr. Jervis," said he, " to find you and Dr. Thorndyke at home, as I have come on some-what urgent professional business. My name," he con-tinued, entering in response to my invitation, " is Barton, but you don't know me, though I know you both by sight. I have come to ask you if one of you —or, better still, both—could come to-night and see my brother."

" That," said Thorndyke, " depends on the circum-stances and on the whereabouts of your brother."

" The circumstances," said Mr. Barton, " are, in my opinion, highly suspicious, and I will place them before you—of course, in strict confidence."

Thorndyke nodded and indicated a chair.

" My brother," continued Mr. Barton, taking the proffered seat, " has recently married for the second time. His age is fifty-five, and that of his wife twenty-six, and I may say that the marriage has been—well, by no means a success. Now, within the last fort-night, my brother has been attacked by a mysterious and extremely painful affection of the stomach, to which his doctor seems unable to give a name. It has resisted all treatment hitherto. Day by day the pain and distress increase, and I feel that, unless something decisive is done, the end cannot be far off."

"Is the pain worse after taking food?" inquired Thorndyke.

"That's just it!" exclaimed our visitor. "I see what is in your mind, and it has been in mine, too; so much so that I have tried repeatedly to obtain samples of the food that he is taking. And this morning I succeeded." Here he took from his pocket a wide-mouthed bottle, which, disengaging from its paper wrappings, he laid on the table. "When I called, he was taking his breakfast of arrowroot, which he complained had a gritty taste, supposed by his wife to be due to the sugar. Now I had provided myself with this bottle, and, during the absence of his wife, I managed unobserved to convey a portion of the arrowroot that he had left into it, and I should be greatly obliged if you would examine it and tell me if this arrowroot contains anything that it should not."

He pushed the bottle across to Thorndyke, who carried it to the window, and, extracting a small quantity of the contents with a glass rod, examined the pasty mass with the aid of a lens; then, lifting the bell-glass cover from the microscope, which stood on its table by the window, he smeared a small quantity of the suspected matter on to a glass slip, and placed it on the stage of the instrument.

"I observe a number of crystalline particles in this," he said, after a brief inspection, "which have the appearance of arsenious acid."

"Ah!" ejaculated Mr. Barton, "just what I feared. But are you certain?"

"No," replied Thorndyke; "but the matter is easily tested."

He pressed the button of the bell that communicated

with the laboratory, a summons that brought the laboratory assistant from his lair with characteristic promptitude.

"Will you please prepare a Marsh's apparatus, Polton," said Thorndyke.

"I have a couple ready, sir," replied Polton.

"Then pour the acid into one and bring it to me, with a tile."

As his familiar vanished silently, Thorndyke turned to Mr. Barton.

"Supposing we find arsenic in this arrowroot, as we probably shall, what do you want us to do?"

"I want you to come and see my brother," replied our client.

"Why not take a note from me to his doctor?"

"No, no; I want you to come—I should like you both to come—and put a stop at once to this dreadful business. Consider! It's a matter of life and death. You won't refuse! I beg you not to refuse me your help in these terrible circumstances."

"Well," said Thorndyke, as his assistant reappeared, "let us first see what the test has to tell us."

Polton advanced to the table, on which he deposited a small flask, the contents of which were in a state of brisk effervescence, a bottle labelled "calcium hypochlorite," and a white porcelain tile. The flask was fitted with a safety-funnel and a glass tube drawn out to a fine jet, to which Polton cautiously applied a lighted match. Instantly there sprang from the jet a tiny, pale violet flame. Thorndyke now took the tile, and held it in the flame for a few seconds, when the appearance of the surface remained unchanged save for a small circle of condensed moisture. His next proceeding was to thin the arrowroot with distilled water until it was quite fluid, and then pour a small quantity into the funnel. It ran slowly down the tube into the flask, with the bubbling contents of which it became speedily mixed. Almost immediately a change began to appear in the character of the flame, which from a pale violet turned gradually to a sickly blue, while above it hung a faint cloud of white smoke. Once more Thorndyke held the tile above the jet, but this time, no sooner had the pallid flame touched the cold surface of the porcelain, than there appeared on the latter a glistening black stain.

"That is pretty conclusive," observed Thorndyke, lifting the stopper out of the reagent bottle, "but we will apply the final test." He dropped a few drops of the hypochlorite solution on to the tile, and immediately the black stain faded away and vanished. "We can now · answer your question, Mr. Barton," said he, replacing the stopper as he turned to our client. "The specimen that you brought us certainly contains arsenic, and in very considerable quantities."

"Then," exclaimed Mr. Barton, starting from his chair, "you will come and help me to rescue my brother from this dreadful peril. Don't refuse me, Dr. Thorndyke, for mercy's sake, don't refuse."

Thorndyke reflected for a moment.

"Before we decide," said he, "we must see what engagements we have."

With a quick, significant glance at me, he walked into the office, whither I followed in some bewilderment, for I knew that we had no engagements for the evening.

"Now, Jervis," said Thorndyke, as he closed the office door, "what are we to do?"

"We must go, I suppose," I replied. "It seems a pretty urgent case."

"It does," he agreed. "Of course, the man may be telling the truth, after all."

"You don't think he is, then?"

"No. It is a plausible tale, but there is too much arsenic in that arrowroot. Still, I think I ought to go. It is an ordinary professional risk. But there is no reason why you should put your head into the noose."

" Thank you," said I, somewhat huffily. " I don't see what risk there is, but if any exists I claim the right to share it."

" Very well," he answered with a smile, " we will both go. I think we can take care of ourselves."

He re-entered the sitting-room, and announced his decision to Mr. Barton, whose relief and gratitude were quite pathetic.

" But," said Thorndyke, " you have not yet told us where your brother lives."

" Rexford," was the reply—" Rexford, in Essex. It is an out-of-the-way place, but if we catch the seven-fifteen train from Liverpool Street, we shall be there in an hour and a half."

" And as to the return ? You know the trains, I suppose ? "

" Oh yes," replied our client ; " I will see that you don't miss your train back."

" Then I will be with you in a minute," said Thorndyke ; and, taking the still-bubbling flask, he retired to the laboratory, whence he returned in a few minutes carrying his hat and overcoat.

The cab which had brought our client was still waiting, and we were soon rattling through the streets towards the station, where we arrived in time to furnish ourselves with dinner-baskets and select our compartment at leisure.

During the early part of the journey our companion was in excellent spirits. He dispatched the cold fowl from the basket and quaffed the rather indifferent claret with as much relish as if he had not had a single relation in the world, and after dinner he became genial to the verge of hilarity. But, as time went on, there crept into his manner a certain anxious restlessness. He became silent and preoccupied, and several times furtively consulted his watch.

" The train is confoundedly late ! " he exclaimed irritably. " Seven minutes behind time already ! "

" A few minutes more or less are not of much consequence," said Thorndyke.

" No, of course not ; but still—— Ah, thank
Heaven, here we are ! "

He thrust his head out of the off-side window, and
gazed eagerly down the line ; then, leaping to his feet,
he bustled out on to the platform while the train was
still moving.

Even as we alighted a warning bell rang furiously
on the up-platform, and as Mr. Barton hurried us
through the empty booking-office to the outside of the
station, the rumble of the approaching train could
be heard above the noise made by our own train
moving off.

" My carriage doesn't seem to have arrived yet,"
exclaimed Mr. Barton, looking anxiously up the station
approach. " If you will wait here a moment, I will
go and make inquiries."

He darted back into the booking-office and through
it on to the platform, just as the up-train roared into
the station. Thorndyke followed him with quick but
stealthy steps, and, peering out of the booking-office
door, watched his proceedings ; then he turned and
beckoned to me.

" There he goes," said he, pointing to an iron footbridge that spanned the line ; and, as I looked, I saw,
clearly defined against the dim night sky, a flying
figure racing towards the " up " side.

It was hardly two-thirds across when the guard's
whistle rang out its shrill warning.

" Quick, Jervis," exclaimed Thorndyke ; " she's
off ! "

He leaped down on to the line, whither I followed
instantly, and, crossing the rails, we clambered up
together on to the footboard opposite an empty first-
class compartment. Thorndyke's magazine knife, containing, among other implements, a railway-key, was
already in his hand. The door was speedily unlocked,

12*

and, as we entered, Thorndyke ran through and looked out on to the platform.

"Just in time!" he exclaimed. "He is in one of the forward compartments."

He relocked the door, and, seating himself, proceeded to fill his pipe.

"And now," said I, as the train moved out of the station, "perhaps you will explain this little comedy."

"With pleasure," he replied, "if it needs any explanation. But you can hardly have forgotten Mr. James's flattering remarks in his report of the Greek Street incident, clearly giving the impression that the mysterious document was in my possession. When I read that, I knew I must look out for some attempt to recover it, though I hardly expected such promptness. Still, when Mr. Barton called without credentials or appointment, I viewed him with some suspicion. That suspicion deepened when he wanted us both to come. It deepened further when I found an impossible quantity of arsenic in his sample, and it gave place to certainty when, having allowed him to select the trains by which we were to travel, I went up to the laboratory and examined the time-table; for I then found that the last train for London left Rexford ten minutes after we were due to arrive. Obviously this was a plan to get us both safely out of the way while he and some of his friends ransacked our chambers for the missing document."

"I see; and that accounts for his extraordinary anxiety at the lateness of the train. But why did you come, if you knew it was a 'plant'?"

"My dear fellow," said Thorndyke, "I never miss an interesting experience if I can help it. There are possibilities in this, too, don't you see?"

"But supposing his friends have broken into our chambers already?"

"That contingency has been provided for; but I think they will wait for Mr. Barton—and us."

Our train, being the last one up, stopped at every station, and crawled slothfully in the intervals, so that it was past eleven o'clock when we reached Liverpool Street. Here we got out cautiously, and, mingling with the crowd, followed the unconscious Barton up the platform, through the barrier, and out into the street. He seemed in no special hurry, for, after pausing to light a cigar, he set off at an easy pace up New Broad Street.

Thorndyke hailed a hansom, and, motioning me to enter, directed the cabman to drive to Clifford's Inn Passage.

" Sit well back," said he, as we rattled away up New Broad Street. " We shall be passing our gay deceiver presently—in fact, there he is, a living, walking illustration of the folly of underrating the intelligence of one's adversary."

At Clifford's Inn Passage we dismissed the cab, and, retiring into the shadow of the dark, narrow alley, kept an eye on the gate of Inner Temple Lane. In about twenty minutes we observed our friend approaching on the south side of Fleet Street. He halted at the gate, plied the knocker, and after a brief parley with the night-porter vanished through the wicket. We waited yet five minutes more, and then, having given him time to get clear of the entrance, we crossed the road.

The porter looked at us with some surprise.

" There's a gentleman just gone down to your chambers, sir," said he. " He told me you were expecting him."

" Quite right," said Thorndyke, with a dry smile, " I was. Good-night."

We slunk down the lane, past the church, and through the gloomy cloisters, giving a wide berth to all lamps and lighted entries, until, emerging into Paper Buildings, we crossed at the darkest part to King's Bench Walk, where Thorndyke made straight for the chambers of our friend Anstey, which were two doors above our own.

" Why are we coming here ? " I asked, as we ascended the stairs.

But the question needed no answer when we reached the landing, for through the open door of our friend's chambers I could see in the darkened room Anstey himself with two uniformed constables and a couple of plain-clothes men.

" There has been no signal yet, sir," said one of the latter, whom I recognised as a detective-sergeant of our division.

" No," said Thorndyke, " but the M.C. has arrived. He came in five minutes before us."

" Then," exclaimed Anstey, " the ball will open shortly, ladies and gents. The boards are waxed, the fiddlers are tuning up, and——"

" Not quite so loud, if you please, sir," said the sergeant. " I think there is somebody coming up Crown Office Row."

The ball had, in fact, opened. As we peered cautiously out of the open window, keeping well back in the darkened room, a stealthy figure crept out of the shadow, crossed the road, and stole noiselessly into the entry of Thorndyke's chambers. It was quickly followed by a second figure, and then by a third, in which I recognised our elusive client.

" Now listen for the signal," said Thorndyke. " They won't waste time. Confound that clock ! "

The soft-voiced bell of the Inner Temple clock, mingling with the harsher tones of St. Dunstan's and the Law Courts, slowly told out the hour of midnight ; and as the last reverberations were dying away, some metallic object, apparently a coin, dropped with a sharp clink on to the pavement under our window.

At the sound the watchers simultaneously sprang to their feet.

" You two go first," said the sergeant, addressing the uniformed men, who thereupon stole noiselessly, in their rubber-soled boots, down the stone stairs and along the pavement. The rest of us followed, with less attention to silence, and as we ran up to Thorndyke's chambers, we were aware of quick but stealthy footsteps on the stairs above.

" They've been at work, you see," whispered one of the constables, flashing his lantern on to the iron-bound outer door of our sitting-room, on which the marks of a large jemmy were plainly visible.

The sergeant nodded grimly, and, bidding the constables to remain on the landing, led the way upwards.

As we ascended, faint rustlings continued to be audible from above, and on the second-floor landing we met a man descending briskly, but without hurry, from the third. It was Mr. Barton, and I could not but admire the composure with which he passed the two detectives. But suddenly his glance fell on Thorndyke, and his composure vanished. With a wild stare of incredulous horror, he halted as if petrified ; then he broke away and raced furiously down the stairs, and a moment later a muffled shout and the sound of a scuffle told us that he had received a check. On the next flight we met two more men, who, more hurried and less self-possessed, endeavoured to push past ; but the sergeant barred the way.

" Why, bless me ! " exclaimed the latter, " it's Moakey ; and isn't that Tom Harris ? "

" It's all right, sergeant," said Moakey plaintively, striving to escape from the officer's grip. " We've come to the wrong house, that's all."

The sergeant smiled indulgently. " I know," he replied. " But you're always coming to the wrong house, Moakey ; and now you're just coming along with me to the right house."

He slipped his hand inside his captive's coat, and adroitly fished out a large, folding jemmy ; whereupon the discomfited burglar abandoned all further protest.

On our return to the first-floor, we found Mr. Barton

sulkily awaiting us, handcuffed to one of the constables, and watched by Polton with pensive disapproval.

" I needn't trouble you to-night, doctor," said the sergeant, as he marshalled his little troop of captors and captives. " You'll hear from us in the morning. Good-night, sir."

The melancholy procession moved off down the stairs, and we retired into our chambers with Anstey to smoke a last pipe.

" A capable man, that Barton," observed Thorndyke—" ready, plausible, and ingenious, but spoilt by prolonged contact with fools. I wonder if the police will perceive the significance of this little affair."

" They will be more acute than I am if they do," said I.

" Naturally," interposed Anstey, who loved to " cheek" his revered senior, " because there isn't any. It's only Thorndyke's bounce. He is really in a deuce of a fog himself."

However this may have been, the police were a good deal puzzled by the incident, for, on the following morning, we received a visit from no less a person than Superintendent Miller, of Scotland Yard.

" This is a queer business," said he, coming to the point at once—" this burglary, I mean. Why should they want to crack your place, right here in the Temple, too ? You've got nothing of value here, have you ? No ' hard stuff,' as they call it, for instance ? "

" Not so much as a silver teaspoon," replied Thorndyke, who had a conscientious objection to plate of all kinds.

" It's odd," said the superintendent, " deuced odd. When we got your note, we thought these anarchist idiots had mixed you up with the case—you saw the papers, I suppose—and wanted to go through your rooms for some reason. We thought we had our hands on the gang, instead of which we find a party of common crooks that we're sick of the sight of. I tell you, sir, it's annoying when you think you've hooked a salmon, to bring up a blooming eel."

" It must be a great disappointment," Thorndyke agreed, suppressing a smile.

" It is," said the detective. " Not but what we're glad enough to get these beggars, especially Halkett, or Barton, as he calls himself—a mighty slippery customer is Halkett, and mischievous, too—but we're not wanting any disappointments just now. There was that big jewel job in Piccadilly, Taplin and Horne's ; I don't mind telling you that we've not got the ghost of a clue. Then there's this anarchist affair. We're all in the dark there, too."

" But what about the cipher ? " asked Thorndyke.

" Oh, hang the cipher ! " exclaimed the detective irritably. " This Professor Poppelbaum may be a very learned man, but he doesn't help *us* much. He says the document is in Hebrew, and he has translated it into Double Dutch. Just listen to this ! " He dragged out of his pocket a bundle of papers, and, dabbing down a photograph of the document before Thorndyke, commenced to read the Professor's report.

" ' The document is written in the characters of the well-known inscription of Mesha, King of Moab ' (who the devil's he ? Never heard of him. Well known, indeed !) ' The language is Hebrew, and the words are separated by groups of letters, which are meaningless, and obviously introduced to mislead and confuse the reader. The words themselves are not strictly consecutive, but, by the interpellation of certain other words, a series of intelligible sentences is obtained, the meaning of which is not very clear, but is no doubt allegorical. The method of decipherment is shown in the accompanying tables, and the full rendering suggested on the enclosed sheet. It is to be noted that the writer of this document was apparently quite unacquainted with the Hebrew language, as appears from the absence of any grammatical construction.' That's the Professor's report, doctor, and here are the tables showing how he worked it out. It makes my head spin to look at 'em.''

He handed to Thorndyke a bundle of ruled sheets, which my colleague examined attentively for a while, and then passed on to me.

" This is very systematic and thorough," said he. " But now let us see the final result at which he arrives.''

Analysis of the cipher with transliteration into modern square Hebrew characters & a translation into English. N.B. The cipher reads from right to left.

	Space	Word	Space	Word	Space	Word
Moabite	Y7	ꟼꟼ	07	470	94	7Y4
Hebrew		פָּדִים		עִיר		אוֹי
Translation		LIES		CITY		WOE
Moabite	57	6Y9	6Y?	74X	HI	6I7
Hebrew		קוֹל		טָרָח		גֵּזֶל
Translation		NOISE		PREY		ROBBERY
Moabite	w4	57Y&	9P	wo4	70#	XYW
Hebrew		אוֹפָן		רַעַשׁ		שׁוֹט
Translation		WHEEL		RATTLING		WHIP
Moabite	Y7	7YI	07	39747	94X	#Y#
Hebrew		יוֹם		מֶרְכָּבָה		סוּס
Translation		DAY		CHARIOT		HORSE

THE PROFESSOR'S ANALYSIS.

" It may be all very systematic," growled the super-intendent, sorting out his papers, " but I tell you, sir, it's all BOSH ! " The latter word he jerked out viciously, as he slapped down on the table the final product of the Professor's labours. " There," he continued, " that's what he calls the ' full rendering,' and I reckon it'll make your hair curl. It might be a message from Bedlam."

Thorndyke took up the first sheet, and as he compared the constructed renderings with the literal translation, the ghost of a smile stole across his usually immovable countenance.

" The meaning is certainly a little obscure," he observed, " though the reconstruction is highly ingenious ; and, moreover, I think the Professor is probably right. That is to say, the words which he has supplied are probably the omitted parts of the passages from which the words of the cryptogram were taken. What do you think, Jervis ? "

He handed me the two papers, of which one gave the actual words of the cryptogram, and the other a suggested reconstruction, with omitted words supplied. The first read :

" Woe	city	lies	robbery	prey
noise	whip	rattling	wheel	horse
chariot	day	darkness		gloominess
cloud	darkness	morning		mountain
people	strong	fire	them	flame."

Turning to the second paper, I read out the suggested rendering :

" ' Woe *to the bloody* city ! *It is full of* lies *and* robbery ; *the* prey *departeth not. The* noise *of a* whip, *and the noise of the* rattling *of the* wheels, *and of the prancing* horses, *and of the jumping* chariots.

" ' *A* day *of* darkness *and of* gloominess, *a day of* clouds, *and of thick* darkness, *as the* morning *spread upon the* mountains, *a great* people *and a* strong.

" ' *A* fire *devoureth before* them, *and behind them a* flame *burneth.' "

Here the first sheet ended, and, as I laid it down, Thorndyke looked at me inquiringly.

" There is a good deal of reconstruction in proportion to the original matter," I objected. " The Professor has ' supplied ' more than three-quarters of the final rendering."

"Exactly," burst in the superintendent; "it's all Professor and no cryptogram."

"Still, I think the reading is correct," said Thorndyke. "As far as it goes, that is."

"Good Lord!" exclaimed the dismayed detective. "Do you mean to tell me, sir, that that balderdash is the real meaning of the thing?"

"I don't say that," replied Thorndyke. "I say it is correct as far as it goes; but I doubt its being the solution of the cryptogram."

"Have you been studying that photograph that I gave you?" demanded Miller, with sudden eagerness.

"I have looked at it," said Thorndyke evasively, "but I should like to examine the original if you have it with you."

"I have," said the detective. "Professor Poppelbaum sent it back with the solution. You can have a look at it, though I can't leave it with you without special authority."

He drew the document from his pocket-book and handed it to Thorndyke, who took it over to the window and scrutinised it closely. From the window he drifted into the adjacent office, closing the door after him; and presently the sound of a faint explosion told me that he had lighted the gas-fire.

"Of course," said Miller, taking up the translation again, "this gibberish is the sort of stuff you might expect from a parcel of crack-brained anarchists; but it doesn't seem to mean anything."

"Not to us," I agreed; "but the phrases may have some prearranged significance. And then there are the letters between the words. It is possible that they may really form a cipher."

"I suggested that to the Professor," said Miller, "but he wouldn't hear of it. He is sure they are only dummies."

"I think he is probably mistaken, and so, I fancy,

does my colleague. But we shall hear what he has to say presently."

"Oh, I know what he will say," growled Miller. "He will put the thing under the microscope, and tell us who made the paper, and what the ink is composed of, and then we shall be just where we were." The superintendent was evidently deeply depressed.

We sat for some time pondering in silence on the vague sentences of the Professor's translation, until, at length, Thorndyke reappeared, holding the document in his hand. He laid it quietly on the table by the officer, and then inquired :

"Is this an official consultation ? "

"Certainly," replied Miller. "I was authorised to consult you respecting the translation, but nothing was said about the original. Still, if you want it for further study, I will get it for you."

"No, thank you," said Thorndyke. "I have finished with it. My theory turned out to be correct."

"Your theory ! " exclaimed the superintendent, eagerly. "Do you mean to say—— ? "

"And, as you are consulting me officially, I may as well give you this."

He held out a sheet of paper, which the detective took from him and began to read.

"What is this ? " he asked, looking up at Thorndyke with a puzzled frown. "Where did it come from ? "

"It is the solution of the cryptogram," replied Thorndyke.

The detective re-read the contents of the paper, and, with the frown of perplexity deepening, once more gazed at my colleague.

"This is a joke, sir ; you are fooling me," he said sulkily.

"Nothing of the kind," answered Thorndyke. "That is the genuine solution."

"But it's impossible ! " exclaimed Miller. "Just look at it, Dr. Jervis."

I took the paper from his hand, and, as I glanced at it, I had no difficulty in understanding his surprise. It bore a short inscription in printed Roman capitals, thus:

" THE PICKERDILLEY STUF IS UP THE CHIMBLY 416 WARDOUR ST 2ND FLOUR BACK IT WAS HID BECOS OF OLD MOAKEYS JOOD MOAKEY IS A BLITER."

" Then that fellow wasn't an anarchist at all ! " I exclaimed.

" No," said Miller. " He was one of Moakey's gang. We suspected Moakey of being mixed up with that job, but we couldn't fix it on him. By Jove ! " he added, slapping his thigh, " if this is right, and I can lay my hands on the loot ! Can you lend me a bag, doctor ? I'm off to Wardour Street this very moment."

We furnished him with an empty suit-case, and, from the window, watched him making for Mitre Court at a smart double.

" I wonder if he will find the booty," said Thorndyke. " It just depends on whether the hiding-place was known to more than one of the gang. Well, it has been a quaint case and instructive, too. I suspect our friend Barton and the evasive Schönberg were the collaborators who produced that curiosity of literature."

" May I ask how you deciphered the thing ? " I said. " It didn't appear to take long."

" It didn't. It was merely a matter of testing a hypothesis ; and you ought not to have to ask that question," he added, with mock severity, " seeing that you had what turn out to have been all the necessary facts, two days ago. But I will prepare a document and demonstrate to you to-morrow morning."

" So Miller was successful in his quest," said Thorndyke, as we smoked our morning pipes after breakfast. " The ' entire swag,' as he calls it, was ' up the chimbly,' undisturbed."

He handed me a note which had been left, with the empty suit-case, by a messenger, shortly before, and I was about to read it when an agitated knock was heard at our door. The visitor, whom I admitted, was a rather haggard and dishevelled elderly gentleman, who, as he entered, peered inquisitively through his concave spectacles from one of us to the other.

"Allow me to introduce myself, gentlemen," said he. "I am Professor Poppelbaum."

Thorndyke bowed and offered a chair.

"I called yesterday afternoon," our visitor continued, "at Scotland Yard, where I heard of your remarkable decipherment and of the convincing proof of its correctness. Thereupon I borrowed the cryptogram, and have spent the entire night in studying it, but I cannot connect your solution with any of the characters. I wonder if you would do me the great favour of enlightening me as to your method of decipherment, and so save me further sleepless nights? You may rely on my discretion."

"Have you the document with you?" asked Thorndyke.

The Professor produced it from his pocket-book, and passed it to my colleague.

"You observe, Professor," said the latter, "that this is a laid paper, and has no water-mark?"

"Yes, I noticed that."

"And that the writing is in indelible Chinese ink?"

"Yes, yes," said the savant impatiently; "but it is the inscription that interests me, not the paper and ink."

"Precisely," said Thorndyke. "Now, it was the ink that interested me when I caught a glimpse of the document three days ago. 'Why,' I asked myself, 'should anyone use this troublesome medium'—for this appears to be stick ink—'when good writing ink is to be had?' What advantages has Chinese ink over writing ink? It has several advantages as a drawing ink, but for writing purposes it has only one : it is quite unaffected by wet. The obvious inference, then, was that this document was, for some reason, likely to be exposed to wet. But this inference instantly suggested another, which I was yesterday able to put to the test—thus."

He filled a tumbler with water, and, rolling up the document, dropped it in. Immediately there began to appear on it a new set of characters of a curious grey colour. In a few seconds Thorndyke lifted out the wet paper, and held it up to the light, and now there was plainly visible an inscription in transparent letter-ing, like a very distinct water-mark. It was in printed Roman capitals, written across the other writing, and read :

" THE PICKERDILLEY STUF IS UP THE CHIMBLY 416 WARDOUR ST 2ND FLOUR BACK IT WAS HID BECOS OF OLD MOAKEYS JOOD MOAKEY IS A BLITER."

The Professor regarded the inscription with profound disfavour.

" How do you suppose this was done ? " he asked gloomily.

" I will show you," said Thorndyke. " I have pre-pared a piece of paper to demonstrate the process to Dr. Jervis. It is exceedingly simple."

He fetched from the office a small plate of glass, and a photographic dish in which a piece of thin notepaper was soaking in water.

" This paper," said Thorndyke, lifting it out and laying it on the glass, " has been soaking all night, and is now quite pulpy."

He spread a dry sheet of paper over the wet one, and on the former wrote heavily with a hard pencil, " Moakey is a bliter." On lifting the upper sheet, the writing was seen to be transferred in a deep grey to the wet paper, and when the latter was held up to the light the inscription stood out clear and transparent as if written with oil.

" When this dries," said Thorndyke, " the writing will completely disappear, but it will reappear whenever the paper is again wetted."

The Professor nodded.

" Very ingenious," said he—" a sort of artificial palimpsest, in fact. But I do not understand how that illiterate man could have written in the difficult Moabite script."

" He did not," said Thorndyke. " The ' cryptogram ' was probably written by one of the leaders of the gang, who, no doubt, supplied copies to the other members to use instead of blank paper for secret communications. The object of the Moabite writing was evidently to divert attention from the paper itself, in case the communication fell into the wrong hands, and I must say it seems to have answered its purpose very well."

The Professor started, stung by the sudden recollection of his labours.

" Yes," he snorted ; " but I am a scholar, sir, not a policeman. Every man to his trade."

He snatched up his hat, and with a curt " Good-morning," flung out of the room in dudgeon.

Thorndyke laughed softly.

" Poor Professor ! " he murmured. " Our playful friend Barton has much to answer for."

12

THE ALUMINIUM
DAGGER

THE " urgent call "—the instant, peremptory summons to professional duty—is an experience that appertains to the medical rather than the legal practitioner, and I had supposed, when I abandoned the clinical side

of my profession in favour of the forensic, that hence-
forth I should know it no more ; that the interrupted
meal, the broken leisure, and the jangle of the night-
bell were things of the past ; but in practice it was
otherwise. The medical jurist is, so to speak, on the
borderland of the two professions, and exposed to the
vicissitudes of each calling, and so it happened from
time to time that the professional services of my
colleague or myself were demanded at a moment's
notice. And thus it was in the case that I am about
to relate.

The sacred rite of the " tub " had been duly performed, and the freshly-dried person of the present
narrator was about to be insinuated into the first
instalment of clothing, when a hurried step was heard
upon the stair, and the voice of our laboratory assistant,
Polton, arose at my colleague's door.

" There's a gentleman downstairs, sir, who says he
must see you instantly on most urgent business. He
seems to be in a rare twitter, sir——"

Polton was proceeding to descriptive particulars,
when a second and more hurried step became audible,
and a strange voice addressed Thorndyke.

" I have come to beg your immediate assistance,
sir ; a most dreadful thing has happened. A horrible
murder has been committed. Can you come with me
now ? "

" I will be with you almost immediately," said Thorndyke. " Is the victim quite dead ? "

" Quite. Cold and stiff. The police think——"

" Do the police know that you have come for me ? "
interrupted Thorndyke.

" Yes. Nothing is to be done until you arrive."

" Very well. I will be ready in a few minutes."

" And if you would wait downstairs, sir," Polton
added persuasively, " I could help the doctor to get
ready."

With this crafty appeal, he lured the intruder back

to the sitting-room, and shortly after stole softly up the stairs with a small breakfast-tray, the contents of which he deposited firmly in our respective rooms, with a few timely words on the folly of " undertaking murders on an empty stomach." Thorndyke and I had meanwhile clothed ourselves with a celerity known only to medical practitioners and quick-change artists, and in a few minutes descended the stairs together, calling in at the laboratory for a few appliances that Thorndyke usually took with him on a visit of investigation.

As we entered the sitting-room, our visitor, who was feverishly pacing up and down, seized his hat with a gasp of relief. " You are ready to come ? " he asked. " My carriage is at the door " ; and, without waiting for an answer, he hurried out, and rapidly preceded us down the stairs.

The carriage was a roomy brougham which fortunately accommodated the three of us, and as soon as we had entered and shut the door, the coachman whipped up his horse and drove off at a smart trot.

" I had better give you some account of the circumstances, as we go," said our agitated friend. " In the first place, my name is Curtis, Henry Curtis ; here is my card. Ah ! and here is another card, which I should have given you before. My solicitor, Mr. Marchmont, was with me when I made this dreadful discovery, and he sent me to you. He remained in the rooms to see that nothing is disturbed until you arrive."

" That was wise of him," said Thorndyke. " But now tell us exactly what has occurred."

" I will," said Mr. Curtis. " The murdered man was my brother-in-law, Alfred Hartridge, and I am sorry to say he was—well, he was a bad man. It grieves me to speak of him thus—*de mortuis*, you know—but, still, we must deal with the facts, even though they be painful."

" Undoubtedly," agreed Thorndyke.

" I have had a great deal of very unpleasant corre-
spondence with him—Marchmont will tell you about
that—and yesterday I left a note for him, asking for
an interview, to settle the business, naming eight
o'clock this morning as the hour, because I had to
leave town before noon. He replied, in a very singular
letter, that he would see me at that hour, and Mr.
Marchmont very kindly consented to accompany me.
Accordingly, we went to his chambers together this
morning, arriving punctually at eight o'clock. We
rang the bell several times and knocked loudly at the
door, but as there was no response, we went down
and spoke to the hall-porter. This man, it seems, had
already noticed, from the courtyard, that the electric
lights were full on in Mr. Hartridge's sitting-room,
as they had been all night, according to the statement
of the night-porter ; so now, suspecting that something
was wrong, he came up with us, and rang the bell and
battered at the door. Then, as there was still no sign
of life within, he inserted his duplicate key and tried
to open the door—unsuccessfully, however, as it proved
to be bolted on the inside. Thereupon the porter
fetched a constable, and, after a consultation, we
decided that we were justified in breaking open the
door ; the porter produced a crowbar, and by our
united efforts the door was eventually burst open.
We entered, and—my God ! Dr. Thorndyke, what a
terrible sight it was that met our eyes ! My brother-
in-law was lying dead on the floor of the sitting-room.
He had been stabbed—stabbed to death ; and the
dagger had not even been withdrawn. It was still
sticking out of his back."

He mopped his face with his handkerchief, and was
about to continue his account of the catastrophe when
the carriage entered a quiet side-street between West-
minster and Victoria, and drew up before a block of
tall, new, red-brick buildings. A flurried hall-porter

ran out to open the door, and we alighted opposite the main entrance.

" My brother-in-law's chambers are on the second-floor," said Mr. Curtis. " We can go up in the lift."

The porter had hurried before us, and already stood with his hand upon the rope. We entered the lift, and in a few seconds were discharged on to the second-floor, the porter, with furtive curiosity, following us down the corridor. At the end of the passage was a half-open door, considerably battered and bruised. Above the door, painted in white lettering, was the inscription, " Mr Hartridge " ; and through the door-way protruded the rather foxy countenance of Inspector Badger.

" I am glad you have come, sir," said he, as he recognised my colleague. " Mr. Marchmont is sitting inside like a watch-dog, and he growls if any of us even walks across the room."

The words formed a complaint, but there was a certain geniality in the speaker's manner which made me suspect that Inspector Badger was already navigating his craft on a lee shore.

We entered a small lobby or hall, and from thence passed into the sitting-room, where we found Mr. Marchmont keeping his vigil, in company with a constable and a uniformed inspector. The three rose softly as we entered, and greeted us in a whisper ; and then, with one accord, we all looked towards the other end of the room, and so remained for a time without speaking.

There was, in the entire aspect of the room, some-thing very grim and dreadful. An atmosphere of tragic mystery enveloped the most commonplace objects ; and sinister suggestions lurked in the most familiar appearances. Especially impressive was the air of suspense—of ordinary, every-day life suddenly arrested—cut short in the twinkling of an eye. The electric lamps, still burning dim and red, though the summer sunshine streamed in through the windows ;

the half-emptied tumbler and open book by the empty chair, had each its whispered message of swift and sudden disaster, as had the hushed voices and stealthy movements of the waiting men, and, above all, an awesome shape that was but a few hours since a living man, and that now sprawled, prone and motionless, on the floor.

" This is a mysterious affair," observed Inspector Badger, breaking the silence at length, " though it is clear enough up to a certain point. The body tells its own story."

We stepped across and looked down at the corpse. It was that of a somewhat elderly man, and lay, on an open space of floor before the fireplace, face downwards, with the arms extended. The slender hilt of a dagger projected from the back below the left shoulder, and, with the exception of a trace of blood upon the lips, this was the only indication of the mode of death. A little way from the body a clock-key lay on the carpet, and, glancing up at the clock on the mantelpiece, I perceived that the glass front was open.

" You see," pursued the inspector, noting my glance, " he was standing in front of the fireplace, winding the clock. Then the murderer stole up behind him—the noise of the turning key must have covered his movements—and stabbed him. And you see, from the position of the dagger on the left side of the back, that the murderer must have been left-handed. That is all clear enough. What is not clear is how he got in, and how he got out again."

" The body has not been moved, I suppose," said Thorndyke.

" No. We sent for Dr. Egerton, the police-surgeon, and he certified that the man was dead. He will be back presently to see you and arrange about the post-mortem."

" Then," said Thorndyke, " we will not disturb the body till he comes, except to take the temperature and dust the dagger-hilt."

He took from his bag a long, registering chemical thermometer and an insufflator or powder-blower. The former he introduced under the dead man's clothing against the abdomen, and with the latter blew a stream of fine yellow powder on to the black leather handle of the dagger. Inspector Badger stooped eagerly to examine the handle, as Thorndyke blew away the powder that had settled evenly on the surface.

"No finger-prints," said he, in a disappointed tone. "He must have worn gloves. But that inscription gives a pretty broad hint."

He pointed, as he spoke, to the metal guard of the dagger, on which was engraved, in clumsy lettering, the single word, "TRADITORE."

"That's the Italian for 'traitor,'" continued the inspector, "and I got some information from the porter that fits in with that suggestion. We'll have him in presently, and you shall hear."

"Meanwhile," said Thorndyke, "as the position of the body may be of importance in the inquiry, I will take one or two photographs and make a rough plan to scale. Nothing has been moved, you say? Who opened the windows?"

"They were open when we came in," said Mr. Marchmont. "Last night was very hot, you remember. Nothing whatever has been moved."

Thorndyke produced from his bag a small folding camera, a telescopic tripod, a surveyor's measuring-tape, a boxwood scale, and a sketch-block. He set up the camera in a corner, and exposed a plate, taking a general view of the room, and including the corpse. Then he moved to the door and made a second exposure.

"Will you stand in front of the clock, Jervis," he said, "and raise your hand as if winding it? Thanks; keep like that while I expose a plate."

I remained thus, in the position that the dead man was assumed to have occupied at the moment of the murder, while the plate was exposed, and then, before

I moved, Thorndyke marked the position of my feet with a blackboard chalk. He next set up the tripod over the chalk marks, and took two photographs from that position, and finally photographed the body itself.

The photographic operations being concluded, he next proceeded, with remarkable skill and rapidity, to lay out on the sketch-block a ground-plan of the room, showing the exact position of the various objects, on a scale of a quarter of an inch to the foot—a process that the inspector was inclined to view with some impatience.

" You don't spare trouble, doctor," he remarked ; " nor time either," he added, with a significant glance at his watch.

" No," answered Thorndyke, as he detached ' the finished sketch from the block ; " I try to collect all the facts that may bear on a case. They may prove worthless, or they may turn out of vital importance ; one never knows beforehand, so I collect them all. But here, I think, is Dr. Egerton."

The police-surgeon greeted Thorndyke with respectful cordiality, and we proceeded at once to the examination of the body. Drawing out the thermometer, my colleague noted the reading, and passed the instrument to Dr. Egerton.

" Dead about ten hours," remarked the latter, after a glance at it. " This was a very determined and mysterious murder."

" Very," said Thorndyke. " Feel that dagger, Jervis."

I touched the hilt, and felt the characteristic grating of bone.

" It is through the edge of a rib ! " I exclaimed.

" Yes ; it must have been used with extraordinary force. And you notice that the clothing is screwed up slightly, as if the blade had been rotated as it was driven in. That is a very peculiar feature, especially when taken together with the violence of the blow."

" It is singular, certainly," said Dr. Egerton,

" though I don't know that it helps us much. Shall
we withdraw the dagger before moving the body ? "

" Certainly," replied Thorndyke, " or the movement may produce fresh injuries. But wait." He
took a piece of string from his pocket, and, having
drawn the dagger out a couple of inches, stretched the
string in a line parallel to the flat of the blade. Then,
giving me the ends to hold, he drew the weapon out
completely. As the blade emerged, the twist in the
clothing disappeared. " Observe," said he, " that the
string gives the direction of the wound, and that the
cut in the clothing no longer coincides with it. There
is quite a considerable angle, which is the measure
of the rotation of the blade."

" Yes, it is odd," said Dr. Egerton, " though, as I
said, I doubt that it helps us."

" At present," Thorndyke rejoined dryly, " we are
noting the facts."

" Quite so," agreed the other, reddening slightly ;
" and perhaps we had better move the body to the
bedroom, and make a preliminary inspection of the
wound."

We carried the corpse into the bedroom, and, having
examined the wound without eliciting anything new,
covered the remains with a sheet, and returned to the
sitting-room.

" Well, gentlemen," said the inspector, " you have
examined the body and the wound, and you have
measured the floor and the furniture, and taken photographs, and made a plan, but we don't seem much
more forward. Here's a man murdered in his rooms.
There is only one entrance to the flat, and that was
bolted on the inside at the time of the murder. The
windows are some forty feet from the ground ; there is
no rain-pipe near any of them ; they are set flush in
the wall, and there isn't a foothold for a fly on any
part of that wall. The grates are modern, and there
isn't room for a good-sized cat to crawl up any of

the chimneys. Now, the question is, How did the murderer get in, and how did he get out again ? ''

" Still," said Mr. Marchmont, " the fact is that he did get in, and that he is not here now ; and therefore he must have got out ; and therefore it must have been possible for him to get out. And, further, it must be possible to discover how he got out."

The inspector smiled sourly, but made no reply.

" The circumstances," said Thorndyke, " appear to have been these : The deceased seems to have been alone ; there is no trace of a second occupant of the room, and only one half-emptied tumbler on the table. He was sitting reading when apparently he noticed that the clock had stopped—at ten minutes to twelve ; he laid his book, face downwards, on the table, and rose to wind the clock, and as he was winding it he met his death."

" By a stab dealt by a left-handed man, who crept up behind him on tiptoe," added the inspector.

Thorndyke nodded. " That would seem to be so," he said. " But now let us call in the porter, and hear what he has to tell us."

The custodian was not difficult to find, being, in fact, engaged at that moment in a survey of the premises through the slit of the letter-box.

" Do you know what persons visited these rooms last night ? " Thorndyke asked him, when he entered, looking somewhat sheepish.

" A good many were in and out of the building," was the answer, " but I can't say if any of them came to this flat. I saw Miss Curtis pass in about nine."

" My daughter ! " exclaimed Mr. Curtis, with a start. " I didn't know that."

" She left about nine-thirty," the porter added.

" Do you know what she came about ? " asked the inspector.

" I can guess," replied Mr. Curtis.

" Then don't say," interrupted Mr. Marchmont.
" Answer no questions."

" You're very close, Mr. Marchmont," said the
inspector ; " we are not suspecting the young lady.
We don't ask, for instance, if she is left-handed."

He glanced craftily at Mr. Curtis as he made this
remark, and I noticed that our client suddenly turned
deathly pale, whereupon the inspector looked away
again quickly, as though he had not observed the
change.

" Tell us about those Italians again," he said,
addressing the porter. " When did the first of them
come here ? "

" About a week ago," was the reply. " He was a
common-looking man—looked like an organ-grinder—
and he brought a note to my lodge. It was in a dirty
envelope, and was addressed ' Mr. Hartridge, Esq.,
Brackenhurst Mansions,' in a very bad handwriting.
The man gave me the note and asked me to give it
to Mr. Hartridge ; then he went away, and I took the
note up and dropped it into the letter-box."

" What happened next ? "

" Why, the very next day an old hag of an Italian
woman—one of them fortune-telling swines with a
cage of birds on a stand—came and set up just by the
main doorway. I soon sent her packing, but, bless
you ! she was back again in ten minutes, birds and all.
I sent her off again—I kept on sending her off, and she
kept on coming back, until I was reg'lar wore to a
thread."

" You seem to have picked up a bit since then,"
remarked the inspector with a grin and a glance at
the sufferer's very pronounced bow-window.

" Perhaps I have," the custodian replied haughtily.
" Well, the next day there was a ice-cream man—a
reg'lar waster, *he* was. Stuck outside as if he was
froze to the pavement. Kept giving the errand-boys
tasters, and when I tried to move him on, he told me

13

not to obstruct his business. Business, indeed ! Well, there them boys stuck, one after the other, wiping their tongues round the bottoms of them glasses, until I was fit to bust with aggravation. And *he* kept me going all day.

"Then, the day after that there was a barrel-organ, with a mangy-looking monkey on it. He was the worst of all. Profane, too, *he* was. Kept mixing up sacred tunes and comic songs : ' Rock of Ages,' ' Bill Bailey,' ' Cujus Animal,' and ' Over the Garden Wall.' And when I tried to move him on, that little blighter of a monkey made a run at my leg ; and then the man grinned and started playing, ' Wait till the Clouds roll by,' I tell you, it was fair sickening."

He wiped his brow at the recollection, and the inspector smiled appreciatively.

"And that was the last of them ? " said the latter ; and as the porter nodded sulkily, he asked : " Should you recognise the note that the Italian gave you ? "

"I should," answered the porter with frosty dignity.

The inspector bustled out of the room, and returned a minute later with a letter-case in his hand.

"This was in his breast-pocket," said he, laying the bulging case on the table, and drawing up a chair. "Now, here are three letters tied together. Ah ! this will be the one." He untied the tape, and held out a dirty envelope addressed in a sprawling, illiterate hand to " Mr. Hartridge, Esq." " Is that the note the Italian gave you ? "

The porter examined it critically. "Yes," said he ; " that is the one."

The inspector drew the letter out of the envelope, and, as he opened it, his eyebrows went up.

"What do you make of that, doctor ? " he said, handing the sheet to Thorndyke.

Thorndyke regarded it for a while in silence, with deep attention. Then he carried it to the window, and, taking his lens from his pocket, examined the paper closely, first with the low power, and then with the highly magnifying Coddington attachment.

"I should have thought you could see that with the naked eye," said the inspector, with a sly grin at me. "It's a pretty bold design."

"Yes," replied Thorndyke; "a very interesting production. What do you say, Mr. Marchmont?"

The solicitor took the note, and I looked over his shoulder. It was certainly a curious production. Written in red ink, on the commonest notepaper, and in the same sprawling hand as the address, was the following message: "You are given six days to do what is just. By the sign above, know what to expect if you fail." The sign referred to was a skull and cross-bones, very neatly, but rather unskilfully, drawn at the top of the paper.

"This," said Mr. Marchmont, handing the document to Mr. Curtis, "explains the singular letter that he wrote yesterday. You have it with you, I think?"

"Yes," replied Mr. Curtis; "here it is."

He produced a letter from his pocket, and read aloud:

"'Yes: come if you like, though it is an ungodly hour. Your threatening letters have caused me great amusement. They are worthy of Sadler's Wells in its prime.

"'ALFRED HARTRIDGE.'"

"Was Mr. Hartridge ever in Italy?" asked Inspector Badger.

"Oh yes," replied Mr. Curtis. "He stayed at Capri nearly the whole of last year."

"Why, then, that gives us our clue. Look here. Here are these two other letters; E.C. postmark—Saffron Hill is E.C. And just look at that!"

He spread out the last of the mysterious letters, and

we saw that, besides the *memento mori*, it contained only three words : " Beware ! Remember Capri ! "

" If you have finished, doctor, I'll be off and have a look round Little Italy. Those four Italians oughtn't to be difficult to find, and we've got the porter here to identify them."

" Before you go," said Thorndyke, " there are two little matters that I should like to settle. One is the dagger : it is in your pocket, I think. May I have a look at it ? "

The inspector rather reluctantly produced the dagger and handed it to my colleague.

" A very singular weapon, this," said Thorndyke, regarding the dagger thoughtfully, and turning it about to view its different parts. " Singular both in shape and material. I have never seen an aluminium hilt before, and bookbinder's morocco is a little unusual."

" The aluminium was for lightness," explained the inspector, " and it was made narrow to carry up the sleeve, I expect."

" Perhaps so," said Thorndyke.

He continued his examination, and presently, to the inspector's delight, brought forth his pocket lens.

" I never saw such a man ! " exclaimed the jocose detective. " His motto ought to be, ' We magnify thee.' I suppose he'll measure it next."

The inspector was not mistaken. Having made a rough sketch of the weapon on his block, Thorndyke produced from his bag a folding rule and a delicate calliper-gauge. With these instruments he proceeded, with extraordinary care and precision, to take the dimensions of the various parts of the dagger, entering each measurement in its place on the sketch, with a few brief, descriptive details.

" The other matter," said he at length, handing the dagger back to the inspector, " refers to the houses opposite."

He walked to the window, and looked out at the

backs of a row of tall buildings similar to the one we were in. They were about thirty yards distant, and were separated from us by a piece of ground, planted with shrubs and intersected by gravel paths.

" If any of those rooms were occupied last night," continued Thorndyke, " we might obtain an actual eyewitness of the crime. This room was brilliantly lighted, and all the blinds were up, so that an observer at any of those windows could see right into the room, and very distinctly, too. It might be worth inquiring into."

" Yes, that's true," said the inspector ; " though I expect, if any of them have seen anything, they will come forward quick enough when they read the report in the papers. But I must be off now, and I shall have to lock you out of the rooms."

As we went down the stairs, Mr. Marchmont announced his intention of calling on us in the evening, " unless," he added, " you want any information from me now."

" I do," said Thorndyke. " I want to know who is interested in this man's death."

" That," replied Marchmont, " is rather a queer story. Let us take a turn in that garden that we saw from the window. We shall be quite private there."

He beckoned to Mr. Curtis, and, when the inspector had departed with the police-surgeon, we induced the porter to let us into the garden.

" The question that you asked," Mr. Marchmont began, looking up curiously at the tall houses opposite, " is very simply answered. The only person immediately interested in the death of Alfred Hartridge is his executor and sole legatee, a man named Leonard Wolfe. He is no relation of the deceased, merely a friend, but he inherits the entire estate—about twenty thousand pounds. The circumstances are these : Alfred Hartridge was the elder of two brothers, of whom the younger, Charles, died before his father, leaving a widow and three children. Fifteen years ago the father died, leaving the whole of his property to Alfred, with the understanding that he should support his brother's family and make the children his heirs."

" Was there no will ? " asked Thorndyke.

" Under great pressure from the friends of his son's widow, the old man made a will shortly before he died ; but he was then very old and rather childish, so the will was contested by Alfred, on the grounds of undue influence, and was ultimately set aside. Since then Alfred Hartridge has not paid a penny towards the support of his brother's family. If it had not been for my client, Mr. Curtis, they might have starved ; the whole burden of the support of the widow and the education of the children has fallen upon him.

" Well, just lately the matter has assumed an acute form, for two reasons. The first is that Charles's eldest son, Edmund, has come of age. Mr. Curtis had him articled to a solicitor, and, as he is now fully qualified, and a most advantageous proposal for a partnership has been made, we have been putting pressure on Alfred to supply the necessary capital in accordance with his father's wishes. This he had refused to do, and it was with reference to this matter that we were calling on him this morning. The second reason involves a curious and disgraceful story. There is a certain Leonard Wolfe, who has been an intimate friend of the deceased. He is, I may say, a man of bad character, and their association has been of a kind creditable to neither. There is also a certain woman named Hester Greene, who had certain claims upon the deceased, which we need not go into at present. Now, Leonard Wolfe and the deceased, Alfred Hartridge, entered into an agreement, the terms of which were these : (1) Wolfe was to marry Hester Greene, and in consideration of this service (2) Alfred Hartridge was to assign to Wolfe the whole of his property, absolutely, the actual transfer to take place on the death of Hartridge."

"And has this transaction been completed ? " asked Thorndyke.

"Yes, it has, unfortunately. But we wished to see if anything could be done for the widow and the children during Hartridge's lifetime. No doubt, my client's daughter, Miss Curtis, called last night on a similar mission—very indiscreetly, since the matter was in our hands ; but, you know, she is engaged to Edmund Hartridge—and I expect the interview was a pretty stormy one."

Thorndyke remained silent for a while, pacing slowly along the gravel path, with his eyes bent on the ground : not abstractedly, however, but with a searching, attentive glance that roved amongst the shrubs and bushes, as though he were looking for something.

"What sort of man," he asked presently, " is this Leonard Wolfe ? Obviously he is a low scoundrel, but what is he like in other respects ? Is he a fool, for instance ? "

"Not at all, I should say," said Mr. Curtis. " He was formerly an engineer, and, I believe, a very capable mechanician. Latterly he has lived on some property that came to him, and has spent both his time and his money in gambling and dissipation. Consequently, I expect he is pretty short of funds at present."

"And in appearance ? "

" I only saw him once," replied Mr. Curtis, " and all I can remember of him is that he is rather short, fair, thin, and clean-shaven, and that he has lost the middle finger of his left hand."

" And he lives at—— ? "

" Eltham, in Kent. Morton Grange, Eltham," said Mr. Marchmont. "And now, if you have all the information that you require, I must really be off, and so must Mr. Curtis."

The two men shook our hands and hurried away,

leaving Thorndyke gazing meditatively at the dingy flower-beds.

"A strange and interesting case, this, Jervis," said he, stooping to peer under a laurel-bush. "The inspector is on a hot scent—a most palpable red herring on a most obvious string ; but that is his business. Ah, here comes the porter, intent, no doubt, on pumping us, whereas——" He smiled genially at the approaching custodian, and asked : "Where did you say those houses fronted ? "

"Cotman Street, sir," answered the porter. "They are nearly all offices."

"And the numbers ? That open second-floor window, for instance ? "

"That is number six ; but the house opposite Mr. Hartridge's rooms is number eight."

"Thank you."

Thorndyke was moving away, but suddenly turned again to the porter.

"By the way," said he, "I dropped something out of the window just now—a small flat piece of metal, like this." He made on the back of his visiting card a neat sketch of a circular disc, with a hexagonal hole through it, and handed the card to the porter. "I can't say where it fell," he continued ; "these flat things scale about so ; but you might ask the gardener to look for it. I will give him a sovereign if he brings it to my chambers, for, although it is of no value to anyone else, it is of considerable value to me."

The porter touched his hat briskly, and as we turned out at the gate, I looked back and saw him already wading among the shrubs.

The object of the porter's quest gave me considerable mental occupation. I had not seen Thorndyke drop anything, and it was not his way to finger carelessly any object of value. I was about to question him on the subject, when, turning sharply round into Cotman Street, he drew up at the doorway of number six, and began attentively to read the names of the occupants.

" ' Third-floor,' " he read out, " ' Mr. Thomas Barlow, Commission Agent.' Hum ! I think we will look in on Mr. Barlow."

He stepped quickly up the stone stairs, and I followed, until we arrived, somewhat out of breath, on the third-floor. Outside the Commission Agent's door he paused for a moment, and we both listened curiously to an irregular sound of shuffling feet from within. Then he softly opened the door and looked into the room. After remaining thus for nearly a minute, he looked round at me with a broad smile, and noiselessly set the door wide open. Inside, a lanky youth of fourteen was practising, with no mean skill, the manipulation of an appliance known by the appropriate name of diabolo ; and so absorbed was he in his occupation that we entered and shut the door without being observed. At length the shuttle missed the string and flew into a large waste-paper basket ; the boy turned and confronted us, and was instantly covered with confusion.

" Allow me," said Thorndyke, rooting rather unnecessarily in the waste-paper basket, and handing the toy to its owner. " I need not ask if Mr. Barlow is in," he added, " nor if he is likely to return shortly."

" He won't be back to-day," said the boy, perspiring with embarrassment ; " he left before I came. I was rather late."

" I see," said Thorndyke. " The early bird catches the worm, but the late bird catches the diabolo. How did you know he would not be back ? "

" He left a note. Here it is."

He exhibited the document, which was neatly written in red ink. Thorndyke examined it attentively, and then asked :

" Did you break the inkstand yesterday ? "

The boy stared at him in amazement. " Yes, I did," he answered. " How did you know ? "

13*

" I didn't, or I should not have asked. But I see that he has used his stylo to write this note."

The boy regarded Thorndyke distrustfully, as he continued :

" I really called to see if your Mr. Barlow was a gentleman whom I used to know ; but I expect you can tell me. My friend was tall and thin, dark, and clean-shaved."

" This ain't him, then," said the boy. " He's thin, but he ain't tall or dark. He's got a sandy beard, and he wears spectacles and a wig. I know a wig when I see one," he added cunningly, " 'cause my father wears one. He puts it on a peg to comb it, and he swears at me when I larf."

" My friend had injured his left hand," pursued Thorndyke.

" I dunno about that," said the youth. " Mr. Barlow nearly always wears gloves ; he always wears one on his left hand, anyhow."

" Ah well ! I'll just write him a note on the chance, if you will give me a piece of notepaper. Have you any ink ? "

" There's some in the bottle. I'll dip the pen in for you."

He produced, from the cupboard, an opened packet of cheap notepaper and a packet of similar envelopes, and, having dipped the pen to the bottom of the ink-bottle, handed it to Thorndyke, who sat down and hastily scribbled a short note. He had folded the paper, and was about to address the envelope, when he appeared suddenly to alter his mind.

" I don't think I will leave it, after all," he said, slipping the folded paper into his pocket. " No. Tell him I called—Mr. Horace Budge—and say I will look in again in a day or two."

The youth watched our exit with an air of per-plexity, and he even came out on to the landing, the better to observe us over the balusters ; until, unexpectedly catching Thorndyke's eye, he withdrew his head with remarkable suddenness, and retired in disorder.

To tell the truth, I was now little less perplexed than the office-boy by Thorndyke's proceedings; in which I could discover no relevancy to the investigation that I presumed he was engaged upon : and the last straw was laid upon the burden of my curiosity when he stopped at a staircase window, drew the note out of his pocket, examined it with his lens, held it up to the light, and chuckled aloud.

" Luck," he observed, " though no substitute for care and intelligence, is a very pleasant addition. Really, my learned brother, we are doing uncommonly well."

When we reached the hall, Thorndyke stopped at the housekeeper's box, and looked in with a genial nod.

" I have just been up to see Mr. Barlow," said he. " He seems to have left quite early."

" Yes, sir," the man replied. " He went away about half-past eight."

" That was very early ; and presumably he came earlier still ? "

" I suppose so," the man assented, with a grin ; " but I had only just come on when he left."

" Had he any luggage with him ? "

" Yes, sir. There was two cases, a square one and a long, narrow one, about five foot long. I helped him to carry them down to the cab."

" Which was a four-wheeler I suppose ? "

" Yes, sir."

" Mr. Barlow hasn't been here very long, has he ? " Thorndyke inquired.

" No. He only came in last quarter-day—about six weeks ago."

" Ah well ! I must call another day. Good-morning " ; and Thorndyke strode out of the building, and made directly for the cab-rank in the adjoining street. Here he stopped for a minute or two to parley with the driver of a four-wheeled cab, whom he finally commissioned to convey us to a shop in New Oxford Street. Having dismissed the cabman with his blessing and a half-sovereign, he vanished into the shop, leaving me to gaze at the lathes, drills, and bars of metal displayed in the window. Presently he emerged with a small parcel, and explained, in answer to my inquiring look : " A strip of tool steel and a block of metal for Polton."

His next purchase was rather more eccentric. We were proceeding along Holborn when his attention was suddenly arrested by the window of a furniture shop, in which was displayed a collection of obsolete French small-arms—relics of the tragedy of 1870—which were being sold for decorative purposes. After a brief inspection, he entered the shop, and shortly reappeared carrying a long sword-bayonet and an old Chassepot rifle.

" What may be the meaning of this martial display ? " I asked, as we turned down Fetter Lane.

" House protection," he replied promptly. " You will agree that a discharge of musketry, followed by a bayonet charge, would disconcert the boldest of burglars."

I laughed at the absurd picture thus drawn of the strenuous house-protector, but nevertheless continued to speculate on the meaning of my friend's eccentric proceedings, which I felt sure were in some way related to the murder in Brackenhurst Chambers, though I could not trace the connection.

After a late lunch, I hurried out to transact such of my business as had been interrupted by the stirring events of the morning, leaving Thorndyke busy with a drawing-board, squares, scale, and compasses, making accurate, scaled drawings from his rough sketches ; while Polton, with the brown-paper parcel

in his hand, looked on at him with an air of anxious
expectation.

As I was returning homeward in the evening by way
of Mitre Court, I overtook Mr. Marchmont, who was
also bound for our chambers, and we walked on together.

"I had a note from Thorndyke," he explained,
"asking for a specimen of handwriting, so I thought
I would bring it along myself, and hear if he has any
news."

When we entered the chambers, we found Thorndyke
in earnest consultation with Polton, and on the table
before them I observed, to my great surprise, the dagger
with which the murder had been committed.

"I have got you the specimen that you asked for,"
said Marchmont. "I didn't think I should be able

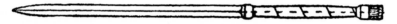

THE ALUMINIUM DAGGER.

to, but, by a lucky chance, Curtis kept the only letter
he ever received from the party in question."

He drew the letter from his wallet, and handed it
to Thorndyke, who looked at it attentively and with
evident satisfaction.

"By the way," said Marchmont, taking up the
dagger, "I thought the inspector took this away with
him."

"He took the original," replied Thorndyke. "This
is a duplicate, which Polton has made, for experimental
purposes, from my drawings."

"Really!" exclaimed Marchmont, with a glance of
respectful admiration at Polton; "it is a perfect
replica—and you have made it so quickly, too."

"It was quite easy to make," said Polton, "to a
man accustomed to work in metal."

"Which," added Thorndyke, "is a fact of some
evidential value."

At this moment a hansom drew up outside. A moment later flying footsteps were heard on the stairs. There was a furious battering at the door, and, as Polton threw it open, Mr. Curtis burst wildly into the room.

"Here is a frightful thing, Marchmont!" he gasped. "Edith—my daughter—arrested for the murder. Inspector Badger came to our house and took her. My God! I shall go mad!"

Thorndyke laid his hand on the excited man's shoulder. "Don't distress yourself, Mr. Curtis," said he. "There is no occasion, I assure you. I suppose," he added, "your daughter is left-handed?"

"Yes, she is, by a most disastrous coincidence. But what are we to do? Good God! Dr. Thorndyke, they have taken her to prison—to prison—think of it! My poor Edith!"

"We'll soon have her out," said Thorndyke. "But listen; there is someone at the door."

A brisk rat-tat confirmed his statement, and when I rose to open the door, I found myself confronted by Inspector Badger. There was a moment of extreme awkwardness, and then both the detective and Mr. Curtis proposed to retire in favour of the other.

"Don't go, inspector," said Thorndyke; "I want to have a word with you. Perhaps Mr. Curtis would look in again, say, in an hour. Will you? We shall have news for you by then, I hope."

Mr. Curtis agreed hastily, and dashed out of the room with his characteristic impetuosity. When he had gone, Thorndyke turned to the detective, and remarked dryly:

"You seem to have been busy, inspector?"

"Yes," replied Badger; "I haven't let the grass grow under my feet; and I've got a pretty strong case against Miss Curtis already. You see, she was the last person seen in the company of the deceased; she had a grievance against him; she is left-handed, and you remember that the murder was committed by a left-handed person."

" Anything else ? "

" Yes. I have seen those Italians, and the whole thing was a put-up job. A woman, in a widow's dress and veil, paid them to go and play the fool outside the building, and she gave them the letter that was left with the porter. They haven't identified her yet, but she seems to agree in size with Miss Curtis."

" And how did she get out of the chambers, with the door bolted on the inside ? "

" Ah, there you are ! That's a mystery at present— unless you can give us an explanation." The inspector made this qualification with a faint grin, and added : " As there was no one in the place when we broke into it, the murderer must have got out somehow. You can't deny that."

" I do deny it, nevertheless," said Thorndyke. " You look surprised," he continued (which was undoubtedly true), " but yet the whole thing is exceedingly obvious. The explanation struck me directly I looked at the body. There was evidently no practicable exit from the flat, and there was certainly no one in it when you entered. Clearly, then, *the murderer had never been in the place at all.*"

" I don't follow you in the least," said the inspector.

" Well," said Thorndyke, " as I have finished with the case, and am handing it over to you, I will put the evidence before you *seriatim*. Now, I think we are agreed that, at the moment when the blow was struck, the deceased was standing before the fireplace, winding the clock. The dagger entered obliquely from the left, and, if you recall its position, you will remember that its hilt pointed directly towards an open window."

" Which was forty feet from the ground."

" Yes. And now we will consider the very peculiar character of the weapon with which the crime was committed."

He had placed his hand upon the knob of a drawer, when we were interrupted by a knock at the door. I sprang up, and, opening it, admitted no less a person than the porter of Brackenhurst Chambers. The man looked somewhat surprised on recognising our visitors, but advanced to Thorndyke, drawing a folded paper from his pocket.

" I've found the article you were looking for, sir," said he, " and a rare hunt I had for it. It had stuck in the leaves of one of them shrubs."

Thorndyke opened the packet, and, having glanced inside, laid it on the table.

" Thank you," said he, pushing a sovereign across to the gratified official. " The inspector has your name, I think ? "

" He have, sir," replied the porter ; and, pocketing his fee, he departed, beaming.

" To return to the dagger," said Thorndyke, opening the drawer. " It was a very peculiar one, as I have said, and as you will see from this model, which is an exact duplicate." Here he exhibited Polton's production to the astonished detective. " You see that it is extraordinarily slender, and free from projections, and of unusual materials. You also see that it was obviously not made by an ordinary dagger-maker ; that, in spite of the Italian word scrawled on it, there is plainly written all over it ' British mechanic.' The blade is made from a strip of common three-quarter-inch tool steel ; the hilt is turned from an aluminium rod ; and there is not a line of engraving on it that could not be produced in a lathe by any engineer's apprentice. Even the boss at the top is mechanical, for it is just like an ordinary hexagon nut. Then, notice the dimensions, as shown on my drawing. The parts A and B, which just project beyond the blade, are exactly similar in diameter—and such exactness could hardly be accidental. They are each parts of a circle having a diameter of 10.9 milli-metres—a dimension which happens, by a singular coincidence, to be exactly the calibre of the old Chassepot rifle, specimens of which are now on sale at several shops in London. Here is one, for instance."

He fetched the rifle that he had bought, from the corner in which it was standing, and, lifting the dagger by its point, slipped the hilt into the muzzle. When he let go, the dagger slid quietly down the barrel, until its hilt appeared in the open breech.

" Good God ! " exclaimed Marchmont. " You don't suggest that the dagger was shot from a gun ? "

" I do, indeed ; and you now see the reason for the aluminium hilt—to diminish the weight of the already heavy projectile—and also for this hexagonal boss on the end ? "

" No, I do not," said the inspector ; " but I say that you are suggesting an impossibility."

" Then," replied Thorndyke, " I must explain and demonstrate. To begin with, this projectile had to travel point foremost ; therefore it had to be made to spin—and it certainly was spinning when it entered the body, as the clothing and the wound showed us. Now, to make it spin, it had to be fired from a rifled barrel ; but as the hilt would not engage in the rifling, it had to be fitted with something that would. That something was evidently a soft metal washer, which fitted on to this hexagon, and which would be pressed into the grooves of the rifling, and so spin the dagger, but would drop off as soon as the weapon left the barrel. Here is such a washer, which Polton has made for us."

He laid on the table a metal disc, with a hexagonal hole through it.

" This is all very ingenious," said the inspector, " but I say it is impossible and fantastic."

" It certainly sounds rather improbable," Marchmont agreed.

" We will see," said Thorndyke. " Here is a make-shift cartridge of Polton's manufacture, containing an eighth charge of smokeless powder for a 20-bore gun."

He fitted the washer on to the boss of the dagger in the open breech of the rifle, pushed it into the barrel, inserted the cartridge, and closed the breech. Then, opening the office-door, he displayed a target of padded strawboard against the wall.

" The length of the two rooms," said he, " gives us a distance of thirty-two feet. Will you shut the windows, Jervis ? "

I complied, and he then pointed the rifle at the target. There was a dull report—much less loud than I had expected—and when we looked at the target, we saw the dagger driven in up to its hilt at the margin of the bull's-eye.

" You see," said Thorndyke, laying down the rifle, " that the thing is practicable. Now for the evidence as to the actual occurrence. First, on the original dagger there are linear scratches which exactly correspond with the grooves of the rifling. Then there is the fact that the dagger was certainly spinning from left to right—in the direction of the rifling, that is—when it entered the body. And then there is this, which, as you heard, the porter found in the garden."

He opened the paper packet. In it lay a metal disc, perforated by a hexagonal hole. Stepping into the office, he picked up from the floor the washer that he had put on the dagger, and laid it on the paper beside the other. The two discs were identical in size, and the margin of each was indented with identical markings, corresponding to the rifling of the barrel.

The inspector gazed at the two discs in silence for a while ; then, looking up at Thorndyke, he said :

" I give in, doctor. You're right, beyond all doubt ; but how you came to think of it beats me into fits. The only question now is, Who fired the gun, and why wasn't the report heard ? "

" As to the latter," said Thorndyke, " it is probable that he used a compressed-air attachment, not only to diminish the noise, but also to prevent any traces of the explosive from being left on the dagger. As to the former, I think I can give you the murderer's name ; but we had better take the evidence in order. You may remember," he continued, " that when Dr. Jervis stood as if winding the clock, I chalked a mark on the floor where he stood. Now, standing on that marked spot, and looking out of the open window, I could see two of the windows of a house nearly opposite. They were the second- and third-floor windows of No. 6 Cotman Street. The second-floor is occupied by a firm of architects ; the third-floor by a commission agent named Thomas Barlow. I called on Mr. Barlow, but before describing my visit, I will refer to another matter. You haven't those threatening letters about you, I suppose ? "

" Yes, I have," said the inspector ; and he drew forth a wallet from his breast-pocket.

" Let us take the first one, then," said Thorndyke. " You see that the paper and envelope are of the very commonest, and the writing illiterate. But the ink does not agree with this. Illiterate people usually buy their ink in penny bottles. Now, this envelope is addressed with Draper's dichroic ink—a superior office ink, sold only in large bottles—and the red ink in which the note is written is an unfixed, scarlet ink, such as is used by draughtsmen, and has been used, as you can see, in a stylographic pen. But the most interesting thing about this letter is the design drawn at the top. In an artistic sense, the man could not draw, and the anatomical details of the skull are ridiculous. Yet the drawing is very neat. It has the clean, wiry line of a machine drawing, and is done with a steady, practised hand. It is also perfectly symmetrical ; the skull, for instance, is exactly in the centre, and, when we examine it through a lens, we see why it is so, for we discover traces of a pencilled centre-line and ruled cross-lines. Moreover, the lens reveals a tiny particle of draughtsman's soft, red rubber, with which the pencil lines were taken out; and all these facts, taken together, suggest that the drawing was made by someone accustomed to making accurate mechanical drawings. And now we will return to Mr. Barlow. He was out when I called, but I took the liberty of glancing round the office, and this is what I saw. On the mantelshelf was a twelve-inch flat boxwood rule, such as engineers use, a piece of soft, red rubber, and a stone bottle of Draper's dichroic ink. I obtained, by a simple ruse, a specimen of the office notepaper and the ink. We will examine it presently. I found that Mr. Barlow is a new tenant, that he is rather short, wears a wig and spectacles, and always wears a glove on his left hand. He left the office at 8.30 this morning, and no one saw him arrive. He had with him a square case, and a narrow, oblong one about five feet in length; and he took a cab to Victoria, and apparently caught the 8.51 train to Chatham."

"Ah!" exclaimed the inspector.

"But," continued Thorndyke, "now examine those three letters, and compare them with this note that I wrote in Mr. Barlow's office. You see that the paper is of the same make, with the same water-mark, but that is of no great significance. What is of crucial importance is this: You see, in each of these letters, two tiny indentations near the bottom corner. Somebody has used compasses or drawing-pins over the packet of notepaper, and the points have made little indentations, which have marked several of the sheets. Now, notepaper is cut to its size after it is folded, and if you stick a pin into the top sheet of a section, the indentations on all the underlying sheets will be at exactly similar distances from the edges and corners of the sheet. But you see that these little dents are all at the same distance from the edges and the corner." He demonstrated the fact with a pair of compasses. "And now look at this sheet, which I obtained at Mr. Barlow's office. There are two little indentations—rather faint, but quite visible—near the bottom corner, and when we measure them with the compasses, we find that they are exactly the same distance apart as the others, and the same distance from the edges and the bottom corner. The irresistible conclusion is that these four sheets came from the same packet."

The inspector started up from his chair, and faced Thorndyke. "Who is this Mr. Barlow?" he asked.

"That," replied Thorndyke, "is for you to determine; but I can give you a useful hint. There is only one person who benefits by the death of Alfred Hartridge, but he benefits to the extent of twenty thousand pounds. His name is Leonard Wolfe, and, I learn from Mr. Marchmont that he is a man of indifferent character—a gambler, and a spendthrift. By profession he is an engineer, and he is a capable mechanician. In appearance he is thin, short, fair, and clean-shaven, and he has lost the middle finger of his left hand. Mr. Barlow is also short, thin, and fair, but wears a wig, a beard, and spectacles, and always wears a glove on his left hand. I have seen the handwriting of both these gentlemen, and should say that it would be difficult to distinguish one from the other."

"That's good enough for me," said the inspector. "Give me his address, and I'll have Miss Curtis released at once."

The same night Leonard Wolfe was arrested at Eltham, in the very act of burying in his garden a large and powerful compressed-air rifle. He was never brought to trial, however, for he had in his pocket a more portable weapon—a large-bore Derringer pistol—with which he managed to terminate an exceedingly ill-spent life.

"And, after all," was Thorndyke's comment, when he heard of the event, "he had his uses. He has relieved society of two very bad men, and he has given us a most instructive case. He has shown us how a clever and ingenious criminal may take endless pains to mislead and delude the police, and yet, by inattention to trivial details, may scatter clues broadcast. We can only say to the criminal class generally, in both respects, ' Go thou and do likewise.' "

13   THE MAGIC CASKET

IT was in the near neighbourhood of King's Road, Chelsea, ، that chance, aided by Thorndyke's sharp and observant eyes, introduced us to the dramatic story of the Magic Casket. Not that there was anything strikingly dramatic in the opening phase of the affair, nor even in the story of the casket itself. It was Thorndyke who added the dramatic touch, and most of the magic, too ; and I record the affair principally as an illustration of his extraordinary capacity for producing odd items of out-of-the-way knowledge and instantly applying them in the most unexpected manner.

Eight o'clock had struck on a misty November night when we turned out of the main road, and, leaving behind the glare of the shop windows, plunged into the maze of dark and narrow streets to the north. The abrupt change impressed us both, and Thorndyke proceeded to moralise on it in his pleasant, reflective fashion.

" London is an inexhaustible place," he mused. " Its variety is infinite. A minute ago we walked in a glare of light, jostled by a multitude. And now look at this little street. It is as dim as a tunnel, and we have got it absolutely to ourselves. Anything might happen in a place like this."

Suddenly he stopped. We were, at the moment,

passing a small church or chapel, the west door of which was enclosed in an open porch ; and as my observant friend stepped into the latter and stooped, I perceived, in the deep shadow against the wall, the object which had evidently caught his eye.

" What is it ? " I asked, following him in.

" It is a handbag," he replied ; " and the question is, what is it doing here ? "

He tried the church door, which was obviously locked, and coming out, looked at the windows.

" There are no lights in the church," said he ; " the place is locked up, and there is nobody in sight. Apparently the bag is derelict. Shall we have a look at it ? "

Without waiting for an answer, he picked it up and brought it out into the mitigated darkness of the street, where we proceeded to inspect it.   But at the first glance it told its own tale ; for it had evidently been locked, and it bore unmistakable traces of having been forced open.

" It isn't empty," said Thorndyke. " I think we had better see what is in it. Just catch hold while I get a light."

He handed me the bag while he felt in his pocket for the tiny electric lamp which he made a habit of carrying—and an excellent habit it is. I held the mouth of the bag open while he illuminated the interior, which we then saw to be occupied by several objects neatly wrapped in brown paper. One of these Thorndyke lifted out, and untying the string and removing the paper, displayed a Chinese stoneware jar. Attached to it was a label, bearing the stamp of the Victoria and Albert Museum, on which was written :

" MISS MABEL BONNEY,
168 Willow Walk, Fulham Road, W."

" That tells us all that we want to know," said Thorndyke, re-wrapping the jar and tenderly replacing it in the bag. " We can't do wrong in delivering the things to their owner, especially as the bag itself is evidently her property, too," and he pointed to the gilt initials, " M. B.," stamped on the morocco.

It took us but a few minutes to reach the Fulham Road, but we then had to walk nearly a mile along that thoroughfare before we arrived at Willow Walk —to which an obliging shopkeeper had directed us ; and, naturally, No. 168 was at the farther end.

As we turned into the quiet street we almost collided with two men, who were walking at a rapid pace, but both looking back over their shoulders. I noticed that they were both Japanese—well-dressed, gentlemanly-looking men—but I gave them little attention, being interested, rather, in what they were looking at. This was a taxicab which was dimly visible by the light of a street lamp at the farther end of the " Walk," and from which four persons had just alighted. Two of these had hurried ahead to knock at a door, while the other two walked very slowly across the pavement and up the steps to the threshold. Almost immediately the door was opened ; two of the shadowy figures entered, and the other two returned slowly to the cab ; and as we came nearer, I could see that these latter were policemen in uniform. I had just time to note this fact when they both got into the cab and were forthwith spirited away.

" Looks like a street accident of some kind," I re-marked ; and then, as I glanced at the number of the house we were passing, I added : " Now, I wonder if that house happens to be—yes, by Jove ! it is. It is 168 ! Things have been happening, and this bag of ours is one of the dramatis personæ."

The response to our knock was by no means prompt. I was, in fact, in the act of raising my hand to the knocker to repeat the summons when the door opened and revealed an elderly servant-maid, who regarded us inquiringly, and, as I thought, with something approaching alarm.

" Does Miss Mabel Bonney live here ? " Thorndyke asked.

" Yes, sir," was the reply ; " but I am afraid you can't see her just now, unless it is something urgent. She is rather upset, and particularly engaged at present."

" There is no occasion whatever to disturb her," said Thorndyke. " We have merely called to restore this bag, which seemed to have been lost ; " and with this he held it out towards her. She grasped it eagerly, with a cry of surprise, and as the mouth fell open, she peered into it.

" Why," she exclaimed, " they don't seem to have taken anything, after all. Where did you find it, sir ? "

" In the porch of a church in Spelton Street," Thorndyke replied, and was turning away when the servant said earnestly :

" Would you kindly give me your name and address, sir ? Miss Bonney will wish to write and thank you."

" There is really no need," said he ; but she interrupted anxiously :

" If you would be so kind, sir. Miss Bonney will be so vexed if she is unable to thank you ; and besides, she may want to ask you some questions about it."

" That is true," said Thorndyke (who was restrained only by good manners from asking one or two questions, himself). He produced his card-case, and having handed one of his cards to the maid, wished her " goodevening " and retired.

" That bag had evidently been pinched," I remarked, as we walked back towards the Fulham Road.

" Evidently," he agreed, and was about to enlarge on the matter when our attention was attracted to a taxi, which was approaching from the direction of the main road. A man's head was thrust out of the window, and as the vehicle passed a street lamp, I observed that the head appertained to an elderly gentleman with very white hair and a very fresh-coloured face.

"Did you see who that was ?" Thorndyke asked.

"It looked like old Brodribb," I replied.

"It did; very much. I wonder where he is off to."

He turned and followed, with a speculative eye, the receding taxi, which presently swept alongside the kerb and stopped, apparently opposite the house from which we had just come. As the vehicle came to rest, the door flew open and the passenger shot out like an elderly, but agile, Jack-in-the-box, and bounced up the steps.

"That is Brodribb's knock, sure enough," said I, as the old-fashioned flourish reverberated up the quiet street. "I have heard it too often on our own knocker to mistake it. But we had better not let him see us watching him."

As we went once more on our way, I took a sly glance, now and again, at my friend, noting with a certain malicious enjoyment his profoundly cogitative air. I knew quite well what was happening in his mind; for his mind reacted to observed facts in an invariable manner. And here was a group of related facts : the bag, stolen, but deposited intact; the museum label; the injured or sick person—probably Miss Bonney, herself—brought home under police escort; and the arrival, post-haste, of the old lawyer; a significant group of facts. And there was Thorndyke, under my amused and attentive observation, fitting them together in various combinations to see what general conclusion emerged. Apparently my own mental state was equally clear to him, for he remarked, presently, as if replying to an unspoken comment :

"Well, I expect we shall know all about it before many days have passed if Brodribb sees my card, as he most probably will. Here comes an omnibus that will suit us. Shall we hop on ?"

He stood at the kerb and raised his stick; and as the accommodation on the omnibus was such that our seats were separated, there was no opportunity to pursue the subject further, even if there had been anything to discuss.

But Thorndyke's prediction was justified sooner than I had expected. For we had not long finished our supper, and had not yet closed the " oak," when there was heard a mighty flourish on the knocker of our inner door.

" Brodribb, by Jingo ! " I exclaimed, and hurried across the room to let him in.

" No, Jervis," he said as I invited him to enter, " I am not coming in. Don't want to disturb you at this time of night. I've just called to make an appointment for to-morrow with a client."

" Is the client's name Bonney ? " I asked.

He started and gazed at me in astonishment. " Gad, Jervis ! " he exclaimed, " you are getting as bad as Thorndyke. How the deuce did you know that she was my client ? "

" Never mind how I know. It is our business to know everything in these chambers. But if your appointment concerns Miss Mabel Bonney, for the Lord's sake come in and give Thorndyke a chance of a night's rest. At present, he is on broken bottles, as Mr. Bumble would express it."

On this persuasion, Mr. Brodribb entered, nothing loath—very much the reverse, in fact—and having bestowed a jovial greeting on Thorndyke, glanced approvingly round the room.

" Ha ! " said he, " you look very cosy. If you are really sure I am not——"

I cut him short by propelling him gently towards the fire, beside which I deposited him in an easy chair, while Thorndyke pressed the electric bell which rang up in the laboratory.

" Well," said Brodribb, spreading himself out comfortably before the fire like a handsome old Tom-cat, " if you are going to let me give you a few particulars—but perhaps you would rather that I should not talk shop."

"Now you know perfectly well, Brodribb," said Thorndyke, "that 'shop' is the breath of life to us all. Let us have those particulars."

Brodribb sighed contentedly and placed his toes on the fender (and at this moment the door opened softly and Polton looked into the room. He took a single, understanding glance at our visitor, and withdrew, shutting the door without a sound).

"I am glad," pursued Brodribb, "to have this opportunity of a preliminary chat, because there are certain things that one can say better when the client is not present; and I am deeply interested in Miss Bonney's affairs. The crisis in those affairs which has brought me here is of quite recent date—in fact, it dates from this evening. But I know your partiality for having events related in their proper sequence, so I will leave to-day's happenings for the moment and tell you the story—the whole of which is material to the case—from the beginning."

Here there was a slight interruption, due to Polton's noiseless entry with a tray on which was a decanter, a biscuit box, and three port glasses. This he deposited on a small table, which he placed within convenient reach of our guest. Then, with a glance of altruistic satisfaction at our old friend, he stole out like a benevolent ghost.

"Dear, dear!" exclaimed Brodribb, beaming on the decanter, "this is really too bad. You ought not to indulge me in this way."

"My dear Brodribb," replied Thorndyke, "you are a benefactor to us. You give us a pretext for taking a glass of port. We can't drink alone, you know."

"I should, if I had a cellar like yours," chuckled Brodribb, sniffing ecstatically at his glass. He took a sip, with his eyes closed, savoured it solemnly, shook his head, and set the glass down on the table.

"To return to our case," he resumed; "Miss Bonney is the daughter of a solicitor, Harold Bonney

—you may remember him. He had offices in Bedford Row ; and there, one morning, a client came to him and asked him to take care of some property while he, the said client, ran over to Paris, where he had some urgent business. The property in question was a collection of pearls of most unusual size and value, forming a great necklace, which had been unstrung for the sake of portability. It is not clear where they came from, but as the transaction occurred soon after the Russian Revolution, we may make a guess. At any rate, there they were, packed loosely in a leather bag, the string of which was sealed with the owner's seal.

" Bonney seems to have been rather casual about the affair. He gave the client a receipt for the bag, stating the nature of the contents, which he had not seen, and deposited it, in the client's presence, in the safe in his private office. Perhaps he intended to take it to the bank or transfer it to his strong-room, but it is evident that he did neither ; for his managing clerk, who kept the second key of the strong-room—without which the room could not be opened—knew nothing of the transaction. When he went home at about seven o'clock, he left Bonney hard at work in his office, and there is no doubt that the pearls were still in the safe.

" That night, at about a quarter to nine, it happened that a couple of C.I.D. officers were walking up Bedford Row when they saw three men come out of one of the houses. Two of them turned up towards Theobald's Road, but the third came south, towards them. As he passed them, they both recognised him as a Japanese named Uyenishi, who was believed to be a member of a cosmopolitan gang and whom the police were keeping under observation. Naturally, their suspicions were aroused. The first two men had hurried round the corner and were out of sight ; and when they turned to look after Uyenishi, he had mended his pace considerably and was looking back at them. There-upon one of the officers, named Barker, decided to follow the Jap, while the other, Holt, reconnoitred the premises.

" Now, as soon as Barker turned, the Japanese broke into a run. It was just such a night as this : dark and slightly foggy. In order to keep his man in sight, Barker had to run, too ; and he found that he had a sprinter to deal with. From the bottom of Bedford Row, Uyeni-shi darted across and shot down Hand Court like a lamp-lighter. Barker followed, but at the Holborn end his man was nowhere to be seen. However, he pre-sently learned from a man at a shop door that the fugi-tive had run past and turned up Brownlow Street, so off he went again in pursuit. But when he got to the top of the street, back in Bedford Row, he was done. There was no sign of the man, and no one about from whom he could make inquiries. All he could do was to cross the road and walk up Bedford Row to see if Holt had made any discoveries.

" As he was trying to identify the house, his colleague came out on to the doorstep and beckoned him in ; and this was the story that he told. He had recognised the house by the big lamp-standard ; and as the place was all dark, he had gone into the entry and tried the office door. Finding it unlocked, he had entered the clerks' office, lit the gas, and tried the door of the private office, but found it locked. He knocked at it, but getting no answer, had a good look round the clerks' office ; and there, presently, on the floor in a dark corner, he found a key. This he tried in the door of the private office, and finding that it fitted, turned it and opened the door. As he did so, the light from the outer office fell on the body of a man lying on the floor just inside.

" A moment's inspection showed that the man had been murdered—first knocked on the head and then finished with a knife. Examination of the pockets showed that the dead man was Harold Bonney, and also that no robbery from the person seemed to have been committed. Nor was there any sign of any other kind of robbery. Nothing seemed to have been disturbed, and the safe had not been broken into, though that was not very conclusive, as the safe key was in the dead man's pocket. However, a murder had been committed, and obviously Uyenishi was either the murderer or an accessory ; so Holt had, at once, rung up Scotland Yard on the office telephone, giving all the particulars.

" I may say at once that Uyenishi disappeared completely and at once. He never went to his lodgings at Limehouse, for the police were there before he could have arrived. A lively hue and cry was kept up. Photographs of the wanted man were posted outside every police-station, and a watch was set at all the ports. But he was never found. He must have got away at once on some outward-bound tramp from the Thames. And there we will leave him for the moment.

" At first it was thought that nothing had been stolen, since the managing clerk could not discover that anything was missing. But a few days later the client returned from Paris, and presenting his receipt, asked for his pearls. But the pearls had vanished. Clearly they had been the object of the crime. The robbers must have known about them and traced them to the office. Of course the safe had been opened with its own key, which was then replaced in the dead man's pocket.

" Now, I was poor Bonney's executor, and in that capacity I denied his liability in respect of the pearls on the ground that he was a gratuitous bailee—there being no evidence that any consideration had been demanded—and that being murdered cannot be construed as negligence. But Miss Mabel, who was practically the sole legatee, insisted on accepting liability. She said that the pearls could have been secured in the bank or the strong-room, and that she was morally, if not legally, liable for their loss; and she insisted on handing to the owner the full amount at which he valued them. It was a wildly foolish proceeding, for he would certainly have accepted half the sum. But still I take my hat off to a person—man or woman—who can accept poverty in preference to a broken covenant "; and here Brodribb, being in fact that sort of person himself, had to be consoled with a replenished glass.

"And mind you," he resumed, "when I speak of poverty, I wish to be taken literally. The estimated value of those pearls was fifty thousand pounds—if you can imagine anyone out of Bedlam giving such a sum for a parcel of trash like that; and when poor Mabel Bonney had paid it, she was left with the prospect of having to spread her butter mighty thin for the rest of her life. As a matter of fact, she has had to sell one after another of her little treasures to pay just her current expenses, and I'm hanged if I can see how she is going to carry on when she has sold the last of them. But there, I mustn't take up your time with her private troubles. Let us return to our muttons.

"First, as to the pearls. They were never traced, and it seems probable that they were never disposed of. For, you see, pearls are different from any other kind of gems. You can cut up a big diamond, but you can't cut up a big pearl. And the great value of this necklace was due not only to the size, the perfect shape and 'orient' of the separate pearls, but to the fact that the whole set was perfectly matched. To break up the necklace was to destroy a good part of its value.

"And now as to our friend Uyenishi. He disappeared, as I have said; but he reappeared at Los Angeles, in custody of the police, charged with robbery and murder. He was taken red-handed and was duly convicted and sentenced to death; but for some reason —or more probably, for no reason, as we should think

—the sentence was commuted to imprisonment for life. Under these circumstances, the English police naturally took no action, especially as they really had no evidence against him.

" Now Uyenishi was, by trade, a metal-worker ; a maker of those pretty trifles that are so dear to the artistic Japanese, and when he was in prison he was allowed to set up a little workshop and practise his trade on a small scale. Among other things that he made was a little casket in the form of a seated figure, which he said he wanted to give to his brother as a keepsake. I don't know whether any permission was granted for him to make this gift, but that is of no consequence ; for Uyenishi got influenza and was carried off in a few days by pneumonia ; and the prison authorities learned that his brother had been killed, a week or two previously, in a shooting affair at San Francisco. So the casket remained on their hands.

" About this time, Miss Bonney was invited to accompany an American lady on a visit to California, and accepted gratefully. While she was there she paid a visit to the prison to inquire whether Uyenishi had ever made any kind of statement concerning the missing pearls. Here she heard of Uyenishi's recent death ; and the governor of the prison, as he could not give her any information, handed over to her the casket as a sort of memento. This transaction came to the knowledge of the press, and—well, you know what the Californian press is like. There were ' some comments,' as they would say, and quite an assortment of Japanese, of shady antecedents, applied to the prison to have the casket ' restored ' to them as Uyenishi's heirs. Then Miss Bonney's rooms at the hotel were raided by burglars —but the casket was in the hotel strong-room—and Miss Bonney and her hostess were shadowed by various undesirables in such a disturbing fashion that the two ladies became alarmed and secretly made their way to New York. But there another burglary occurred, with

14

the same unsuccessful result, and the shadowing began again.   Finally, Miss Bonney, feeling that her presence was a danger to her friend, decided to return to England, and managed to get on board the ship without letting her departure be known in advance.

"But even in England she has not been left in peace. She has had an uncomfortable feeling of being watched and attended, and has seemed to be constantly meeting Japanese men in the streets, especially in the vicinity of her house.   Of course, all the fuss is about this infernal casket ; and when she told me what was happening, I promptly popped the thing in my pocket and took it to my office, where I stowed it in the strong-room. And there, of course, it ought to have remained.   But it didn't.   One day Miss Bonney told me that she was sending some small things to a loan exhibition of oriental works of art at the South Kensington Museum, and she wished to include the casket.   I urged her strongly to do nothing of the kind, but she persisted ; and the end of it was that we went to the museum together, with her pottery and stuff in a handbag and the casket in my pocket.

"It was a most imprudent thing to do, for there the beastly casket was, for several months, exposed in a glass case for anyone to see, with her name on the label ; and what was worse, full particulars of the origin of the thing.   However, nothing happened while it was there—the museum is not an easy place to steal from—and all went well until it was time to remove the things after the close of the exhibition.   Now, to-day was the appointed day, and, as on the previous occasion, she and I went to the museum together.   But the unfortunate thing is that we didn't come away together. Her other exhibits were all pottery, and these were dealt with first, so that she had her handbag packed and was ready to go before they had begun on the metal-work cases.   As we were not going the same way, it didn't seem necessary for her to wait ; so she went off with her bag and I stayed behind until the casket was released, when I put it in my pocket and went home, where I locked the thing up again in the strong-room.

"It was about seven when I got home. A little after eight I heard the telephone ring down in the office, and down I went, cursing the untimely ringer, who turned out to be a policeman at St. George's Hospital. He said he had found Miss Bonney lying unconscious in the street and had taken her to the hospital, where she had been detained for a while, but she was now recovered and he was taking her home. She would like me, if possible, to go and see her at once. Well, of course, I set off forthwith and got to her house a few minutes after her arrival, and just after you had left.

"She was a good deal upset, so I didn't worry her with many questions, but she gave me a short account of her misadventure, which amounted to this: She had started to walk home from the museum along the Brompton Road, and she was passing down a quiet street between that and Fulham Road when she heard soft footsteps behind her. The next moment, a scarf or shawl was thrown over her head and drawn tightly round her neck. At the same moment, the bag was snatched from her hand. That is all that she remembers, for she was half-suffocated and so terrified that she fainted, and knew no more until she found herself in a cab with two policemen, who were taking her to the hospital.

"Now it is obvious that her assailants were in search of that damned casket, for the bag had been broken open and searched, but nothing taken or damaged ; which suggests the Japanese again, for a British thief would have smashed the crockery. I found your card there, and I put it to Miss Bonney that we had better ask you to help us—I told her all about you—and she agreed emphatically. So that is why I am here, drinking your port and robbing you of your night's rest."

"And what do you want me to do?" Thorndyke asked.

"Whatever you think best," was the cheerful reply. "In the first place, this nuisance must be put a stop to—this shadowing and hanging about. But apart from that, you must see that there is something queer about this accursed casket. The beastly thing is of no intrinsic value. The museum man turned up his nose at it. But it evidently has some extrinsic value, and no small value either. If it is good enough for these devils to follow it all the way from the States, as they seem to have done, it is good enough for us to try to find out what its value is. That is where you come in. I propose to bring Miss Bonney to see you to-morrow, and I will bring the infernal casket, too. Then you will ask her a few questions, take a look at the casket—through the microscope, if necessary—and tell us all about it in your usual necromantic way."

Thorndyke laughed as he refilled our friend's glass. "If faith will move mountains, Brodribb," said he, "you ought to have been a civil engineer. But it is certainly a rather intriguing problem."

"Ha!" exclaimed the old solicitor; "then it's all right. I've known you a good many years, but I've never known you to be stumped; and you are not going to be stumped now. What time shall I bring her? Afternoon or evening would suit her best."

"Very well," replied Thorndyke; "bring her to tea —say, five o'clock. How will that do?"

"Excellently; and here's good luck to the adventure." He drained his glass, and the decanter being now empty, he rose, shook our hands warmly, and took his departure in high spirits.

It was with a very lively interest that I looked forward to the prospective visit. Like Thorndyke, I found the case rather intriguing. For it was quite clear, as our shrewd old friend had said, that there was something more than met the eye in the matter of this casket.

Hence, on the following afternoon, when, on the stroke of five, footsteps became audible on our stairs, I awaited the arrival of our new client with keen curiosity, both as to herself and her mysterious property.

To tell the truth, the lady was better worth looking at than the casket. At the first glance, I was strongly prepossessed in her favour, and so, I think, was Thorndyke. Not that she was a beauty, though comely enough. But she was an example of a type that seems to be growing rarer ; quiet, gentle, soft-spoken, and a lady to her finger-tips ; a little sad-faced and careworn, with a streak or two of white in her prettily-disposed black hair, though she could not have been much over thirty-five. Altogether a very gracious and winning personality.

When we had been presented to her by Brodribb—who treated her as if she had been a royal personage—and had enthroned her in the most comfortable easy-chair, we inquired as to her health, and were duly thanked for the salvage of the bag. Then Polton brought in the tray, with an air that seemed to demand an escort of choristers ; the tea was poured out, and the informal proceedings began.

She had not, however, much to tell ; for she had not seen her assailants, and the essential facts of the case had been fully presented in Brodribb's excellent summary. After a very few questions, therefore, we came to the next stage ; which was introduced by Brodribb's taking from his pocket a small parcel which he proceeded to open.

" There," said he, " that is the *fons et origo mali*. Not much to look at, I think you will agree." He set the object down on the table and glared at it malevolently, while Thorndyke and I regarded it with a more impersonal interest. It was not much to look at. Just an ordinary Japanese casket in the form of a squat, shapeless figure with a silly little grinning face, of which the head and shoulders opened on a hinge ; a pleasant enough object, with its quiet, warm colouring, but certainly not a masterpièce of art.

Thorndyke picked it up and turned it over slowly for a preliminary inspection ; then he went on to examine it detail by detail, watched closely, in his turn, by Brodribb and me. Slowly and methodically, his eye —fortified by a watchmaker's eyeglass—travelled over every part of the exterior. Then he opened it, and having examined the inside of the lid, scrutinised the bottom from within, long and attentively. Finally, he turned the casket upside down and examined the bottom from without, giving to it the longest and most rigorous inspection of all—which puzzled me somewhat, for the bottom was absolutely plain. At length, he passed the casket and the eyeglass to me without comment.

" Well," said Brodribb, " what is the verdict ? "

" It is of no value as a work of art," replied Thorndyke. " The body and lid are just castings of common white metal—an antimony alloy, I should say. The bronze colour is lacquer."

" So the museum man remarked," said Brodribb.

" But," continued Thorndyke, " there is one very odd thing about it. The only piece of fine metal in it is in the part which matters least. The bottom is a separate plate of the alloy known to the Japanese as Shakudo—an alloy of copper and gold."

" Yes," said Brodribb, " the museum man noted that, too, and couldn't make out why it had been put there."

" Then," Thorndyke continued, " there is another anomalous feature ; the inside of the bottom is covered with elaborate decoration—just the place where decoration is most inappropriate, since it would be covered up by the contents of the casket. And, again, this decoration is etched ; not engraved or chased. But etching is a very unusual process for this purpose, if it is ever used at all by Japanese metal-workers. My impression is that it is not ; for it is most unsuitable for decorative purposes. That is all that I observe, so far."

" And what do you infer from your observations ? "
Brodribb asked.

" I should like to think the matter over," was the
reply. " There is an obvious anomaly, which must
have some significance. But I won't embark on speculative opinions at this stage. I should like, however,
to take one or two photographs of the casket, for reference ; but that will occupy some time. You will hardly
want to wait so long."

" No," said Brodribb. " But Miss Bonney is coming
with me to my office to go over some documents and
discuss a little business. When we have finished, I
will come back and fetch the confounded thing."

" There is no need for that," replied Thorndyke.
" As soon as I have done what is necessary, I will bring
it up to your place."

To this arrangement Brodribb agreed readily, and he
and his client prepared to depart. I rose, too, and as
I happened to have a call to make in Old Square, Lincoln's Inn, I asked permission to walk with them.

As we came out into King's Bench Walk I noticed a
smallish, gentlemanly-looking man who had just passed
our entry and now turned in at the one next door ; and
by the light of the lamp in the entry he looked to me
like a Japanese. I thought Miss Bonney had observed
him, too, but she made no remark, and neither did I.
But, passing up Inner Temple Lane, we nearly overtook
two other men, who—though I got but a back view of
them and the light was feeble enough—aroused my
suspicions by their neat, small figures. As we approached, they quickened their pace, and one of them
looked back over his shoulder ; and then my suspicions
were confirmed, for it was an unmistakable Japanese
face that looked round at us. Miss Bonney saw that I
had observed the men, for she remarked, as they turned
sharply at the Cloisters and entered Pump Court :

" You see, I am still haunted by Japanese."

" I noticed them," said Brodribb. " They are

probably law students. But we may as well be companionable "; and with this, he, too, headed for Pump Court.

We followed our oriental friends across the Lane into Fountain Court, and through that and Devereux Court out to Temple Bar, where we parted from them ; they turning westward and we crossing to Bell Yard, up which we walked, entering New Square by the Carey Street gate. At Brodribb's doorway we halted and looked back, but no one was in sight. I accordingly went my way, promising to return anon to hear Thorndyke's report, and the lawyer and his client disappeared through the portal.

My business occupied me longer than I had expected, but nevertheless, when I arrived at Brodribb's premises —where he lived in chambers over his office—Thorndyke had not yet made his appearance. A quarter of an hour later, however, we heard his brisk step on the stairs, and as Brodribb threw the door open, he entered and produced the casket from his pocket.

" Well," said Brodribb, taking it from him and locking it, for the time being, in a drawer, " has the oracle spoken ; and if so, what did he say ? "

" Oracles," replied Thorndyke, " have a way of being more concise than explicit. Before I attempt to interpret the message, I should like to view the scene of the escape ; to see if there was any intelligible reason why this man Uyenishi should have returned up Brownlow Street into what must have been the danger zone. I think that is a material question."

" Then," said Brodribb, with evident eagerness, " let us all walk up and have a look at the confounded place. It is quite close by."

We all agreed instantly, two of us, at least, being on the tip-toe of expectation. For Thorndyke, who habitually understated his results, had virtually admitted that the casket had told him something ; and as we walked up the Square to the gate in Lincoln's Inn Fields,

I watched him furtively, trying to gather from his impassive face a hint as to what the something amounted to, and wondering how the movements of the fugitive bore on the solution of the mystery. Brobribb was similarly occupied, and as we crossed from Great Turnstile and took our way up Brownlow Street, I could see that his excitement was approaching bursting-point.

At the top of the street Thorndyke paused and looked up and down the rather dismal thoroughfare which forms a continuation of Bedford Row and bears its name. Then he crossed to the paved island surrounding the pump which stands in the middle of the road, and from thence surveyed the entrances to Brownlow Street and Hand Court ; and then he turned and looked thoughtfully at the pump.

" A quaint old survivor, this," he remarked, tapping the iron shell with his knuckles. " There is a similar one, you may remember, in Queen Square, and another at Aldgate. But that is still in use."

" Yes," Brodribb assented, almost dancing with impatience and inwardly damning the pump, as I could see, " I've noticed it."

" I suppose," Thorndyke proceeded, in a reflective tone, " they had to remove the handle. But it was rather a pity."

" Perhaps it was," growled Brodribb, whose complexion was rapidly developing affinities to that of a pickled cabbage, " but what the d——"

Here he broke off short and glared silently at Thorndyke, who had raised his arm and squeezed his hand into the opening once occupied by the handle. He groped in the interior with an expression of placid interest, and presently reported : " The barrel is still there, and so, apparently, is the plunger "—(Here I heard Brodribb mutter huskily, " Damn the barrel and the plunger too ! ") " but my hand is rather large for the exploration. Would you, Miss Bonney, mind slipping your hand in and telling me if I am right ? "

14*

We all gazed at Thorndyke in dismay, but in a moment Miss Bonney recovered from her astonishment, and with a deprecating smile, half shy, half amused, she slipped off her glove, and reaching up—it was rather high for her—inserted her hand into the narrow slit. Brodribb glared at her and gobbled like a turkey-cock, and I watched her with a sudden suspicion that something was going to happen. Nor was I mistaken. For, as I looked, the shy, puzzled smile faded from her face and was succeeded by an expression of incredulous astonishment. Slowly she withdrew her hand, and as it came out of the slit it dragged something after it. I started forward, and by the light of the lamp above the pump I could see that the object was a leather bag secured by a string from which hung a broken seal.

"It can't be!" she gasped as, with trembling fingers, she untied the string. Then, as she peered into the open mouth, she uttered a little cry.

"It is! It is! It is the necklace!"

Brodribb was speechless with amazement. So was I; and I was still gazing open-mouthed at the bag in Miss Bonney's hands when I felt Thorndyke touch my arm. I turned quickly and found him offering me an automatic pistol.

"Stand by, Jervis," he said quietly, looking towards Gray's Inn.

I looked in the same direction, and then perceived three men stealing round the corner from Jockey's Fields. Brodribb saw them, too, and snatching the bag of pearls from his client's hands, buttoned it into his breast pocket and placed himself before its owner, grasping his stick with a war-like air. The three men filed along the pavement until they were opposite us, when they turned simultaneously and bore down on the pump, each man, as I noticed, holding his right hand behind him. In a moment, Thorndyke's hand, grasping a pistol, flew up—as did mine, also—and he called out sharply:

" Stop ! If any man moves a hand, I fire."

The challenge brought them up short, evidently unprepared for this kind of reception. What would have happened next it is impossible to guess. But at this moment a police whistle sounded and two constables ran out from Hand Court. The whistle was instantly echoed from the direction of Warwick Court, whence two more constabulary figures appeared through the postern gate of Gray's Inn. Our three attendants hesitated but for an instant. Then, with one accord, they turned tail and flew like the wind round into Jockey's Fields, with the whole posse of constables close on their heels.

" Remarkable coincidence," said Brodribb, " that those policemen should happen to be on the look-out. Or isn't it a coincidence ? "

" I telephoned to the station superintendent before I started," replied Thorndyke, " warning him of a possible breach of the peace at this spot."

Brodribb chuckled. " You're a wonderful man, Thorndyke. You think of everything. I wonder if the police will catch those fellows."

" It is no concern of ours," replied Thorndyke. " We've got the pearls, and that finishes the business. There will be no more shadowing, in any case."

Miss Bonney heaved a comfortable little sigh and glanced gratefully at Thorndyke. " You can have no idea what a relief that is ! " she exclaimed ; " to say nothing of the treasure-trove."

We waited some time, but as neither the fugitives nor the constables reappeared, we presently made our way back down Brownlow Street. And there it was that Brodribb had an inspiration.

" I'll tell you what," said he. " I will just pop these things in my strong-room—they will be perfectly safe there until the bank opens to-morrow—and then we'll go and have a nice little dinner. I'll pay the piper."

" Indeed you won't ! " exclaimed Miss Bonney.
" This is my thanksgiving festival, and the benevolent
wizard shall be the guest of the evening."

" Very well, my dear," agreed Brodribb. " I will
pay and charge it to the estate. But I stipulate that
the benevolent wizard shall tell us exactly what the
oracle said. That is essential to the preservation of my
sanity."

" You shall have his *ipsissima verba*," Thorndyke
promised ; and the resolution was carried, *nem. con.*

An hour and a half later we were seated around a
table in a private room of a café to which Mr. Brodribb
had conducted us. I may not divulge its whereabouts,
though I may, perhaps, hint that we approached it by
way of Wardour Street. At any rate, we had dined,
even to the fulfilment of Brodribb's ideal, and coffee and
liqueurs furnished a sort of gastronomic doxology.
Brodribb had lighted a cigar and Thorndyke had produced a vicious-looking little black cheroot, which he
regarded fondly and then returned to its abiding-place
as unsuited to the present company.

" Now," said Brodribb, watching Thorndyke fill his
pipe (as understudy of the cheroot aforesaid), " we are
waiting to hear the words of the oracle."

" You shall hear them," Thorndyke replied. " There
were only five of them. But first, there are certain
introductory matters to be disposed of. The solution
of this problem is based on two well-known physical
facts, one metallurgical and the other optical."

" Ha ! " said Brodribb. " But you must temper the
wind to the shorn lamb, you know, Thorndyke. Miss
Bonney and I are not scientists."

" I will put the matter quite simply, but you must
have the facts. The first relates to the properties of
malleable metals—excepting iron and steel—and especially of copper and its alloys. If a plate of such metal
or alloy—say, bronze, for instance—is made red-hot and
quenched in water, it becomes quite soft and flexible—

the reverse of what happens in the case of iron. Now, if such a plate of softened metal be placed on a steel anvil and hammered, it becomes extremely hard and brittle."

" I follow that," said Brodribb.

" Then see what follows. If, instead of hammering the soft plate, you put on it the edge of a blunt chisel and strike on that chisel a sharp blow, you produce an indented line. Now the plate remains soft ; but the metal forming the indented line has been hammered and has become hard. There is now a line of hard metal on the soft plate. Is that clear ? "

" Perfectly," replied Brodribb ; and Thorndyke accordingly continued :

" The second fact is this : If a beam of light falls on a polished surface which reflects it, and if that surface is turned through a given angle, the beam of light is deflected through double that angle."

" H'm ! " grunted Brodribb. " Yes. No doubt. I hope we are not going to get into any deeper waters, Thorndyke."

" We are not," replied the latter, smiling urbanely. " We are now going to consider the application of these facts. Have you ever seen a Japanese magic mirror ? "

" Never ; nor even heard of such a thing."

" They are bronze mirrors, just like the ancient Greek or Etruscan mirrors—which are probably ' magic ' mirrors, too. A typical specimen consists of a circular or oval plate of bronze, highly polished on the face and decorated on the back with chased ornament—commonly a dragon or some such device—and furnished with a handle. The ornament is, as I have said, chased ; that is to say, it is executed in indented lines made with chasing tools, which are, in effect, small chisels, more or less blunt, which are struck with a chasing-hammer.

" Now these mirrors have a very singular property. Although the face is perfectly plain, as a mirror should be, yet, if a beam of sunlight is caught on it and reflected, say, on to a white wall, the round or oval patch of light on the wall is not a plain light patch. It shows quite clearly the ornament on the back of the mirror."

" But how extraordinary ! " exclaimed Miss Bonney. " It sounds quite incredible."

" It does," Thorndyke agreed. " And yet the explanation is quite simple. Professor Sylvanus Thompson pointed it out years ago. It is based on the facts which I have just stated to you. The artist who makes one of these mirrors begins, naturally, by annealing the metal until it is quite soft. Then he chases the design on the back, and this design then shows slightly on the face. But he now grinds the face perfectly flat with fine emery and water so that the traces of the design are completely obliterated. Finally, he polishes the face with rouge on a soft buff.

" But now observe that wherever the chasing-tool has made a line, the metal is hardened right through, so that the design is in hard metal on a soft matrix. But the hardened metal resists the wear of the polishing buff more than the soft metal does. The result is that the act of polishing causes the design to appear in faint relief on the face. Its projection is infinitesimal—less than the hundred-thousandth of an inch—and totally invisible to the eye. But, minute as it is, owing to the optical law which I mentioned—which, in effect, doubles the projection—it is enough to influence the reflection of light. As a consequence, every chased line appears on the patch of light as a dark line with a bright border, and so the whole design is visible. I think that is quite clear."

" Perfectly clear," Miss Bonney and Brodribb agreed.

" But now," pursued Thorndyke, " before we come to the casket, there is a very curious corollary which I must mention. Supposing our artist, having finished the mirror, should proceed with a scraper to erase the design from the back ; and on the blank, scraped surface to etch a new design. The process of etching does not harden the metal, so the new design does not appear on the reflection. But the old design would. For although it was invisible on the face and had been erased from the back, it would still exist in the substance of the metal and continue to influence the reflection. The odd result would be that the design which would be visible in the patch of light on the wall would be a different one from that on the back of the mirror.

"No doubt, you see what I am leading up to. But I will take the investigation of the casket as it actually occurred. It was obvious, at once, that the value of the thing was extrinsic. It had no intrinsic value, either in material or workmanship. What could that value be? The clear suggestion was that the casket was the vehicle of some secret message or information. It had been made by Uyenishi, who had almost certainly had possession of the missing pearls, and who had been so closely pursued that he never had an opportunity to communicate with his confederates. It was to be given to a man who was almost certainly one of those confederates; and, since the pearls had never been traced, there was a distinct probability that the (presumed) message referred to some hiding-place in which Uyenishi had concealed them during his flight, and where they were probably still hidden.

"With these considerations in my mind, I examined the casket, and this was what I found. The thing, itself, was a common white-metal casting, made presentable by means of lacquer. But the white metal bottom had been cut out and replaced by a plate of fine bronze—Shakudo. The inside of this was covered with an etched design, which immediately aroused my suspicions. Turning it over, I saw that the outside of the bottom was not only smooth and polished; it was a true mirror. It gave a perfectly undistorted reflection of my face. At once, I suspected that the mirror held the secret; that the message, whatever it was, had been chased on the back, had then been scraped away and an etched design worked on it to hide the traces of the scraper.

" As soon as you were gone, I took the casket up to the laboratory and threw a strong beam of parallel light from a condenser on the bottom, catching the reflection on a sheet of white paper. The result was just what I had expected. On the bright oval patch on the paper could be seen the shadowy, but quite distinct, forms of five words in the Japanese character.

" I was in somewhat of a dilemma, for I have no knowledge of Japanese, whereas the circumstances were such as to make it rather unsafe to employ a translator. However, as I do just know the Japanese characters and possess a Japanese dictionary, I determined to make an attempt to fudge out the words myself. If I failed, I could then look for a discreet translator.

" However, it proved to be easier than I had expected, for the words were detached ; they did not form a sentence, and so involved no questions of grammar. I spelt out the first word and then looked it up in the dictionary. The translation was ' pearls.' This looked hopeful, and I went on to the next, of which the translation was ' pump.' The third word floored me. It seemed to be ' jokkis,' or ' jokkish,' but there was no such word in the dictionary ; so I turned to the next word, hoping that it would explain its predecessor. And it did. The fourth word was ' fields,' and the last word was evidently ' London.' So the entire group read : ' Pearls, Pump, Jokkis, Fields, London.'

" Now, there is no pump, so far as I know, in Jockey's Fields, but there is one in Bedford Row close to the corner of the Fields, and exactly opposite the end of Brownlow Street. And by Mr. Brodribb's account, Uyenishi, in his flight, ran down Hand Court and re-turned up Brownlow Street, as if he were making for the pump. As the latter is disused and the handle-hole is high up, well out of the way of children, it offers quite a good temporary hiding-place, and I had no doubt that the bag of pearls had been poked into it and was probably there still. I was tempted to go at once and explore ;

but I was anxious that the discovery should be made by Miss Bonney, herself, and I did not dare to make a preliminary exploration for fear of being shadowed. If I had found the treasure I should have had to take it and give it to her ; which would have been a flat ending to the adventure. So I had to dissemble and be the occasion of much smothered objurgation on the part of my friend Brodribb. And that is the whole story of my interview with the oracle."

Our mantelpiece is becoming a veritable museum of trophies of victory, the gifts of grateful clients. Among them is a squat, shapeless figure of a Japanese gentleman of the old school, with a silly grinning little face—The Magic Casket. But its possession is no longer a menace. Its sting has been drawn ; its magic is exploded ; its secret is exposed, and its glory departed.

14   THE CONTENTS OF A MARE'S NEST

" IT is very unsatisfactory," said Mr. Stalker, of the ' Griffin ' Life Assurance Company, at the close of a consultation on a doubtful claim. " I suppose we shall have to pay up."

" I am sure you will," said Thorndyke. " The death was properly certified, the deceased is buried, and you have not a single fact with which to support an application for further inquiry."

" No," Stalker agreed. " But I am not satisfied. I don't believe that doctor really knew what she died from. I wish cremation were more usual."

" So, I have no doubt, has many a poisoner," Thorndyke remarked dryly.

Stalker laughed, but stuck to his point. " I know you don't agree," said he, " but from our point of view it is much more satisfactory to know that the extra precautions have been taken. In a cremation case, you have not to depend on the mere death certificate ; you have the cause of death verified by an independent authority, and it is difficult to see how any miscarriage can occur."

Thorndyke shook his head. " It is a delusion, Stalker. You can't provide in advance for unknown contingencies. In practice, your special precautions degenerate into mere formalities. If the circumstances of a death appear normal, the independent authority will certify ; if they appear abnormal, you won't get a certificate at all. And if suspicion arises only after the cremation has taken place, it can neither be confirmed nor rebutted."

" My point is," said Stalker, " that the searching examination would lead to discovery of a crime before cremation."

" That is the intention," Thorndyke admitted. " But no examination, short of an exhaustive post-mortem, would make it safe to destroy a body so that no recon-sideration of the cause of death would be possible.'

Stalker smiled as he picked up his hat. " Well," he said, " to a cobbler there is nothing like leather, and I suppose that to a toxicologist there is nothing like an exhumation," and with this parting shot he took his leave.

We had not seen the last of him, however. In the course of the same week he looked in to consult us on a fresh matter.

" A rather queer case has turned up," said he. " I don't know that we are deeply concerned in it, but we should like to have your opinion as to how we stand. The position is this : Eighteen months ago, a man named Ingle insured with us for fifteen hundred pounds, and he was then accepted as a first-class life. He has recently died—apparently from heart failure, the heart being described as fatty and dilated—and his wife, Sibyl, who is the sole legatee and executrix, has claimed payment.

But just as we were making arrangements to pay, a caveat has been entered by a certain Margaret Ingle, who declares that she is the wife of the deceased and claims the estate as next-of-kin. She states that the alleged wife, Sibyl, is a widow named Huggard who contracted a bigamous marriage with the deceased, knowing that he had a wife living."

" An interesting situation," commented Thorndyke, " but, as you say, it doesn't particularly concern you. It is a matter for the Probate Court."

" Yes," agreed Stalker. " But that is not all. Margaret Ingle not only charges the other woman with bigamy ; she accuses her of having made away with the deceased."

" On what grounds ? "

" Well, the reasons she gives are rather shadowy. She states that Sibyl's husband, James Huggard, died under suspicious circumstances—there seems to have been some suspicion that he had been poisoned—and she asserts that Ingle was a healthy, sound man and could not have died from the causes alleged."

" There is some reason in that," said Thorndyke, " if he was really a first-class life only eighteen months ago. As to the first husband, Huggard, we should want some particulars : as to whether there was an inquest, what was the alleged cause of death, and what grounds there were for suspecting that he had been poisoned. If there really were any suspicious circumstances, it would be advisable to apply to the Home Office for an order to exhume the body of Ingle and verify the cause of death."

Stalker smiled somewhat sheepishly. " Unfortunately," said he, " that is not possible. Ingle was cremated."

" Ah ! " said Thorndyke, " that is, as you say, unfortunate. It clearly increases the suspicion of poisoning, but destroys the means of verifying that suspicion."

" I should tell you," said Stalker, " that the cremation was in accordance with the provisions of the will."

" That is not very material," replied Thorndyke.
" In fact, it rather accentuates the suspicious aspect of
the case ; for the knowledge that the death of the deceased
would be followed by cremation might act as a further
inducement to get rid of him by poison.   There were two
death certificates, of course ? "

" Yes.   The confirmatory certificate was given by
Dr. Halbury, of Wimpole Street.   The medical attendant
was a Dr. Barber, of Howland Street.   The deceased lived
in Stock-Orchard Crescent, Holloway."

" A good distance from Howland Street," Thorndyke
remarked.   " Do you know if Halbury made a post-
mortem ? I don't suppose he did."

" No, he didn't," replied Stalker.

" Then," said Thorndyke, " his certificate is worthless.
You can't tell whether a man has died from heart failure
by looking at his dead body.   He must have just accepted
the opinion of the medical attendant.   Do I understand
that you want me to look into this case ? "

" If you will.   It is not really our concern whether
or not the man was poisoned, though I suppose we should
have a claim on the estate of the murderer.   But we
should like you to investigate the case ; though how the
deuce you are going to do it I don't quite see."

" Neither do I," said Thorndyke.   " However, we
must get into touch with the doctors who signed the
certificates, and possibly they may be able to clear the
whole matter up."

" Of course," said I, " there is the other body—that
of Huggard—which might be exhumed—unless he was
cremated, too."

" Yes," agreed Thorndyke ; " and for the purposes of
the criminal law, evidence of poisoning in that case would
be sufficient.   But it would hardly help the Griffin
Company, which is concerned exclusively with Ingle
deceased.   Can you let us have a précis of the facts
relating to this case, Stalker ? "

" I have brought one with me," was the reply ; " a

short statement, giving names, addresses, dates, and other particulars. Here it is "; and he handed Thorndyke a sheet of paper bearing a tabulated statement.

When Stalker had gone Thorndyke glanced rapidly through the précis and then looked at his watch. " If we make our way to Wimpole Street at once," said he, " we ought to catch Halbury. That is obviously the first thing to do. He signed the ' C ' certificate, and we shall be able to judge from what he tells us whether there is any possibility of foul play. Shall we start now ? "

As I assented, he slipped the précis in his pocket and we set forth. At the top of Middle Temple Lane we chartered a taxi by which we were shortly deposited at Dr. Halbury's door and a few minutes later were ushered into his consulting room, and found him shovelling a pile of letters into the waste-paper basket.

" How d'ye do ? " he said briskly, holding out his hand. " I'm up to my eyes in arrears, you see. Just back from my holiday. What can I do for you ? "

" We have called," said Thorndyke, " about a man named Ingle."

" Ingle—Ingle," repeated Halbury. " Now, let me see—— "

" Stock-Orchard Crescent, Holloway," Thorndyke explained.

" Oh, yes. I remember him. Well, how is he ? "

" He's dead," replied Thorndyke.

" Is he really ? " exclaimed Halbury. " Now that shows how careful one should be in one's judgments. I half suspected that fellow of malingering. He was sup-posed to have a dilated heart, but I couldn't make out any appreciable dilatation. There was excited, irregular action. That was all. I had a suspicion that he had been dosing himself with trinitrine. Reminded me of the cases of cordite chewing that I used to meet with in South Africa. So he's dead, after all. Well, it's queer. Do you know what the exact cause of death was ? "

" Failure of a dilated heart is the cause stated on the

certificates—the body was cremated ; and the ' C '
Certificate was signed by you."

" By me ! " exclaimed the physician. " Nonsense !
It's a mistake. I signed a certificate for a Friendly
Society—Mrs. Ingle brought it here for me to sign—but
I didn't even know he was dead. Besides, I went away
for my holiday a few days after I saw the man and only
came back yesterday. What makes you think I signed
the death certificate ? "

Thorndyke produced Stalker's précis and handed it
to Halbury, who read out his own name and address with
a puzzled frown. " This is an extraordinary affair,"
said he. " It will have to be looked into."

" It will, indeed," assented Thorndyke ; " especially
as a suspicion of poisoning has been raised."

" Ha ! " exclaimed Halbury. " Then it was trinitrine,
you may depend. But I suspected him unjustly. It was
somebody else who was dosing him ;, perhaps that sly-
looking baggage of a wife of his. Is anyone in particular
suspected ? "

" Yes. The accusation, such as it is, is against the
wife."

" H'm. Probably a true bill. But she's done us.
Artful devil. You can't get much evidence out of an
urnful of ashes. Still, somebody has forged my signature. I suppose that is what the hussy wanted that
certificate for—to get a specimen of my handwriting.
I see the ' B ' certificate was signed by a man named
Meeking. Who's he ? It was Barber who called me in
for an opinion."

" I must find out who he is," replied Thorndyke.
" Possibly Dr. Barber will know. I shall go and call
on him now."

" Yes," said Dr. Halbury, shaking hands as we rose
to depart, " you ought to see Barber. He knows the
history of the case, at any rate."

From Wimpole Street we steered a course for Howland
Street, and here we had the good fortune to arrive just

as Dr. Barber's car drew up at the door. Thorndyke introduced himself and me, and then introduced the subject of his visit, but said nothing, at first, about our call on Dr. Halbury.

" Ingle," repeated Dr. Barber. " Oh, yes, I remember him. And you say he is dead. Well, I'm rather surprised. I didn't regard his condition as serious."

" Was his heart dilated ? " Thorndyke asked.

" Not appreciably. I found nothing organic ; no valvular disease. It was more like a tobacco heart. But it's odd that Meeking didn't mention the matter to me—he was my locum, you know. I handed the case over to him when I went on my holiday. And you say he signed the death certificate ? "

" Yes ; and the ' B ' certificate for cremation, too."

" Very odd," said Dr. Barber. " Just come in and let us have a look at the day book."

We followed him into the consulting room, and there, while he was turning over the leaves of the day book, I ran my eye along the shelf over the writing-table from which he had taken it ; on which I observed the usual collection of case books and books of certificates and notification forms, including the book of death certificates.

" Yes," said Dr. Barber, " here we are ; ' Ingle, Mr., Stock-Orchard Crescent." The last visit was on the 4th of September, and Meeking seems to have given some sort of certificate. Wonder if he used a printed form." He took down two of the books and turned over the counterfoils.

" Here we are," he said presently ; " ' Ingle, Jonathan, 4th September. Now recovered and able to resume duties.' That doesn't look like dying, does it ? Still, we may as well make sure."

He reached down the book of death certificates and began to glance through the most recent entries.

" No," he said, turning over the leaves, " there doesn't seem to be—— Hullo ! What's this ? Two blank counterfoils ; and about the date, too ; between the

2nd and 13th of September. Extraordinary ! Meeking is such a careful, reliable man."

He turned back to the day book and read through the fortnight's entries. Then he looked up with an anxious frown.

" I can't make this out," he said.   " There is no record of any patient having died in that period."

" Where is Dr. Meeking at present ? " I asked.

" Somewhere in the South Atlantic," replied Barber. " He left here three weeks ago to take up a post on a Royal Mail Boat. So he couldn't have signed the certificate in any case."

That was all that Dr. Barber had to tell us, and a few minutes later we took our departure.

" This case looks pretty fishy," I remarked, as we turned down Tottenham Court Road.

" Yes," Thorndyke agreed. " There is evidently something radically wrong. And what strikes me especially is the cleverness of the fraud ; the knowledge and judgment and foresight that are displayed."

" She took pretty considerable risks," I observed.

" Yes, but only the risks that were unavoidable. Everything that could be foreseen has been provided for. All the formalities have been complied with—in appearance.   And you must notice, Jervis, that the scheme did actually succeed. The cremation has taken place. Nothing but the incalculable accident of the appearance of the real Mrs. Ingle, and her vague and apparently groundless suspicions, prevented the success from being final.   If she had not come on the scene, no questions would ever have been asked."

" No," I agreed.   " The discovery of the plot is a matter of sheer bad luck.   But what do you suppose has really happened ? "

Thorndyke shook his head.

" It is very difficult to say.   The mechanism of the affair is obvious enough, but the motives and purpose are rather incomprehensible.   The illness was apparently a sham, the symptoms being produced by nitro-glycerine or some similar heart poison. The doctors were called in, partly for the sake of appearances and partly to get specimens of their handwriting. The fact that both the doctors happened to be away from home and one of them at sea at the time when verbal questions might have been asked—by the undertaker, for instance—suggests that this had been ascertained in advance. The death certificate forms were pretty certainly stolen by the woman when she was left alone in Barber's consulting-room, and, of course, the cremation certificates could be obtained on application to the crematorium authorities. That is all plain sailing. The mystery is, what is it all about ? Barber or Meeking would almost certainly have given a death certificate, although the death was unexpected, and I don't suppose Halbury would have refused to confirm it. They would have assumed that their diagnosis had been at fault."

" Do you think it could have been suicide, or an inadvertent overdose of trinitrine ? "

" Hardly. If it was suicide, it was deliberate, for the purpose of getting the insurance money for the woman, unless there was some further motive behind. And the cremation, with all its fuss and formalities, is against suicide ; while the careful preparation seems to exclude inadvertent poisoning. Then, what was the motive for the sham illness except as a preparation for an abnormal death ? "

" That is true," said I. " But if you reject suicide, isn't it rather remarkable that the victim should have provided for his own cremation ? "

" We don't know that he did," replied Thorndyke. " There is a suggestion of a capable forger in this business. It is quite possible that the will itself is a forgery."

" So it is ! " I exclaimed. " I hadn't thought of that."

" You see," continued Thorndyke, " the appearances suggest that cremation was a necessary part of the programme ; otherwise these extraordinary risks would not have been taken. The woman was sole executrix and could have ignored the cremation clause. But if the cremation was necessary, why was it necessary ? The suggestion is that there was something suspicious in the appearance of the body ; something that the doctors would certainly have observed or that would have been discovered if an exhumation had taken place."

" You mean some injury or visible signs of poisoning ? "

" I mean something discoverable by examination even after burial."

" But what about the undertaker ? Wouldn't he have noticed anything palpably abnormal ? "

" An excellent suggestion, Jervis. We must see the undertaker. We have his address : Kentish Town Road—a long way from deceased's house, by the way. We had better get on a bus and go there now."

A yellow omnibus was approaching as he spoke. We hailed it and sprang on, continuing our discussion as we were borne northward.

Mr. Burrell, the undertaker, was a pensive-looking, profoundly civil man who was evidently in a small way, for he combined with his funeral functions general carpentry and cabinet making. He was perfectly willing to give any required information, but he seemed to have very little to give.

" I never really saw the deceased gentleman," he said in reply to Thorndyke's cautious inquiries. " When I took the measurements, the corpse was covered with a sheet ; and as Mrs. Ingle was in the room, I made the business as short as possible."

" You didn't put the body in the coffin, then ? "

" No. I left the coffin at the house, but Mrs. Ingle said that she and the deceased gentleman's brother would lay the body in it."

" But didn't you see the corpse when you screwed the coffin-lid down ? "

" I didn't screw it down. When I got there it was

screwed down already. Mrs. Ingle said they had to close up the coffin, and I dare say it was necessary. The weather was rather warm ; and I noticed a strong smell of formalin."

" Well," I said, as we walked back down the Kentish Town Road, " we haven't got much more forward."

" I wouldn't say that," replied Thorndyke. " We have a further instance of the extraordinary adroitness with which this scheme was carried out ; and we have confirmation of our suspicion that there was something unusual in the appearance of the body. It is evident that this woman did not dare to let even the undertaker see it. But one can hardly help admiring the combination of daring and caution, the boldness with which these risks were taken, and the care and judgment with which they were provided against. And again I point out that the risks were justified by the result. The secret of that man's death appears to have been made secure for all time."

It certainly looked as if the mystery with which we were concerned were beyond the reach of investigation. Of course, the woman could be prosecuted for having forged the death certificates, to say nothing of the charge of bigamy. But that was no concern of ours or Stalker's. Jonathan Ingle was dead, and no one could say how he died.

On our arrival at our chambers we found a telegram that had just arrived, announcing that Stalker would call on us in the evening ; and as this seemed to suggest that he had some fresh information we looked forward to his visit with considerable interest. Punctually at six o'clock he made his appearance and at once opened the subject.

" There are some new developments in this Ingle case," said he. " In the first place, the woman, Huggard, has bolted. I went to the house to make a few inquiries and found the police in possession. They had come to arrest her on the bigamy charge, but she had got wind of their intentions and cleared out. They made a search of the premises, but I don't think they found anything of interest except a number of rifle cartridges ; and I don't know that they are of much interest either, for she could hardly have shot him with a rifle."

" What kind of cartridges were they ? " Thorndyke asked.

Stalker put his hand in his pocket.

" The inspector let me have one to show you," said he ; and he laid on the table a military cartridge of the pattern of some twenty years ago. Thorndyke picked it up, and taking from a drawer a pair of pliers drew the bullet out of the case and inserted into the latter a pair of dissecting forceps. When he withdrew the forceps, their points grasped one or two short strings of what looked like cat-gut.

" Cordite ! " said I. " So Halbury was probably right, and this is how she got her supply." Then, as Stalker looked at me inquiringly, I gave him a short account of the results of our investigations.

" Ha ! " he exclaimed, " the plot thickens. This juggling with the death certificates seems to connect itself with another kind of juggling that I came to tell you about. You know that Ingle was Secretary and Treasurer to a company that bought and sold land for building estates. Well, I called at their office after I left you and had a little talk with the chairman. From him I learned that Ingle had practically complete control of the financial affairs of the company, that he received and paid all moneys and kept the books. Of late, however, some of the directors have had a suspicion that all was not well with the finances, and at last it was decided to have the affairs of the company thoroughly overhauled by a firm of chartered accountants. This decision was communicated to Ingle, and a couple of days later a letter arrived from his wife saying that he had had a severe heart attack and asking that the audit of the books might be postponed until he recovered and was able to attend at the office."

" And was it postponed ? " I asked.

" No," replied Stalker. " The accountants were asked to get to work at once, which they did ; with the result that they discovered a number of discrepancies in the books and a sum of about three thousand pounds unaccounted for. It isn't quite obvious how the frauds were carried out, but it is suspected that some of the returned cheques are fakes with forged endorsements."

" Did the company communicate with Ingle on the subject ? " asked Thorndyke.

" No. They had a further letter from Mrs. Ingle— that is, Huggard—saying that Ingle's condition was very serious ; so they decided to wait until he had recovered. Then, of course, came the announcement of his death, on which the matter was postponed pending the probate of the will. I suppose a claim will be made on the estate, but as the executrix has absconded, the affair has become rather complicated."

" You were saying," said Thorndyke, " that the fraudulent death certificates seem to be connected with these frauds on the company. What kind of connection do you assume ? "

" I assume—or, at least, suggest," replied Stalker, " that this was a case of suicide. The man, Ingle, saw that his frauds were discovered, or were going to be, and that he was in for a long term of penal servitude, so he just made away with himself. And I think that if the murder charge could be dropped, Mrs. Huggard might be induced to come forward and give evidence as to the suicide."

Thorndyke shook his head.

" The murder charge couldn't be dropped," said he. " If it was suicide, Huggard was certainly an accessory ; and in law, an accessory to suicide is an accessory to murder. But, in fact, no official charge of murder has been made, and at present there are no means of sustaining

such a charge. The identity of the ashes might be assumed to be that stated in the cremation order, but the
difficulty is the cause of death. Ingle was admittedly ill.
He was attended for heart disease by three doctors.
There is no evidence that he did not die from that
illness."

" But the illness was due to cordite poisoning," said I.

" That is what we believe. But no one could swear
to it. And we certainly could not swear that he died
from cordite poisoning."

" Then," said Stalker, " apparently there is no means
of finding out whether his death was due to natural
causes, suicide, or murder ? "

" There is only one chance," replied Thorndyke.
" It is just barely possible that the cause of death might
be ascertainable by an examination of the ashes."

" That doesn't seem very hopeful," said I. " Cordite
poisoning would certainly leave no trace."

" We mustn't assume that he died from cordite
poisoning," said Thorndyke. " Probably he did not.
That may have masked the action of a less obvious poison,
or death might have been produced by some new agent."

" But," I objected, " how many poisons are there
that could be detected in the ashes ? No organic poison
would leave any traces, nor would metallic poisons such
as mercury, antimony, or arsenic."

" No," Thorndyke agreed. " But there are other
metallic poisons which could be easily recovered from
the ashes ; lead, tin, gold, and silver, for instance.
But it is useless to discuss speculative probabilities. The
only chance that we have of obtaining any new facts is
by an examination of the ashes. It seems infinitely
improbable that we shall learn anything from it, but there
is the bare possibility and we ought not to leave it untried."

Neither Stalker nor I made any further remark, but I
could see that the same thought was in both our minds.
It was not often that Thorndyke was " gravelled " ; but
apparently the resourceful Mrs. Huggard had set him a

problem that was beyond even his powers. When an investigator of crime is reduced to the necessity of examining a potful of ashes in the wild hope of ascertaining from them how the deceased met his death, one may assume that he is at the very end of his tether. It is a forlorn hope indeed.

Nevertheless, Thorndyke seemed to view the matter quite cheerfully, his only anxiety being lest the Home Secretary should refuse to make the order authorising the examination. And this anxiety was dispelled a day or two later by the arrival of a letter giving the necessary authority, and informing him that a Dr. Hemming— known to us both as an expert pathologist—had been deputed to be present at the examination and to confer with him as to the necessity for a chemical analysis.

On the appointed day Dr. Hemming called at our chambers and we set forth together for Liverpool Street ; and as we drove thither it became evident to me that his view of our mission was very similar to my own. For, though he talked freely enough, and on professional topics, he maintained a most discreet silence on the subject of the forthcoming inspection ; indeed, the first reference to the subject was made by Thorndyke himself just as the train was approaching Corfield, where the crematorium was situated.

" I presume," said he, " you have made all necessary arrangements, Hemming ? "

" Yes," was the reply. " The superintendent will meet us and will conduct us to the catacombs, and there, in our presence, will take the casket from its niche in the columbarium and have it conveyed to the office, where the examination will be made. I thought it best to use these formalities, though, as the casket is sealed and bears the name of the deceased, there is not much point in them."

" No," said Thorndyke, " but I think you were right. It would be easy to challenge the identity of a mass

of ashes if all precautions were not taken, seeing that the
ashes themselves are unidentifiable."

" That was what I felt," said Hemming ; and then,
as the train slowed down, he added : " This is our station,
and that gentleman on the platform, I suspect, is the
superintendent."

The surmise turned out to be correct ; but the cemetery
official was not the only one present bearing that title ;
for as we were mutually introducing ourselves, a familiar
tall figure approached up the platform from the rear of
the train—our old friend Superintendent Miller of the
Criminal Investigation Department.

" I don't wish to intrude," said he, as he joined the
group and was presented by Thorndyke to the strangers,
" but we were notified by the Home Office that an
investigation was to be made, so I thought I would be
on the spot to pick up any crumbs of information that
you may drop.   Of course, I am not asking to be present
at the examination."

" You may as well be present as an additional witness
to the removal of the urn," said Thorndyke ; and
Miller accordingly joined the party, which now made its
way from the station to the cemetery.

The catacombs were in a long, low arcaded building
at the end of the pleasantly-wooded grounds, and on our
way thither we passed the crematorium, a smallish,
church-like edifice with a perforated chimney-shaft
partly concealed by the low spire.   Entering the catacombs, we were conducted to the " columbarium," the
walls of which were occupied by a multitude of niches or
pigeon-holes, each niche accommodating a terra-cotta
urn or casket.   The superintendent proceeded to near the
end of the gallery, where he halted, and opening the
register, which he had brought with him, read out a
number and the name " Jonathan Ingle," and then led
us to a niche bearing that number and name, in which
reposed a square casket, on which was inscribed the name
and date of death.   When we had verified these par-

ticulars, the casket was tenderly lifted from its place by two attendants, who carried it to a well-lighted room at the end of the building, where a large table by a window had been covered with white paper. Having placed the casket on the table, the attendants retired, and the superintendent then broke the seals and removed the cover.

For a while we all stood looking in at the contents of the casket without speaking ; and I found myself contrasting them with what would have been revealed by the lifting of a coffin-lid. Truly corruption had put on incorruption. The mass of snow-white, coral-like fragments, delicate, fragile, and lace-like in texture, so far from being repulsive in aspect, were almost attractive. I ran my eye, with an anatomist's curiosity, over these dazzling remnants of what had lately been a man, half-unconsciously seeking to identify and give a name to particular fragments, and a little surprised at the difficulty of determining that this or that irregularly-shaped white object was a part of any one of the bones with which I had thought myself so familiar.

Presently Hemming looked up at Thorndyke and asked : "Do you observe anything abnormal in the appearance of these ashes ? I don't."

"Perhaps," replied Thorndyke, "we had better turn them out on to the table, so that we can see the whole of them."

This was done very gently, and then Thorndyke proceeded to spread out the heap, touching the fragments with the utmost delicacy—for they were extremely fragile and brittle—until the whole collection was visible.

"Well," said Hemming, when we had once more looked them over critically, "what do you say ? I can see no trace of any foreign substance. Can you ? "

"No," replied Thorndyke. "And there are some other things that I can't see. For instance, the medical referee reported that the proposer had a good set of sound teeth. Where are they ? I have not seen a single frag-

15

ment of a tooth.   Yet teeth are far more resistant to fire
than bones, especially the enamel caps."

Hemming ran a searching glance over the mass of
fragments and looked up with a perplexed frown.

" I certainly can't see any sign of teeth," he admitted ;
" and it *is* rather curious, as you say.   Does the fact
suggest any particular significance to you ? "

By way of reply, Thorndyke delicately picked up a
flat fragment and silently held it out towards us.   I
looked at it and said nothing ; for a very strange suspicion
was beginning to creep into my mind.

" A piece of a rib," said Hemming.   " Very odd that
it should have broken across so cleanly.   It might have
been cut with a saw."

Thorndyke laid it down and picked up another, larger
fragment, which I had already noticed.

" Here is another example," said he, handing it to our
colleague.

" Yes," agreed Hemming.   " It is really rather
extraordinary.   It looks exactly as if it had been sawn
across."

" It does," agreed Thorndyke.   " What bone should
you say it is ? "

" That is what I was just asking myself," replied
Hemming, looking at the fragment with a sort of half-
vexed smile.   " It seems ridiculous that a competent
anatomist should be in any doubt with as large a portion
as this, but really I can't confidently give it a name.   The
shape seems to me to suggest a tibia, but of course it is
much too small.   Is it the upper end of the ulna ? "

" I should say no," answered Thorndyke.   Then he
picked out another of the larger fragments, and handing
it to Hemming, asked him to name it.

Our friend began to look somewhat worried.

" It is an extraordinary thing, you know," said he,
" but I can't tell you what bone it is part of.   It is clearly
the shaft of a long bone, but I'm hanged if I can say
which.   It is too big for a metatarsal and too small for any

of the main limb bones. It reminds one of a diminutive thigh bone."

"It does," agreed Thorndyke; "very strongly." While Hemming had been speaking he had picked out four more large fragments, and these he now laid in a row with the one that had seemed to resemble a tibia in shape. Placed thus together, the five fragments bore an obvious resemblance.

"Now," said he, "look at these. There are five of them. They are parts of limb bones, and the bones of which they are parts were evidently exactly alike, excepting that three were apparently from the left side and two from the right. Now, you know, Hemming, a man has only four limbs and of those only two contain similar bones. Then two of them show distinct traces of what looks like a saw-cut."

Hemming gazed at the row of fragments with a frown of deep cogitation.

"It is very mysterious," he said. "And looking at them in a row they strike me as curiously like tibiæ—in shape ; not in size."

"The size," said Thorndyke, "is about that of a sheep's tibia."

"A sheep's !" exclaimed Hemming, staring in amazement, first at the calcined bones and then at my colleague.

"Yes ; the upper half, sawn across in the middle of the shank."

Hemming was thunderstruck.

"It is an astounding affair !" he exclaimed. "You mean to suggest——"

"I suggest," said Thorndyke, "that there is not a sign of a human bone in the whole collection. But there are very evident traces of at least five legs of mutton."

For a few moments there was a profound silence, broken only by a murmur of astonishment from the cemetery official and a low chuckle from Superintendent

Miller, who had been listening with absorbed interest. At length Hemming spoke.

" Then, apparently, there was no corpse in the coffin at all ? "

" No," answered Thorndyke. " The weight was made up, and the ashes furnished, by joints of butcher's meat. I dare say, if we go over the ashes carefully, we shall be able to judge what they were. But it is hardly necessary. The presence of five legs of mutton and the absence of a single recognisable fragment of a human skeleton, together with the forged certificates, gives us a pretty conclusive case. The rest, I think we can leave to Superintendent Miller."

" I take it, Thorndyke," said I, as the train moved out of the station, " that you came here expecting to find what you did find ? "

" Yes," he replied. " It seemed to me the only possibility, having regard to all the known facts."

" When did it first occur to you ? "

" It occurred to me as a possibility as soon as we discovered that the cremation certificates had been forged ; but it was the undertaker's statement that seemed to clench the matter."

" But he distinctly stated that he measured the body."

" True. But there was nothing to show that it was a dead body. What was perfectly clear was that there was something that must on no account be seen ; and when Stalker told us of the embezzlement we had a body of evidence that could point to only one conclusion. Just consider that evidence.

" Here we had a death, preceded by an obviously sham illness and followed by cremation with forged certificates. Now, what was it that had happened ? There were four possible hypotheses. Normal death, suicide, murder, and fictitious death. Which of these hypotheses fitted the facts ?

" Normal death was apparently excluded by the forged certificates.

" The theory of suicide did not account for the facts. It did not agree with the careful, elaborate preparation. And why the forged certificates ? If Ingle had really died, Meeking would have certified the death. And why the cremation ? There was no purpose in taking those enormous risks.

" The theory of murder was unthinkable. These certificates were almost certainly forged by Ingle himself, who we know was a practised forger. But the idea of the victim arranging for his own cremation is an absurdity.

" There remained only the theory of fictitious death ; and that theory fitted all the facts perfectly. First, as to the motive. Ingle had committed a felony. He had to disappear. But what kind of disappearance could be so effectual as death and cremation ? Both the prosecutors and the police would forthwith write him off and forget him. Then there was the bigamy—a criminal offence in itself. But death would not only wipe that off ; after ' death ' he could marry Huggard regularly under another name, and he would have shaken off his deserted wife for ever. And he stood to gain fifteen hundred pounds from the Insurance Company. Then see how this theory explained the other facts. A fictitious death made necessary a fictitious illness. It necessitated the forged certificates, since there was no corpse. It made cremation highly desirable ; for suspicion might easily have arisen, and then the exhumation of a coffin containing a dummy would have exploded the fraud. But successful cremation would cover up the fraud for ever. It explained the concealment of the corpse from the undertaker, and it even explained the smell of formalin which he noticed."

" How did it ? " I asked.

" Consider, Jervis," he replied. " The dummy in this coffin had to be a dummy of flesh and bone which would yield the correct kind of ash. Joints of butcher's meat would fulfil the conditions. But the quantity required would be from a hundred and fifty to two hundred pounds. Now Ingle could not go to the butcher and order a whole sheep to be sent the day before the funeral. The joints would have to be bought gradually and stored. But the storage of meat in warm weather calls for some kind of preservative ; and formalin is highly effective, as it leaves no trace after burning.

" So you see that the theory of fictitious death agreed with all the known circumstances, whereas the alternative theories presented inexplicable discrepancies and contradictions. Logically, it was the only possible theory, and, as you have seen, experiment proved it to be the true one."

As Thorndyke concluded, Dr. Hemming took his pipe from his mouth and laughed softly.

" When I came down to-day," said he, " I had all the facts which you had communicated to the Home Office, and I was absolutely convinced that we were coming to examine a mare's nest. And yet, now I have heard your exposition, the whole thing looks perfectly obvious."

" That is usually the case with Thorndyke's conclusions," said I. " They are perfectly obvious—when you have heard the explanation."

Within a week of our expedition, Ingle was in the hands of the police. The apparent success of the cremation adventure had misled him to a sense of such complete security that he had neglected to cover his tracks, and he had accordingly fallen an easy prey to our friend Superintendent Miller. The police were highly gratified, and so were the directors of the Griffin Life Assurance Company.

As Thorndyke and I descended the stairs of the footbridge at Densford Junction we became aware that
something unusual had happened. The platform was
nearly deserted save at one point, where a small but
dense crowd had collected around the open door of a
first-class compartment of the down train ; heads were
thrust out of the windows of the other coaches, and at
intervals doors opened and inquisitive passengers ran
along to join the crowd, from which an excited porter
detached himself just as we reached the platform.

" You'd better go for Dr. Pooke first," the station-
master called after him.

On this, Thorndyke stepped forward.

" My friend and I," said he, " are medical men.
Can we be of any service until the local doctor arrives ? "

" I'm very much afraid not, sir," was the reply,
" but you'll see." He cleared a way for us and we
approached the open door.

At the first glance there appeared to be nothing to
account for the awe-stricken expression with which the
bystanders peered into the carriage and gazed at its
solitary occupant. For the motionless figure that sat
huddled in the corner seat, chin on breast, might have
been a sleeping man. But it was not. The waxen
pallor of the face and the strange, image-like immobility
forbade the hope of any awakening.

" It looks almost as if he had passed away in his
sleep," said the station-master when we had concluded
our brief examination and ascertained certainly that the
man was dead. " Do you think it was a heart attack,
sir ? "

Thorndyke shook his head and touched with his finger
a depressed spot on the dead man's waistcoat. When
he withdrew his finger it was smeared with blood.

" Good God ! " the official gasped, in a horrified

447

whisper. " The man has been murdered ! " He stared incredulously at the corpse for a few moments and then turned and sprang out of the compartment, shutting the door behind him, and we heard him giving orders for the coach to be separated and shunted into the siding.

" This is a gruesome affair, Jervis," my colleague said as he sat down on the seat opposite the dead man and cast a searching glance round the compartment. " I wonder who this poor fellow was and what was the object of the murder ? It looks almost too determined for a common robbery ; and, in fact, the body does not appear to have been robbed." Here he stooped suddenly to pick up one or two minute fragments of glass which seemed to have been trodden into the carpet, and which he examined closely in the palm of his hand. I leaned over and looked at the fragments, and we agreed that they were portions of the bulb of an electric torch or flash-lamp.

" The significance of these—if they have any," said Thorndyke, " we can consider later. But if they are recent, it would appear that the metal part of the bulb has been picked up and taken away. That might be an important fact. But, on the other hand, the fragments may have been here some time and have no connection with the tragedy ; though you notice that they were lying opposite the body and opposite the seat which the murderer must have occupied when the crime was committed."

As he was speaking, the uncoupled coach began slowly to move towards the siding, and we both stooped to make a further search for the remainder of the lamp-bulb. And then, almost at the same moment, we perceived two objects lying under the opposite seat—the seat occupied by the dead man. One was a small pocket-handkerchief, the other a sheet of notepaper.

" This," said I, as I picked up the former, " accounts for the strong smell of scent in the compartment."

" Possibly," Thorndyke agreed, " though you will

notice that the odour does not come principally from the handkerchief, but from the back cushion of the corner seat. But here is something more distinctive— a most incriminating piece of evidence, unless it can be answered by an undeniable alibi." He held out to me a sheet of letter paper, both pages of which were covered with writing in bright blue ink, done with a Hectograph or some similar duplicator. It was evidently a circular letter, for it bore the printed heading, "Women's Emancipation League, 16 Barnabas Square, S.W.," and the contents appeared to refer to a "militant demonstration" planned for the near future.

"It is dated the day before yesterday," commented Thorndyke, "so that it might have been lying here for twenty-four hours, though that is obviously improbable ; and as this is neither the first sheet nor the last, there are —or have been—at least two more sheets. The police will have something to start on, at any rate."

He laid the letter on the seat and explored both of the hat-racks, taking down the dead man's hat, gloves, and umbrella, and noting in the hat the initials "F. B." He had just replaced them when voices became audible outside, and the station-master climbed up on the foot-board and opened the door to admit two men, one of whom I assumed to be a doctor, the other being a police inspector.

"The station-master tells me that this is a case of homicide," said the former, addressing us jointly.

"That is what the appearances suggest," replied Thorndyke. "There is a bullet wound, inflicted apparently at quite short range—the waistcoat is perceptibly singed—and we have found no weapon in the compartment."

The doctor stepped past us and proceeded to make a rapid examination of the body.

"Yes," he said, "I agree with you. The position of the wound and the posture of the body both suggest that death was practically instantaneous. If it had been

15*

suicide, the pistol would have been in the hand or on the floor. There is no clue to the identity of the murderer, I suppose ? ”

“ We found these on the floor under the dead man's seat,” replied Thorndyke, indicating the letter and the handkerchief ; “ and there is some glass trodden into the carpet—apparently the remains of an electric flash-lamp.”

The inspector pounced on the handkerchief and the letter, and having scrutinised the former vainly in search of name or initials, turned to the letter.

“ Why, this is a suffragist's letter ! ” he exclaimed. “ But it can't have anything to do with this affair. They are mischievous beggars, but they don't do this sort of thing.” Nevertheless, he carefully bestowed both articles in a massive wallet, and approaching the corpse, remarked: “ We may as well see who he is while we are waiting for the stretcher.”

With a matter-of-fact air, which seemed somewhat to shock the station-master, he unbuttoned the coat of the passive figure in the corner and thrust his hand into the breast pocket, drawing out a letter-case which he opened, and from which he extracted a visiting card. As he glanced at it, his face suddenly took on an expression of amazement.

“ God ! ” he exclaimed in a startled tone. “ Who do you think he is, doctor ? He is Mr. Francis Burnham ! ”

The doctor looked at him with an interrogative frown. “ Burnham—Burnham,” he repeated. “ Let me see, now——”

“ Don't you know ? The anti-suffrage man. Surely——”

“ Yes, yes,” interrupted the doctor. “ Of course I remember him. The arch-enemy of the suffrage movement and—yes, of course.” The doctor's brisk speech changed abruptly into a hesitating mumble. Like the inspector, he had suddenly “ seen a great light ” ;

and again, like the officer, his perception had begotten a sudden reticence.

Thorndyke glanced at his watch. "Our train is a minute overdue," said he. "We ought to get back to the platform." Taking a card from his case, he handed it to the inspector, who looked at it and slightly raised his eyebrows.

"I don't think my evidence will be of much value," said he; "but, of course, I am at your service if you want it." With this and a bow to the doctor and the station-master, he climbed down to the ground; and when I had given the inspector my card, I followed, and we made our way to the platform.

The case was not long in developing. That very evening, as Thorndyke and I were smoking our after-dinner pipes by the fire, a hurried step was heard on the stair and was followed by a peremptory knock on our door. The visitor was a man of about thirty, with a clean-shaved face, an intense and rather neurotic expression, and a restless, excited manner. He introduced himself by the name of Cadmus Bawley, and thereby, in effect, indicated the purpose of his visit.

"You know me by name, I expect," he said, speaking rapidly and with a sharp, emphatic manner, "and probably you can guess what I have come about. You have seen the evening paper, of course?"

"I have not," replied Thorndyke.

"Well," said Mr. Bawley, "you know about the murder of the man Burnham, because I see that you were present at the discovery; and you know that part of a circular letter from our League was found in the compartment. Perhaps you will not be surprised to learn that Miss Isabel Dalby has been arrested and charged with the murder."

"Indeed!" said Thorndyke.

"Yes. It's an infamous affair! A national disgrace!" exclaimed Bawley, banging the table with his fist. " A manifest plot of the enemies of social reform to get rid of a high-minded, noble-hearted lady whose championship of this great Cause they are unable to combat by fair means in the open. And it is a wild absurdity, too. As to the fellow, Burnham, I can't pretend to feel any regret——"

" May I suggest "—Thorndyke interrupted somewhat stiffly—" that the expression of personal sentiments is neither helpful nor discreet ? My methods of defence —if that is what you have come about—are based on demonstration rather than rhetoric. Could you give us the plain facts ? "

Mr. Cadmus Bawley looked unmistakably sulky, but after a short pause, he began his recital in a somewhat lower key.

" The bald facts," he said, " are these : This afternoon, at half-past two, Miss Dalby took the train from King's Cross to Holmwood. This is the train that stops at Densford Junction and is the one in which Burnham travelled. She took a first-class ticket and occupied a compartment for ladies only, of which she was the only occupant. She got out at Holmwood and went straight to the house of our Vice-President, Miss Carleigh—who has been confined to her room for some days—and stayed there about an hour. She came back by the four-fifteen train, and I met her at the station—King's Cross—at a quarter to five. We had tea at a restaurant opposite the station, and over our tea we discussed the plans for the next demonstration, and arranged the rendezvous and the most convenient routes for retreat and dispersal when the police should arrive. This involved the making of sketch plans, and these Miss Dalby drew on a sheet of paper that she took from her pocket, and which happened to be part of the circular letter referring to the raid. After tea we walked together down Gray's Inn Road and parted at Theobald's Road, I going on to the head-quarters and she to her rooms in Queen Square. On her arrival home, she found two detectives waiting outside her house, and then—and then, in short, she was arrested, like a common criminal, and taken to the police station, where she was searched and the remainder of the circular letter found in her pocket. Then she was formally charged with the murder of the man Burnham, and she was graciously permitted to send a telegram to head-quarters. It arrived just after I got there, and, of course, I at once went to the police station. The police refused to accept bail, but they allowed me to see her to make arrangements for the defence."

" Does Miss Dalby offer any suggestion," asked Thorndyke, " as to how a sheet of her letter came to be in the compartment with the murdered man ? "

" Oh, yes ! " replied Mr. Bawley. " I had forgotten that. It wasn't her letter at all. She destroyed her copy of the letter as soon as she had read it."

" Then," inquired Thorndyke, " how came the letter to be in her pocket ? "

" Ah," replied Bawley, " that is the mystery. She thinks someone must have slipped it into her pocket to throw suspicion on her."

" Did she seem surprised to find it in her pocket when you were having tea together ? "

" No. She had forgotten having destroyed her copy. She only remembered it when I told her that the sheet had been found in Burnham's carriage."

" Can she produce the fragments of the destroyed letter ? "

" No, she can't. Unfortunately she burned it."

" Do these circular letters bear any distinguishing mark ? Are they addressed to members by name ? "

" Only on the envelopes. The letters are all alike. They are run off a duplicator. Of course, if you don't believe the story——"

" I am not judging the case," interrupted Thorndyke ; " I am simply collecting the facts. What do you want me to do ? "

" If you feel that you could undertake the defence,

I should like you to do so. We shall employ the solicitors
to the League, Bird & Marshall, but I know they will be
willing and glad to act with you."

" Very well," said Thorndyke. " I will investigate
the case and consult with your solicitors. By the way,
do the police know about the sheet of the letter on
which the plans were drawn ? "

" No. I thought it best to say nothing about that,
and I have told Miss Dalby not to mention it."

" That is just as well," said Thorndyke. " Have you
the sheet with the plan on it ? "

" I haven't it about me," was the reply. " It is in
my desk at my chambers."

" You had better let me have it to look at," said
Thorndyke.

" You can have it if you want it, of course," said
Bawley, " but it won't help you. The letters are all
alike, as I have told you."

" I should like to see it, nevertheless," said
Thorndyke ; " and perhaps you could give me some
account of Mr. Burnham. What do you know about
him ? "

Mr. Bawley shut his lips tightly, and his face took on
an expression of vindictiveness verging on malignity.

" All I know about Burnham," he said, " is that he
was a fool and a ruffian. He was not only an enemy of
the great reform that our League stands for ; he was a
treacherous enemy—violent, crafty, and indefatigably
active. I can only regard his death as a blessing to
mankind."

" May I ask," said Thorndyke, " if any members of
your League have ever publicly threatened to take
personal measures against him ? "

" Yes," snapped Bawley. " Several of us—including
myself—have threatened to give him the hiding that he
deserved. But a hiding is a different thing from murder,
you know."

" Yes," Thorndyke agreed somewhat dryly ; then he

asked : " Do you know anything about Mr. Burnham's occupation and habits ? "

" He was a sort of manager of the London and Suburban Bank. His job was to supervise the suburban branches, and his habit was to visit them in rotation. He was probably going to the branch at Holmwood when he was killed. That is all I can tell you about him."

" Thank you," said Thorndyke ; and as our visitor rose to depart he continued : " Then I will look into the case and arrange with your solicitors to have Miss Dalby properly represented at the inquest ; and I shall be glad to have that sheet of the letter as soon as you can send or leave it."

" Very well," said Bawley, " though, as I have told you, it won't be of any use to you. It is only a duplicated circular."

" Possibly," Thorndyke assented. " But the other sheets will be produced in Court, so I may as well have an opportunity of examining it beforehand."

For some minutes after our client had gone Thorndyke remained silent and reflective, copying his rough notes into his pocket-book and apparently amplifying and arranging them. Presently he looked up at me with an unspoken question in his eyes.

" It is a queer case," said I. " The circumstantial evidence seems to be strongly against Miss Dalby, but it is manifestly improbable that she murdered the man."

" It seems so," he agreed. " But the case will be decided on the evidence ; and the evidence will be considered by a judge, not by a Home Secretary. You notice the importance of Burnham's destination ? "

" Yes. He was evidently dead when the train arrived at Holmwood. But it isn't clear how long he had been dead."

" The evidence," said Thorndyke, " points strongly to the tunnel between Cawden and Holmwood as the place where the murder was committed. You will remember that the up-express passed our train in the tunnel. If the adjoining compartments were empty, the sound of a pistol shot would be completely drowned by the noise of the express thundering past. Then you will remember the fragments of the electric bulb that we picked up, and that there was no light on in the carriage. That is rather significant. It not only suggests that the crime was committed in the dark, but there is a distinct suggestion of preparation—arrangement and premeditation. It suggests that the murderer knew what the circumstances would be and provided for them."

" Yes ; and that is rather a point against our client. But I don't quite see what you expect to get out of that sheet of the letter. It is the presence of the letter, rather than its matter, that constitutes the evidence against Miss Dalby."

" I don't expect to learn anything from it," replied Thorndyke ; " but the letter will be the prosecution's trump card, and it is always well to know in advance exactly what cards your opponent holds. It is a mere matter of routine to examine everything, relevant or irrelevant."

The inquest was to be held at Densford on the third day after the discovery of the body. But in the interval certain new facts had come to light. One was that the deceased was conveying to the Holmwood branch of the bank a sum of three thousand pounds, of which one thousand was in gold and the remainder in Bank of England notes, the whole being contained in a leather handbag. This bag had been found, empty, in a ditch by the side of the road which led from the station to the house of Miss Carleigh, the Vice-President of the Women's Emancipation League. It was further stated that the ticket-collector at Holmwood had noticed that Miss Dalby—whom he knew by sight—was carrying a bag of the kind described when she passed the barrier, and that when she returned, about an hour later, she had no bag with her. On the other hand, Miss Carleigh had stated that the bag which Miss Dalby brought to her house was her (Miss Carleigh's) property, and she had produced it for the inspection of the police. So that already there was some conflict of evidence, with a balance distinctly against Miss Dalby.

" There is no denying," said Thorndyke, as we discussed the case at the breakfast table on the morning of the inquest, " that the circumstantial evidence is formidably complete and consistent, while the rebutting evidence is of the feeblest. Miss Dalby's statement that the letter had been put into her pocket by some unknown person will hardly be taken seriously, and even Miss Carleigh's statement with reference to the bag will not carry much weight unless she can furnish corroboration."

" Nevertheless," said I, " the general probabilities are entirely in favour of the accused. It is grossly improbable that a lady like Miss Dalby would commit a robbery with murder of this cold-blooded, deliberate type."

" That may be," Thorndyke retorted, " but a jury has to find in accordance with the evidence."

" By the way," said I, " did Bawley ever send you that sheet of the letter that you asked for ? "

" No, confound him ! But I have sent Polton round to get it from him, so that I can look it over carefully in the train. Which reminds me that I can't get down in time for the opening of the inquest. You had better travel with the solicitors and see the shorthand writers started. I shall have to come down by a later train."

Half an hour later, just as I was about to start, a familiar step was heard on the stair, and then our laboratory assistant, Polton, let himself in with his key.

" Just caught him, sir, as he was starting for the station," he said, with a satisfied, crinkly smile, laying an envelope on the table, and added, " Lord ! how he did swear ! "

Thorndyke chuckled, and having thanked his assistant, opened the envelope and handed it to me. It contained a single sheet of letter-paper, exactly similar to the one that we had found in the railway carriage, excepting that the writing filled one side and a quarter only, and, since it concluded with the signature " Letitia Humboe, President," it was evidently the last sheet. There was no water-mark nor anything, so far as I could see, to distinguish it from the dozens of other impressions that had been run off on the duplicator with it, excepting the roughly-pencilled plan on the blank side of the sheet.

" Well," I said as I put on my hat and walked towards the door, " I suspect that Bawley was right. You won't get much help from this to support Miss Dalby's rather improbable statement." And Thorndyke agreed that appearances were not very promising.

The scene in the coffee-room of " The Plough " Inn at Densford was one with which I was familiar enough. The quiet, business-like coroner, the half-embarrassed jurors, the local police and witnesses and the spectators, penned up at one end of the room, were all well-known characters. The unusual feature was the handsome, distinguished-looking young lady who sat on a plain Windsor chair between two inscrutable policemen, watched intently by Mr. Cadmus Bawley. Miss Dalby was pale and obviously agitated, but quiet, resolute, and somewhat defiant in manner. She greeted me with a pleasant smile when I introduced myself, and hoped that I and my colleague would have no difficulty in disposing of " this grotesque and horrible accusation."

I need not describe the proceedings in detail. Evidence of the identity of the deceased having been taken, Dr. Pooke deposed that death was due to a wound of the heart produced by a spherical bullet, apparently fired from a small, smooth-bore pistol at very short range. The wound was in his opinion not self-inflicted. The coroner then produced the sheet of the circular letter found in the carriage, and I was called to testify to the finding of it. The next witness was Superintendent Miller of the Criminal Investigation Department, who produced the two sheets of the letter which were taken from Miss Dalby's pocket when she was arrested. These he handed to the coroner for comparison with the one found in the carriage with the body of deceased.

"There appear," said the coroner, after placing the three sheets together, " to be one or more sheets missing. The two you have handed me are sheets one and three, and the one found in the railway carriage is sheet two."

" Yes," the witness agreed, " sheet four is missing, but I have a photograph of it. Here is a set of the complete letter," and he laid four unmounted prints on the table.

The coroner examined them with a puzzled frown. "May I ask," he said, "how you obtained these photographs ? "

" They are not photographs of the copy that you have," the witness explained, " but of another copy of the same letter which we intercepted in the post. That letter was addressed to a stationer's shop to be called for. We have considered it necessary to keep ourselves informed of the contents of these circulars, so that we can take the necessary precautions ; and as the envelopes are marked with the badge and are invariably addressed in blue ink, it is not difficult to identify them."

" I see," said the coroner, glaring stonily at Mr. Bawley, who had accompanied the superintendent's statement with audible and unfavourable comments. " Is that the whole of your evidence ? Thank you. Then, if there is no cross-examination, I will call the next witness. Mr. Bernard Parsons."

Mr. Parsons was the general manager of the London and Suburban Bank, and he deposed that deceased was, on the day when he met his death, travelling to Holmwood to visit and inspect the new local branch of the bank, and that he was taking thither the sum of three thousand pounds, of which one thousand was in gold and the remainder in Bank of England notes—mostly

five-pound notes. He carried the notes and specie in
a strong leather handbag.

" Can you say if either of these is the bag that he
carried ? " the coroner asked, indicating two largish,
black leather bags that his officer had placed on the table.

Mr. Parsons promptly pointed to the larger of the two,
which was smeared externally with mud. The coroner
noted the answer and then asked :

" Did anyone besides yourself know that deceased was
making this visit ? "

" Many persons must have known," was the reply.
" Deceased visited the various branches in a fixed order.
He came to Holmwood on the second Tuesday in the
month."

" And would it be known that he had this great sum
of money with him ? "

" The actual amount would not be generally known,
but he usually took with him supplies of specie and notes
—sometimes very large sums—and this would be known
to many of the bank staff, and probably to a good many
persons outside. The Holmwood Branch consumes a
good deal of specie, as most of the customers pay in
cheques and draw out cash for local use."

This was the substance of Mr. Parsons' evidence,
and when he sat down the ticket-collector was called.
That official identified Miss Dalby as one of the passengers
by the train in which the body of deceased was found.
She was carrying a bag when she passed the barrier.
He could not identify either of the bags, but both
were similar to the one that she was carrying. She
returned about an hour later and caught an up-train,
and he noticed that she was then not carrying a bag.
He could not say whether any of the other passengers
was carrying a bag. There were very few first-class
passengers by that train, but a large number of third-
class—mostly fruit-pickers—and they made a dense
crowd at the barrier so that he did not notice individual
passengers particularly. He noticed Miss Dalby because

he knew her by sight, as she often came to Holmwood with other suffragist ladies. He did not see which carriage Miss Dalby came from, and he did not see any first-class compartment with an open door.

The coroner noted down this evidence with thoughtful deliberation, and I was considering whether there were any questions that it would be advisable to ask the witness when I felt a light touch on my shoulder, and looking up perceived a constable holding out a telegram. Observing that it was addressed to " Dr. Jervis, Plough Inn, Densford," I nodded to the constable, and taking the envelope from him, opened it and unfolded the paper. The telegram was from Thorndyke, in the simple code that he had devised for our private use. I was able to decode it without referring to the key—which each of us always carried in his pocket—and it then read :

" I am starting for Folkestone *in re* Burnham deceased. Follow immediately and bring Miller if you can for possible arrest. Meet me on pier near Ostend boat. Thorndyke."

Accustomed as I was to my colleague's inveterate habit of acting in the least expected manner, I must confess that I gazed at the decoded message in absolute stupefaction. I had been totally unaware of the faintest clue beyond the obvious evidence to which I had been listening, and behold ! here was Thorndyke with an entirely fresh case, apparently cut-and-dried, and the unsuspected criminal in the hollow of his hand. It was astounding.

Unconsciously I raised my eyes—and met those of Superintendent Miller, fixed on me with devouring curiosity. I held up the telegram and beckoned, and immediately he tip-toed across and took a seat by my side. I laid the decoded telegram before him, and when he had glanced through it, I asked in a whisper : " Well, what do you say ? "

By way of reply, he whisked out a time-table, conned it eagerly for a few minutes, and then held it towards me with his thumb-nail on the words "Densford Junction."

"There's a fast train up in seven minutes," he whispered hoarsely. "Get the coroner to excuse us and let your solicitors carry on for you."

A brief, and rather vague, explanation secured the assent of the coroner—since we had both given our evidence—and the less willing agreement of my clients. In another minute the superintendent and I were heading for the station, which we reached just as the train swept up alongside the platform.

"This is a queer start," said Miller, as the train moved out of the station; "but, Lord! there is never any calculating Dr. Thorndyke's moves. Did you know that he had anything up his sleeve?"

"No; but then one never does know. He is as close as an oyster. He never shows his hand until he can play a trump card. But it is possible that he has struck a fresh clue since I left."

"Well," rejoined Miller, "we shall know when we get to the other end And I don't mind telling you that it will be a great relief to me if we can drop this charge against Miss Dalby."

From time to time during the journey to London, and from thence to Folkestone, the superintendent reverted to Thorndyke's mysterious proceedings. But it was useless to speculate. We had not a single fact to guide us; and when, at last, the train ran into Folkestone Central Station we were as much in the dark as when we started.

Assuming that Thorndyke would have made any necessary arrangements for assistance from the local police, we chartered a cab and proceeded direct to the end of Rendez-vous Street—a curiously appropriate destination, by the way. Here we alighted in order that we might make our appearance at the meeting-place as inconspicuously as possible, and, walking towards the harbour, perceived Thorndyke waiting on the quay,

THE STALKING HORSE 463

ostensibly watching the loading of a barge, and putting in their case a pair of prismatic binoculars with which he had apparently observed our arrival.

"I am glad you have come, Miller," he said, shaking the superintendent's hand. "I can't make any promises, but I have no doubt that it is a case for you even if it doesn't turn out all that I hope and expect. The *Cornflower* is our ship, and we had better go on board separately in case our friends are keeping a look-out. I have arranged matters with the captain, and the local superintendent has got some plain-clothes men on the pier."

With this we separated. Thorndyke went on in advance, and Miller and I followed at a discreet interval.

As I descended the gangway a minute or so after Miller, a steward approached me, and having asked my name requested me to follow him, when he conducted me to the purser's office, in which I found Thorndyke and Miller in conversation with the purser.

"The gentlemen you are inquiring for," said the latter, "are in the smoking-room playing cards with another passenger. I have put a tarpaulin over one of the ports, in case you want to have a look at them without being seen."

"Perhaps you had better make a preliminary inspection, Miller," said Thorndyke. "You may know some of them."

To this suggestion the superintendent agreed, and forthwith went off with the purser, leaving me and Thorndyke alone. I at once took the opportunity to demand an explanation.

"I take it that you struck some new evidence after I left you?"

"Yes," Thorndyke replied. "And none too soon, as you see. I don't quite know what it will amount to, but I think we have secured the defence, at any rate; and that is really all that we are concerned with. The positive aspects of the case are the business of the police.

But here comes Miller, looking very pleased with himself, and with the purser."

The superintendent, however, was not only pleased ; he was also not a little puzzled.

" Well ! " he exclaimed, " this is a quaint affair. We have got two of the leading lights of the suffrage movement in there. One is Jameson, the secretary of the Women's Emancipation League, the other is Pinder, their chief bobbery-monger. Then there are two men named Dorman and Spiller, both of them swell crooks, I am certain, though we have never been able to fix anything on them. The fifth man I don't know."

" Neither do I," said Thorndyke. " My repertoire includes only four. And now we will proceed to sort them out. Could we have a few words with Mr. Thorpe —in here, if you don't mind."

" Certainly," replied the purser. "I'll go and fetch him." He bustled away in the direction of the smoking-room, whence he presently reappeared, accompanied by a tall, lean man who wore large bi-focal spectacles of the old-fashioned, split-lens type, and was smoking a cigar. As the new-comer approached down the alley-way, it was evident that he was nervous and uneasy, though he maintained a certain jaunty swagger that accorded ill with a pronounced, habitual stoop. As he entered the cabin, however, and became aware of the portentous group of strangers, the swagger broke down completely ; suddenly his face became ashen and haggard, and he peered through his great spectacles from one to the others with an expression of undisguisable terror.

" Mr. Thorpe ? " queried Thorndyke ; and the superintendent murmured : " Alias Pinder."

" Yes," was the reply, in a husky undertone. " What can I do for you ? "

Thorndyke turned to the superintendent.

" I charge this man," said he, " with having murdered Francis Burnham in the train between London and Holmwood."

The superintendent was visibly astonished, but not more so than the accused, on whom Thorndyke's statement produced the most singular effect. In a moment, his terror seemed to drop from him ; the colour returned to his face, the haggard expression of which gave place to one of obvious relief.

Miller stood up, and addressing the accused, began : " It is my duty to caution you—— " but the other interrupted :

" Caution your grandmother ! You are talking a parcel of dam' nonsense. I was in Birmingham when the murder was committed. I can prove it, easily."

The superintendent was somewhat taken aback, for the accused spoke with a confidence that carried conviction.

" In that case," said Thorndyke, " you can probably explain how a letter belonging to you came to be found in the carriage with the murdered man."

" Belonging to me ! " exclaimed Thorpe. " What the deuce do you mean ? That letter belonged to Miss Dalby. The rest of it was found in her pocket."

" Precisely," said Thorndyke. " One sheet had been placed in the railway carriage and the remainder in Miss Dalby's pocket to fix suspicion on her. But it was your letter, and the inference is that you disposed of it in that manner for the purpose that I have stated."

" But," persisted Thorpe, with visibly-growing uneasiness, " this was a duplicated circular. You couldn't tell one copy from another."

" Mr. Pinder," said Thorndyke, in an impressively quiet tone, " if I tell you that I ascertained from that letter that you had taken a passage on this ship in the name of Thorpe, you will probably understand what I mean."

Apparently he did understand, for, once more, the colour faded from his face and he sat down heavily on a locker, fixing on Thorndyke a look of undisguised dismay. Thus he sat for some moments, motionless and silent, apparently thinking hard.

Suddenly he started up. " My God ! " he exclaimed,
" I see now what has happened. The infernal scoundrel !
First he put it on to Miss Dalby, and now he has put it
on to me. Now I understand why he looked so startled
when I ran against him."

" What do you mean ? " asked Thorndyke.

" I'll tell you," replied Pinder. " As I move about
a good deal—and for other reasons—I used to have my
suffrage letters sent to a stationer's shop in Barlow
Street—— "

" I know," interrupted the superintendent ; " Bedall's.
I used to look them over and take photographs of them."
He grinned craftily as he made this statement, and,
rather to my surprise, the accused grinned too. A little
later I understood that grin.

" Well," continued Pinder, " I used to collect these
letters pretty regularly. But this last letter was delivered
while I was away at Birmingham. Before I came back
I met a man who gave me certain—er—instructions—
you know what they were," he added, addressing Thorndyke—" so I did not need the letter. But, of course, I
couldn't leave it there uncollected, so when I got back
to London, I called for it. That was two days ago. To
my astonishment Miss Bedall declared that I had collected it three days previously. I assured her that I
was not in London on that day, but she was positive that
I had called. ' I remember clearly,' she said, ' giving
you the letter myself.' Well, there was no arguing.
Evidently she had given the letter to the wrong person—
she is very near-sighted, I should say, judging by the
way she holds things against her nose—but how it
happened I couldn't understand. But I think I understand now. There is one person only in the world who
knew that I had my letters addressed there : a sort
of pal of mine named Payne. He happened to be with
me one evening when I called to collect my letters.
Now, Payne chanced to be a good deal like me—at least
he is tall and thin and stoops a bit ; but he does not wear

spectacles. He tried on my spectacles once for a joke, and then he really looked extremely like me. He looked in a mirror and remarked on the resemblance himself. Now, Payne did not belong to the Women's League, and I suggest that he took advantage of this resemblance to get possession of this letter. He got a pair of spectacles like mine and personated me at the shop."

" Why should he want to get possession of that letter ? " Miller demanded.

" To plant it as he has planted it," replied Pinder, " and set the police on a false trail."

" This sounds pretty thin," said Miller. " You are accusing this man of having murdered Mr. Burnham. What grounds have you for this accusation ? "

" My grounds," replied Pinder, " are, first, that he stole this letter which has been found, obviously planted ; and, second, that he had a grudge against Burnham and knew all about his movements."

" Indeed ! " said Miller, with suddenly increased interest. " Then who and what is this man Payne ? "

" Why," replied Pinder, " until a month ago, he was assistant cashier at the Streatham branch of the bank. Then Burnham came down and hoofed him out without an hour's notice. I don't know what for, but I can guess."

" Do you happen to know where Payne is at this moment ? "

" Yes, I do. He is on this ship, in the smoking-room —only he is Mr. Shenstone now. And mighty sick he was when he found me on board."

The superintendent looked at Thorndyke.

" What do you think about it, doctor ? " he asked.

" I think," said Thorndyke, " that we had better have Mr. Shenstone in here and ask him a few questions. Would you see if you can get him to come here ? " he added, addressing the purser, who had been listening with ecstatic enjoyment.

" I'll get him to come along all right," replied the

purser, evidently scenting a new act in this enthralling drama ; and away he bustled, all agog. In less than a minute we saw him returning down the alley-way, with a tall, thin man, who, at a distance, was certainly a good deal like Pinder, though the resemblance diminished as he approached. He, too, was obviously agitated, and seemed to be plying the purser with questions. But when he came opposite the door of the cabin he stopped dead and seemed disposed to shrink back.

" Is that the man ? " Thorndyke demanded sharply and rather loudly, springing to his feet as he spoke.

The effect of the question was electrical. As Thorndyke rose, the new-comer turned, and, violently thrusting the purser aside, raced madly down the alley-way and out on to the deck.

" Stop that man ! " roared Miller, darting out in pursuit ; and at the shout a couple of loitering deck-hands headed the fugitive off from the gangway. Following, I saw the terrified man swerving this way and that across the littered deck to avoid the seamen, who joined in the pursuit ; I saw him make a sudden frantic burst for a baggage-slide springing from a bollard up to the bulwark-rail. Then his foot must have tripped on a lashing, for he staggered for a moment, flung out his arms with a wild shriek, and plunged headlong into the space between the ship's side and the quay wall.

In an instant the whole ship was in an uproar. An officer and two hands sprang to the rail with ropes and a boathook, while others manned the cargo derrick and lowered a rope with a running bowline between the ship and the quay.

" He's gone under," a hoarse voice proclaimed from below ; " but I can see him jammed against the side."

There were a couple of minutes of sickening suspense. Then the voice from below was heard again.

" Heave up ! "

The derrick-engine rattled, the taut rope came up slowly, and at length out of that horrid gulf arose a limp and dripping shape that, as it cleared the bulwark, was swung inboard and let down gently on the deck. Thorndyke and I stooped over him. But it was a dead man's face that we looked into ; and a tinge of blood on the lips told the rest of the tale.

"Cover him up," said the superintendent. "He's out of our jurisdiction now. But what's going on there ?"

Following his look, I perceived a small scattered crowd of men all running furiously along the quay towards the town. Some of them I judged to be the late inmates of the smoking-room and some plain-clothes men. The only figure that I recognised was that of Mr. Pinder, and he was already growing small in the distance.

"The local police will have to deal with them," said Miller. Then turning to the purser, he asked : "What baggage had this man ?"

"Only two cabin trunks," was the reply. "They are both in his state-room."

To the state-room we followed the purser, when Miller had possessed himself of the dead man's keys, and the two trunks were hoisted on to the bunk and opened. Each trunk contained a large cash-box, and each cash-box contained five hundred pounds in gold and a big bundle of notes. The latter Miller examined closely, checking their numbers by a column of entries in his pocket-book.

"Yes," he reported at length ; "it's a true bill. These are the notes that were stolen from Mr. Burnham. And now I will have a look at the baggage of those other four sportsmen."

This being no affair of ours, Thorndyke and I went ashore and slowly made our way towards the town. But presently the superintendent overtook us in high glee, with the news that he had discovered what appeared to be the accumulated "swag" of a gang of swell burglars for whom he had been for some months vainly on the look-out.

" How was it done ? " repeated Thorndyke in reply
to Miller's question, as we sat at a retired table in the
" Lord Warden " Hotel. " Well, it was really very
simple. I am afraid I shall disappoint you if you
expect anything ingenious and recondite. Of course,
it was obvious that Miss Dalby had not committed this
atrocious murder and robbery ; and it was profoundly
improbable that this extremely incriminating letter had
been dropped accidentally. That being so, it was
almost certain that the letter had been ' planted,' as
Pinder expressed it. But that was a mere opinion that
helped us not at all. The actual solution turned upon
a simple chemical fact with which I happened to be
acquainted ; which is this : that all the basic coal-tar
dyes, and especially methylene blue, dye oxycellulose
without requiring a mordant, but do not react in this
way on cellulose. Now, good paper is practically pure
cellulose ; and if you dip a sheet of such paper into
certain oxidising liquids, such as a solution of potassium
chlorate with a slight excess of hydrochloric acid, the
paper is converted into oxycellulose. But if instead of
immersing the paper, you write on it with a quill or
glass pen dipped in the solution, only the part which
has been touched by the pen is changed into oxycellulose. No change is visible to the eye : but if a sheet of
paper written on with this colourless fluid is dipped in
a solution of, say, methylene blue, the invisible writing
immediately becomes visible. The oxycellulose takes
up the blue dye.

" Now, when I picked up that sheet of the letter
in the railway carriage and noted that the ink used
appeared to be methylene blue, this fact was recalled
to my mind. Then, on looking at it closely, I seemed
to detect a certain slight spottiness in the writing.
There were points on some of the letters that were a
little deeper in colour than the rest ; and it occurred to
me that it was possible that these circulars might be used
to transmit secret messages of a less innocent kind than

those that met the unaided eye, just as these political societies might form an excellent cover for the operations of criminal associations. But if the circulars had been so used, it is evident that the secret writing would not be on all the circulars. The prepared sheets would be used only for the circulars that were to be sent to particular persons, and in those cases the secret writing would probably be in the nature of a personal communication, either to a particular individual or to a small group. The possible presence of a secret message thus became of vital evidential importance ; for if it could be shown that this letter was addressed to some person other than Miss Dalby, that would dispose of the only evidence connecting her with the crime.

" It happened, most fortunately, that I was able to get possession of the final sheet of this letter——"

" Of course it did," growled Miller, with a sour smile.

" It reached me," continued Thorndyke, " only after Dr. Jervis had started for Densford. The greater part of one side was blank, excepting for a rough plan drawn in pencil, and this blank side I laid down on a sheet of glass and wetted the written side with a small wad of cotton-wool dipped in distilled water. Of course, the blue writing began to run and dissolve out ; and then, very faintly, some other writing began to show through in reverse. I turned the paper over, and now the new writing, though faint, was quite legible, and became more so when I wiped the blue-stained cotton-wool over it a few times. A solution of methylene blue would have made it still plainer, but I used water only, as I judged that the blue writing was intended to furnish the dye for development. Here is the final result."

He drew from his pocket a letter-case, from which he extracted a folded paper which he opened and laid on the table. It was stained a faint blue, through which the original writing could be seen, dim and blurred, while the secret message, though very pale, was quite sharp and clear. And this was the message :

" . . . so although we are not actually blown on, the position is getting risky and it's time for us to hop. I have booked passages for the four of us to Ostend by the *Cornflower*, which sails on Friday evening next (20th). The names of the four illustrious passengers are, Walsh (that's me), Grubb (Dorman), Jenkins (Spiller) and Thorpe (that's you). Get those names well into your canister—better make a note of them—and turn up in good time on Friday."

" Well," said Miller, as he handed back the letter, " we can't know everything—unless we are Dr. Thorndyke. But there's one thing I do know."
" What is that ? " I asked.
" I know why that fellow Pinder grinned when I told him that I had photographed his confounded letters."

16   THE NATURALIST
                                                   AT LAW

A HUSH had fallen on the court as the coroner concluded his brief introductory statement and the first witness took up his position by the long table. The usual preliminary questions elicited that Simon Moffet, the witness aforesaid, was fifty-eight years of age, that he followed the calling of a shepherd and that he was engaged in supervising the flocks that fed upon the low-lying meadows adjoining the little town of Bantree in Buckinghamshire.
" Tell us how you came to discover the body," said the coroner.
" 'Twas on Wednesday morning, about half-past

five," Moffet began. " I was getting the sheep through the gate into the big meadow by Reed's farm, when I happened to look down the dyke, and then I noticed a boot sticking up out of the water. Seemed to me as if there was a foot in it by the way it stuck up, so as soon as all the sheep was in, I shut the gate and walked down the dyke to have a look at un. When I got close I see the toe of another boot just alongside. Looks a bit queer, I thinks, but I couldn't see anything more, 'cause the duck-weed is that thick as it looks as if you could walk on it. Howsever, 1 clears away the weed with my stick, and then I see 'twas a dead man. Give me a rare turn, it did. He was a-layin' at the bottom of the ditch with his head near the middle and his feet up close to the bank. Just then young Harry Walker comes along the cart-track on his way to work, so I shows him the body and sends him back to the town for to give notice at the police station."

" And is that all you know about the affair ? "

" Ay. Later on I see the sergeant come along with a man wheelin' the stretcher, and I showed him where the body was and helped to pull it out and load it on the stretcher. And that's all I know about it."

On this the witness was dismissed and his place taken by a shrewd-looking, business-like police sergeant, who deposed as follows :

" Last Wednesday, the 8th of May, at 6.15 a.m., I received information from Henry Walker that a dead body was lying in the ditch by the cart-track leading from Ponder's Road to Reed's farm. I proceeded there forthwith, accompanied by Police-Constable Ketchum, and taking with us a wheeled stretcher. On the track I was met by the last witness, who conducted me to the place where the body was lying and where I found it in the position that he has described ; but we had to clear away the duck-weed before we could see it distinctly. I examined the bank carefully, but could see no trace of footprints, as the grass grows thickly right

16

down to the water's edge. There were no signs of a struggle or any disturbance on the bank. With the aid of Moffet and Ketchum, I drew the body out and placed it on the stretcher. I could not see any injuries or marks of violence on the body or anything unusual about it. I conveyed it to the mortuary, and with Constable Ketchum's assistance removed the clothing and emptied the pockets, putting the contents of each pocket in a separate envelope and writing the description on each. In a letter-case from the coat pocket were some visiting cards bearing the name and address of Mr. Cyrus Pedley, of 21 Hawtrey Mansions, Kensington, and a letter signed Wilfred Pedley, apparently from deceased's brother. Acting on instructions, I communicated with him and served a summons to attend this inquest."

" With regard to the ditch in which you found the body," said the coroner, " can you tell us how deep it is ? "

" Yes ; I measured it with Moffet's crook and a tape measure. In the deepest part, where the body was lying, it is four feet two inches deep. From there it slopes up pretty sharply to the bank."

" So far as you can judge, if a grown man fell into the ditch by accident, would he have any difficulty in getting out ? "

" None at all, I should say, if he were sober and in ordinary health. A man of medium height, standing in the middle at the deepest part, would have his head and shoulders out of water ; and the sides are not too steep to climb up easily, especially with the grass and rushes on the bank to lay hold of."

" You say there were no signs of disturbance on the bank. Were there any in the ditch itself ? "

" None that I could see. But, of course, signs of disturbance soon disappear in water. The duck-weed drifts about as the wind drives it, and there are creatures moving about on the bottom. I noticed that deceased had some weed grasped in one hand."

This concluded the sergeant's evidence, and as he retired, the name of Dr. Albert Parton was called. The new witness was a young man of grave and professional aspect, who gave his evidence with an extreme regard for clearness and accuracy.

" I have made an examination of the body of the deceased," he began, after the usual preliminaries. " It is that of a healthy man of about forty-five. I first saw it about two hours after it was found. It had then been dead from twelve to fifteen hours. Later I made a complete examination. I found no injuries, marks of violence or any definite bruises, and no signs of disease."

" Did you ascertain the cause of death ? " the coroner asked.

" Yes. The cause of death was drowning."

" You are quite sure of that ? "

" Quite sure. The lungs contained a quantity of water and duck-weed, and there was more than a quart of water mixed with duck-weed and water-weed in the stomach. That is a clear proof of death by drowning. The water in the lungs was the immediate cause of death, by making breathing impossible, and as the water and weed in the stomach must have been swallowed, they furnish conclusive evidence that deceased was alive when he fell into the water."

" The water and weed could not have got into the stomach after death ? "

" No, that is quite impossible. They must have been swallowed when the head of the deceased was just below the surface ; and the water must have been drawn into the lungs by spasmodic efforts to breathe when the mouth was under water."

" Did you find any signs indicating that deceased might have been intoxicated ? "

" No. I examined the water from the stomach very carefully with that question in view, but there was no trace of alcohol—or, indeed, of anything else. It was simple ditch-water. As the point is important I have preserved it, and——" here the witness produced a paper parcel which he unfastened, revealing a large glass jar containing about a quart of water plentifully sprinkled with duck-weed. This he presented to the coroner, who waved it away hastily and indicated the jury; to whom it was then offered and summarily rejected with emphatic head-shakes. Finally it came to rest on the table by the place where I was sitting with my colleague, Dr. Thorndyke, and our client, Mr. Wilfred Pedley. I glanced at it with faint interest, noting how the duck-weed plants had risen to the surface and floated, each with its tassel of roots hanging down into the water, and how a couple of tiny, flat shells, like miniature ammonites, had sunk and lay on the bottom of the jar. Thorndyke also glanced at it; indeed, he did more than glance, for he drew the jar towards him and examined its contents in the systematic way in which it was his habit to examine everything. Meanwhile the coroner asked:

" Did you find anything abnormal or unusual, or anything that could throw light on how deceased came to be in the water? "

" Nothing whatever," was the reply. " I found simply that deceased met his death by drowning."

Here, as the witness seemed to have finished his evidence, Thorndyke interposed.

" The witness states, sir, there were no definite bruises. Does he mean that there were any marks that might have been bruises? "

The coroner glanced at Dr. Parton, who replied:

" There was a faint mark on the outside of the right arm, just above the elbow, which had somewhat the appearance of a bruise, as if the deceased had been struck with a stick. But it was very indistinct. I shouldn't like to swear that it was a bruise at all."

This concluded the doctor's evidence, and when he had retired, the name of our client, Wilfred Pedley, was called. He rose, and having taken the oath and given his name and address, deposed :

" I have viewed the body of deceased. It is that of my brother, Cyrus Pedley, who is forty-three years of age. The last time I saw deceased alive was on Tuesday morning, the day before the body was found."

" Did you notice anything unusual in his manner or state of mind ? "

The witness hesitated but at length replied :

" Yes. He seemed anxious and depressed. He had been in low spirits for some time past, but on this occasion he seemed more so than usual."

" Had you any reason to suspect that he might contemplate taking his life ? "

" No," the witness replied, emphatically, " and I do not believe that he would, under any circumstances, have contemplated suicide."

" Have you any special reason for that belief ? "

" Yes. Deceased was a highly conscientious man and he was in my debt. He had occasion to borrow two thousand pounds from me, and the debt was secured by an insurance on his life. If he had committed suicide that insurance would be invalidated and the debt would remain unpaid. From my knowledge of him, I feel certain that he would not have done such a thing."

The coroner nodded gravely, and then asked :

" What was deceased's occupation ? "

" He was employed in some way by the Foreign Office, I don't know in what capacity. I know very little about his affairs."

" Do you know if he had any money worries or any troubles or embarrassments of any kind ? "

" I have never heard of any ; but deceased was a very reticent man. He lived alone in his flat, taking his meals at his club, and no one knew—at least, I did not—how he spent his time or what was the state of his finances. He was not married, and I am his only near relative."

" And as to deceased's habits. Was he ever addicted to taking more stimulants than was good for him ? "

" Never," the witness replied emphatically. " He was a most temperate and abstemious man."

" Was he subject to fits of any kind, or fainting attacks ? "

" I have never heard that he was."

" Can you account for his being in this solitary place at this time—apparently about eight o'clock at night ? "

" I cannot. It is a complete mystery to me. I know of no one with whom either of us was acquainted in this district. I had never heard of the place until I got the summons to the inquest."

This was the sum of our client's evidence, and, so far, things did not look very favourable from our point of view—we were retained on the insurance question, to rebut, if possible, the suggestion of suicide. However, the coroner was a discreet man, and having regard to the obscurity of the case—and perhaps to the interests involved—summed up in favour of an open verdict ; and the jury, taking a similar view, found that deceased met his death by drowning, but under what circumstances there was no evidence to show.

" Well," I said, as the court rose, " that leaves it to the insurance people to make out a case of suicide if they can. I think you are fairly safe, Mr. Pedley. There is no positive evidence."

" No," our client replied. " But it isn't only the money I am thinking of. It would be some consolation to me for the loss of my poor brother if I had some idea how he met with his death, and could feel sure that it was an unavoidable misadventure. And for my own satisfaction—leaving the insurance out of the question—I should like to have definite proof that it was not suicide."

He looked half-questioningly at Thorndyke, who nodded gravely.

" Yes," the latter agreed, " the suggestion of suicide

ought to be disposed of if possible, both for legal and sentimental reasons. How far away is the mortuary ? "

" A couple of minutes' walk," replied Mr. Pedley. " Did you wish to inspect the body ? "

" If it is permissible," replied Thorndyke ; " and then I propose to have a look at the place where the body was found."

" In that case," our client said, " I will go down to the Station Hotel and wait for you. We may as well travel up to town together, and you can then tell me if you have seen any further light on the mystery."

As soon as he was gone, Dr. Parton advanced, tying the string of the parcel which once more enclosed the jar of ditch-water.

" I heard you say, sir, that you would like to inspect the body," said he. " If you like, I will show you the way to the mortuary. The sergeant will let us in, won't you, sergeant ? This gentleman is a doctor as well as a lawyer."

" Bless you, sir," said the sergeant, " I know who Dr. Thorndyke is, and I shall feel it an honour to show him anything he wishes to see."

Accordingly we set forth together, Dr. Parton and Thorndyke leading the way.

" The coroner and the jury didn't seem to appreciate my exhibit," the former remarked with a faint grin, tapping the parcel as he spoke.

" No," Thorndyke agreed ; " and it is hardly reasonable to expect a layman to share our own matter-of-fact outlook. But you were quite right to produce the specimen. That ditch-water furnishes conclusive evidence on a vitally material question. Further, I would advise you to preserve that jar for the present, well covered and under lock and key."

Parton looked surprised.

" Why ? " he asked. " The inquest is over and the verdict pronounced."

" Yes, but it was an open verdict, and an open ver-

dict leaves the case in the air. The inquest has thrown
no light on the question as to how Cyrus Pedley came
by his death."

"There doesn't seem to me much mystery about it,"
said the doctor. "Here is a man found drowned in a
shallow ditch which he could easily have got out of if
he had fallen in by accident. He was not drunk.
Apparently he was not in a fit of any kind. There are
no marks of violence and no signs of a struggle, and the
man is known to have been in an extremely depressed
state of mind. It looks like a clear case of suicide,
though I admit that the jury were quite right, in the
absence of direct evidence."

"Well," said Thorndyke, "it will be my duty to
contest that view if the insurance company dispute the
claim on those grounds."

"I can't think what you will have to offer in answer
to the suggestion of suicide," said Parton.

"Neither can I, at present," replied Thorndyke.
"But the case doesn't look to me quite so simple as it
does to you."

"You think it possible that an analysis of the contents
of this jar may be called for?"

"That is a possibility," replied Thorndyke. "But
I mean that the case is obscure, and that some further
inquiry into the circumstances of this man's death is
by no means unlikely."

"Then," said Parton, "I will certainly follow your
advice and lock up this precious jar. But here we are
at the mortuary. Is there anything in particular that
you want to see?"

"I want to see all that there is to see," Thorndyke
replied. "The evidence has been vague enough so far.
Shall we begin with that bruise or mark that you mentioned?"

Dr. Parton advanced to the grim, shrouded figure
that lay on the slate-topped table, like some solemn
effigy on an altar tomb, and drew back the sheet that

covered it. We all approached, stepping softly, and stood beside the table, looking down with a certain awesome curiosity at the still, waxen figure that, but a few hours since, had been a living man like ourselves. The body was that of a good-looking, middle-aged man with a refined, intelligent face—slightly disfigured by a scar on the cheek—now set in the calm, reposeful expression that one so usually finds on the faces of the drowned ; with drowsy, half-closed eyes and slightly parted lips that revealed a considerable gap in the upper front teeth.

Thorndyke stood awhile looking down on the dead man with a curious questioning expression. Then his eye travelled over the body, from the placid face to the marble-like torso and the hand which, though now relaxed, still lightly grasped a tuft of water-weed. The latter Thorndyke gently disengaged from the limp hand, and, after a glance at the dark green, feathery fronds, laid it down and stooped to examine the right arm at the spot above the elbow that Parton had spoken of.

" Yes," he said, " I think I should call it a bruise, though it is very faint. As you say, it might have been produced by a blow with a stick or rod. I notice that there are some teeth missing. Presumably he wore a plate ? "

" Yes," replied Parton ; " a smallish gold plate with four teeth on it—at least, so his brother told me. Of course, it fell out when he was in the water, but it hasn't been found ; in fact, it hasn't been looked for."

Thorndyke nodded and then turned to the sergeant.

" Could I see what you found in the pockets ? " he asked.

The sergeant complied readily, and my colleague watched his orderly procedure with evident approval. The collection of envelopes was produced from an attaché-case and conveyed to a side table, where the sergeant emptied out the contents of each into a little heap, opposite which he placed the appropriate envelope.

16*

with its written description. Thorndyke ran his eye
over the collection—which was commonplace enough—
until he came to the tobacco pouch, from which protruded the corner of a scrap of crumpled paper. This
he drew forth and smoothed out the creases, when it
was seen to be a railway receipt for an excess fare.

"Seems to have lost his ticket or travelled without
one," the sergeant remarked. "But not on this line."

"No," agreed Thorndyke. "It is the Tilbury and
Southend line. But you notice the date. It is the
18th; and the body was found on the morning of
Wednesday, the 19th. So it would appear that he must
have come into this neighbourhood in the evening; and
that he must have come either by way of London or
by a very complicated cross-country route. I wonder
what brought him here."

He produced his notebook and was beginning to
copy the receipt when the sergeant said :

"You had better take the paper, sir. It is of no use
to us now, and it isn't very easy to make out."

Thorndyke thanked the officer, and, handing me the
paper, asked :

"What do you make of it, Jervis ? "

I scrutinised the little crumpled scrap and deciphered
with difficulty the hurried scrawl, scribbled with a hard,
ill-sharpened pencil.

"It seems to read Ldn to ' C.B. or S.B., Hlt '—that
is some ' Halt,' I presume. But the amount, 4/9, is
clear enough, and that will give us a clue if we want
one." I returned the paper to Thorndyke, who bestowed
it in his pocket-book and then remarked :

"I don't see any keys."

"No, sir," replied the sergeant, "there aren't any.
Rather queer, that, for he must have had at least a latchkey. They must have fallen out into the water."

"That is possible," said Thorndyke, "but it would
be worth while to make sure. Is there anyone who
could show us the place where the body was found ? "

" I will walk up there with you myself, sir, with pleasure," said the sergeant, hastily repacking the envelopes. " It is only a quarter of an hour's walk from here."

" That is very good of you, sergeant," my colleague responded ; " and as we seem to have seen everything here, I propose that we start at once. You are not coming with us, Parton ? "

" No," the doctor replied. " I have finished with the case and I have got my work to do." He shook hands with us heartily and watched us—with some curiosity, I think—as we set forth in company with the sergeant.

His curiosity did not seem to me to be unjustified. In fact, I shared it. The presence of the police officer precluded discussion, but as we took our way out of the town I found myself speculating curiously on my colleague's proceedings. To me, suicide was written plainly on every detail of the case. Of course, we did not wish to take that view, but what other was possible ? Had Thorndyke some alternative theory ? Or was he merely, according to his invariable custom, making an impartial survey of everything, no matter how apparently trivial, in the hope of lighting on some new and informative fact ?

The temporary absence of the sergeant, who had stopped to speak to a constable on duty, enabled me to put the question :

" Is this expedition intended to clear up anything in particular ? "

" No," he replied, " excepting the keys, which ought to be found. But you must see for yourself that this is not a straightforward case. That man did not come all this way merely to drown himself in a ditch. I am quite in the dark at present, so there is nothing for it but to examine everything with our own eyes and see if there is anything that has been overlooked that may throw some light on either the motive or the circum-

stances. · It is always desirable to examine the scene of
a crime or a tragedy."

Here the return of the sergeant put a stop to the discussion and we proceeded on our way in silence. Already
we had passed out of the town, and we now turned out
of the main road into a lane or by-road, bordered by
meadows and orchards and enclosed by rather high
hedgerows.

"This is Ponder's Road," said the sergeant. "It
leads to Renham, a couple of miles farther on, where it
joins the Aylesbury Road. The cart track is on the left
a little way along."

A few minutes later we came to our turning, a narrow
and rather muddy lane, the entrance to which was
shaded by a grove of tall elms. Passing through this
shady avenue, we came out on a grass-covered track,
broken by deep wagon-ruts and bordered on each side
by a ditch, beyond which was a wide expanse of marshy
meadows.

"This is the place," said the sergeant, halting by
the side of the right-hand ditch and indicating a spot
where the rushes had been flattened down. "It was
just as you see it now, only the feet were just visible
sticking out of the duck-weed, which had drifted back
after Moffet had disturbed it."

We stood awhile looking at the ditch, with its thick
mantle of bright green, spotted with innumerable small
dark objects and showing here and there a faint track
where a water-vole had swum across.

"Those little dark objects are water-snails, I suppose," said I, by way of making some kind of remark.

"Yes," replied Thorndyke; "the common Amber
shell, I think—*Succinea putris*." He reached out his
stick and fished up a sample of the duck-weed, on which
one or two of the snails were crawling. "Yes," he repeated. "*Succinea putris* it is; a queer little left-
handed shell, with the spire, as you see, all lop-sided.
They have a habit of swarming in this extraordinary

way. You notice that the ditch is covered with them."

I had already observed this, but it hardly seemed to be worth commenting on under the present circumstances—which was apparently the sergeant's view also, for he looked at Thorndyke with some surprise, which developed into impatience when my colleague proceeded further to expand on the subject of natural history.

" These water-weeds," he observed, " are very remarkable plants in their various ways. Look at this duck-weed, for instance. Just a little green oval disc with a single root hanging down into the water, like a tiny umbrella with a long handle ; and yet it is a complete plant, and a flowering plant, too." He picked a specimen off the end of his stick and held it up by its root to exhibit its umbrella-like form ; and as he did so, he looked in my face with an expression that I felt to be somehow significant ; but of which I could not extract the meaning. But there was no difficulty in interpreting the expression on the sergeant's face. He had come here on business and he wanted to " cut the cackle and get to the hosses."

" Well, sergeant," said Thorndyke, " there isn't much to see, but I think we ought to have a look for those keys. He must have had keys of some kind, if only a latchkey ; and they must be in this ditch."

The sergeant was not enthusiastic. " I've no doubt you are right, sir," said he ; " but I don't see that we should be much forrader if we found them. However, we may as well have a look, only I can't stay more than a few minutes. I've got my work to do at the station."

" Then," said Thorndyke, " let us get to work at once. We had better hook out the weed and look it over ; and if the keys are not in that, we must try to expose the bottom where the body was lying. You must tell us if we are working in the right place."

With this he began, with the crooked handle of his

stick, to rake up the tangle of weed that covered the
bottom of the ditch and drag the detached masses
ashore, piling them on the bank and carefully looking
them through to see if the keys should chance to be
entangled in their meshes. In this work I took my
part under the sergeant's direction, raking in load after
load of the delicate, stringy weed, on the pale green
ribbon-like leaves of which multitudes of the water-
snails were creeping ; and sorting over each batch in
hopeless and fruitless search for the missing keys. In
about ten minutes we had removed the entire weedy
covering from the bottom of the ditch over an area of
from eight to nine feet—the place which, according to
the sergeant, the body had occupied ; and as the duck-
weed had been caught by the tangled masses of water-
weed that we had dragged ashore, we now had an uninterrupted view of the cleared space save for the clouds
of mud that we had stirred up.

" We must give the mud a few minutes to settle,"
said Thorndyke.

" Yes," the sergeant agreed, " it will take some time ;
and as it doesn't really concern me now that the inquest
is over, I think I will get back to the station if you will
excuse me."

Thorndyke excused him very willingly, I think,
though politely and with many thanks for his help.
When he had gone I remarked :

" I am inclined to agree with the sergeant. If we find
the keys we shan't be much forrader."

" We shall know that he had them with him," he
replied. " Though, of course, if we don't find them,
that will not prove that they are not here. Still, I think
we should try to settle the question."

His answer left me quite unconvinced ; but the
care with which he searched the ditch and sorted out
the weed left me in no doubt that, to him, the matter
seemed to be of some importance. However, nothing
came of the search. If the keys were there they were

buried in the mud, and eventually we had to give up the search and make our way back towards the station.

As we passed out of the lane into Ponder's Road, Thorndyke stopped at the entrance, under the trees, by a little triangle of turf which marked the beginning of the lane, and looked down at the muddy ground.

"Here is quite an interesting thing, Jervis," he remarked, "which shows us how standardised objects tend to develop an individual character. These are the tracks of a car, or more probably a tradesman's van, which was fitted with Barlow tyres. Now there must be thousands of vans fitted with these tyres; they are the favourite type for light covered vans, and when new they are all alike and indistinguishable. Yet this tyre—of the off hind-wheel—has acquired a character which would enable one to pick it out with certainty from ten thousand others. First, you see, there is a deep cut in the tyre at an angle of forty-five, then a kidney-shaped 'Blakey' has stuck in the outer tyre without puncturing the inner; and finally some adhesive object—perhaps a lump of pitch from a newly-mended road—has become fixed on just behind the 'Blakey.' Now, if we make a rough sketch of those three marks and indicate their distance apart, thus "—here he made a rapid sketch in his notebook, and wrote in the intervals in inches—" we have the means of swearing to the identity of a vehicle which we have never seen."

"And which," I added, "had for some reason swerved over to the wrong side of the road. Yes, I should say that tyre is certainly unique. But surely most tyres are identifiable when they have been in use for some time."

"Exactly," he replied. "That was my point. The standardised thing is devoid of character only when it is new."

It was not a very subtle point, and as it was fairly obvious I made no comment, but presently reverted to the case of Pedley deceased.

" I don't quite see why you are taking all this trouble. The insurance claim is not likely to be contested. No one can prove that it was a case of suicide, though I should think no one will feel any doubt that it was, at least that is my own feeling."

Thorndyke looked at me with an expression of reproach.

" I am afraid that my learned friend has not been making very good use of his eyes," said he. " He has allowed his attention to be distracted by superficial appearances."

" You don't think that it was suicide, then ? " I asked, considerably taken aback.

" It isn't a question of thinking," he replied. " It was certainly not suicide. There are the plainest indications of homicide ; and, of course, in the particular circumstances, homicide means murder."

I was thunderstruck. In my own mind I had dismissed the case somewhat contemptuously as a mere commonplace suicide. As my friend had truly said, I had accepted the obvious appearances and let them mislead me, whereas Thorndyke had followed his golden rule of accepting nothing and observing everything. But what was it that he had observed ? I knew that it was useless to ask, but still I ventured on a tentative question.

" When did you come to the conclusion that it was a case of homicide ? "

" As soon as I had had a good look at the place where the body was found," he replied promptly.

This did not help me much, for I had given very little attention to anything but the search for the keys. The absence of those keys was, of course, a suspicious fact, if it was a fact. But we had not proved their absence ; we had only failed to find them.

" What do you propose to do next ? " I asked.

" Evidently," he answered, " there are two things to be done. One is to test the murder theory—to look for more evidence for or against it ; the other is to identify

THE NATURALIST AT LAW 489

the murderer, if possible. But really the two problems
are one, since they involve the questions, Who had a
motive for killing Cyrus Pedley? and Who had the
opportunity and the means?"

Our discussion brought us to the station, where,
outside the hotel, we found Mr. Pedley waiting for us.

"I am glad you have come," said he. "I was beginning to fear that we should lose this train. I suppose
there is no new light on this mysterious affair?"

"No," Thorndyke replied. "Rather there is a
new problem. No keys were found in your brother's
pockets, and we have failed to find them in the ditch;
though, of course, they may be there."

"They must be," said Pedley. "They must have
fallen out of his pocket and got buried in the mud,
unless he lost them previously, which is most unlikely.
It is a pity, though. We shall have to break open his
cabinets and drawers, which he would have hated.
He was very fastidious about his furniture."

"You will have to break into his flat, too," said I.

"No," he replied, "I shan't have to do that. I
have a duplicate of his latchkey. He had a spare
bedroom which he let me use if I wanted to stay in
town." As he spoke, he produced his key-bunch and
exhibited a small Chubb latchkey. "I wish we had
the others, though," he added.

Here the up-train was heard approaching and we
hurried on to the platform, selecting an empty first-
class compartment as it drew up. As soon as the train
had started, Thorndyke began his inquiries, to which I
listened attentively.

"You said that your brother had been anxious and
depressed lately. Was there anything more than this?
Any nervousness or foreboding?"

"Well, yes," replied Pedley. "Looking back, I seem
to see that the possibility of death was in his mind.
A week or two ago he brought his will to me to see if it
was quite satisfactory to me as the principal beneficiary;

and he handed to me his last receipt for the insurance premium. That looks a little suggestive."

"It does," Thorndyke agreed. "And as to his occupation and his associates, what do you know about them ?"

"His private friends are mostly my own, but of his official associates I know nothing. He was connected with the Foreign Office ; but in what capacity I don't know at all. He was extremely reticent on the subject. I only know that he travelled about a good deal, presumably on official business."

This was not very illuminating, but it was all our client had to tell ; and the conversation languished somewhat until the train drew up at Marylebone, when Thorndyke said, as if by an after-thought :

"You have your brother's latchkey. How would it be if we just took a glance at the flat ? Have you time now ?"

"I will make time," was the reply, "if you want to see the flat. I don't see what you could learn from inspecting it ; but that is your affair. I am in your hands."

"I should like to look round the rooms," Thorndyke answered ; and as our client assented, we approached a taxi-cab and entered while Pedley gave the driver the necessary directions. A quarter of an hour later we drew up opposite a tall block of buildings, and Mr. Pedley, having paid off the cab, led the way to the lift.

The dead man's flat was on the third floor, and, like the others, was distinguished only by the number on the door. Mr. Pedley inserted the key into the latch, and having opened the door, preceded us across the small lobby into the sitting-room.

"Ha !" he exclaimed, as he entered, "this solves your problem." As he spoke, he pointed to the table, on which lay a small bunch of keys, including a latchkey similar to the one that he had shown us.

"But," he continued, "it is rather extraordinary.

It just shows what a very disturbed state his mind must have been in."

"Yes," Thorndyke agreed, looking critically about the room ; " and as the latchkey is there, it raises the question whether the keys may have been out of his possession. Do you know what the various locked receptacles contain ? "

"I know pretty well what is in the bureau ; but as to the cupboard above it, I have never seen it open and don't know what he kept in it. I always assumed that he reserved it for his official papers. I will just see if anything seems to have been disturbed."

He unlocked and opened the flap of the old-fashioned bureau and pulled out the small drawers one after the other, examining the contents of each. Then he opened each of the larger drawers and turned over the various articles in them. As he closed the last one, he reported : "Everything seems to be in order—cheque-book, insurance policy, a few share certificates, and so on. Nothing seems to have been touched. Now we will try the cupboard, though I don't suppose its contents would be of much interest to anyone but himself. I wonder which is the key."

He looked at the keyhole and made a selection from the bunch, but it was evidently the wrong key. He tried another and yet another with a like result, until he had exhausted the resources of the bunch.

"It is very remarkable," he said. "None of these keys seems to fit. I wonder if he kept this particular key locked up or hidden. It wasn't in the bureau. Will you try what you can do ? "

He handed the bunch to Thorndyke, who tried all the keys in succession with the same result. None of them was the key belonging to the lock. At length, having tried them all, he inserted one and turned it as far as it would go. Then he gave a sharp pull ; and immediately the door came open.

"Why, it was unlocked after all ! " exclaimed Mr.

Pedley. " And there is nothing in it. That is why there was no key on the bunch. Apparently he didn't use the cupboard."

Thorndyke looked critically at the single vacant shelf, drawing his finger along it in two places and inspecting his finger-tips. Then he turned his attention to the lock, which was of the kind that is screwed on the inside of the door, leaving the bolt partly exposed. He took the bolt in his fingers and pushed it out and then in again ; and by the way it moved I could see that the spring was broken. On this he made no comment, but remarked :

" The cupboard has been in use pretty lately. You can see the trace of a largish volume—possibly a box-file—on the shelf. There is hardly any dust there, whereas the rest of the shelf is fairly thickly coated. However, that does not carry us very far ; and the appearance of the rooms is otherwise quite normal."

" Quite," agreed Pedley. " But why shouldn't it be ? You didn't suspect——"

" I was merely testing the suggestion offered by the absence of the keys," said Thorndyke. " By the way, have you communicated with the Foreign Office ? "

" No," was the reply, " but I suppose I ought to. What had I better say to them ? "

" 1 should merely state the facts in the first instance. But you can, if you like, say that I definitely reject the idea of suicide."

" I am glad to hear you say that," said Pedley. " Can I give any reasons for your opinion ? "

" Not in the first place," replied Thorndyke. " I will consider the case and let you have a reasoned report in a day or two, which you can show to the Foreign Office and also to the insurance company."

Mr. Pedley looked as if he would have liked to ask some further questions, but as Thorndyke now made his way to the door, he followed in silence, pocketing the keys as we went out. He accompanied us down to the entry and there we left him, setting forth in the direction of South Kensington Station.

" It looked to me," said I, as soon as we were out of ear-shot, " as if that lock had been forced. What do you think ? "

" Well," he answered, " locks get broken in ordinary use, but taking all the facts together, I think you are right. There are too many coincidences for reasonable probability. First, this man leaves his keys, including his latchkey, on the table, which is an extraordinary thing to do. On that very occasion, he is found dead under inexplicable circumstances. Then, of all the locks in his rooms, the one which happens to be broken is the one of which the key is not on the bunch. That is a very suspicious group of facts."

" It is," I agreed. " And if there is, as you say —though I can't imagine on what grounds—evidence of foul play, that makes it still more suspicious. But what is the next move ? Have you anything in view ? "

" The next move," he replied, " is to clear up the mystery of the dead man's movements on the day of his death. The railway receipt shows that on that day he travelled down somewhere into Essex. From that place, he took a long, cross-country journey of which the destination was a ditch by a lonely meadow in Buckinghamshire. The questions that we have to answer are, What was he doing in Essex ? Why did he make that strange journey ? Did he make it alone ? and, if not, Who accompanied him ?

" Now, obviously, the first thing to do is to locate that place in Essex ; and when we have done that, to go down there and see if we can pick up any traces of the dead man."

" That sounds like a pretty vague quest," said I ; " but if we fail, the police may be able to find out something. By the way, we want a new *Bradshaw*."

" An excellent suggestion, Jervis," said he. " I will get one as we go into the station."

A few minutes later, as we sat on a bench waiting for our train, he passed to me the open copy of *Bradshaw*, with the crumpled railway receipt.

"You see," said he, "it was apparently ' G.B.Hlt.,' and the fare from London was four and ninepence. Here is Great Buntingfield Halt, the fare to which is four and ninepence. That must be the place. At any rate, we will give it a trial. May I take it that you are coming to lend a hand ? I shall start in good time to-morrow morning."

I assented emphatically. Never had I been more completely in the dark than I was in this case, and seldom had I known Thorndyke to be more positive and confident. Obviously, he had something up his sleeve ; and I was racked with curiosity as to what that something was.

On the following morning we made a fairly early start, and half-past ten found us seated in the train, looking out across a dreary waste of marshes, with the estuary of the Thames a mile or so distant. For the first time in my recollection Thorndyke had come unprovided with his inevitable "research case," but I noted that he had furnished himself with a botanist's vasculum—or tin collecting-case—and that his pocket bulged as if he had some other appliances concealed about his person. Also that he carried a walking-stick that was strange to me.

"This will be our destination, I think," he said, as the train slowed down ; and sure enough it presently came to rest beside a little makeshift platform on which was displayed the name "Great Buntingfield Halt." We were the only passengers to alight, and the guard, having noted the fact, blew his whistle and dismissed the little station with a contemptuous wave of his flag.

Thorndyke lingered on the platform after the train had gone, taking a general survey of the country. Half a mile away to the north a small village was visible ;

while to the south the marshes stretched away to the
river, their bare expanse unbroken save by a solitary
building whose unredeemed hideousness proclaimed it
a factory of some kind. Presently the station-master
approached deferentially, and as we proffered our tickets,
Thorndyke remarked :

" You don't seem overburdened with traffic here."

" No, sir. You're right," was the emphatic reply.
" 'Tis a dead-alive place. Excepting the people at the
Golomite Works and one now and then from the village,
no one uses the halt. You're the first strangers I've seen
for more than a month."

" Indeed," said Thorndyke. " But I think you are
forgetting one. An acquaintance of mine came here
last Tuesday—and by the same token, he hadn't got a
ticket and had to pay his fare."

" Oh, I remember," the station-master replied.
" You mean a gentleman with a scar on his cheek. But
I don't count him as a stranger. He has been here
before ; I think he is connected with the works, as he
always goes up their road."

" Do you happen to remember what time he came
back ? " Thorndyke asked.

" He didn't come back at all," was the reply. " I
am sure of that, because I work the halt and level crossing by myself. I remember thinking it queer that he
didn't come back, because the ticket that he had lost
was a return. He must have gone back in the van
belonging to the works—that one that you see coming
towards the crossing."

As he spoke, he pointed to a van that was approaching
down the factory road—a small covered van with the
name " Golomite Works " painted, not on the cover,
but on a board that was attached to it. The station-
master walked towards the crossing to open the gates,
and we followed ; and when the van had passed, Thorndyke wished our friend " Good morning," and led the
way along the road, looking about him with lively interest

and rather with the air of one looking for something in particular.

We had covered about two-thirds of the distance to the factory when the road approached a wide ditch ; and from the attention with which my friend regarded it, I suspected that this was the something for which he had been looking. It was, however, quite unapproachable, for it was bordered by a wide expanse of soft mud thickly covered with rushes and trodden deeply by cattle. Nevertheless, Thorndyke followed its margin, still looking about him keenly, until, about a couple of hundred yards from the factory, I observed a small decayed wooden staging or quay, apparently the remains of a vanished footbridge. Here Thorndyke halted, and unbuttoning his coat, began to empty out his pockets, producing first the vasculum, then a small case containing three wide-mouthed bottles—both of which he deposited on the ground—and finally a sort of miniature landing-net, which he proceeded to screw on to the ferrule of his stick.

"I take it," said I, "that these proceedings are a blind to cover some sort of observations."

"Not at all," he replied. "We are engaged in the study of pond and ditch natural history, and a most fascinating and instructive study it is. The variety of forms is endless. This ditch, you observe, like the one at Bantree, is covered with a dense growth of duck-weed : but whereas that ditch was swarming with succineæ, here there is not a single succinea to be seen."

I grunted a sulky assent, and watched suspiciously as he filled the bottles with water from the ditch and then made a preliminary sweep with his net.

"Here is a trial sample," said he, holding the loaded net towards me. "Duck-weed, horn-weed, Planorbis nautileus, but no succineæ. What do you think of it, Jervis ? "

I looked distastefully at the repulsive mess, but yet with attention, for I realised that there was a meaning in his question. And then, suddenly, my attention sharpened. I picked out of the net a strand of dark green, plumy weed and examined it.

"So this is horn-weed," I said. "Then it was a piece of horn-weed that Cyrus Pedley held grasped in his hand; and now I come to think of it, I don't remember seeing any horn-weed in the ditch at Bantree."

He nodded approvingly. "There wasn't any," said he.

"And these little ammonite-like shells are just like those that I noticed at the bottom of Dr. Parton's jar. But I don't remember seeing any in the Bantree ditch."

"There were none there," said he. "And the duck-weed?"

"Oh, well," I replied, "duck-weed is duck-weed, and there's an end of it."

He chuckled aloud at my answer, and quoting:

"A primrose by the river's brim
A yellow primrose was to him,"

bestowed a part of the catch in the vasculum, then turned once more to the ditch and began to ply his net vigorously, emptying out each netful on the grass, looking it over quickly and then making a fresh sweep, dragging the net each time through the mud at the bottom. I watched him now with a new and very lively interest; for enlightenment was dawning, mingled with some self-contempt and much speculation as to how Thorndyke had got his start in this case.

But I was not the only interested watcher. At one of the windows of the factory I presently observed a man who seemed to be looking our way. After a few seconds' inspection he disappeared, to reappear almost immediately with a pair of field-glasses, through which he took a long look at us. Then he disappeared again, but in less than a minute I saw him emerge from a side door and advance hurriedly towards us.

"We are going to have a notice of ejectment served on us, I fancy," said I.

Thorndyke glanced quickly at the approaching stranger but continued to ply his net, working, as I noticed, methodically from left to right. When the man came within fifty yards he hailed us with a brusque inquiry as to what our business was. I went forward to meet him and, if possible, to detain him in conversation ; but this plan failed, for he ignored me and bore straight down on Thorndyke.

"Now, then," said he, "what's the game ? What are you doing here ? "

Thorndyke was in the act of raising his net from the water, but he now suddenly let it fall to the bottom of the ditch while he turned to confront the stranger.

"I take it that you have some reason for asking," said he.

"Yes, I have," the other replied angrily and with a slight foreign accent that agreed with his appearance— he looked like a Slav of some sort. "This is private land. It belongs to the factory. I am the manager."

"The land is not enclosed," Thorndyke remarked.

"I tell you the land is private land," the fellow retorted excitedly. "You have no business here. I want to know what you are doing."

"My good sir," said Thorndyke, "there is no need to excite yourself. My friend and I are just collecting botanical and other specimens."

"How do I know that ? " the manager demanded. He looked round suspiciously and his eye lighted on the vasculum. "What have you got in that thing ? " he asked.

"Let him see what is in it," said Thorndyke, with a significant look at me.

Interpreting this as an instruction to occupy the man's attention for a few moments, I picked up the vasculum and placed myself so that he must turn his back to Thorndyke to look into it. I fumbled awhile with the catch, but at length opened the case and began to pick out the weed strand by strand. As soon as the stranger's back was turned Thorndyke raised his net and quickly picked out of it something which he slipped into his pocket. Then he advanced towards us, sorting out the contents of his net as he came.

"Well," he said, "you see we are just harmless naturalists. By the way, what did you think we were looking for ? "

"Never mind what I thought," the other replied fiercely. "This is private land. You have no business here, and you have got to clear out."

"Very well," said Thorndyke. "As you please. There are plenty of other ditches." He took the vasculum and the case of bottles, and having put them in his pocket, unscrewed his net, wished the stranger "Good-morning," and turned back towards the station. The man stood watching us until we were near the level crossing, when he, too, turned back and retired to the factory.

"I saw you take something out of the net," said I. "What was it ? "

He glanced back to make sure that the manager was out of sight. Then he put his hand in his pocket, drew it out closed, and suddenly opened it. In his palm lay a small gold dental plate with four teeth on it.

"My word ! " I exclaimed ; "this clenches the matter with a vengeance. That is certainly Cyrus Pedley's plate. It corresponds exactly to the description."

"Yes," he replied, "it is practically a certainty. Of course, it will have to be identified by the dentist who made it. But it is a foregone conclusion."

I reflected as we walked towards the station on the singular sureness with which Thorndyke had followed what was to me an invisible trail. Presently I said :

"What is puzzling me is how you got your start in this case. What gave you the first hint that it was homicide and not suicide or misadventure ? "

"It was the old story, Jervis," he replied ; "just

a matter of observing and remembering apparently trivial details. Here, by the way, is a case in point."

He stopped and looked down at a set of tracks in the soft, earth road—apparently those of the van which we had seen cross the line. I followed the direction of his glance and saw the clear impression of a Blakey's protector, preceded by that of a gash in the tyre and followed by that of a projecting lump.

" But this is astounding ! " I exclaimed. " It is almost certainly the same track that we saw in Ponder's Road."

" Yes," he agreed. " I noticed it as we came along." He brought out his spring-tape and notebook, and handing the latter to me, stooped and measured the distances between the three impressions. I wrote them down as he called them out, and then we compared them with the note made in Ponder's Road. The measurements were identical, as were the relative positions of the impressions.

" This is an important piece of evidence," said he. " I wish we were able to take casts, but the notes will be pretty conclusive. And now," he continued as we resumed our progress towards the station, " to return to your question. Parton's evidence at the inquest proved that Cyrus Pedley was drowned in water which contained duck-weed. He produced a specimen and we both saw it. We saw the duck-weed in it and also two Planorbis shells. The presence of those two shells proved that the water in which he was drowned must have swarmed with them. We saw the body, and observed that one hand grasped a wisp of horn-weed. Then we went to view the ditch and we examined it. That was when I got, not a mere hint, but a crucial and conclusive fact. The ditch was covered with duck-weed, as we expected. *But it was the wrong duck-weed.*"

" The wrong duck-weed ! " I exclaimed. " Why, how many kinds of duck-weed are there ? "

" There are four British species," he replied. " The Greater Duck-weed, the Lesser Duck-weed, the Thick

Duck-weed, and the Ivy-leaved Duck-weed. Now the specimens in Parton's jar I noticed were the Greater Duck-weed, which is easily distinguished by its roots, which are multiple and form a sort of tassel. But the duck-weed on the Bantree ditch was the Lesser Duck-weed, which is smaller than the other, but is especially distinguished by having only a single root. It is impossible to mistake one for the other.

" Here, then, was practically conclusive evidence of murder. Cyrus Pedley had been drowned in a pond or ditch. But not in the ditch in which his body was found. Therefore his dead body had been conveyed from some other place and put into this ditch. Such a proceeding furnishes *prima facie* evidence of murder. But as soon as the question was raised, there was an abundance of confirmatory evidence. There was no horn-weed or Planorbis shells in the ditch, but there were swarms of succineæ, some of which would inevitably have been swallowed with the water. There was an obscure linear pressure mark on the arm of the dead man, just above the elbow : such a mark as might be made by a cord if a man were pinioned to render him helpless. Then the body would have had to be conveyed to this place in some kind of vehicle ; and we found the traces of what appeared to be a motor-van, which had approached the cart-track on the wrong side of the road, as if to pull up there. It was a very conclusive mass of evidence ; but it would have been useless but for the extraordinarily lucky chance that poor Pedley had lost his railway ticket and preserved the receipt ; by which we were able to ascertain where he was on the day of his death and in what locality the murder was probably committed. But that is not the only way in which Fortune has favoured us. The station-master's information was, and will be, invaluable. Then it was most fortunate for us that there was only one ditch on the factory land ; and that that ditch was accessible at only one point, which must have been the place where Pedley was drowned."

" The duck-weed in this ditch is, of course, the Greater Duck-weed ? "

" Yes. I have taken some specimens as well as the horn-weed and shells."

He opened the vasculum and picked out one of the tiny plants, exhibiting the characteristic tassel of roots.

" I shall write to Parton and tell him to preserve the jar and the horn-weed if it has not been thrown away. But the duck-weed alone, produced in evidence, would be proof enough that Pedley was not drowned in the Bantree ditch ; and the dental plate will show where he was drowned."

" Are you going to pursue the case any farther ? " I asked.

" No," he replied. " I shall call at Scotland Yard on my way home and report what I have learned and what I can prove in court. Then I shall have finished with the case. The rest is for the police, and I imagine they won't have much difficulty. The circumstances seem to tell their own story. Pedley was employed by the Foreign Office, probably on some kind of secret service. I imagine that he discovered the existence of a gang of evil-doers—probably foreign revolutionaries, of whom we may assume that our friend the manager of the factory is one ; that he contrived to associate himself with them and to visit the factory occasionally to ascertain what was made there besides Golomite—if Golomite is not itself an illicit product. Then I assume that he was discovered to be a spy, that he was lured down here ; that he was pinioned and drowned some time on Tuesday night and his body put into the van and conveyed to a place miles away from the scene of his death, where it was deposited in a ditch apparently identical in character with that in which he was drowned. It was an extremely ingenious and well-thought-out plan. It seemed to have provided for every kind of inquiry, and it very narrowly missed being successful."

" Yes," I agreed. " But it didn't provide for Dr. John Thorndyke."

" It didn't provide for a searching examination of all the details," he replied ; " and no criminal plan that I have ever met has done so. The completeness of the scheme is limited by the knowledge of the schemers, and, in practice, there is always something overlooked. In this case, the criminals were unlearned in the natural history of ditches."

Thorndyke's theory of the crime turned out to be substantially correct. The Golomite Works proved to be a factory where high explosives were made by a gang of cosmopolitan revolutionaries who were all known to the police. But the work of the latter was simplified by a detailed report which the dead man had deposited at his bank and which was discovered in time to enable the police to raid the factory and secure the whole gang. When once they were under lock and key, further information was forthcoming ; for a charge of murder against them jointly soon produced King's Evidence sufficient to procure a conviction of the three actual perpetrators of the murder.

17   MR. PONTING'S ALIBI

THORNDYKE looked doubtfully at the pleasant-faced, athletic-looking clergyman who had just come in, bearing Mr. Brodribb's card as an explanatory credential.

" I don't quite see," said he, " why Mr. Brodribb sent you to me. It seems to be a purely legal matter which he could have dealt with himself, at least as well as I can."

" He appeared to think otherwise," said the clergyman. (" The Revd. Charles Meade " was written on the card.) " At any rate," he added with a persuasive smile, " here I am, and I hope you are not going to send me away."

"I shouldn't offer that affront to my old friend Brodribb," replied Thorndyke, smiling in return; "so we may as well get to business, which, in the first place, involves the setting out of all the particulars. Let us begin with the lady who is the subject of the threats of which you spoke."

"Her name," said Mr. Meade, "is Miss Millicent Fawcett. She is a person of independent means, which she employs in works of charity. She was formerly a hospital sister, and she does a certain amount of voluntary work in the parish as a sort of district nurse. She has been a very valuable help to me and we have been close friends for several years; and I may add, as a very material fact, that she has consented to marry me in about two months' time. So that, you see, I am properly entitled to act on her behalf."

"Yes," agreed Thorndyke. "You are an interested party. And now, as to the threats. What do they amount to?"

"That," replied Meade, "I can't tell you. I gathered quite by chance, from some words that she dropped, that she had been threatened. But she was unwilling to say more on the subject, as she did not take the matter seriously. She is not at all nervous. However, I told her I was taking advice; and I hope you will be able to extract more details from her. For my own part, I am decidedly uneasy."

"And as to the person or persons who have uttered the threats. Who are they? and out of what circumstances have the threats arisen?"

"The person is a certain William Ponting, who is Miss Fawcett's step-brother—if that is the right term. Her father married, as his second wife, a Mrs. Ponting, a widow with one son. This is the son. His mother died before Mr. Fawcett, and the latter, when he died, left his daughter, Millicent, sole heir to his property. That has always been a grievance to Ponting. But now he has another. Miss Fawcett made a will some years ago by which the bulk of her rather considerable property is left to two cousins, Frederick and James Barnett, the sons of her father's sister. A comparatively small amount goes to Ponting. When he heard this he was furious. He demanded a portion at least equal to the others, and has continued to make this demand from time to time. In fact, he has been extremely troublesome, and appears to be getting still more so. I gathered that the threats were due to her refusal to alter the will."

"But," said I, "doesn't he realise that her marriage will render that will null and void ? "

"Apparently not," replied Meade ; "nor, to tell the truth, did I realise it myself. Will she have to make a new will ? "

"Certainly," I replied. "And as that new will may be expected to be still less favourable to him, that will presumably be a further grievance."

"One doesn't understand," said Thorndyke, "why he should excite himself so much about her will. What are their respective ages ? "

"Miss Fawcett is thirty-six and Ponting is about forty."

"And what kind of man is he ? " Thorndyke asked.

"A very unpleasant kind of man, I am sorry to say. Morose, rude, and violent-tempered. A spendthrift and a cadger. He has had quite a lot of money from Miss Fawcett—loans, which, of course, are never repaid. And he is none too industrious, though he has a regular job on the staff of a weekly paper. But he seems to be always in debt."

"We may as well note his address," said Thorndyke.

"He lives in a small flat in Bloomsbury—alone now, since he quarrelled with the man who used to share it with him. The address is 12 Borneo House, Devonshire Street."

"What sort of terms is he on with the cousins, his rivals ? "

"No sort of terms now," replied Meade. "They

17

used to be great friends. So much so that he took his present flat to be near them—they live in the adjoining flat, number 12 Sumatra House. But since the trouble about the will, he is hardly on speaking terms with them."

"They live together, then?"

"Yes, Frederick and his wife and James, who is unmarried. They are rather a queer lot, too. Frederick is a singer on the variety stage, and James accompanies him on various instruments. But they are both sporting characters of a kind, especially James, who does a bit on the turf and engages in other odd activities. Of course, their musical habits are a grievance to Ponting. He is constantly making complaints of their disturbing him at his work."

Mr. Meade paused and looked wistfully at Thorndyke, who was making full notes of the conversation.

"Well," said the latter, "we seem to have got all the facts excepting the most important—the nature of the threats. What do you want us to do?"

"I want you to see Miss Fawcett—with me, if possible —and induce her to give you such details as would enable you to put a stop to the nuisance. You couldn't come to-night, I suppose? It is a beast of a night, but I would take you there in a taxi—it is only to Tooting Bec. What do you say?" he added eagerly, as Thorndyke made no objection. "We are sure to find her in, because her maid is away on a visit to her home and she is alone in the house."

Thorndyke looked reflectively at his watch.

"Half-past eight," he remarked, "and half an hour to get there. These threats are probably nothing but ill-temper. But we don't know. There may be something more serious behind them; and, in law as in medicine, prevention is better than a post-mortem. What do you say, Jervis?"

What could I say? I would much sooner have sat by the fire with a book than turn out into the murk of a November night. But I felt it necessary, especially as Thorndyke had evidently made up his mind. Accordingly I made a virtue of necessity ; and a couple of minutes later we had exchanged the cosy room for the chilly darkness of Inner Temple Lane, up which the gratified parson was speeding ahead to capture a taxi. At the top of the Lane we perceived him giving elaborate instructions to a taxi-driver as he held the door of the cab open ; and Thorndyke, having carefully disposed of his research-case—which, to my secret amusement, he had caught up, from mere force of habit, as we started—took his seat, and Meade and I followed.

As the taxi trundled smoothly along the dark streets, Mr. Meade filled in the details of his previous sketch, and, in a simple, manly, unaffected way dilated upon his good fortune and the pleasant future that lay before him. It was not, perhaps, a romantic marriage, he admitted ; but Miss Fawcett and he had been faithful friends for years, and faithful friends they would remain till death did them part. So he ran on, now gleefully, now with a note of anxiety, and we listened by no means unsympathetically, until at last the cab drew up at a small, unpretentious house, standing in its own little grounds in a quiet suburban road.

" She is at home, you see," observed Meade, pointing to a lighted ground-floor window. He directed the taxi-driver to wait for the return journey, and striding up the path, delivered a characteristic knock at the door. As this brought no response, he knocked again and rang the bell. But still there was no answer, though twice I thought I heard the sound of a bolt being either drawn or shot softly. Again Mr. Meade plied the knocker more vigorously, and pressed the push of the bell, which we could hear ringing loudly within.

" This is very strange," said Meade, in an anxious tone, keeping his thumb pressed on the bell-push. " She can't have gone out and left the electric light on. What had we better do ? "

" We had better enter without more delay," Thorndyke replied. " There were certainly sounds from within. Is there a side gate ? "

Meade ran off towards the side of the house, and Thorndyke and I glanced at the lighted window, which was slightly open at the top.

" Looks a bit queer," I remarked, listening at the letter-box.

Thorndyke assented gravely, and at this moment Meade returned, breathing hard.

" The side gate is bolted inside," said he ; and at this I recalled the stealthy sound of the bolt that I had heard. " What is to be done ? "

Without replying, Thorndyke handed me his research-case, stepped across to the window, sprang up on the sill, drew down the upper sash and disappeared between the curtains into the room. A moment later the street door opened and Meade and I entered the hall. We glanced through the open doorway into the lighted room, and I noticed a heap of needlework thrown hastily on the dining-table. Then Meade switched on the hall light, and Thorndyke walked quickly past him to the half-open door of the next room. Before entering, he reached in and switched on the light ; and as he stepped into the room he partly closed the door behind him.

" Don't come in here, Meade ! " he called out. But the parson's eye, like my own, had seen something before the door closed : a great, dark stain on the carpet just within the threshold. Regardless of the admonition, he pushed the door open and darted into the room. Following him, I saw him rush forward, fling his arms up wildly, and with a dreadful, strangled cry, sink upon his knees beside a low couch on which a woman was lying.

" Merciful God ! " he gasped. " She is dead ! Is she dead, doctor ? Can nothing be done ? "

Thorndyke shook his head. " Nothing," he said in a low voice. " She is dead."

Poor Meade knelt by the couch, his hands clutching at his hair and his eyes riveted on the dead face, the very embodiment of horror and despair.

"God Almighty!" he exclaimed in the same strangled undertone. "How frightful! Poor, poor Millie! Dear, sweet friend!" Then suddenly—almost savagely—he turned to Thorndyke. "But it can't be, doctor! It is impossible—unbelievable. That, I mean!" and he pointed to the dead woman's right hand, which held an open razor.

Our poor friend had spoken my own thought. It was incredible that this refined, pious lady should have inflicted those savage wounds, that gaped scarlet beneath the waxen face. There, indeed, was the razor lying in her hand. But what was its testimony worth? My heart rejected it; but yet, unwillingly, I noted that the wounds seemed to support it; for they had been made from left to right, as they would have been if self-inflicted.

"It is hard to believe," said Thorndyke, "but there is only one alternative. Someone should acquaint the police at once."

"I will go," exclaimed Meade, starting up. "I know the way and the cab is there." He looked once more with infinite pity and affection at the dead woman. "Poor, sweet girl!" he murmured. "If we can do no more for you, we can defend your memory from calumny and call upon the God of Justice to right the innocent and punish the guilty."

With these words and a mute farewell to his dead friend, he hurried from the room, and immediately afterwards we heard the street door close.

As he went out, Thorndyke's manner changed abruptly. He had been deeply moved—as who would not have been—by this awful tragedy that had in a moment shattered the happiness of the genial, kindly parson. Now he turned to me with a face set and stern.

"This is an abominable affair, Jervis," he said in an ominously quiet voice.

"You reject the suggestion of suicide, then ? " said I, with a feeling of relief that surprised me.

"Absolutely," he replied. "Murder shouts at us from everything that meets our eye. Look at this poor woman, in her trim nurse's dress, with her unfinished needlework lying on the table in the next room and that preposterous razor loose in her limp hand. Look at the savage wounds. Four of them, and the first one mortal. The great bloodstain by the door, the great bloodstain on her dress from the neck to the feet. The gashed collar, the cap-string cut right through. Note that the bleeding had practically ceased when she lay down. That is a group of visible facts that is utterly inconsistent with the idea of suicide. But we are wasting time. Let us search the premises thoroughly. The murderer has pretty certainly got away, but as he was in the house when we arrived, any traces will be quite fresh."

As he spoke he took his electric lamp from the research-case and walked to the door.

"We can examine this room later," he said, "but we had better look over the house. If you will stay by the stairs and watch the front and back doors, I will look through the upper rooms."

He ran lightly up the stairs while I kept watch below, but he was absent less than a couple of minutes.

"There is no one there," he reported, "and as there is no basement we will just look at this floor and then examine the grounds."

After a rapid inspection of the ground-floor rooms, including the kitchen, we went out by the back door, which was unbolted, and inspected the grounds. These consisted of a largish garden with a small orchard at the side. In the former we could discover no traces of any kind, but at the end of the path that crossed the orchard we came on a possible clue. The orchard was enclosed by a five-foot fence, the top of which bristled with hooked nails ; and at the point opposite to the path, Thorndyke's lantern brought into view one or two wisps of cloth caught on the hooks.

"Someone has been over here," said Thorndyke, "but as this is an orchard, there is nothing remarkable in the fact. However, there is no fruit on the trees now, and the cloth looks fairly fresh. There are two kinds, you notice : a dark blue and a black and white mixture of some kind."

"Corresponding, probably, to the coat and trousers," I suggested.

"Possibly," he agreed, taking from his pocket a couple of the little seed-envelopes of which he always carried a supply. Very delicately he picked the tiny wisps of cloth from the hooks and bestowed each kind in a separate envelope. Having pocketed these, he leaned over the fence and threw the light of his lamp along the narrow lane or alley that divided the orchard from the adjoining premises. It was ungravelled and covered with a growth of rank grass, which suggested that it was little frequented. But immediately below was a small patch of bare earth, and on this was a very distinct impression of a foot, covering several less distinct prints.

"Several people have been over here at different times," I remarked.

"Yes," Thorndyke agreed. "But that sharp foot-print belongs to the last one over, and he is our concern. We had better not confuse the issues by getting over ourselves. We will mark the spot and explore from the other end." He laid his handkerchief over the top of the fence and we then went back to the house.

"You are going to take a plaster cast, I suppose ? " said I ; and as he assented, I fetched the research-case from the drawing-room. Then we fixed the catch of the front-door latch and went out, drawing the door to after us.

We found the entrance to the alley about sixty yards from the gate, and entering it, walked slowly forwards, scanning the ground as we went. But the bright lamplight showed nothing more than the vague marks of trampling feet on the grass until we came to the spot marked by the handkerchief on the fence.

" It is a pity," I remarked, " that this footprint has obliterated the others."

" On the other hand," he replied, " this one, which is the one that interests us, is remarkably clear and characteristic : a circular heel and a rubber sole of a recognisable pattern mended with a patch of cement paste. It is a footprint that could be identified beyond a doubt."

As he was speaking, he took from the research-case the water-bottle, plaster-tin, rubber mixing-bowl and spoon, and a piece of canvas with which to " reinforce " the cast. Rapidly, he mixed a bowlful—extra thick, so that it should set quickly and hard—dipped the canvas into it, poured the remainder into the footprint, and laid the canvas on it.

" I will get you to stay here, Jervis," said he, " until the plaster has set. I want to examine the body rather more thoroughly before the police arrive, particularly the back."

" Why the back ? " I asked.

" Did not the appearance of the body suggest to you the advisability of examining the back ? " he asked, and then, without waiting for a reply, he went off, leaving the inspection-lamp with me.

His words gave me matter for profound thought during my short vigil. I recalled the appearance of the dead woman very vividly—indeed, I am not likely ever to forget it—and I strove to connect that appearance with his desire to examine the back of the corpse. But there seemed to be no connection at all. The visible injuries were in front, and I had seen nothing to suggest the existence of any others. From time to time I tested the condition of the plaster, impatient to rejoin my colleague but fearful of cracking the thin cast by raising it prematurely. At length the plaster seemed to be hard enough, and trusting to the strength of the canvas, I prised cautiously at the edge, when, to my relief, the brittle plate came up safely and I lifted it clear. Wrapping it carefully in some spare rag, I packed it in the research-case, and then, taking this and the lantern, made my way back to the house.

When I had let down the catch and closed the front door, I went to the drawing-room, where I found Thorndyke stooping over the dark stain at the threshold and scanning the floor as if in search of something. I reported the completion of the cast and then asked him what he was looking for.

" I am looking for a button," he replied. " There is one missing from the back ; the one to which the collar was fastened."

" Is it of any importance ? " I asked.

" It is important to ascertain when and where it became detached," he replied. " Let us have the inspection-lamp."

I gave him the lamp, which he placed on the floor, turning it so that its beam of light travelled along the surface. Stooping to follow the light, I scrutinised the floor minutely but in vain.

" It may not be here at all," said I ; but at that moment the bright gleam, penetrating the darkness under a cabinet, struck a small object close to the wall. In a moment I had thrown myself prone on the carpet, and reaching under the cabinet, brought forth a largish mother-of-pearl button.

" You notice," said Thorndyke, as he examined it, " that the cabinet is near the window, at the opposite end of the room to the couch. But we had better see that it is the right button."

He walked slowly towards the couch, still stooping and searching the floor with the light. The corpse, I noticed, had been turned on its side, exposing the back and the displaced collar. Through the strained button-

17*

hole of the latter Thorndyke passed the button without difficulty.

"Yes," he said, "that is where it came from. You will notice that there is a similar one in front. By the way," he continued, bringing the lamp close to the surface of the grey serge dress, "I picked off one or two hairs—animal hairs ; cat and dog they looked like. Here are one or two more. Will you hold the lamp while I take them off ? "

"They are probably from some pets of hers," I remarked, as he picked them off with his forceps and deposited them in one of the invaluable seed-envelopes. "Spinsters are a good deal addicted to pets, especially cats and dogs."

"Possibly," he replied. "But I could see none in front, where you would expect to find them, and there seem to be none on the carpet. Now let us replace the body as we found it and just have a look at our material before the police arrive. I expected them here before this."

We turned the body back into its original position, and taking the research-case and the lamp, went into the dining-room. Here Thorndyke rapidly set up the little travelling microscope, and bringing forth the seed-envelopes, began to prepare slides from the contents of some while I prepared the others. There was time only for a very hasty examination, which Thorndyke made as soon as the specimens were mounted.

"The clothing," he reported, with his eye at the microscope, "is woollen in both cases. Fairly good quality. The one a blue serge, apparently indigo dyed ; the other a mixture of black and white, no other colour. Probably a fine tabby or a small shepherd's plaid."

"Serge coat and shepherd's plaid trousers," I suggested. "Now see what the hairs are." I handed him the slide, on which I had roughly mounted the collection in oil of lavender, and he placed it on the stage.

"There are three different kinds of hairs here," he

reported, after a rapid inspection. "Some are obviously from a cat—a smoky Persian. Others are long, rather fine tawny hairs from a dog. Probably a Pekinese. But there are two that I can't quite place. They look like monkey's hairs, but they are a very unusual colour. There is a perceptible greenish tint, which is extremely uncommon in mammalian hairs. But I hear the taxi approaching. We need not be expansive to the local police as to what we have observed. This will probably be a case for the C.I.D."

I went out into the hall and opened the door as Meade came up the path, followed by two men; and as the latter came into the light, I was astonished to recognise in one of them our old friend, Detective-Superintendent Miller, the other being, apparently, the station superintendent.

"We have kept Mr. Meade a long time," said Miller, "but we knew you were here, so the time wouldn't be wasted. Thought it best to get a full statement before we inspected the premises. How do, doctor?" he added, shaking hands with Thorndyke. "Glad to see you here. I suppose you have got all the facts. I understood so from Mr. Meade."

"Yes," replied Thorndyke, "we have all the antecedents of the case, and we arrived within a few minutes of the death of the deceased."

"Ha!" exclaimed Miller. "Did you? And I expect you have formed an opinion on the question as to whether the injuries were self-inflicted?"

"I think," said Thorndyke, "that it would be best to act on the assumption that they were not—and to act promptly."

"Pre—cisely," Miller agreed emphatically. "You mean that we had better find out at once where a certain person was at—— What time did you arrive here?"

"It was two minutes to nine when the taxi stopped," replied Thorndyke; "and, as it is now only twenty-five minutes to ten, we have good time if Mr. Meade can spare us the taxi. I have the address."

" The taxi is waiting for you," said Mr. Meade, " and the man has been paid for both journeys. I shall stay here in case the superintendent wants anything." He shook our hands warmly, and as we bade him farewell and noted the dazed, despairing expression and lines of grief that had already eaten into the face that had been so blithe and hopeful, we both thought bitterly of the few fatal minutes that had made us too late to save the wreckage of his life.

We were just turning away when Thorndyke paused and again faced the clergyman.

" Can you tell me," he asked, " whether Miss Fawcett had any pets ? Cats, dogs, or other animals ? "

Meade looked at him in surprise, and Superintendent Miller seemed to prick up his ears. But the former answered simply : " No. She was not very fond of animals ; she reserved her affections for men and women."

Thorndyke nodded gravely, and picking up the research-case walked slowly out of the room, Miller and I following.

As soon as the address had been given to the driver and we had taken our seats in the taxi, the superintendent opened the examination-in-chief.

" I see you have got your box of magic with you, doctor," he said, cocking his eye at the research-case. " Any luck ? "

" We have secured a very distinctive footprint," replied Thorndyke, " but it may have no connection with the case."

" I hope it has," said Miller. " A good cast of a foot-print which you can let the jury compare with the boot is first-class evidence." He took the cast, which I had produced from the research-case, and turning it over tenderly and gloatingly, exclaimed : " Beautiful ! beautiful ! Absolutely distinctive ! There can't be another exactly like it in the world. It is as good as a finger-print. For the Lord's sake take care of it. It means a conviction if we can find the boot."

The superintendent's efforts to engage Thorndyke in discussion were not very successful, and the conversational brunt was borne by me. For we both knew my colleague too well to interrupt him if he was disposed to be meditative. And such was now his disposition. Looking at him as he sat in his corner, silent but obviously wrapped in thought, I knew that he was mentally sorting out the data and testing the hypotheses that they yielded.

"Here we are," said Miller, opening the door as the taxi stopped. "Now what are we going to say? Shall I tell him who I am?"

"I expect you will have to," replied Thorndyke, "if you want him to let us in."

"Very well," said Miller. "But I shall let you do the talking, because I don't know what you have got up your sleeve."

Thorndyke's prediction was verified literally. In response to the third knock, with an obbligato accompaniment on the bell, wrathful footsteps—I had no idea footsteps could be so expressive—advanced rapidly along the lobby, the door was wrenched open—but only for a few inches—and an angry, hairy face appeared in the opening.

"Now then," the hairy person demanded, "what the deuce do you want?"

"Are you Mr. William Ponting?" the superintendent inquired.

"What the devil is that to do with you?" was the genial answer—in the Scottish mode.

"We have business," Miller began persuasively.

"So have I," the presumable Ponting replied, "and mine won't wait."

"But our business is very important," Miller urged.

"So is mine," snapped Ponting, and would have

shut the door but for Miller's obstructing foot, at which he kicked viciously, but with unsatisfactory results, as he was shod in light slippers, whereas the superintendent's boots were of constabulary solidity.

"Now, look here," said Miller, dropping his conciliatory manner very completely, "you'd better stop this nonsense. I am a police officer, and I am going to come in"; and with this he inserted a massive shoulder and pushed the door open.

"Police officer, are you?" said Ponting. "And what might your business be with me?"

"That is what I have been waiting to tell you," said Miller. "But we don't want to do our talking here."

"Very well," growled Ponting. "Come in. But understand that I am busy. I've been interrupted enough this evening."

He led the way into a rather barely furnished room with a wide bay-window in which was a table fitted with a writing-slope and lighted by an electric standard lamp. A litter of manuscript explained the nature of his business and his unwillingness to receive casual visitors. He sulkily placed three chairs, and then, seating himself, glowered at Thorndyke and me.

"Are they police officers, too?" he demanded.

"No," replied Miller, "they are medical gentlemen. Perhaps you had better explain the matter, doctor," he added, addressing Thorndyke, who thereupon opened the proceedings.

"We have called," said he, "to inform you that Miss Millicent Fawcett died suddenly this evening."

"The devil!" exclaimed Ponting. "That's sudden with a vengeance. What time did this happen?"

"About a quarter to nine."

"Extraordinary!" muttered Ponting. "I saw her only the day before yesterday, and she seemed quite well then. What did she die of?"

"The appearances," replied Thorndyke, "suggest suicide."

" Suicide ! " gasped Ponting. " Impossible ! I can't believe it. Do you mean to tell me she poisoned herself ? "

" No," said Thorndyke, " it was not poison. Death was caused by injuries to the throat inflicted with a razor."

" Good God ! " exclaimed Ponting. " What a horrible thing ! But," he added, after a pause, " I can't believe she did it herself, and I don't. Why should she commit suicide ? She was quite happy, and she was just going to be married to that mealy-faced parson. And a razor, too ! How do you suppose she came by a razor ? Women don't shave. They smoke and drink and swear, but they haven't taken to shaving yet. I don't believe it. Do you ? "

He glared ferociously at the superintendent, who replied :

" I am not sure that I do. There's a good deal in what you've just said, and the same objections had occurred to us. But you see, if she didn't do it herself, someone else must have done it, and we should like to find out who that someone is. So we begin by ascertaining where any possible persons may have been at a quarter to nine this evening."

Ponting smiled like an infuriated cat.

" So you think me a possible person, do you ? " said he.

" Everyone is a possible person," Miller replied blandly, " especially when he is known to have uttered threats."

The reply sobered Ponting considerably. For a few moments he sat, looking reflectively at the superintendent ; then, in comparatively quiet tones, he said :

" I have been working here since six o'clock. You can see the stuff for yourself, and I can prove that it has been written since six."

The superintendent nodded, but made no comment, and Ponting gazed at him fixedly, evidently thinking hard. Suddenly he broke into a harsh laugh.

" What is the joke ? " Miller inquired stolidly.

" The joke is that I have got another alibi—a very complete one. There are compensations in every evil. I told you I had been interrupted in my work already this evening. It was those fools next door, the Barnetts—cousins of mine. They are musicians, save the mark ! Variety stage, you know. Funny songs and jokes for mental defectives. Well, they practise their infernal ditties in their rooms, and the row comes into mine, and an accursed nuisance it is. However, they have agreed not to practise on Thursdays and Fridays—my busy nights—and usually they don't. But to-night, just as I was in the thick of my writing, I suddenly heard the most unholy din ; that idiot, Fred Barnett, bawling one of his imbecile songs—' When the pigs their wings have folded,' and balderdash of that sort—and the other donkey accompanying him on the clarinet, if you please ! I stuck it for a minute or two. Then I rushed round to their flat and raised Cain with the bell and knocker. Mrs. Fred opened the door, and I told her what I thought of it. Of course she was very apologetic, said they had forgotten that it was Thursday and promised that she would make her husband stop. And I suppose she did, for by the time I got back to my rooms the row had ceased. I could have punched the whole lot of them into a jelly, but it was all for the best as it turns out."

" What time was it when you went round there ? " asked Miller.

" About five minutes past nine," replied Ponting. " The church bell had struck nine when the row began."

" Hm ! " grunted Miller, glancing at Thorndyke. " Well, that is all we wanted to know, so we need not keep you from your work any longer."

He rose, and being let out with great alacrity, stumped down the stairs, followed by Thorndyke and me. As we came out into the street, he turned to us with a deeply disappointed expression.

" Well," he exclaimed, " this is a suck-in. I was in

hopes that we had pounced on our quarry before he had got time to clear away the traces. And now we've got it all to do. You can't get round an alibi of that sort."

I glanced at Thorndyke to see how he was taking this unexpected check. He was evidently puzzled, and I could see by the expression of concentration in his face that he was trying over the facts and inferences in new combinations to meet this new position. Probably he had noticed, as I had, that Ponting was wearing a tweed suit, and that therefore the shreds of clothing from the fence could not be his unless he had changed. But the alibi put him definitely out of the picture, and, as Miller had said, we now had nothing to give us a lead.

Suddenly Thorndyke came out of his reverie and addressed the superintendent.

" We had better put this alibi on the basis of ascertained fact. It ought to be verified at once. At present we have only Ponting's unsupported statement."

" It isn't likely that he would risk telling a lie," Miller replied gloomily.

" A man who is under suspicion of murder will risk a good deal," Thorndyke retorted, " especially if he is guilty. I think we ought to see Mrs. Barnett before there is any opportunity of collusion."

" There has been time for collusion already," said Miller. " Still, you are quite right, and I see there is a light in their sitting-room, if that is it, next to Ponting's. Let us go up and settle the matter now. I shall leave you to examine the witness and say what you think it best to say."

We entered the building and ascended the stairs to the Barnetts' flat, where Miller rang the bell and executed a double knock. After a short interval the door was opened and a woman looked out at us inquisitively.

" Are you Mrs. Frederick Barnett ? " Thorndyke inquired. The woman admitted her identity in a tone of some surprise, and Thorndyke explained : " We have

called to make a few inquiries concerning your neigh-
bour, Mr. Ponting, and also about certain matters relating to your family. I am afraid it is a rather unseason-
able hour for a visit, but as the affair is of some importance
and time is an object, I hope you will overlook that."

Mrs. Barnett listened to this explanation with a
puzzled and rather suspicious air. After a few moments'
hesitation, she said :

" I think you had better see my husband. If you
will wait here a moment I will go and tell him." With
this, she pushed the door to, without actually closing it,
and we heard her retire along the lobby, presumably
to the sitting-room. For, during the short colloquy, I
had observed a door at the end of the lobby, partly open,
through which I could see the end of a table covered
with a red cloth.

The " moment " extended to a full minute, and the
superintendent began to show signs of impatience.

" I don't see why you didn't ask her the simple question straight out," he said, and the same question had
occurred to me. But at this point footsteps were heard
approaching, the door opened, and a man confronted
us, holding the door open with his left hand, his right
being wrapped in a handkerchief. He looked suspiciously from one to the other of us, and asked stiffly :

" What is it that you want to know ? And would
you mind telling me who you are ? "

" My name is Thorndyke," was the reply. " I am
the legal adviser of the Reverend Charles Meade, and
these two gentlemen are interested parties. I want to
know what you can tell me of Mr. Ponting's recent
movements—to-day, for instance. When did you last
see him ? "

The man appeared to be about to refuse any conversation, but suddenly altered his mind, reflected for a few
moments, and then replied :

" I saw him from my window at his—they are bay-
windows—about half-past eight. But my wife saw him

later than that. If you will come in she can tell you the time exactly." He led the way along the lobby with an obviously puzzled air. But he was not more puzzled than I, or than Miller, to judge by the bewildered glance that the superintendent cast at me, as he followed our host along the lobby. I was still meditating on Thorndyke's curiously indirect methods when the sitting-room door was opened ; and then I got a minor surprise of another kind. When I had last looked into the room, the table had been covered by a red cloth. It was now bare ; and when we entered the room I saw that the red cover had been thrown over a side table, on which was some bulky and angular object. Apparently it had been thought desirable to conceal that object, whatever it was, and as we took our seats beside the bare table, my mind was busy with conjectures as to what that object could be.

Mr. Barnett repeated Thorndyke's question to his wife, adding : " I think it must have been a little after nine when Ponting came round. What do you say ? "

" Yes," she replied, " it would be, for I heard it strike nine just before you began your practice, and he came a few minutes after."

" You see," Barnett explained, " I am a singer, and my brother, here, accompanies me on various instruments, and of course we have to practise. But we don't practise on the nights when Ponting is busy—Thursdays and Fridays—as he said that the music disturbed him. To-night, however, we made a little mistake. I happen to have got a new song that I am anxious to get ready —it has an illustrative accompaniment on the clarinet, which my brother will play. We were so much taken up with the new song that we all forgot what day of the week it was, and started to have a good practice. But before we had got through the first verse, Ponting came round, battering at the door like a madman. My wife went out and pacified him, and of course we shut down for the evening."

While Mr. Barnett was giving his explanation, I looked about the room with vague curiosity. Somehow —I cannot tell exactly how—I was sensible of something queer in the atmosphere of this place ; of a certain indefinite sense of tension. Mrs. Barnett looked pale and flurried. Her husband, in spite of his volubility, seemed ill at ease, and the brother, who sat huddled in an easy-chair, nursing a dark-coloured Persian cat. stared into the fire, and neither moved nor spoke. And again I looked at the red table-cloth and wondered what it covered.

" By the way," said Barnett, after a brief pause, " what is the point of these inquiries of yours ? About Ponting, I mean. What does it matter to you where he was this evening ? "

As he spoke, he produced a pipe and tobacco-pouch and proceeded to fill the former, holding it in his bandaged right hand and filling it with his left. The facility with which he did this suggested that he was left-handed, an inference that was confirmed by the ease with which he struck the match with his left hand, and by the fact that he wore a wrist-watch on his right wrist.

" Your question is a perfectly natural one," said Thorndyke. " The answer to it is that a very terrible thing has happened. Miss Millicent Fawcett, who is, I think, a connection of yours, met her death this evening under circumstances of grave suspicion. She died, either by her own hand or by the hand of a murderer, a few minutes before nine o'clock. Hence it has become necessary to ascertain the whereabouts at that time of any persons on whom suspicion might reasonably fall."

" Good God ! " exclaimed Barnett. " What a shocking thing ! "

The exclamation was followed by a deep silence, amidst which I could hear the barking of a dog in an adjacent room, the unmistakable sharp, treble yelp of a Pekinese. And again I seemed to be aware of a

strange sense of tension in the occupants of this room.
On hearing Thorndyke's answer, Mrs. Barnett had
turned deadly pale and let her head fall forward on her
hand. Her husband had sunk on to a chair, and he,
too, looked pale and deeply shocked, while the brother
continued to stare silently into the fire.

At this moment Thorndyke astonished me by an
exhibition of what seemed—under the tragic circumstances—the most outrageous bad manners and bad
taste. Rising from his chair with his eyes fixed on a
print which hung on the wall above the red-covered
table, he said :

" That looks like one of Cameron's etchings," and
forthwith stepped across the room to examine it, resting
his hand, as he leaned forward, on the object covered by
the cloth.

" Mind where you are putting your hand, sir ! "
Fred Barnett called out, springing to his feet.

Thorndyke looked down at his hand, and deliberately
raising a corner of the cloth, looked under. " There
is no harm done," he remarked quietly, letting the
cloth drop ; and with another glance at the print, he
went back to his chair.

Once more a deep silence fell upon the room, and I
had a vague feeling that the tension had increased.
Mrs. Barnett was as white as a ghost and seemed to
catch at her breath. Her husband watched her with a
wild, angry expression and smoked furiously, while the
superintendent—also conscious of something abnormal
in the atmosphere of the room—looked furtively from
the woman to the man and from him to Thorndyke.

Yet again in the silence the shrill barking of the
Pekinese dog broke out, and somehow that sound connected itself in my mind with the Persian cat that dozed
on the knees of the immovable man by the fire. I looked
at the cat and at the man, and even as I looked, I was
startled by a most extraordinary apparition. Above the
man's shoulder, slowly rose a little round head like the

head of a diminutive, greenish-brown man. Higher and higher the tiny monkey raised itself, resting on its little hands to peer at the strangers. Then, with sudden coyness, like a shy baby, it popped down out of sight.

I was thunderstruck. The cat and the dog I had noted merely as a curious coincidence. But the monkey —and such an unusual monkey, too—put coincidences out of the question. I stared at the man in positive stupefaction. Somehow that man was connected with that unforgettable figure lying upon the couch miles away. But how? When that deed of horror was doing, he had been here in this very room. Yet, in some way, he had been concerned in it. And suddenly a suspicion dawned upon me that Thorndyke was waiting for the actual perpetrator to arrive.

" It is a most ghastly affair," Barnett repeated presently in a husky voice. Then, after a pause, he asked : " Is there any sort of evidence as to whether she killed herself or was killed by somebody else ? "

" I think that my friend, here, Detective-Superintendent Miller, has decided that she was murdered." He looked at the bewildered superintendent, who replied with an inarticulate grunt.

" And is there any clue as to who the—the murderer may be ? You spoke of suspected persons just now."

" Yes," replied Thorndyke, " there is an excellent clue, if it can only be followed up. We found a most unmistakable footprint ; and what is more, we took a plaster cast of it. Would you like to see the cast ? "

Without waiting for a reply, he opened the research-case and took out the cast, which he placed in my hands.

" Just take it round and show it to them," he said.

The superintendent had witnessed Thorndyke's amazing proceedings with an astonishment that left him speechless. But now he sprang to his feet, and, as I walked round the table, he pressed beside me to guard the precious cast from possible injury. I laid it carefully down on the table, and as the light fell on it obliquely, it presented a most striking appearance—that of a snow-white boot-sole on which the unshapely patch, the circular heel, and the marks of wear were clearly visible.

The three spectators gathered round, as near as the superintendent would let them approach, and I observed them closely, assuming that this incomprehensible move of Thorndyke's was a device to catch one or more of them off their guard. Fred Barnett looked at the cast stolidly enough, though his face had gone several shades paler, but Mrs. Barnett stared at it with starting eye-balls and dropped jaw—the very picture of horror and dismay. As to James Barnett, whom I now saw clearly for the first time, he stood behind the woman with a singularly scared and haggard face, and his eyes riveted on the white boot-sole. And now I could see that he wore a suit of blue serge and that the front both of his coat and waistcoat were thickly covered with the shed hairs of his pets.

There was something very uncanny about this group of persons gathered around that accusing footprint, all as still and rigid as statues and none uttering a sound. But something still more uncanny followed. Suddenly the deep silence of the room was shattered by the shrill notes of a clarinet, and a brassy voice burst forth :

> " When the pigs their wings have folded
> And the cows are in their nest——"

We all spun round in amazement, and at the first glance the mystery of the crime was solved. There stood Thorndyke with the red table-cover at his feet, and at his side, on the small table, a massively-constructed phonograph of the kind used in offices for dictating letters, but fitted with a convoluted metal horn in place of the rubber ear-tubes.

A moment of astonished silence was succeeded by a wild confusion. Mrs. Barnett uttered a piercing shriek and fell back on to a chair, her husband broke away and rushed at Thorndyke, who instantly gripped his wrist and pinioned him, while the superintendent, taking in the situation at a glance, fastened on the unresisting James and forced him down into a chair. I ran round, and having stopped the machine—for the preposterous song was hideously incongruous with the tragedy that was enacting—went to Thorndyke's assistance and helped him to remove his prisoner from the neighbourhood of the instrument.

"Superintendent Miller," said Thorndyke, still maintaining a hold on his squirming captive, "I believe you are a justice of the peace?"

"Yes," was the reply, "ex officio."

"Then," said Thorndyke, "I accuse these three persons of being concerned in the murder of Miss Millicent Fawcett; Frederick Barnett as the principal who actually committed the murder, James Barnett as having aided him by holding the arms of the deceased, and Mrs. Barnett as an accessory before the fact in that she worked this phonograph for the purpose of establishing a false alibi."

"I knew nothing about it!" Mrs. Barnett shrieked hysterically. "They never told me why they wanted me to work the thing."

"We can't go into that now," said Miller. "You will be able to make your defence at the proper time and place. Can one of you go for assistance or must I blow my whistle?"

"You had better go, Jervis," said Thorndyke. "I can hold this man until reinforcements arrive. Send a constable up and then go on to the station. And leave the outer door ajar."

I followed these directions, and having found the police station, presently returned to the flat with four constables and a sergeant in two taxis.

When the prisoners had been removed, together with the three animals—the latter in charge of a zoophilist constable—we searched the bedrooms. Frederick Barnett had changed his clothing completely, but in a locked drawer—the lock of which Thorndyke picked neatly, to the superintendent's undisguised admiration —we found the discarded garments, including a pair of torn shepherd's plaid trousers, covered with blood-stains, and a new, empty razor-case. These things, together with the wax cylinder of the phonograph, Miller made up into a neat parcel and took away with him.

" Of course," said I, as we walked homewards, " the general drift of this case is quite obvious. But it seemed to me that you went to the Barnetts' flat with a definite purpose already formed, and with a definite suspicion in your mind. Now, I don't see how you came to suspect the Barnetts."

" I think you will," he replied, " if you will recall the incidents in their order from the beginning, including poor Meade's preliminary statement. To begin with the appearances of the body : the suggestion of suicide was transparently false. To say nothing of its incon-gruity with the character and circumstances of the deceased and the very unlikely weapon used, there were the gashed collar and the cut cap-string. As you know, it is a well-established rule that suicides do not damage their clothing. A man who cuts his own throat doesn't cut his collar. He takes it off. He removes all obstruc-tions. Naturally, for he wishes to complete the act as easily and quickly as possible, and he has time for preparation. But the murderer must take things as he finds them and execute his purpose as best he can.

" But further ; the wounds were inflicted near the door, but the body was on the couch at the other end of the room. We saw, from the absence of bleeding, that she was dying—in fact, apparently dead—when she lay down. She must therefore have been carried to the couch after the wounds were inflicted.

" Then there were the blood-stains. They were all in front, and the blood had run down vertically. Then she must have been standing upright while the blood was flowing. Now there were four wounds, and the first one was mortal. It divided the common carotid artery and the great veins. On receiving that wound she would ordinarily have fallen down. But she did not fall, or there would have been a blood-stain across the neck. Why did she not fall ? The obvious suggestion was that someone was holding her up. This suggestion was confirmed by the absence of cuts on her hands—which would certainly have been cut if someone had not been holding them. It was further confirmed by the rough crumpling of the collar at the back : so rough that the button was torn off. And we found that button near the door.

" Further, there were the animal hairs. They were on the back only. There were none on the front— where they would have been if derived from the animals —or anywhere else. And we learned that she kept no animals. All these appearances pointed to the presence of two persons, one of whom stood behind her and held her arms while the other stood in front and committed the murder. The cloth on the fence supported this view, being probably derived from two different pairs of trousers. The character of the wounds made it nearly certain that the murderer was left-handed.

" While we were returning in the cab, I reflected on these facts and considered the case generally. First, what was the motive ? There was nothing to suggest robbery, nor was it in the least like a robber's crime. What other motive could there be ? Well, here was a comparatively rich woman who had made a will in favour of certain persons, and she was going to be married. On her marriage the will would automatically become void, and she was not likely to make another will so favourable to those persons. Here, then, was a possible motive, and that motive applied to Ponting, who had actually uttered threats and was obviously suspect.

" But, apart from those threats, Ponting was not the principal suspect, for he benefited only slightly under the will. The chief beneficiaries were the Barnetts, and Miss Fawcett's death would benefit them, not only by securing the validity of the will, but by setting the will into immediate operation. And there were two of them. They therefore fitted the circumstances better than Ponting did. And when we came to interview Ponting, he went straight out of the picture. His manuscript would probably have cleared him—with his editor's confirmation. But the other alibi was conclusive.

" What instantly struck me, however, was that Ponting's alibi was also an alibi for the Barnetts. But there was this difference : Ponting had been seen ; the Barnetts had only been heard. Now, it has often occurred to me that a very effective false alibi could be worked with a gramophone or a phonograph—especially with one on which one can make one's own records. This idea now recurred to me ; and at once it was supported by the appearance of an arranged effect. Ponting was known to be at work. It was practically certain that a blast of ' music ' would bring him out. Then he would be available, if necessary, as a witness to prove an alibi. It seemed to be worth while to investigate.

" When we came to the flat we encountered a man with an injured hand—the right. It would have been more striking if it had been his left. But it presently turns out that he is left-handed ; which is still more striking as a coincidence. This man is extraordinarily ready to answer questions which most persons would have refused to answer at all. Those answers contain the alibi.

" Then there was the incident of the table-cover— I think you noticed it. That cover was on the large table when we arrived, but it was taken off and thrown over something, evidently to conceal it. But I need not pursue the details. When I had seen the cat, heard

the dog, and then seen the monkey, I determined to see
what was under the table-cover ; and finding that it
was a phonograph with the cylinder record still on the
drum, I decided to ' go Nap ' and chance making a
mistake. For until we had tried the record, the alibi
remained. If it had failed, I should have advised
Miller to hold a boot parade. Fortunately we struck
the right record and completed the case."

Mrs. Barnett's defence was accepted by the magistrate
and the charge against her was dismissed. The other
two were committed for trial, and in due course paid
the extreme penalty. " Yet another illustration," was
Thorndyke's comment, " of the folly of that kind of
criminal who won't let well alone, and who will create
false clues. If the Barnetts had not laid down those
false tracks, they would probably never have been suspected. It was their clever alibi that led us straight to
their door."

18
PANDORA'S
BOX

" I SEE our friend, S. Chapman, is still a defaulter," said
I, as I ran my eye over the " personal " column of *The
Times*.

Thorndyke looked up interrogatively.

" Chapman ? " he repeated ; " let me see, who is
he ? "

" The man with the box. I read you the advertise-
ment the other day. Here it is again. ' If the box left
in the luggage-room by S. Chapman is not claimed
within a week from this date, it will be sold to defray
expenses.—Alexander Butt, " Red Lion " Hotel, Stoke
Varley, Kent.' That sounds like an ultimatum ; but it
has been appearing at intervals for the last month. As

Printed in the United Kingdom
by Lightning Source UK Ltd.
102559UKS00002B/33